BLOOD MONEY

A STUNNED SILENCE settled upon the street as the echoing report of the handgun slowly faded away. Brunner stalked across the mud, crouched down beside the body of the Tilean and pulled the large knife from his belt. The serrated edge gleamed in the light for a moment before he brought the blade against the neck of the dead man. A woman screamed as Brunner set about his gruesome labour.

'Always make sure that the man you want to kill is playing by the same rules,' the bounty hunter said as he lifted Savio's head from the corpse.

*To Durango, who I know will appreciate a
well-armed protagonist. Thanks, Old Man.*

A BLACK LIBRARY PUBLICATION

First published in Great Britain
in 2003 by The Black Library,
an imprint of Games Workshop Ltd.,
Willow Road, Lenton,
Nottingham, NG7 2WS, UK

10 9 8 7 6 5 4 3 2 1

Cover illustration by Martin Hanford

A CIP record for this book
is available from the British Library

ISBN 1 84154 267 9

Set in ITC Giovanni

Printed and bound in Great Britain by
Cox & Wyman Ltd, Cardiff Rd, Reading, Berkshire RG1 8EX, UK

See the Black Library on the Internet at
www.blacklibrary.com

Find out more about Games Workshop
and the world of Warhammer at
www.games-workshop.com

THIS IS A DARK age, a bloody age, an age of daemons
and of sorcery. It is an age of battle and death, and of the
world's ending. Amidst all of the fire, flame and fury
it is a time, too, of mighty heroes, of bold deeds
and great courage.

AT THE HEART of the Old World sprawls the Empire, the
largest and most powerful of the human realms. Known
for its engineers, sorcerers, traders and soldiers, it is
a land of great mountains, mighty rivers, dark forests
and vast cities. And from his throne in Altdorf reigns
the Emperor Karl-Franz, sacred descendant of the
founder of these lands, Sigmar, and wielder
of his magical warhammer.

BUT THESE ARE far from civilised times. Across the
length and breadth of the Old World, from the knightly
palaces of Bretonnia to ice-bound Kislev in the far north,
come rumblings of war. In the towering World's Edge
Mountains, the orc tribes are gathering for another assault.
Bandits and renegades harry the wild southern lands of
the Border Princes. There are rumours of rat-things, the
skaven, emerging from the sewers and swamps across the
land. And from the northern wildernesses there is the
ever-present threat of Chaos, of daemons and beastmen
corrupted by the foul powers of the Dark Gods.
As the time of battle draws ever near,
the Empire needs heroes
like never before.

PROLOGUE

FOR ME, IT all began one hot summer night in the sweltering back streets of the Tilean city of Miragliano. I was in my second year of exile from the place of my birth, grand Altdorf, that emperor of all cities, that symbol of human endeavour, might, learning and faith. It followed, as some may recall, the publication of my own retelling of history's most fearsome villain: *A True History of the Life of Count Vlad von Carstein of Sylvania – the Vampyre* that my troubles began.

True, the name of Ehrhard Stoecker became known far and wide across the Empire. There was even an invitation to visit the tsarina in Kislev, a land fascinated by tales of the aristocracy of the night. But in my own land, even as fame and fortune crept towards me, implacable foes arose between me and the rewards of my labours. My work was denounced by no less a personage than the Grand Theogonist himself, and the High Priest of Ulric in Middenheim even called the novel 'contemptible'. Literary critics, ever bowing their craven heads to the mood of the

7

pulpit, decried my work as doggerel and claptrap, the work of a barely literate hack who 'doubtless thinks Sylvania is a province in Bretonnia'.

I could contend with such spiteful and petty detractors, for my publishers happily informed me that with every harsh word the Grand Theogonist deigned to hurl upon my volume, another five hundred copies were sold. And it is in the matter of coin, perhaps, that public opinion has always been, and shall ever be, expressed. No, it was not the vitriol of the critics, nor the scorn of the pulpit that drove me to distant lands to lose myself from the Empire. It was one late night in a darkened street, when I discovered that there were others who had taken offence at my work, and that not all my detractors were human. It was then that I distanced myself from the land of my birth.

So it was that I, Ehrhard Stoecker, came to be sitting in the burrow-like interior of a filthy tavern in the seediest district in Miragliano, that notorious port of merchant princes, swashbuckling privateers and dastardly smugglers. I had found my status much reduced. I, who had once put to pen some of the most well-known and sinister tales of horror to ever grace the libraries of the Empire.

The last of my monies from *A True History of Vlad* were fast failing and I had been impressed upon by a most unscrupulous Tilean by the name of Ernesto – a publisher of thin tomes foisted upon seafarers to lessen the tedium of their ocean voyages – to turn my talents to furnishing him with fodder for his schilling dreadfuls. I found my days spent lurking in the taverns of Miragliano, dutifully committing to memory the tales of seamen and mercenaries as they sank into their cups, wading through their crude dialects and inveterate boasting to seize any germ of truth behind the stories they related.

It was not unlike being put to the question by an Estalian torturer, those long hours of trying to endure some simpleton's vanity as he explained how he was the mightiest hero since Sigmar, or at least Konrad. Still, Ernesto needed as much material as I could furnish, and the pittance he paid for each page ensured that I furnished him with as many manuscripts as I could compose.

I was deep in my cups one evening, sitting in a dockside dive known as the Maid of Albion. I was not, however, as deep as my companion, a petty banditti named Ferrini, who was drunkenly slobbering out his life story. He explained to me how he had become a veritable bandit prince after being villainously spirited away from the household of a noble family in Tobaro by agents of his younger brother, who desired the title for himself. I was finding myself unable to decide if even Ernesto would be able to swallow the lout's lies, when the door of the tavern opened and my companion suddenly became sober as a priest of Morr. I followed his ashen gaze to the figure that had made its way into the room.

He was a tall man, lean yet muscular, after the fashion of a professional duellist, or a professional assassin – men whose need of strength is seconded to their need for agility. The man wore a suit of brigandine armour about his body, a breastplate of gromril, that fabulous metal of the dwarfs, over his chest. Belts of knives, crossbow bolts and other weapons encircled his waist and crossed his chest above the armour. A heavy falchion sword swung from his hip. The man's face was partially obscured, the region above his upper lip hidden behind the rounded surface of his black steel helm. As I gazed upon him, he turned and for a moment the icy blue eyes that stared from behind the visor met my own. The man at my side muttered a word under his breath.

'Brunner,' Ferrini croaked. He cast a desperate look at the two brutish men who had been with him before my arrival. The pair of bandits was already in motion, one pulling a long-bladed dagger from his belt, the other hefting a heavy club of steel and oak. As the man Ferrini had identified as Brunner began to walk towards our table, Ferrini's comrades assaulted him. There was a flash of light as a knife whipped from one of the armoured man's gloved hands and I saw the club-wielder drop his weapon as the blade sank into his forearm. Even as he screamed, Brunner turned on him, kicking in his teeth with a steel-toed boot. The other bandit charged the killer from behind. Brunner dodged the stabbing blade. I did not see what transpired next, however, though I could hear the man screaming a moment later. For I was hurrying out of the side door of the Maid of Albion, hastening after my drinking partner who had risen from the table and scurried away the instant Brunner's attention had been diverted to the other bandits.

Had I been even a moment tardier in my pursuit, I should never have caught up with the weasel-faced bandit. The door opened upon a narrow alley, and my former companion was already half way down its length. It took a tremendous effort to catch him. When I did, he spun on me, a dagger clenched in his fist. He recognised me in an instant and withdrew the blade, then turned to run. I placed a hand on his shoulder and told him I knew of a place where he could hide. He sighed a moan of thanks through heavy breaths and the two of us slid down a dank alleyway toward the dingy little hostel where I kept my rooms.

Ferrini immediately went to the single window that looked down upon the street, quickly searching for any sign of pursuit. Finding none, he hastily slammed the shutters, sealing off the window. Then, feeling a bit safer, some of the old bravado wormed its way up in the bandit, and he began to tell me about this figure of dread, this walking herald of death and judgement.

Brunner was a bounty hunter, Ferrini explained. The man's name was a fearful whisper among bandits, pirates and highwaymen as far away as the forests of Bretonnia and the villages of the Reikland. It was said that once Brunner had set out to catch a man, that man's days were numbered not in years, but in weeks. It was said that the bounty hunter had spirited a buccaneer captain from the sanctuary of the pirate stronghold of Sartosa, that he had brought down a traitor to the King of Bretonnia in the court of an Arabyan sheik, and that he had pursued one notorious smuggler to the depths of Black Crag and returned with his prey from the bowels of the goblin fortress. Or at least, the man's head... With sword and bow, there were few men who could match him, and none who could claim supremacy over him in both. The tales went on, each more terrible and grim than the last.

Then Ferrini's face went white once more. I turned to see what had horrified the bandit so. Standing in the doorway was the armoured figure of the bounty hunter. So silently had he come, I never heard even the softest footfall, the merest creak of the door. It was as if some daemon prince had snapped his fingers and summoned the man from thin air.

Ferrini fumbled for his sword. I heard the rasp of steel as the bounty hunter drew his own. Ferrini shrieked and threw down his weapon, scrambling for the window, and throwing open the shutters.

The bounty hunter was on him in an instant. Ferrini became a dead weight in Brunner's gloved hands, sobbing like a child. A liquid stench rose from the bandit's trousers. The bounty hunter did not hold onto his prey, but hurled him screaming through the window. There was a dull thud as the man landed on the cobblestones three floors below.

The bounty hunter leaned from the window as screams of pain rose from the street.

'Just his leg,' I heard a voice as cold and chill as an open grave grumble. 'Thought he'd break his neck. Guess I'll just have to drag him back up here and try again.' The armoured figure turned from the window and began to stalk towards the door with long, pantherish steps.

Brunner exuded an aura of menace, a tangible feeling of impending violence, a promise of death. But there was something about him that at once captivated and fascinated me. I thought of the sparrow who sees the serpent, knows it for what it is, yet cannot tear its eyes away and fly from its company. I was also reminded of an old saying, a favourite of my father's: 'The Great and the Good are not always one and the same.' I at once decided that I must speak with this man. The idea had sprung into my mind that the exploits of such a man would be no boastful lies told by some loutish ruffian seeking to enlarge a drunken ego. No, whatever words might pass between myself and a man like this, they would be the truth. A dark, brutal, murderous truth, but truth is not always a pleasant thing. And Ernesto was not paying me to pen parables for the cult of Shallya.

I must confess that my voice was like the squeak of a mouse when I addressed the bounty hunter for the first time. The man's face, clothed as ever in the steel mask of his helm, fixed upon me, as if becoming aware of my presence for the first time.

The breath caught in my throat, and for a moment I was certain that I had foolishly invited Morr to reach up from the shadows and pull me into the kingdom of the dead. But after a second, the bounty hunter relaxed his grip on the hilt of his sword. The icy voice spoke again, demanding to know what I wanted.

I stumbled over my words several times as I tried to relate the idea. It seemed no less suicidal than walking up to a sleeping dragon, knocking it upon the head and loudly proclaiming its mother to be the lowest form of lizard. The bounty hunter listened for a moment, and I watched as a curious light crept into his eyes, as if the blue glaciers behind the visor of his steel face were melting. There was silence. I finally said that I could pay him, and proffered the leather purse that contained monies I had earned from a month of prying stories from the addled memories of pirates and thieves deep in their cups.

A gloved hand closed about the bag, and stuffed it into his belt. I later came to understand how unusual a gesture this was, for Brunner did not count what I had given him. Whatever moved him to speak with me that night in my dingy little room, the money was nothing more than a dressing, a garnish.

The bounty hunter walked back into the room, closed a hand about the back of the single wooden chair that was a part of my furnishings, and set it beside the window, in order that he might keep an eye on the moaning man in the street below. I hastened to my table, digging quill, ink and parchment from their cubby holes and set myself upon the floor, eager to begin recording the bounty hunter's adventures before he thought better of such a charitable impulse. He waited until I was ready, and then the icy voice began to speak...

THE MONEY-LENDER'S PRICE

WE TALKED LONG *into the dark hours. I am still uncertain what motivated the bounty hunter to confide in me, for as he related a lengthy and gruesome catalogue of bloodshed and depravity, I was certain that no other ears had heard these things before. I was momentarily reminded of a pilgrim listing his misdeeds to a confessor in one of Verena's temples. I cannot help but wonder if Brunner spoke to me out of a similar need to unburden his soul of the filth that encrusted it. As I came to know him better, I often wondered at this grim parody of penitent and confessor, but I am certain that Brunner has never asked anyone – man or god – to absolve him of anything he has ever done. For him, the gold that crosses his palm is absolution enough.*

Brunner told me many tales that night, of his travels across the Known World and his battles with hideous beasts and equally vile things that were more horrible for their humanity. He told me about his lengthy service under another bounty hunter, a fellow man of the Empire, named Kristov Leopold, until he at last learned all he could from the crafty veteran and surpassed his teacher in the skills of his gory trade.

At one point during the night, Brunner suddenly rose from his chair and removed the crossbow from the clamp on his left vambrace. He leaned out the window, snarling down at Ferrini in a voice more laden with threat than any red-eyed thing I had encountered in the darkened streets of Altdorf. I heard the bandit sob, and the bounty hunter hiss a second command. Then he fired the crossbow and Ferrini's wails of pain rose from the street, lingering on for sometime before shock and fatigue caused the bandit to fall silent. I later learned that Ferrini had started to crawl away, seeking to escape while we spoke. By what means the bounty hunter knew his prey was escaping, I do not know, but it was almost as if some sixth sense warned him. The sight of the crossbow aimed at him from the window instantly caused the bandit to plead for his life. Brunner ordered the man to place his hand against the wall next to him, holding it above his prone body. Without a moment's hesitation, the bounty hunter fired, the bolt smashing through Ferrini's hand, pinning the man to the wall.

Satisfied that his prey would be going nowhere, and seemingly paying him no further thought, the bounty hunter resumed his tale, telling me about a money-lender named Volonté...

THE LITTLE, SHARP-EYED man scuttled through the grimy, manure-ridden back streets of Miragliano. He wore an ill-tended dark purple tunic above coarse homespun breeches. A slender poniard graced a leather sheath attached to a belt around his emaciated waist. The man did not seem particularly nervous as he passed a band of bois-terous mercenary marines on leave from some wealthy merchant vessel berthed in the harbour. The frail-looking man kept his eyes averted from the mercenaries as they lurched their way to the next tavern on this, Miragliano's most notorious street: the Strada dei Cento Peccati. Taverns, brothels, weirdroot dens, fighting pits and other, even less savoury, places of diversion prospered here. It was said that even the most dour priest of Morr could not walk the breadth of the street without discovering some-thing to make him forget his clerical vows.

This lane of illicit pleasure was the most dangerous in the entire city. Murder was more rampant than venereal disease and alcoholism, and not a night passed without a cart of bodies being removed in the morning, destined for the lime pits outside the city. It was whispered that many more died without their bodies being found, slaughtered in dark rituals or spirited away to the abodes of necromancers. It was also rumoured that some of the taverns and brothels, and especially weirdroot dens, were not above drugging their patrons, the unlucky victims waking up to find themselves in the secret holds of some barque bound for the slave markets of distant Araby – a fate perhaps worse than death.

It was a lawless district, where even the watch did not dare to come during the hours of night. It was just the sort of place where the most wretched and depraved of men would thrive. And it was precisely where Rocha would find the man his master had sent him to look for.

The sound of loud, volatile cursing intruded into his thoughts as a gaudily dressed sailor was flung from the darkened doorway of a beer hall to his left. The man landed noisily in the dung-ridden gutter. He raised a soiled hand and screamed obscenities at the massive figure looming in the door, his high, nasally tones carrying the accent of a Sartosan. The bearded man in a grimy suit of armour glowered at the cursing sailor for a moment, then stalked from the doorway, his steps swift, his hands clenching and unclenching at his sides.

The Sartosan started to rise, nervous fear stalking through his anger. Even as he tried to scuttle away, the bearded man was upon him. Rocha heard the sound of a mallet-like fist crashing into the sailor's face, but he ignored the violent scene, having seen its like too often to be interested in its finale. His gaze drifted away from the brawlers and came to rest upon the wooden sign swinging beside the doorway. Depicted upon it was a dark, massive porcine creature. Crude characters beneath the slavering brute spelled out the name 'The Black Boar' in Reikspiel.

Stepping around the huge man raining punches upon the now slack form of the Sartosan sailor, Rocha entered the beer hall. Merchants and ships from all over the Old World came to Miragliano, from Marienburg and the Empire, to Araby and the near mythical elf realm of Ulthuan. And for every breed that came to Miragliano's cluttered markets and swarming docks, there could be found a drinking hole to match their particular cultural tastes. The Black Boar, Rocha knew, was a beer hall operated by a displaced Reiklander brewer, and catered especially to the needs of men from the Empire – a familiar setting in a foreign land. Rocha was certain that at some point, the man he was looking for would show himself in the beer hall.

Rocha entered the dark building. The ceiling was much higher than might have been expected, for the floor was set well below street level. The cause of this architectural irregularity was clustered about the end of the massive bar. It was a bar that sloped from the chest height of a man, to terminate at just above knee-height at its far end. Numerous dwarfs, their dress ranging from the robes of tradesmen to the armour of mercenaries, were clustered about the short end of the bar, downing overflowing steins of white-capped beer.

The dwarfs were not the only ones who clustered within the tunnel-like hall, seeking a taste more substantial than the thin Tilean wines and Bretonnian ales of other taverns. Rocha could see men from such diverse places as Marienburg, Altdorf and Nuln. A dour group seated about a large round table had the fur caps and drooping moustaches of the far north: Kislevite horsemen, come to sell their martial prowess to the merchants of the south.

The Tilean turned his eyes from the Kislevites and scanned the dark niches cut into the far wall of the beer hall. There were small private tables for those who wanted to see what manner of patron entered the Black Boar without themselves being seen first. The gleam of steel reflected in the dim light cast by the hanging lanterns of the tavern caught Rocha's eye and he advanced upon one of the darkened niches.

Rocha removed his hat as he approached, wringing it in both hands. It was partially a gesture of nervousness, but also a measure of caution, lest he accidentally make any motion that might be construed as a play for the dagger in his belt.

'Say your piece,' a steel voice intoned from the shadows, halting Rocha in his steps.

'My master, the most esteemed merchantman Ennio Corbucci Volonté...' Rocha began, bowing slightly to his shadowy accoster.

'Volonté,' the shadow scoffed. Rocha could see a head leer from the darkness. It was clothed in steel, a black helm in the rounded sallet style favoured by Imperial militia. Cold eyes stared out from the visor of the helm. A gloved hand raised a small clay cup to the exposed mouth below the edge of the helm. 'Volonté is a leech and a parasite, who lends money to men who can ill afford to repay what they have borrowed, let alone the extortionate interest.'

The man in the shadows shifted forward still more, exposing a lean, muscular body clothed in a suit of brigandine armour, a heavy-bladed falchion sword strapped to his side, a belt of long knives crossing his chest. 'That bloodworm has never been one to spend the gold he makes. My price is more than he can stomach. Let him deal with street thugs and unemployed duellists, let him look to the gutter trash he knows so well.'

Rocha smiled fawningly, diplomatically overlooking the slights upon the name and reputation of his master. He bobbed his head in appeasement. 'It is true, my master has never had cause to engage a – collector – of your calibre. But he now finds himself set upon by a matter not only of errant debitry, but also of familial honour.'

The bounty hunter mulled over the Tilean's words for a moment, keeping to himself any dubious thoughts about Volonté's familial honour. He rose from the darkness, striding towards Rocha from the depths of the niche.

'You have earned my interest,' Brunner stated, retrieving a small compact crossbow from the bench. 'Lead on,' he gestured with a gloved hand towards the steps leading back up to the street. 'But your master had better have conquered his miserly ways,' the bounty hunter warned. 'Men who take me from my vices only to waste my time do not find me agreeable company.'

THE ROOM WAS cold and clammy, almost like the preparation room in a temple of Morr. A lavish portrait of nubile wood nymphs consorting with horned satyrs dominated one wall, its gilded frame tarnished in the gloom, its colours overtaken by mildew and rot. A similar fate seemed destined for the exquisite marble statue of some slender and naked maiden that loomed beside a massive oak table that formed the focal point of the room. Behind it, seated in a high-backed chair, was a great greasy puddle of flesh that might once have resembled a man. He stared at the bounty hunter.

Ennio Corbucci Volonté was one of many moneylenders in Miragliano, but his were the fattest fingers, the greasiest thumbs. His bribes went higher than most men, his retinue of thugs and enforcers more brutal than any. It was said that Volonté would loan a gold crown to anyone, because he would see five returned to him before the month was out. And if he did not, the streets of Miragliano were teeming with beggars who sought to placate the toad-like man, even after his enforcers had reduced them to penury. And, darker rumours averred, the money-lender even had ways to turn a profit from the dead – passing their parts off to alchemists and herbalists for use in the concoction of remedies and elixirs, and selling the refuse to sausage makers who, it was also said, had never laid eyes upon a hog.

The fat man rolled forward in his chair. His maggot-like fingers were fitted with rings, the rolls of fat flesh almost engulfing the bands of gold.

Volonté swept a greasy lock of black hair from his face, staring into the eyes of the bounty hunter with his own swine-like orbs.

'Bertolucci,' the fat man wheezed, as if every breath spent away from the plate of roast fowl set before him came at great exertion. 'I want Bertolucci, bounty killer.'

'So your minion explained,' Brunner returned, unfazed by the money-lender's attempt to affect an air of superiority. His gloved hand casually rested about the pommel of the heavy falchion sword at his side.

'He has wronged me terribly,' the money-lender croaked. 'I lent him a tremendous sum, in good faith, to fund a business venture I wanted to invest in.' Brunner noted that Volonté was careful not to mention the exact sum, lest he give the bounty hunter any ideas about his own fee. 'But more than this, he insisted that I allow my daughter, my lovely Giana, my only child...' The thin, rasping noises issuing from Volonté's throat resembled belching more than sobbing and were silenced quickly as the money-lender continued to speak. 'Bertolucci insisted that I make my daughter wed his pig of a son! To seal our pact with blood! As if his were some great and noble house!'

'Get to the quick of it, fat man,' Brunner's icy voice intoned.

'Ninety in silver,' the money-lender croaked. 'Ninety in silver when you bring me Bertolucci's heart.' Volonté's fat fist opened in a clutching, clawing motion. 'When you place it in my hand.'

'Ninety it is,' the bounty hunter said, his voice level and emotionless. 'But it will be gold, not silver.' Brunner gestured with his gloved hand. 'This is a matter of revenge, not restitution, as I understand it. Passion such as that is costly. And besides,' Brunner said as he turned away from the scowling face of Volonté, 'she was your only daughter.'

THE DINGY CELLAR beneath the tannery stank of rotten cabbage and spoiled fruit. Strips of wet cloth were hung from the beams that supported the floor above, in a desperate attempt to fend off the heat of day. Brunner picked his way through the wet strips of cloth, penetrating the maze-like veils to reach his goal – a shabby wooden cot that crouched like a crippled beast in the far corner of the cellar, where the stench was less and the shadows more. A form stirred upon that cot, and Brunner watched as it reached out to light a stubby candle with a strange device of flint and steel.

'Ah, Brunner,' the voice of the figure called out as the light of the candle revealed the bounty hunter's armoured shape. The form on the cot was revealed as well: an emaciated thing, little more than a bag of bones, withered by age and unnatural disease alike. The face of the man was skull-like, his skin dark with small bony growths like little nubs of teeth embedded in the flesh of cheek and forehead. One hand was a perfectly natural, albeit shrunken and gaunt. The other was a trio of long, worm-like digits, short tentacles that gripped the candle in a loathsome parody of fingers. The bounty hunter strode forward, undisturbed by the sight of the mutant.

'I need information, Tessari,' the bounty hunter said, seating himself in a battered wooden chair opposite the cot.

'No one ever just comes just to visit me,' the mutant sighed, his watery eyes rolling skyward. 'They always come because they want something.'

'Maybe it is because your son charges three pieces of copper to let anyone come down here,' Brunner replied. Tessari drew himself up as straight as his frame would allow.

'Hmph! That bastard! I should have brained him when he was a babe in arms!' The mutant leaned toward the bounty hunter. 'Do you know that that rascal has started letting children pay their way down here? "See the Beast in the Cellar", let the urchins have their morbid little eyes gawk at my affliction.'

'I came here to ask what you knew about Ennio Volonté and Goffredo Bertolucci,' the bounty hunter snapped. 'There was a time, before your *affliction*, when you knew quite a bit about everyone in Miragliano. But perhaps the rot has crawled into your brain as well as your hand.' Brunner rose from the chair, but Tessari's human hand beckoned him to sit once more.

'Not going to grace me with the pleasure of human company and a few kind words?' the mutant asked, his voice heavy. Noting the lack of compassion on the bounty hunter's face, the mutant sighed. 'You always were a ruthless bastard, Brunner. What do you want to know?' Brunner leaned forward, his helm gleaming in the candlelight.

'Bertolucci has fled Miragliano,' the sharp voice of the killer rasped. 'Where would he have gone?'

'How can you be certain he has left the city?' the mutant challenged.

'Because if he hadn't, Volonté's men would have found him by now. Bertolucci, his son, Volonté's daughter and about twenty of his household have vanished. Almost as if the Chaos gods plucked them from his villa and whisked them away to the Wastes.'

'Bertolucci does not have much money,' Tessari mused. 'After this thing with Volonté, he is almost as badly off as myself. Now where might he go?' Tessari turned his face to stare into Brunner's eyes. The palm of his human hand was turned upwards. Brunner placed a pair of silver coins in the mutant's hand.

'In better days, many of the wealthy families of Miragliano kept villas in the country, before the beastmen and the orcs drove them back into the stink of the city.' The mutant laughed, the sound dry and moist at the same time. 'The Bertoluccis had a villa somewhere to the north of here, a winery as I recall. Perhaps he has decided that the dangers of the city outweigh those of the country. Perhaps he has gone home.'

'Thank you,' Brunner said, plucking the coins from Tessari's hand. The mutant sat bolt upright, snarling at the bounty hunter. His face twisted into something as bestial as his tentacled hand.

'Don't worry, I'll be back,' Brunner said. 'You'll get paid when I return.'

'Do you actually think Volonté is going to pay you for killing Bertolucci?' the mutant sneered. 'Did he tell you why he wants Bertolucci dead?'

Brunner turned back towards the mutant. 'Something about his daughter and a broken business deal.'

Tessari laughed again, the sound both louder and more liquid-laden than before.

'Is that what he told you?' the mutant gasped between cacklings. 'Volonté's daughter and Bertolucci's son had for months been secretly attending one another in the long hours before dawn. They are in love, you see. But that toad Volonté was not about to give away his only daughter without a substantial profit. I think the reptile had thoughts that he might marry her off to some petty lord and thereby ooze his way into the noble classes. Be that as it may, he at last relented, but only on condition that Bertolucci allow Volonté into a business dealing that promised a great reward.

'Spices. Spices from Araby, Brunner, worth their weight in gold. That was what Volonté wanted. For his consent to the marriage, he was allowed to invest in Bertolucci's enterprise, though the money-lender forced Bertolucci to squeeze out all of the other investors. The money-hungry maggot could not bear the thought that other men might profit alongside himself. This destroyed Bertolucci's reputation and made enemies of many that were once his friends. And many of those laughed when news arrived that the ship bearing the spices from Araby was lost – claimed by pirates, storm, or some horror of the deep. You can imagine that Volonté was the most upset of them all. He had lost his investment and the chance to marry his daughter to some great advantage. So now he sends you, the wolfhound, to bring his prey to ground and slake his thirst for retribution.' The mutant's eyes glittered in the flickering candlelight, studying the reaction his words had caused.

After a moment, the bounty hunter turned his back to the mutant.

'I care not for the whys of it,' Brunner said, stalking away. 'Only that there is money waiting at the end.'

* * *

THE COUNTRYSIDE BEYOND Miragliano was rolling, hilly terrain, marked by isolated pockets of humanity, but, more often, vast stretches of uninhabited wildland. Streams and brooks snaked their way along the deep hollows between the hills, encouraging the thick woods that filled each of the valleys. To the north side of the boulder-strewn hills and their forested hollows was a great plain of sandy, level ground. Stands of thin, scraggly trees were scattered in clumps, sometimes only a few dozen, other times a few hundred, forming an irregular forest.

The occasional stretch of level, grassy earth showed where farms had once stood, or, more rarely, where some hardy peasant still fought to wrest a living from the land. A path of brown dirt snaked its way between the trees and rocks, passing each of the farms, deserted or occupied, a relic of the time when there had been peace and safety in the hills of Tilea.

Two travellers made their way along the path, haste warring with caution for mastery over their steeds. One of the travellers was a large man, his powerful body encased in a tunic of hardened leather further toughened by strips of steel riveted to the garment. A rounded helm covered the man's head, the low cheek-guards fanning outward to join the rounded rim. A long sabre hung from a scabbard at his side and a heavy crossbow was strapped to the saddle of his horse. The man cast wary glances to right and left as they proceeded on their journey, his hard features betraying none of the fear that gripped him. There were things abroad, the soldier knew, things inhuman and unclean.

The other rider was mounted upon a short, shaggy-pelted burro. The little creature kept pace with its larger kin with great effort, its shorter steps causing it to fall behind several lengths before a brief burst of speed would bring it beside the horseman once more. No saddle graced the burro's back, only a thick blanket of wool. Seated upon that blanket, her legs thrown across the left side of the animal, rode a woman dressed in a hooded robe of pure white. Her face, framed by the fringe of her hood, was not unhandsome, but the stamp of age was creeping into it, the first webwork of wrinkles trickling away from the corners of her eyes.

Elisia had been a priestess in the service of Shallya for most of her life. Her family had been taken from her by plague; a husband and three children lost to an outbreak of the dreaded red pox. Somehow, though she too had become ill, she had recovered, and in her survival had seen the mercy of the goddess. She had devoted her life to Shallya, joining a shrine deep in the countryside, catering to the needs of the poor peasants and farmers who braved the wild to feed the swarming cities. Somewhere, in the long years of healing the sick, tending the wounded and soothing the bereft, Elisia had discovered within herself another woman, a woman far different from the one whose life the red pox had ravaged.

The priestess brought her burro to a halt as the soldier reined in his horse. She looked up at the armed man, a questioning look on her face.

'What is it, Gramsci?' she asked. 'Do you see the villa?'

The soldier kept his armoured head staring down the path even as he replied to the priestess. 'There is a man on the road ahead.' He pointed his finger toward a figure, only distantly visible, ahead of them upon the road. The horseman slapped the reins in his hand against his steed's neck, urging it forward.

'Stay here, sister,' he called back as he left, 'I shall see what he is about.'

Gramsci rode towards the man he had seen, scanning the trees and brush for any sign of lurking banditti. He doubted that any brigands would be so bold as to attack a priestess, but it was not unknown for some follower of Ranald to return the contempt of Shallya's followers with the edge of a knife.

'That is close enough,' a cold voice arrested Gramsci. The soldier came to a halt as the armoured man before him pointed a crossbow in his direction. Gramsci tried to peer at the face of the man, but it was hidden behind the steel mask of his Imperial-style helmet.

'I mean you no harm, sir,' Gramsci offered, raising his hands. 'I am but escorting yon priestess upon an errand. Let us pass and we shall be upon our way.'

The bounty hunter stared at the soldier, then his attention turned away from Gramsci. The soldier stifled an annoyed groan as he heard the clopping steps of the burro draw up beside him.

'It is true, sir,' Elisia stated, not at all intimidated or threatened by the crossbow aimed at her. 'I am a servant of Shallya on a mission of mercy to aid this worthy swordsman's household. Please, sir, let us pass, for we bear you no threat.'

Brunner lowered the crossbow, striding back to the horses he had left tethered at the side of the road. 'If your travel takes you north of here,' the bounty hunter remarked as he returned the crossbow to a scabbard set into the harness of his packhorse, 'I should advise you to turn back now. Just this afternoon, I was set upon by three beastmen. Their numbers will only grow when the sun fades.'

The bounty hunter's words brought a gasp of alarm from the priestess, who for the first time noticed the slight limp in the bounty hunter's gait, the small flecks of crimson staining his leggings. At her side, Gramsci glowered at the armoured killer, suspicion in his eyes.

'And what became of these beastmen?' the soldier asked. Brunner favoured him with a cold stare.

'They will not trouble you,' he said, 'but I cannot speak for whatever friends they might have.'

'What causes you to be abroad in the wilds alone?' Gramsci persisted, trying to inch his hand towards the sword at his side. The bounty hunter's eyes locked upon the slight motion. Gramsci scowled and let his hand drift away from the hilt of his blade.

'My business is my own affair,' Brunner stated.

Elisia interposed herself between the two men.

'This fencing with words is pointless,' she declared. 'We are yet distant from our destination, are we not, Gramsci?' The soldier, eyes and scowl still trained on Brunner nodded his head reluctantly.

Elisia turned to face the bounty hunter. 'What you say about beastmen alarms me greatly, and it seems to me that you are just as far from shelter as we. Please, ride with us and make camp in our company this evening. We shall be safer with a second sword should the fell creatures chance upon us in the night. And I can tend your wound, for I see that you did not emerge from your combat unscathed.' The priestess's eyes were bright, pleading and hopeful. Brunner inclined his helmed head.

'I shall join you, at least for the present,' he said, striding back towards his animals.

'And what are you named?' Gramsci called at the bounty hunter, his voice betraying his belligerence and suspicion. The bounty hunter halted, one hand upon the horn of his saddle.

'I am named Habermas,' the bounty hunter said, raising himself into the saddle.

'Then be warned, Habermas,' the Tilean soldier continued. 'Do not think to take advantage of us.'

Brunner turned the head of his steed, facing the Tileans once more. 'If I did,' the bounty hunter's voice was as frigid as a Norse breeze, 'you would not stop me.'

BRUNNER SAT BESIDE the fallen rubble of a chimney, all that remained of a long-departed farmstead. He let his gaze pass warily from the dark shadows beyond the light of the fire the priestess and her companion had started. He locked eyes with the scowling Gramsci, then let his stare linger on the tired, frightened features of the priestess. He let his hand rest for a moment on the compress the woman had pressed against the injury in his leg. Elisia did good work, the bounty hunter had to admit as he flexed his knee, noting only the faintest trace of pain. It was just as well for her that he had discovered them. And just as well for him, if their destination was the one that he suspected.

'Still annoyed by my fire, Habermas?' Gramsci snorted from his place beside the fire pit.

'I have already told you that it is unwise,' the cold voice beneath the steel helm responded.

The Tilean soldier favoured the other warrior with a friendless smile, heedless of the fact that the man was not looking at him. 'A good fire will keep any animal away. They fear flame. Anyone knows that.'

'Your knowledge of woodcraft is quite good for a city dweller,' Brunner stated. He focused his attention on a patch of shadow. His keen ears could not be certain, but had there been the whisper of a sound from there? The bounty hunter fingered one of his knives.

'Is it possible that the question of the fire could be put to rest?' asked Elisia, her patient temperament worn away by the long verbal skirmish.

'This fool thinks the fire will drive away the haunters of the night,' the bounty hunter said, almost under his breath, his eyes still focused on the shadow. 'Beastmen are not so craven as wolves or wild cats. Far from keeping them away, your fire is attracting them. It is like a beacon letting them know that there is food to be had here.'

The priestess stifled a gasp as she heard Brunner's words, so firm and sure was his tone. Gramsci just scowled anew, tossing another branch into the blaze.

'If that is so,' the Tilean said, 'then where are they?'

In that instant, the darkness exploded into life as howls, bleats and whinnies sounded from the shadows surrounding the camp. The noise of hooves, feet and claws crashing through the underbrush told of the swift and hurried advance of many large bodies. A thin, whiny and inhuman voice shrieked above the clamour. 'Skulls for the Skull Throne! Blood for the Blood God!'

The first beastman broke from the patch of midnight. A wiry brute with a mangy pelt of tawny fur, its face like a housecat, save for the glittering, multi-faceted eyes that gleamed in the dancing light of the campfire like two diamonds. A massive stone-headed axe was gripped in its long-fingered, clawless hands, a ghastly skull rune worked into the crude edge of the blade. The creature let a snarl, like the drone of a wasp, emerge from its fanged mouth as it sprang into the clearing. A moment later, the axe fell from slackened hands and the droning challenge faded into a bubbling gurgle as Brunner's throwing knife sank into the fiend's throat.

But even as the cat-beast died, its fellows swarmed into the camp: things with goat-like heads, others with dog faces, and still others sporting a twisted, almost human form. Brunner did not hesitate. He fell back toward his horses, sending another throwing knife whirling into the Chaos throng. The blade embedded itself in the long snout of a slavering hound-headed creature. The beastman dropped its swords to tear at the steel that had bitten into its face. A towering brute turned a goat-like face in the direction of the bounty hunter as it heard its fellow cry out in pain. The monster roared, pushing its companions aside to charge towards the knife thrower.

Gramsci rose from beside the fire, sword in his hand. A small beastman, its form more human than many of its fellows, its lope more steady and regular, fell upon the Tilean, smashing at him with a bone club. Gramsci's blade slashed through the crude weapon, and bit through the forearm behind the cudgel. The beastman wailed in pain as gore slopped from the stump of its arm, a look of agony frozen on its features as a quick thrust of Gramsci's blade pierced the monster's heart.

But the soldier did not have time to savour the beastman's death, for already more of its fellows had surrounded him, jabbing at him with spears, gesturing at him with rusted swords and stone axes. Fanged mouths drooled froth and spittle as the creatures of Chaos promised the soldier a bloody death in their inhuman voices.

Elisia fled from the fire and ran towards Brunner, instinctively hurrying to the side of the more capable of her two defenders. As she did so, one of the beastmen, a smaller version of the goat-headed horror that led the throng, capered after her, snarling and snapping at her heels. The monster swung a heavy wooden club at the woman, missed, and raised its paw to try again. A cry of pain arrested its attack, and the brute rolled against the ground, clawing at the small crossbow bolt that had smashed into his breast. Elisia, with a last burst of speed, reached the bounty hunter, as he lowered the small crossbow pistol he had fired into the inhuman attacker.

'I had meant that for him,' Brunner gestured with the point of his sword at the huge goat-headed thing that was now so near that the stink of its lice-ridden fur brought tears to the priestess's eyes. The bounty hunter handed the pistol to Elisia, pushing her behind him. The beastman's yellow eyes narrowed as it watched its foe, its fanged mouth twisting in a parody of a smile.

'Blood for the Blood God,' it hissed, its voice low and rumbling. The monster stepped forward, the lengths of chainmail dripping from the crude hide armour that encased its twisted form swaying and clattering with its every step. A mask, daubed with the skull rune of Khorne clothed the monster's face. Small lengths of chain had been driven into the brute's horns, and from the end of each dripped a fresh human scalp. The monster slapped the massive axe into the palm of its left hand. No thing of wood and stone, but a weapon of bronze, haft and head, and it seemed to call out for blood.

Brunner gestured at the beast with his sword, a motion that he was certain this debased thing would interpret as challenge. The beastman showed the rows of fangs, wicked and sharp, gleaming in its muzzle. One of the smaller creatures that had gathered about their leader shrieked and leapt forward, a rusted sword in its hands. The hulking leader split its minion in half with a sweep of its axe, the bloodied debris thrown across the clearing. The meaning was clear: none but the goat-headed chieftain would be allowed to offer this skull before their gory god.

The beastman loped forward, its hooves punching into the ground with every step. Brunner stood defiant, his sword in a guarding position, his left hand held immobile at his side.

Brunner smiled up at the hulking brute. The chieftain raised its bronze axe, gripping it with both hands. With a last snarl it leapt forward. Brunner's left hand rose in tandem with the brute's attack.

A white cloud engulfed the masked face of the beastman as it charged. The bounty hunter had quietly worked the packet of salt kept in the sleeve of his tunic into his palm, puncturing the little pouch of sackcloth with his fingernail. Now the mineral did its work, stinging and biting into the Chaos monster's eyes. Brunner lashed out with his sword, taking advantage of his enemy's blindness and surprise. The sword stabbed at the monster's belly, but the bounty hunter's strike was deflected by the crude armour of hide and steel – upon which had been carved all manner of strange and loathsome runes. Instead of opening up the monster's belly, Brunner's falchion gored a patch of the monster's thigh. The beastman let a howl of pain, terrifying like a human scream, rise from its throat before toppling backward. Its brutish followers stood in a stunned silence.

'Come on!' Brunner snapped, spinning and racing toward his horses, dragging the stunned priestess with him. 'They won't be confused for long, and they will be twice as enraged when they recover!' Brunner slashed the tether of his steed with the edge of his sword, spinning and doing the same for his packhorse. He scrambled into the saddle, pulling Elisia up behind him. The woman pulled at his arm, trying to direct him back toward the fire, back into the camp. He spared a look to where the Tileans' animals had been tied, seeing the swarm of beastmen upon them. His gaze canvassed the clearing, noting Gramsci holding off the press of monsters, though he was cut in both leg and arm, and his blade was not as quick in warding away adversaries as it had been.

'Do you know the way he was taking you?' Brunner asked.

'Y–yes,' Elisia muttered, her gaze wavering between Brunner, the beastmen and her embattled bodyguard.

'Good,' the bounty hunter said as he saw a beastman's spear puncture Gramsci's side. 'Because your guide is dead.' Brunner turned and quickly brought the horse to full gallop, dragging his packhorse behind them as they raced through the midnight wilds.

Behind them, a monstrous shape rose, snarling beneath its mask of flayed skin. The beastman chieftain watched as its chosen offering to Khorne escaped into the night. Infuriated, the monster reached out, snapping the neck of one of its fellows that had come closer to examine its master's wound. As the creature died, and the blood bubbled from its mouth, the wound in the beastman's thigh stopped bleeding. The masked brute turned its head, gazing at the still gaping wound. No, it thought, the wound shall remain until it is salved by the blood of a proper offering. The chieftain turned its head in the direction of the vanished bounty hunter. Its sharp bark of wrath and command brought the other brutes loping away from the gory, butchered bodies.

The hulking monster pointed its axe into the night, in the direction its prey had retreated.

'Blood for the Blood God!'

THE VILLA CROUCHED on the summit of a lonely round-topped hill. The overgrown ruin of the vinefields that had surrounded the estate formed a buffer zone between hill and forest, a few scraggly, thin trees ignoring the boundary and providing patches of shadow upon the grassy expanse. The crumbling remains of a wall appeared beside the dirt path that had once been a road, a narrow strip of dirt wending its way from the rotten wooden gate through the overgrown fields to the hill at their centre.

It had taken Brunner and his guide the better part of two days to reach this place, and once again the dark cloak of night was falling upon the land. They had ridden long and hard, with the bounty hunter pausing only long enough to give the animals such rest as they might require to keep up the pace. And even those brief stops had been forsaken since the afternoon, when Brunner had sighted the first of their pursuers. The beastman had loped off before the bounty hunter could get a shot at it. Not long after, the sound of many bodies crashing through the brush to either side of the path had lent speed to the horses' efforts. The beastmen were masters of the wild, and where the path turned and twisted like some serpentine river, the Chaos creatures could travel through the undergrowth and hidden trails known only to these children of the wild.

Many times, Brunner had heard hooting and snarling, and was certain that an ambush was about to be sprung. But the anticipated attack never came. Recalling the hulking chieftain's casual slaughter of its overeager follower, the bounty hunter could guess the reason for the reluctance of the monsters to attack.

Now, as they at last reached the villa, the sounds of pursuit had grown louder, and Brunner guessed that the entire pack had caught up with them now – even the brute he had crippled during their brief encounter. The sanctuary of the ruined Bertolucci villa had come none too soon. Brunner whipped his steed into a final effort, the packhorse obediently following after the leading horse.

The villa had been opulent and splendid in its day. A two-storey structure, the upper floors had been devoted to bed chambers, music rooms, dining halls and the every pleasure of its noble owners, while the larger lower floor had served as quarters for servants, as stables and kennels, kitchens and store-rooms. The villa's walls were still intact, but its wooden shutters and doors had long ago collapsed into rotten ruin. As Brunner rode up, he could see swarthy Tilean faces peering out at him from every opening. But a loud cry from the woods forced the attention of the watching men away from the bounty hunter and his companion for a moment – all eyes were trained upon the tree-line. Brunner rode his horse through the gaping maw of the old main entrance, whose double doors rotted on the floor just inside the portal. He lowered Elisia from the saddle, then dismounted after her and led the horses to where ten other steeds were tethered.

'Praise be to Shallya!', a voice cried out. A young man, wearing a suit of well-tailored clothes and a leather jupon studded with steel raced from one of the four doorways leading into the entrance hall. He was fair-featured, his black hair short, after the style favoured by the merchant princes themselves. He had the air of a man used to quality in his life, but as Brunner's gaze took in the newcomer's appearance, he noted the calluses upon his hands, the worn spots in the knees of his breeches, the abrasions on his boots. Here may be a man of quality, but he had not shirked from his part in labour, now that things were not so prosperous as before.

The young man strode towards the priestess. 'I feared that you would never come! My wife is very near her time, please hurry!' Then, as if noticing Brunner for the first time, the young man froze. 'Who are you? And where is Gramsci?'

'Questions which I was about to ask,' a second voice spoke from another doorway. The speaker was an older man, but shared the facial qualities of the younger. He was dressed like the other, his fine clothing perhaps not quite so well worn. His aged hands had been hardened by a life in which pleasure and comfort had been all too infrequent.

'His name is Habermas,' the priestess said. 'Your man and I met him on the road as we journeyed here. We were set upon by beastmen.' A sad look crossed Elisia's face and she bowed her hooded head in the direction of the older man. 'I fear that the monsters killed Gramsci. We barely escaped with our lives.'

'We have not escaped yet,' the bounty hunter's cold voice sounded for the first time. He turned his helmeted head towards the elder man. 'The monsters that set upon us have followed us here.' The news brought startled and fearful expressions to both men's faces. 'Even now they surround this ruin.'

The older man quickly recovered himself. 'Alberto,' he snapped, 'lead the priestess to Giana, then find me! I'll get the men together.' He turned toward the bounty hunter. 'I am no soldier, sir,' he addressed Brunner. 'The house of Bertolucci has seldom produced military men. If you have any notion of how best we might defend this place, I would like to hear it.'

SEVEN BODYGUARDS HAD remained loyal to Bertolucci after his fall from grace, and one of these had been Gramsci. That left only eight men apart from Brunner himself to hold the ruined villa. The bounty hunter snapped his orders as quickly as he could. Below, in the woods, the grunting and lowing of the monsters reached the villa's occupants, indicating that others were making their plans as well.

It was decided that those armed with crossbows would be positioned in the upper floor, descending when the brutes crossed the clear ground surrounding the hill. This accounted for five men. The remaining men, including Bertolucci and his son, were to stand with Brunner. They would guard two chambers: the larger entry hall where the horses were tethered, and the small parlour that abutted it and gave entry to the stairs leading to the upper floor. It was where the non-combatant servants and Alberto's expectant wife had retreated.

Hasty barricades were thrown across the windows and doorways, leaving only narrow places from which the defenders could peer out and Brunner could fire his own crossbows. It was a ramshackle defence, but it was the best Brunner could manage. Two things favoured their chances: the fact that most beastmen were too simple to manage

even the most rude missile weapon, and the fact that the
notion of burning the villa down about their ears would
likewise not occur to them. The brilliant blue-silver light
cast by a full and engorged Mannsleib did much to favour
the defenders; it made the grounds of the villa almost as
visible as under the noonday sun. Only beneath the surrounding trees were the shadows still long and the grip of
darkness tight.

No sooner had the preparations been made, and the
Tileans sent to their posts, than the beasts began their
attack. Brunner watched as a number of the brutes loped
from the edge of the trees, a lanky thing with a snake's
head squirming from its shoulders bearing a standard of
flayed skin. Brunner raised a clumsy-looking contraption
of wood and steel. He aimed the tube-like barrel at the
creature. The weapon sparked and a loud crack of thunder
sounded with the brilliant flash of its discharge.

The standard bearer howled and fell, crushing its flag
beneath its bleeding body. The other beastmen gave bleats
of fright and capered back into the woods.

'That should give them pause,' the bounty hunter said.
'Though I don't think that leader of theirs will let them hide
for long.' As if in response, ten brutes stole from the trees
once more. The bounty hunter watched as several of them
cried out, dropping as crossbow bolts pierced their flesh.
The wounded hastened back into the trees, leaving the dead
ones lying in the field. The scene was repeated on each side
of the villa, and soldiers shouted down news of the monsters' advance and retreat in the face of each volley.

'What are they doing?' Alberto asked the bounty hunter,
unable to find a reason for the beastmen's tactics.

'Testing us,' replied Brunner. 'They are trying to see what
kind of defence we have, how many archers. Where we are
strongest and where we are weakest.'

'But their probing has cost them ten of their number,'
marvelled the elder Bertolucci.

'No doubt they can spare twice as many,' Brunner
responded, watching the trees. 'I had the ill fortune to face

the thing that leads these animals, a worshipper of the
Blood God. Like its god, it cares not whose blood it sheds.'

A loud cry of savagery rose from the darkness, and the
beating of drums rolled from the woods. Horns sounded,
their moans low and warped. Shouts both near-human
and unhuman roared into the night sky. At the edges of the
trees, shapes appeared.

'Looks like our friends are done playing strategist,'
Brunner remarked, raising his crossbow. Then the frenzied,
inhuman mob burst from the shadows.

THE BATTLE WAS short, but fierce. Ten more beastmen were
wounded or slain by crossbow bolts before they could
reach the hill. Brunner had added his own fire to that of the
Bertolucci soldiers. As the monsters reached the ruin,
Brunner gave the first one to try and batter down the barricade in front of the wide entry a blast from his handgun.
The monster shrieked and toppled backwards, its chest a
mass of chewed meat. Others were quick to follow it. A second beast perished, its body draped across the barricade as
Brunner's crossbow pistol sent a bolt slamming into its eye.
Then he drew his sword and joined the other defenders.

Four of the bodyguards had descended, two of them
joining Bertolucci and their other comrade in the far room
to protect the stairs. The others joined Alberto and the
bounty hunter in the makeshift stable. The horses whin-
nied in fear as the stench of blood and the mangy pelts of
the beastmen reached them. One of the soldiers broke
away to try and quiet the animals that were straining at
their tethers.

'Leave them to their fear,' Brunner called to the man. 'If
you want to help, help us drive this scum away.'

Despite the best efforts of the men, the barricades were
not holding. Great holes had been chopped and clawed
into the wooden debris, and at each opening a slavering
monster snarled. One hound-like thing with a spider-like
assemblage of legs and a single clawed hand erupting from
its belly leaped through an opening. It capered wildly

about in the room, and snapped at the men with its claw before a blow from Alberto's sword sent the deformed limb sailing away from its body. A stroke from the nearest bodyguard's blade detached the snapping dog-head from its body. The thing's abnormal corpse sagged, as a bubble of blood oozed from the stump of its neck.

One of the soldiers cried out. Brunner looked round to see the man's torso fly away from his legs, and land in a bloody smear against the far wall of the chamber. A massive shape smashed its way through the barricade, its goat-like head craning from side to side, scanning the room for its prey. The monster now wore the severed head of Gramsci about its neck, a length of the man's intestines tying the trophy to the monster's neck.

The sight of the gruesome ornament caused Alberto and the remaining bodyguard to fall back in fear. Brunner met the monster's gaze, his icy stare unflinching before the yellow orbs peering from the beastman's mask. As the two locked eyes, the sounds of battle died away. The other beastmen fell back, their eyes gleaming in expectation and fear. Each howled for blood, but none of the beastmen wanted that blood to be their own.

The chieftain gestured with its gory bronze axe, a crude parody of Brunner's own challenge. The bounty hunter raised his sword and closed upon the beast. He circled the monster, as it circled him, its steps uneven as it favoured its uninjured leg. Then it roared and attacked. The axe swung down in a gleaming arc of death – only Brunner's quick reaction saved him from a blow that would have split him down the middle. Sparks flew as the axe bit into the tile floor.

The beastman recovered as Brunner lashed out at it, catching the killer's strike on the haft of its great bronze axe. The beastman spat bloody phlegm into Brunner's face, the gory drool trickling down the side of the bounty hunter's helm. Brunner replied by kicking a steel-toed boot at the monster's injured leg. The beast staggered, roaring in anger and pain. Brunner darted in once more, but the monster proved quicker than its great bulk would suggest, and the axe was slashing towards Brunner even as he began to move. The bronze blade scraped across the gromril breastplate, digging a deep scratch in the hard metal.

The bounty hunter arrested his charge; the beastman regained its feet.

Brunner glared at the monster, taunting it with his sword. The beastman snarled back and tensed itself, preparing for some brutal effort. Then it noticed Brunner's left hand, lying slack and immobile at his side. A flash of warning widened the monster's eyes and it raised both its hands to ward off the coming attack as Brunner thrust his left arm forward. This time, however, no cloud of salt enveloped the creature's face. Instead, Brunner slashed the creature's good leg, cutting through its knee with the blade held in his right hand.

The Chaos abomination screamed as it staggered from the maiming blow. It lashed out at Brunner once more, but the weight of the bronze axe overbalanced the crippled thing and it fell. The bounty hunter was quick to pounce upon his fallen adversary, slashing its right arm with his sword as his left hand stabbed a dagger across the brute's face. Thick blood streamed from the ruptured eye, and the beastman's body twitched in spasms of agony. The Tileans watched in horror as it strove to rise again. But its right arm was nearly severed, and the terrible bronze axe slipped from its slackened grasp.

As the axe clattered to the floor, Brunner darted in once more, stabbing his blade into the monster's throat, above the gruesome necklace it had crafted. The beastman's head sagged forward as the bounty hunter withdrew the blade, and it crumpled to the floor like a wilting flower.

The mutant throng at the barricade watched in silence as their champion died. Then a few loped into the room, their clawed hands empty. Brunner and the Tileans watched warily as the creatures converged on the body of their leader. Gripping the carcass under the arms and by the legs, two brutes carried it back through the doorway. A third beastman, its face almost human but for the horns sprouting along the bridge of its nose, grabbed the bronze axe with its clawed arms and followed its comrades.

Slowly, the brutish throng retreated. When the horses at last grew quiet, the men knew that the last of their foes had truly gone.

Brunner made his way to the barricade and peered down on the moonlit clearing below.

'I truly hate working for free,' the bounty hunter muttered to himself.

BRUNNER WATCHED AS the silent beastmen bore the corpse of their champion into the gloom of the trees. He looked over at the younger Bertolucci leaning against the doorway. The young man's face was smeared with dirt and dried bestial blood, his clothing ragged and torn, his leather tunic sporting a gash that had nearly penetrated the skin beneath.

'Think they will come again?' the merchant asked. 'Slink back into the woods and rally?'

Brunner shook his head. 'No,' he replied. 'They take their hero away for their own profane rites, which is more important to them than the prospect of man-flesh for their bellies. They will take that monster that led them and tonight, when the rot has had a chance to set in that creature's carcass, they will take their fangs and their knives to him.' Brunner saw Alberto recoil in horror, his face blanching at the image. 'They think that if they consume the meat of a champion like that, they will absorb his strength. There will be a great falling out as they try to determine who will partake in the feast. By this time tomorrow, that rabble will have scattered, none of them in the same pack.'

The sound of rustling cloth brought both men away from the view afforded by the doorway. Elisia stepped from the room beyond and moved toward Alberto. The youth hastened to the priestess's side.

'My father?' he asked, his voice heavy with concern. The priestess shook her head, smiling.

'No, your son,' she replied. It took a moment for the import of her words to sink in, then a light of joy and understanding gleamed in Alberto's face. He grabbed the priestess's arms.

'My son? When? How?'

'Yes, a boy, as healthy and wonderful as any I have seen,' Elisia responded. 'He arrived during the night.' A dour look came upon her. 'Battle or no, he had decided this was his time.' A smug smile replaced her dour look. 'As to the how of it, perhaps you might ask your wife about that, if you have forgotten. She is with your son in the far room.'

With hardly another look at either Brunner or Elisia, Alberto hurried from the chamber.

The priestess watched him go, recalling for an instant the many hundreds of times she had seen men, great or poor, react in the same manner when she bore such tidings.

'And what of the elder Bertolucci?' the cold voice of the bounty hunter intruded. Elisia turned and stared into the emotionless face beneath the mask of steel.

'He is down in the kitchen, warming some porridge. He was injured, but his wound is not serious, and I have taken precautions so that infection should not set in,' she answered. A sudden questioning look entered her eyes. 'You have not troubled yourself about anyone else in the brief time since I have met you. Even when you rescued me from the beastmen, it seemed more for your own convenience than any concern for me. Why does Bertolucci interest you so?'

The bounty hunter made no reply, leaving the priestess's question unanswered as he strode into the inner chambers of the ruined villa.

THE OLD KITCHEN was a shambles. Its tiled floor was cracked and broken, and grass peeped from between broken squares. Dead, ragged brambles were strewn in the corners where Bertolucci and his men had cast them hurriedly away. From dozens of places, sunlight shone down into the chamber, bringing light into the shadowy ruin, but also the chill of the dawn dew.

In the old hearth, a small fire smouldered, heating a large black cauldron. It was an original implement of the villa, a relic of the old days that neither time, nor weather, nor looter had touched. And it had served the exiled merchant well; he boiled a mash of grain and vegetable into something that might feed his retinue after their long, hard night of battle. But Bertolucci was not so altruistic as to think only of his men. He sat before a cracked, leaning wooden table, on an even more feeble bench, and noisily slopped the contents of the wooden bowl with a jagged piece of brown bread.

The sound of armour caused the merchant to look up from his meal. His eyes focused upon those of the man who had entered the kitchen.

Bertolucci stared into the helmed visage of the stranger who had arrived with the priestess. A premonition of dread froze him for a moment, but he soon recovered, reaching forward and ladling some of the porridge into a second bowl.

'I hope that you do not mind,' the merchant apologised, 'but I felt I should do something useful if I could not be at the wall. And, since I did make it...' Bertolucci finished his statement by biting down on the dripping bread.

Brunner stepped towards the table.

'I'll eat later,' the bounty hunter said, the eyes behind the visor of his helm burning into Bertolucci's. The merchant finished his mouthful of food and rose from the table.

'I should have guessed,' the man said, the dread once more crawling down his spine. 'Couldn't you just tell Volonté you didn't find us?' His look was resigned; he already knew the killer's answer before it was spoken.

'I have a commission,' Brunner explained. 'The only thing in this world I honour. But Volonté only wants you. Your children are not my concern.'

Bertolucci was thoughtful for a moment, some measure of relief and hope filling him even as fear gnawed at his guts. 'I saw you fight,' the man said. He placed a hand on his wounded arm. 'Even whole, you would have made short work of me.' The merchant reached into his tunic, noticing the bounty hunter's grip tighten about the hilt of his blade. He continued anyway, drawing a leather purse from his clothing.

'Tell me, what is the market value of a swine in the streets of Miragliano these days?' the merchant asked, his eyes returning Brunner's icy gaze with a hateful flame.

'Eighty copper pieces, when last I passed the swineherd's lane,' the bounty killer responded. The merchant carefully counted out an equivalent measure of gold and set the coins on the table. He sighed and set the leather pouch beside them. Brunner nodded at the man, and drew his sword.

Bertolucci never saw the blade that sliced through his neck, so swift were the bounty hunter's movements. As blood spread from his cloven neck, the last thing the merchant's eyes saw were the gloved hands scooping up the coins he had placed on the table, never disturbing the leather purse beside them.

THE SOUND OF booted feet brought Brunner up from his gory labour. He spun about, seeing the joy fade from Alberto's features. He had rushed here, after tearing himself away from his wife and child to usher his father upstairs to see his grandson. Now a different purpose filled the youth.

'Assassin!' he hissed, ripping his sabre from its scabbard. Brunner did not wait to trade words with the boy, but met Alberto's first strike with a parry. The youth did not fully recover from the fended-off attack, but turned the deflection into a sideways swipe at the bounty hunter. His mind clouded with rage, Alberto had forgotten all his schooling in the art of swordplay and duelling. It would have been easy for Brunner to kill him.

The bounty hunter's sword licked out, penetrating Alberto's almost non-existent guard, and lashing upwards towards the boy's head. At the last moment, however, Brunner adjusted his strike, smashing the flat of his blade into the boy's shoulder, rather than the edge. Alberto dropped to his knees, staggered by the blow. Brunner smashed the pommel of his sword into the stunned man's head, rendering him insensible. Under the care of the priestess of Shallya, he knew, the boy would recover. But not until long after he had gone.

The sound of more running feet announced the hurried advance of the remaining retainers. The men cast murderous looks at the bounty hunter when they saw the two bodies lying behind him. They drew their blades as one.

'It is the elder I came for,' Brunner stated in a voice like a chill winter wind. 'Alberto Bertolucci will recover.' One of the men sheathed his sword and cautiously manoeuvred his way around the bounty killer. He reached the prone form of Alberto, clasped its wrist and nodded at his fellows.

'If you wish to die for your former master, I shall oblige you,' Brunner declared, his piercing gaze meeting each of the guards in turn. 'But it seems to me that your duty lies with your living master now.' It took but a moment for the men to reluctantly return blades to scabbards. They too had seen the contest between the bounty hunter and the beastman.

Brunner strode down the hall, towards the cavernous entry chamber where the horses were stabled. As he passed the stairs, he met the accusing glare of Elisia.

'You never cared about any of us,' she snarled. Brunner smiled at her and stalked away.

'Only about Bertolucci, and the price on his head,' the bounty hunter said, making his way toward his animals. 'Pray to your goddess that I never have cause to care about you.'

THE BLOATED FIGURE stood before the slowly mildewing painting of nymphs and satyrs, studying the painting, and its creeping corruption. A pity, the money-lender thought for a moment, for it had been a very vibrant and arousing piece, in its day. He had accepted it in exchange for not breaking the owner's hands for missing a payment – though that rendezvous with mutilation was only deferred by a few months, when the man again fell behind in his debt. Volonté sucked at his teeth. Yes, soon he would have to see about having this one replaced. It never occurred to him to actually see to the care of his possessions. The acquisition was all that mattered to him. And now he wondered which of his debtors might be the owner of something of equal style and quality.

A sound in the shadowy room caused the massive man to turn. He could dimly see a figure standing in the flickering candlelight, light dancing upon a helmet of steel.

'Who's there?' the money-lender choked, fear seizing him. As the bounty hunter stepped more fully into the light, Volonté breathed a deep sigh of relief. 'Brunner,' he laughed. 'My servants did not announce you.'

'I found my own way in,' the bounty hunter explained. He lifted his hand, showing Volonté the leather-wrapped object he had carved from Bertolucci. The money-lender's piggish eyes settled upon the gruesome thing, a smile widening across his face.

'You have it!' he chortled. 'Bertolucci's heart!' He held out his hand, gesturing for the bounty hunter to give him his grisly trophy. Brunner stepped forward, dropping the leather-wrapped object in the fat-man's swollen paw. Volonté hurriedly unwrapped it, revealing the gruesome, blood-soaked organ within. The fat man laughed deeply.

'Your daughter was there as well,' the bounty hunter said. 'She has just given birth to a child, by Bertolucci's son.'

'Ha!' the money-lender laughed. 'With that old thief dead, the slut will come crawling back to me soon enough. Her husband can keep their bastard whelp for all I care.' The fat man leaned over the disembodied heart, sniffing at it with flared nostrils, and savouring the stench of the butchered flesh. He snapped his head about, reaching into the table, withdrawing a cloth pouch, his hand trembling with the weight as he lifted it.

'Your price, bounty hunter,' the money-lender said. 'You have done a good, if expensive, job for me.' A sudden gleam of hate flickered across Volonté's face, and he drew the bag close to his breast. 'But before I pay you, I want to hear about his death. I want to hear how Bertolucci grovelled before you and begged for his life. I want you to describe his screams as you cut his heart out!'

Brunner took another step forward. 'Then I must disappoint you.' A sullen look of anger contorted Volonté's obese features. 'Bertolucci did not beg, nor did he grovel. When he learned who I was, and what I had come for, he did not try to run.' Brunner looked into Volonté's eyes, seeing the dissatisfied look there. 'He simply asked me what the market value of swine was in Miragliano these days.'

A puzzled look replaced the scowl on Volonté's face. Brunner took another step closer.

'He paid me eighty pieces of copper before he died,' Brunner said, his hand gripping the pommel of the long-bladed and serrated-edged knife sheathed at his hip. Volonté laughed nervously.

'Not enough to buy a man like you, eh?' the money-lender stammered, sweat beading along his brow.

'It is the quarry that determines a bounty hunter's price,' Brunner said, closing the distance between the men. 'A pig is worth much less than a man.'

Volonté's servants roused in their slumbers as a sharp scream echoed through the walls. The sound seemed to come from the study where their master was in the habit of going over his records of debts late at night. Apparently he was not alone this evening. The thought did not unduly disturb Volonté's household, and many of them went back to sleep. There would be time enough to divide up the money-lender's possessions in the morning.

THE DOOM OF GNASHRAK

PROWLING THE STREETS *of Miragliano one day, in search of an elusive merchant who had a supply of Arabyian inks at a suspiciously low price, I found myself unexpectedly staring into the black steel face of Brunner's helmet. I was surprised at our sudden meeting; it had been some months since our last conversation. The bounty hunter nodded, relaxing the grip his hand had assumed on the hilt of his sword as he saw my own unarmed condition. I believe that the bounty hunter had a certain fondness for me, but I doubt if he trusted anyone.*

I greeted Brunner warmly, happy indeed to have stumbled upon him, thoughts of stolen ink at once banished from my head. My initial recounting of the man's exploits had proven extremely popular. Indeed, I was still living off some of the proceeds the pamphlet had won me, and I was eager to repeat my past success. I wasted no time in unleashing a barrage of questions, asking him where he had gone these past months, what feats of bravery (and avarice, though I kept that thought firmly to myself) he had accomplished. Brunner batted away my questions, saying that the street was no place to talk. He began to walk away, and as he did so, I noticed the stiff manner in which he moved and the fact that some pieces of his armour appeared to be new, as though the old ones had required replacements. The thought occurred to me that perhaps his lengthy absence had not been due to some long and difficult string of hunts, but because this grim and forbidding man had actually encountered a foe who was his equal. Perhaps he had spent these long months recovering from injuries received in battle?

Thrilled by the prospect of such a tale, I hurried after him, a feat made easy by the slowed nature of his stride. As I had half expected, Brunner's path led me to the Black Boar. I found the bounty hunter seated, as usual, at one of the rear tables, a tankard of beer set before him. I noticed a second tankard opposite him and quietly chastised myself for being so foolish as to think that my contact had not seen me dogging his tracks.

I took the unspoken invitation, and seated myself at his table. I sipped at my beer a moment, noting the dents and scratches on his armour, and observing once more the stiff, awkward movements of his left arm as he lifted the cup to his mouth. I inquired as to what mishap had discomfited Brunner so, not daring to suggest that he had fallen prey to injury or illness.

The bounty hunter sipped at his beer for a moment then set his tankard down, fixing me with cold blue eyes. In a low voice that was kindred to the sound of a raven gliding toward a gallows, he asked me if I had ever hunted orcs...

SMOKE BILLOWED FROM the blazing rubble, fingers of flame clutching at the darkening, overcast sky. Screams and sounds of slaughter rose into the darkness, as if to welcome the advent of night. Beside the inferno that had moments before been a barn, a massive, brutish shape loomed, glaring at the burning building.

The dancing flames picked out details of the figure. The shape belonged to no human body. The legs were short, bandy, almost bowed. The arms were long, much longer than a man's: more like the limbs of the fabled apes of the South Lands and rippling with such a quantity of muscle that even the strongest man could not match. The shoulders were broad, nearly four feet in breadth. The head jutted forward from the shoulders, supported by a thick stump of a neck. Its skull was thick, the forehead sloping away so quickly from the creature's face as to be almost nonexistent. Sharp, wolf-like ears adorned the sides of the head. One of them was notched and sported dozens of steel and brass rings, blades of rusting metal dangling from each loop.

The face of the beast was dominated by a massive maw, the lower jaw of the creature's mouth jutting forward, allowing its tusk-like fangs to stab past its upper lips and cheeks. Each of the tusks was tipped by a cap of steel pinned into the living ivory of the fangs. The tips of the two longest fangs rested against the edge of the deep-set eye sockets that sank into the creature's skull from either side of its small, smashed, snout-like nose. Beady red eyes glowered from the shadowed pits of the creature's face, offsetting the dark green hue of its leathery, weathered hide.

The monster had come from the impenetrable depths of the mountains in the south known as the Vaults, and wore the tale of his travels upon his grotesque body. Armour encased his form, armour ripped from the bodies of butchered foes. The shoulder plates that protected his upper arms had been beaten from the helmets of human knights, the chainmail hauberk that dripped about his chest and hung below his waist had once graced an ogre mercenary, the steel leggings had been cobbled together from the greaves of a dozen militiamen who had been unfortunate enough to discover the beings that had been preying upon their mountain village's cattle.

The piecemeal armour was held together by numerous leather straps and bits of wire, and it creaked and groaned as the orc moved. But the blade held in his ham-like fist was no looted and violated craftwork of man. The work of his own people's brutish smiths, it was a massive, cleaver-like blade, its edge nearly three-and-a-half feet in length, honed to a dull sharpness that would punch through bone and steel without notching the blade. A thick, round stump of steel formed a crude handle for the orc's fist to grip at the bottom of the blade. A sideshow strongman would have been hard pressed to even lift the mass of steel. The orc lifted it above his head in one hand without even a grunt of effort from his lungs. The choppa was like the orc who wielded it – and whose people had crafted it – massive, monstrous, ugly and murderous.

The orc's mouth gaped open, exposing bits of rotting meat caught between the fangs. Its voice roared over the screams, over the crackle of the flames. It was like the boom of a cannon, and carried with it the grating harshness of a knife scraping bone. The slobbering, brutal tones sounded like shredding metal. The monster was howling to his minions in the harsh Orrakh tongue.

The orcs had fallen upon the village like one of the Grey Mountains' capricious storms: suddenly, without warning, and utterly devastating. The villagers, peasant farmers and a few craftsmen, had fallen before the orcs like wheat before the scythe, and the greenskin marauders had reaped that harvest in a frenzy of murder and butchery. The terrified Bretonnians had mounted no form of defence. They had run before the orcs, fleeing for their lives rather than standing to fight. The sight of their human adversaries fleeing had driven the raiders into an even more berserk rage. They had come for loot and slaughter, it was true, but above all else, they had come for battle. Now, with the entire hamlet in flames, the last survivors cowered within the quickly burning barn.

Gnashrak turned his attention toward the barn as the wooden door opened. A coughing man emerged, thick black smoke billowing from behind him. Several sootstained, sobbing faces appeared in the doorway behind him, gasping for fresh air.

Gnashrak's beady red eyes studied the man. He was a burly sort for a human, most likely the protector of this nest of cattle. A simple leather contrivance hung about his neck and was tied to his knees. The man held a large hammer in his hands, but one look told Gnashrak that it was a tool, not a weapon. The orc's gruesome face twisted, as though he had eaten something distasteful. He spat a blob of phlegm as if to remove a foulness from his mouth. Still, the warboss hefted his huge blade and shambled forward.

Gnashrak growled at the leather-aproned human. The man hesitated, glancing back at the burning barn. Then he walked forward. He shifted his grip on the hammer, his knuckles turning white as he firmed his grasp. The man spread his legs apart, adopting a combat stance. It had been long years since he had raised a weapon against bandit raiders, but the blacksmith was no coward. He fought down the fear in his breast, staring at the mob of greenskinned monsters with his best defiant glare. Gnashrak and his followers laughed at the pathetic sight. The blacksmith rushed at them, hate overcoming his fear as their grunting laughter washed over him. Gnashrak's lips twisted into a parody of a smile.

The orc warboss loped forward, the brutal length of his choppa held straight up beside him. Thick lines of foamy spittle trickled from the corners of the fiend's mouth as he anticipated the coming fray. The blacksmith was the first man in the entire village to turn and fight him, and Gnashrak intended to savour the moment.

'Orc scum!' the man screamed in a voice filled more with terror than rage. He leapt forward, bringing the hammer down in a smashing blow. The orc leader stepped back, turning his body, and letting the clumsy blow strike the armour of his shoulder guard. Gnashrak glared at the man. The orc's jaws dropped to their full cavernous extent and a deep, rumbling roar issued from its bellows-like lungs. The blacksmith cringed, holding the hammer across his chest, as though to make a barrier between himself and the greenskin marauder.

Gnashrak lifted his massive blade and brought the weapon crashing down. The crude choppa snapped the steel hammer like a twig, and sliced into the flesh of the man cowering behind the crude weapon, crunching through his ribcage and severing him crosswise from shoulder to waist. Blood exploded from the wound that slid apart, the dismembered halves slipping into the dirt. The faces at the doorway of the burning barn wailed in horror. Gnashrak paused to hawk a glob of phlegm on the dead body. He turned and roared at his followers.

The orcs rushed forward, not using their weapons to kill, but to herd the survivors back into the burning barn.

Gnashrak watched his mob for a moment, then craned his bull neck about, casting a last disgusted look at the mutilated blacksmith. He turned his eyes from the body, towards the orcs herding the cowering survivors back into the blazing barn, with the points of spears. The screams brought a slight smile to Gnashrak's face, but it was not enough. As the clouds at last released the slightest of drizzles, the orc nodded to himself.

Somewhere to the north, he would find the knights who owned the sorry cattle he and his mob had claimed. Then there would be a slaughter worthy of an orc, a proper fight to make the name of Gnashrak Headkrusher. The peasants thought the harvest was past, but the orc would teach them and their masters differently. There was a second harvest coming. A harvest reaped not with sickles, but with swords.

Opening his massive maw once more, Gnashrak voiced his bestial howl of ambition into the falling night.

THE CASTLE OF the Marquis de Galfort loomed over the flat meadowlands. Tall towers thrust upward from every corner of the curtain wall, while still taller pillars of stone rose from the keep. From the height of the tallest tower, the marquis could look down upon his entire domain, even to the distant green apparition on the horizon that marked the easternmost limit of his realm, the edge of the faerie-haunted wood of Loren. He could see every farm, every village, every little hovel the peasants of his land called home.

It was a sight the aged marquis never tired of: looking down upon his land, his possessions, knowing that they were his, his by decree of Bretonnia's king and the grace of the Lady, Bretonnia's patron deity. He would drink in the blue of the sky, the gold of the fields, the green of the meadows long into the afternoon. Then the sun would begin its downward descent and the marquis would return to his chambers within the castle and attend to such duties as were necessary to manage his domain and could not be delegated to his wife or his steward.

But this morning, the view had been spoiled, befouled by a thick stream of black smoke rising from the south, in the direction of the distant mountains. This was where a few hamlets stood, dwellings for the rugged peasant miners who clawed salt from the slopes of the Vaults and helped de Galfort's domain prosper. Later in the day, the wasted, worn-out form of a peasant was brought to the castle, discovered by one of de Galfort's game wardens wandering through the forest. Yet this sorry, terrified creature was no poacher and the tale he told the marquis turned his blood to ice. Not since the time of his own grandfather had the domain of the de Galforts been set upon by orcs. When last the marauders had come, it had taken two generations to repair the damage.

Now the aged Marquis de Galfort sat in his throne room, deep in disturbed thoughts. He had ordered messengers to be sent at once to the neighbouring counts, barons and dukes, letting them know of this peril that had come upon his domain and threatened them all. There was no question that all were at risk, for orcs respect no boundaries, and it would not matter to them if the village they plundered belonged to de Galfort or some other. No, his neighbours would react as decent Bretonnian nobles, and would send a company of knights and such armsmen as they might muster to augment de Galfort's own forces and hunt the orcs down. But it would take time, much time, for the aid to arrive. And the orcs would be free to loot and despoil until then. Unless the marquis were to act on his own, without the support of his neighbours.

The marquis looked up from his chair and stared down into the eager young face of his son, Etienne, and wondered if he had ever borne such inexperience and naiveté in his own youth.

The boy had pleaded with him all morning, ever since the tale of orcs and slaughter had been related, to release to him the household knights, to let him ride down these monsters and make them learn the folly of trespassing upon lands protected by the de Galfort name.

The marquis's observation that the peasant had no idea how many orcs were in this raiding party, that an entire army of the greenskinned monsters might have been vomited from the mountains, had done nothing to dim the boy's enthusiasm. He was young, not yet learned in the ways of war; the only blood he had ever shed was that of wolves, wild cats and bandits. He reckoned this to be a similar task, perhaps a bit nobler, putting more faith in the favours of the Lady and good Bretonnian steel than he did in the strength of monsters he only knew from legend and travellers' tales.

Truth to tell, it had been a long time since any in de Galfort's domain had laid eyes upon an orc. Even the marquis himself had only seen stuffed specimens in the castle of the Duc de Vilifere – never a living, breathing greenskin. And the marquis was an old enough hunter and soldier to know that it is folly to pursue a foe, beast or man, whom you know nothing of.

A servant entered, bowing low before the two noblemen and hastened toward the seated marquis.

The marquis raised a thin hand, the fur-trimmed cuff of his voluminous robe falling away, and gestured for the servant to speak.

'By your leave, my lord,' the servant said, his voice low, his eyes downcast. 'I felt that you would like to be informed that the outlander is making ready to depart.'

The marquis rose from his chair, an excited light blazing in his eyes. His wrinkled skin cracked into a smile. 'Of course,' he said. 'Why did I not think of it before?' He fixed his gaze on the servant. 'Hasten to the gate and inform Sir Doneval that the outlander is not to be allowed to leave.' A sly look entered the marquis's eyes. 'Tell him to bring the bounty hunter to me.'

THE MARQUIS STROKED the scraggly moustache that spread from the thick grey hairs of his nostrils to the corners of his chin. It was a nervous habit, a peculiarity of temperament that afflicted him whenever he was discomfited. Normally, it only struck him at balls and masquerades and other such public functions of pomp and pageantry. But there was something decidedly unsettling about the man who stood before him, his face unreadable behind the steel mask of the black helm he had not doffed upon entering the presence of the marquis, as custom demanded. Nor had he bowed, as had the armoured bulk of Sir Doneval, who was now crouched upon one knee.

But the marquis had expected such disregard for his station from the man. Had he not behaved so the previous day? Had he not strode to the marquis's throne with such arrogance that he might have been the Emperor himself? Had he shown any consideration for the delicate sensibilities of the women of the court when he had presented the marquis with the grisly object that had brought him to de Galfort's domain?

No, it was not the contempt for nobility which the bounty hunter showed that unsettled the marquis. There was an aura about the man, something which the aged marquis, with one foot in Morr's domain already, could see with his tired old eyes. It was as if an air of dread hung about the man like a shroud, a miasma of blood and death.

The marquis had not shied from the sword in his younger years, and he had known knights who had been as steeped in blood as any Sartosan corsair or Norse reaver. But there had been reasons for the lives they took, a cause that ennobled their deeds, a chivalry that governed their actions. There was no such honour about the bounty hunter. Though he walked with death, like a comrade in arms, he did not respect it. Death was nothing more than a commodity to him, a ware to be traded at market.

'I understood our business to be at an end,' the bounty hunter rasped icily. Beside him, Sir Doneval tensed, one hand dropping to the pommel of his sword. The bounty hunter let his own gloved hand caress the butt of the pistol nestled against his belly.

'There is another service I would ask of you,' the marquis said, choosing to ignore the bounty hunter's words. 'I shall pay you twice what you collected for Lorca the Estalian and his brigands.'

Brunner stared up at the seated noble. Silence lingered for so long that it seemed to become an almost tangible thing. At last he nodded his head, the gloved hand adopting a slightly more casual position on the butt of the pistol. 'You have my interest,' Brunner said at last. 'Who do you want me to kill?'

'Not who, but what,' the marquis corrected. The bounty hunter's eyes narrowed behind his visor, though from suspicion or interest, the noble could not be sure. 'Yesterday, a band of orcs invaded my land, torched one of my villages, and murdered my peasants. I want you to track them down.'

'I've fought orcs before,' Brunner replied. 'Their raiding parties come in many sizes. A horde numbers thousands and a warband consists of a single bull. I have no desire to trade swords with either.' The bounty hunter touched a finger to the brim of his helm, turning on his heel to leave.

'I do not ask you to kill them yourself,' the marquis hastened to say, hoping to keep the killer from leaving. He wondered whether his men would be able to detain him. Fortunately the bounty hunter stopped and faced him once more. 'I ask only that you lead my son and a company of my finest knights to these brutes.'

'And if they number more than your men can handle?' Brunner asked pointedly. The kneeling Sir Doneval bit down the protest welling up in his massive chest.

'I pay you only to track these monsters, not to fight them. If they are more than the men I send with you and my son can handle, you will return here, to await the reinforcements I have requested from the neighbouring domains.'

'And who shall make the decision as to how many orcs are too many?' Brunner asked, his sharp tone suggesting that he already knew the answer before it was given.

'My son shall be in command, Brunner,' the marquis replied, refusing to be intimidated in his own castle. 'You shall defer to him in all matters of command.'

Brunner stood still for a moment, and the Marquis de Galfort wondered if he would refuse the task. But at last the bounty hunter nodded his armoured head. 'Very well, I agree to the terms. But it will be three times what you paid me for Lorca. More if I have cause to use my sword.' The bounty hunter fixed the marquis with a penetrating gaze. 'With orcs, one is never sure who is the hunter and who the hunted.'

THE COMPANY OF horsemen rode from the yawning maw of the castle gate, the ponderous weight of armoured knight and barded warhorse causing the timbers of the drawbridge to shudder and creak. Fifty of the Marquis de Galfort's knights and their lightly armoured squires had been delegated to accompany Etienne de Galfort and the foreign bounty hunter. The young de Galfort was certain that it was too many noble men to dispatch upon so rude a quest, positive that a dozen knights would be more than an equal for any brutish adversary. Brunner had refrained from commenting on the boy's enthusiasm.

'The thin column of smoke there on the horizon,' Sir Doneval pointed a steel-clothed finger toward the south. Brunner followed the knight's gesture. 'That was the hamlet of Villiers.'

The bounty hunter nodded. 'What is the closest habitation to Villiers?' the icy voice asked.

'Of what concern is that?' interrupted Etienne de Galfort. The visor of his helm had been lifted, exposing his smooth-featured, handsome face, and an eager gleam in his eyes. He did not flinch as the bounty hunter turned in his saddle and fixed him with a cold stare.

'The orcs will head for the next closest village,' Brunner explained. 'With our horses, we should be able to engage them before they reach their destination.'

'Such is your view on the situation,' objected Etienne. 'But what if the orcs do not proceed as you say? We shall have wasted our time, and worn out our steeds in pursuit of phantoms.'

'At least we would be able to warn the peasants,' Sir Doneval said. 'They should be able to retreat back to the safety of your father's castle.'

'And shall we ride across the whole domain and warn every little hovel to pack its belongings and fly to the castle?' Etienne de Galfort responded, shaking his head. 'We would be weeks rounding up every miner, woodsman and shepherd.' The young nobleman clenched his mailed fist. 'No, we serve them best by running these monsters to ground before they can cause further harm.'

Brunner leaned forward, the leather of his saddle creaking, the blue eyes behind the visor glaring at Etienne. 'And how do you propose to accomplish this feat?'

'We shall ride to the hamlet of Villiers,' replied Etienne. 'There you shall do what my father is paying you to do. You shall pick up the trail of the orcs and follow their tracks back to their lair.' The nobleman snorted with contempt. 'Then you will be free to pull back as we attend to the monsters.'

Brunner spat into the dust of the road. 'These are orcs on the march,' he explained. 'They have no lair. They sleep only when fatigue overpowers them, and lie where they fall. They can march for days without rest, and their wind will carry them longer than even the best of your horses. If you try to wear them down, they will wear you down, and fall upon you when you are tired, and most in need of rest. No, it is better to anticipate them, to lie in wait for them.'

'I am in command here,' Etienne snapped. 'We ride for Villiers, and you will find the trail these orcs have taken. That is an order. This is a hunt, bounty killer, not some Tilean pirate prince's game of skulk and dagger. I think you will find these monsters much less capable of matching Bretonnian vigour than you imagine.'

So saying, Etienne reined his steed about and set it galloping down the southward spur of the track. The other knights and their squires followed. With a last, surly look at the castle and the aged marquis who had impressed him into accepting this task, Brunner turned Fiend, his own bay, about and rode after the line of Bretonnians.

OLD MARCEL WHISTLED a tune as he made his way down the rocky terrain, back toward the little mining camp. The heavy wicker basket of salt rocks was lashed to his back, but it was a weight the miner had borne many times, and he no longer even felt the burden except when it was no longer there. The Bretonnian thought about the meal his wife was preparing for him: the small fowl his young son had claimed with his bow the day before would make good eating after boiling over a small flame for the day.

The miner suddenly pitched to the ground, misjudging his step. Marcel crashed onto his belly, skinning his knee on the loose stones, the rocks of salt spilling from his pack. He gave voice to a curse as he crawled toward the nearest of the crystals. But a deep, rumbling sound froze him in place. He turned his face to see what could utter such a harsh, unpleasant sound.

Beady red eyes gleamed back at the man from a scarred visage of fangs and leathery green skin. The orc laughed again. It had not been a misstep that had tripped the old Bretonnian but a shove from the orc's massive paw. Marcel began to crawl away from the hulking monster, noting with alarm the massive axe gripped in its other paw. The monster watched the man retreat. Marcel could see amusement fade from the greenskin's eyes, and a cold look of death creep in. The orc uttered a low snarl and raised the huge axe, taking a step towards the old miner.

THE COLUMN OF armoured men was silent as it emerged from the tree-lined trail that led to the smouldering remains of the tiny village. They had ridden hard from the desolation that had been the hamlet of Villiers. It was shortly after the knights had arrived at the site of the earlier massacre that a squire had spied the plume of smoke rising from the east. At once, the horsemen had set out at a gallop along the narrow track that slithered its way through the trees and grassy fields toward the looming rocky slopes of the mountains.

Etienne de Galfort stared up at the severed head that watched the knights emerge from the wood. It was a grisly thing, the face nearly cleft in half by a gruesome cut that sank deep into the bone of the skull, the flesh darkened by flame. It had been spitted upon a crude spear, from which other ghastly talismans dangled, and swayed in the breeze from the smouldering remains of a large bonfire. The young nobleman's expression was unreadable as he considered the hideous object. He raised a mailed hand to his face, and motioned with his other for a squire to come forward and bury the vile totem.

It was a repetition of the scene they had found at Villiers: every building put to the torch. Butchered bodies lay strewn about the devastation. At the centre of each carnage, a great fire had been built from wood and debris ransacked from the dwellings, and before each fire had been placed a gory talisman of limbs and skulls.

Etienne looked at the hulking figure of Sir Doneval beside him, the older knight's face completely hidden within the great helm he wore. Then he cast a guilty glance at the bounty hunter. Brunner had dismounted and was examining the footprints exactly as he had done at Villiers.

The footprints were all inhuman. They were sunk to a depth even a fully armoured knight's weight did not manage. The feet were broader and shorter than human feet, so that even the smallest betokened an immense size. Some of the feet were shod, others were bare. Brunner had informed Etienne that there had been at least twenty-five individual orcs at Villiers, based upon the prints. Now he rose from a cursory examination and faced the nobleman.

'This was the same mob,' the bounty hunter declared. 'No question. I have both three-toe and the one with the clubbed foot here. There can't be two orcs with feet like that rampaging about in your father's domain.'

Etienne sighed loudly. He looked away from the bounty hunter, staring about the clearing. The lightly armoured squires had spread out, their bows held at the ready, their keen eyes scanning the trees. The knights were moving their steeds through the ruins, examining the handiwork of the orcs. The sight added fire to the outrage boiling in their hearts. Finally, Etienne turned towards Brunner.

'You were right,' he said. 'We should have come here first. This is my fault.'

Brunner stared back. 'We might have saved these people, but the orcs would have only hit someplace else.' The bounty hunter noted the confused look entering Etienne's eyes. He hastened to explain. 'You have to understand something about orcs. It is true they live for plunder and massacre. But above all else, they lust after battle. These totems, those bonfires, they are a challenge.'

'But if they want to fight, why won't they face us?' Etienne demanded, his knightly pride insulted by the thought of such creatures questioning his courage.

'Because whatever bull is leading this mob is no fool,' Brunner said, spitting into the dust and ash. 'An orc leader is a mixture of raw strength, charisma, and cunning. This one seems to have a bit more cunning than usual. He wants a fight, but he is smart enough to want a fight that he can win. He has maybe thirty orcs with him. You have fifty horsemen.' Brunner let a harsh laugh escape his lips. 'He might not be able to count, but he can certainly recognise a lop-sided pairing.'

'Then what do we do?' Etienne asked. 'He won't stand and fight, you say that tracking him would only wear us down, and if we don't give chase, he's just going to burn down every settlement in the domain!'

The bounty hunter's voice became a low, harsh whisper. 'We split the force. We give him a fight more in keeping with what he is looking for.'

BRUNNER RODE AT the front of the small group of horsemen. Five knights and their lightly armoured squires were ranged about along the trail behind him. The bounty hunter looked over at his side, meeting the gaze of Sir Doneval. The knight swatted a horsefly away from his face.

'How long do you think it will take?' the knight asked.

'Not long,' the bounty hunter replied. 'We've been watched since we left the mine.'

The killer's words brought a startled gasp from the knight. He spun about in the saddle, scanning the trees and underbrush that lined the trail. 'If they are out there, what are they waiting for?' Sir Doneval demanded.

Brunner let a short laugh rasp from his throat.

'Oh, the boss of this mob is indeed a rare one,' the bounty hunter said. 'He's holding them back until he is certain that Etienne isn't following us. He's making sure it isn't some sort of trap.'

'And when he is satisfied that Etienne isn't coming?' the knight asked.

As if in answer, a black-fletched arrow shrieked out of the undergrowth, striking the knight's armoured breast-plate and bouncing from the metal. More arrows followed, some striking horses, others striking men. The knights, in their suits of metal plate, were immune to the fusillade of arrows, but the horses and squires were not so fortunate. Screams – human and equine – tore into the breeze.

'Is there open ground near here?' Brunner shouted at Sir Doneval. The knight nodded his helmeted head.

'There is a clearing not far to the north,' the knight shouted, pointing his sword towards the path. A second barrage of arrows sped from the shadows, accompanied now by the grunts and howls of the orc archers.

Brunner lashed his horse into action, racing forward down the path, the knights and their retinue following his lead. Behind them, they left three squires, their bodies pierced by the orc arrows. One of the men, pinned beneath his maimed horse, shouted for aid. Sir Doneval did his best to ignore the squire's plea. To turn back now would mean death to them both and the possible failure of the bounty hunter's plan.

A massive shape appeared in the road before Brunner. The orc was just under six feet in height, a double-bladed axe and a crude wooden shield gripped in his clawed hands. The skin of a bear covered his back and his body was encased in a hodge-podge of metal scraps and bits of chain and ring mail. A battered kettle-helm covered the brute's head.

The monster snarled, and leapt toward Brunner. The bounty hunter drew the pistol from his belt and sent a bullet crashing through the orc's eye, into the tiny brain within his thick skull. The orc moaned, staggering into the middle of the road, his primitive body not understanding that it was dead. The massive shape was bowled under by the charging Bretonnian horses, their hooves smashing and crushing the thick bones underfoot.

As the riders raced along the wooded trail, they could hear the savage cries and snarls of their foes. Brunner risked a look over his shoulder and could see massive shapes racing after them along the trail. One paused to hurl a spear at the retreating cavalry, the shaft just missing the hindmost knight.

Ahead, the sunlight grew brighter; it was the clearing Sir Doneval had spoken of. Brunner lashed at Fiend for a final burst of speed.

The clearing was wide, with a small mound at its centre – a tomb of some long lost tribe. A small circle of standing stones, relics of the Old Faith, had once adorned the top of the mound, but had since toppled into piles of rubble. Brunner turned his horse at once toward the old barrow. The Bretonnians followed his lead once more, less concerned with offending the ancient dead that slept within the mound than with joining them.

The hindmost knight's steed shrieked and fell just as he emerged from the trees. Three arrows had sunk into the animal's flesh and the wounds had at last overcome its strength and noble heart. The knight managed to push the dead animal off and limp away. One of the other knights wheeled about, riding back to his injured comrade. Brunner could hear Sir Doneval shout for the man to come back, but the choice had already been made.

Two greenskinned giants loped out of the trees. Spying the knights, the orcs let savage cries of rage and bloodlust rip through their fanged jaws. The mounted knight drove his steed forward, putting himself between the orcs and the wounded man. The orcs roared with approval, standing their ground before the horseman. The knight lashed downwards with his sword, catching one of the brutes in the shoulder. The blade crunched through the orc's crude shoulder-guard and bit deeply into the flesh and bone beneath. Dark green blood spurted from the injury. The orc stumbled backwards from the force of the blow, a heavy club of metal and bone dropping from his suddenly nerveless arm.

The other orc gave vent to a savage cry of murderous fury. The knight turned his head to see the cleaving blade of the orc's axe swinging towards him. The butchering blow caught the knight just below the knee, the awesome power of the orc's muscles punching the axe-blade through the metal armour, through the leg within and into the side of the knight's charger. Horse and man screamed as one. The orc tugged at his weapon, trying to wrench it from the meat of the steed. The maimed animal whickered shrilly, then toppled onto its side, crushing the greenskin beneath its weight and snapping the neck of its rider.

The dismounted knight saw the fate of his valiant comrade and limped back to the animal. He stared down at the orc, its head and shoulders sticking out from beneath the slain charger. The orc snarled up at him and tried to push and wriggle his way free. The knight raised his sword over his head and stabbed it into the orc's skull with a downward thrust. Then he turned his armoured head to face the howling mob that burst from the trees. The rest of the pack had arrived. Several of the brutes raced forward to see the defiant knight standing over the dead orc, but a towering figure dressed in piecemeal armour and sporting steel-capped fangs pushed and punched his way to the fore.

Gnashrak roared, the sound booming across the clearing. Then he charged, bringing the giant blade of his choppa hurtling toward the knight. To his credit, the knight did not flinch, but brought his own sword up from the skull of the dead orc to meet and parry the warboss's attack. The crude, massive bulk of the orc's weapon slammed into the knight's elegant steel, sparks flying.

The knight staggered backwards, his blade now sporting an inch-deep notch from where the orc's choppa had met it. Gnashrak tensed his powerful frame backward, ready for another strike. The other orcs momentarily grew silent, watching in awe as their fearsome champion demonstrated his incredible strength and power. Across the field, Brunner and the remaining knights and squires did the same; all eyes were drawn to the uneven contest unfolding only a few dozen yards away.

It ended the only way that it could. With another booming roar, Gnashrak slashed at the knight once more. Again, the man tried to meet the orc's crude metal weapon, but this time the notched blade snapped before the orc's massive blow. The choppa continued unhindered, smashing into the mail standard about the Bretonnian's neck. Chain links snapped apart before the blow and a crimson fountain erupted as the choppa passed clean through the neckbone. The knight's helmet flew ten feet from the man's body, rolling into the long grass, blood spurting from the head within.

Gnashrak pulled his choppa back towards him, his beady eyes examining the gory metal. A long, dog-like tongue dropped from his ponderous jaws and licked at the blood. Then the orc fixed his gaze on the small band of men clustered amongst the ancient stones atop the mound. He took a step forward, his foot smashing through the ruin of the fallen orc's skull.

The warboss raised the choppa again, and pointed it at the Bretonnians. His jaws opened again and he roared at the watching soldiers. Though they could not understand the orc's crude language, its meaning was clear – the Bretonnians could expect no mercy from their attackers.

Like hounds loosed from the leash, the orcs under Gnashrak's command howled and began charging across the clearing, swinging their weapons overhead. A few, remembering the bows they carried, sent some black feathered arrows ahead of them, the ill-aimed shots bouncing harmlessly from the stones. The squires nestled among the rocks were more effective with their own longbows; each of their arrows found its way into orcish flesh, but none had enough stopping power to drop their hulking targets. Orcs closed their monstrous paws about the shafts that stuck from the flesh of arm, leg or breast and ripped them free, seemingly immune to the pain. Neither did they heed the meat clinging to the barbed arrowheads that they discarded with contemptuous snarls.

The figure of the bounty hunter emerged from behind the rocks, the long steel barrel of his gun held before him. He set a match to the flashpowder, then braced his legs as the explosive discharge of his weapon shook his body. A huge orc suddenly spun about, green blood bursting from the smoking hole in his chest. The orc slammed into the ground, his body shuddering for a long moment. The beast pressed his hands to either side of his prone body, and started to lift himself, but then he shuddered and dropped once more, his body bleeding out from the gaping crater where his heart had been.

Brunner did not spare the orc a second thought. He dropped the spent handgun, and reached beside him for the loaded crossbow he had leaned against a stone. He raised the weapon to his shoulder, sighted, and sent a steel bolt slamming through the helmet of a second orc as the brute was pulling a Bretonnian arrow from his chest. The orc's head snapped about, with an even more angry leer on his face. His little eyes focused upon Brunner, and widened as they saw the crossbow in the man's hands. The orc snarled, bellowing like a maddened steer. Then the green blood seeping from his helmet blurred his vision.

The orc raised a paw to his head. A clawed finger probed the hole in his helmet and the skull within. The orc's legs suddenly gave out and he fell onto his rump, his finger still lodged within the wound in his head. A slight whimper hissed from the orc's jaws, as the massive body fell onto its side. Then the greenskin was still.

A third orc was nearly at the base of the mound when he dropped, succumbing to the three arrow wounds in his chest. The orc behind him hurdled the body, and then fell as another Bretonnian arrow transfixed his throat. But a full twenty of the marauders reached the mound. And behind them loped the massive steel-toothed figure of their leader, his gory weapon held over his head as he bellowed war cries in his own harsh tongue.

The remaining knights met the charge of the orcs, two of the squires drawing their own swords to stand beside their lords and masters. The third squire let a shriek of terror escape his lips as he sprinted from the cover of the rocks, and raced for the nearer edge of the clearing. Three orcs loped after the fleeing man, their swift gait quickly closing the distance between man and pursuers.

Brunner sent the bolt from his smaller crossbow into the face of the first orc that closed with him, the dart sticking from the monster's cheek like a steel pimple. The orc clutched at the bolt, his clawed fingers working to pull it free. So intent was he upon the bolt, that he did not react as Brunner brought the cleaving edge of his falchion sword slashing through the brute's forearm. The severed limb still had claws locked about the bolt protruding from the orc's face. With the severed arm dangling, the orc snarled, and raised his remaining arm that clutched a savage length of sharpened steel. But the reaction was too slow – already Brunner's falchion was slashing downwards, splitting the orc's skull open like a melon. Green blood and snot-like brain matter bubbled from the ruin and the orc slumped against the side of the toppled stone plinth beside him.

A second orc leapt forward, crying in savage triumph to find a worthy adversary in the bounty hunter. The orc's axe bit down, glancing along the heavy gromril breastplate that encased Brunner's chest. The bounty hunter staggered under the impact of the blow, the dwarf metal resisting the cleaving edge of the orc's weapon.

The orc, unbalanced by the strike, began to recover both his stance and his weapon. Leaning before the shaken but unharmed Imperial warrior, the orc began to rise. With one hand, Brunner plunged a knife into the orc's neck, while his falchion sliced through the beast's backbone. The orc let a whimper of agony sigh from his enormous lungs and fell prone before the bounty hunter. The greenskin twitched for a moment, hands clutching at the knife buried in the back of his neck. Brunner turned away from the dying creature, looking for that next monster to challenge his blade.

The battle was faring badly for the Bretonnians. Both squires and one of the remaining knights were down, and there were only two orcs lying beside the corpses of the men. As the bounty hunter looked, he could see the huge warboss attacking Sir Doneval, the bulky knight dwarfed by the enormous orc's twisted form. The knight dodged the orc's awkward blows, so the orc's huge choppa sparked each time it bit into the old plinths. The knight slashed and thrust at the beast each time it recovered, and the orc was bleeding from numerous cuts in arms and chest. But the monster was hardly slowed, his inhuman vitality and resistance to pain carrying him forward.

Sir Doneval at last misjudged the sweep of the orc's choppa, slipping to the left when he should have dodged to the right. The warboss's choppa mashed the knight's arm, splitting the metal and tearing the flesh beneath. Dark blood oozed from the wound and Sir Doneval staggered away from the triumphant roar of his hulking adversary.

Brunner drew the reloaded pistol from its holster and fired at the orc leader's back. The weapon spat a flare of flame, and emitted a sound like the crack of thunder. An acrid stench wafted from the weapon. The warboss turned his head slightly at the sound, then returned his attention to the reeling knight. Brunner stared in disgust at the Nuln-made weapon, casting the pistol into the face of the horn-helmed reaver closing upon him. The weapon crashed into the monster's face, smashing his nose and splitting his lip. The orc paid no attention to the injury, but swept his massive sword at the bounty hunter. Brunner ducked under the sweep of the orc's blade, stabbing out with his own sword and piercing the crude leather that covered the orc's breast. Dark green liquid bubbled from the wound and the orc fell, his heart cleft by the bounty hunter's blade.

Gnashrak chopped down at the knight. Sir Doneval raised his shield, blocking the blow yet again, but this time the orc was in a position to put his whole weight behind the blow. The knight's arm broke under the impact. Sir Doneval let out a cry of pain from behind his helm. The orc grinned at him – a toothy, comfortless steel smile. Then the orc's massive choppa was swinging downward in a two-handed strike.

The metal of Sir Doneval's breastplate was cut to shreds by the choppa's impact, as was the ribcage beneath. A final scream of agony bubbled from the knight's mouth as the orc raised his weapon from the gory husk of the knight's mangled torso. Gnashrak's beady eyes considered the carnage all around him. Then his red eyes found the black-helmed bounty hunter rising from the corpse of one of his orcs.

Gnashrak let a bloodthirsty leer spread across his leathery face. He remembered him, cowardly trying to shoot him in the back with the fire and smoke weapon. But Gork and Mork had protected their savage child, and the magic of the backshooter's weapon had failed. Gnashrak ran a clawed finger through the gore dripping from his choppa.

He would teach this snivelling cur how a proper fight was conducted.

BRUNNER WATCHED AS the hulking warboss rose from Sir Doneval's body and advanced towards him with heavy, thudding steps. The bounty hunter drew a throwing knife from the belt at his chest and waited, turning his body to present the orc with his side and the blade in his other hand. He doubted if the orc would recognise the purpose of the knife, but he didn't want to take any chances.

The orc shuffled forward, his enormous weapon held across his chest. Brunner let him take a few more steps, then threw the knife. The orc grunted in surprise as the knife streaked across the distance between them. The blade sank into the corner of the orc's eye socket. The huge brute howled in pain, letting go of his choppa, and closed his hand about the knife. Brunner scrambled to reload his crossbow pistol while the orc paused. He looked up as the warboss gave vent to a wild cry of pain. The massive paw came away with the knife, dark green blood flowing from the wound. The orc fingered the knife for a moment, then bent and lifted the huge choppa with his other hand. The orc stared into Brunner's eyes and uttered a deep growl.

'Come try it,' the bounty hunter snarled. The orc roared again, displaying his enormous steel-capped fangs and charged forward like a blood-mad Estalian bull. Brunner fired his crossbow pistol at the oncoming avalanche of greenskin flesh, but the shot was hasty and the bolt smashed into the beast's knee. The orc did not seem to feel the impact of the bolt as it charged onwards. Brunner dropped back, letting the monster crash into the boulder he had been standing before. The stone cracked as Gnashrak struck it. Not even winded by the bone-jarring impact, the orc lashed out with his steel choppa, missing the bounty hunter's body by mere inches.

Brunner struck out with his own weapon, dealing the orc's arm a deep gash that severed tendons in his hand. The huge choppa dropped from the suddenly useless hand. But Gnashrak's other hand was already in motion, feeding Brunner's left shoulder the point of his own knife. Brunner twisted from the injury, a cry of pain ringing out from below his helm. The orc grinned back, his massive paw closing about the armour on the bounty hunter's injured shoulder.

Brunner screamed again as the orc's hand crumpled the steel and bruised the bone beneath. As though tiring from the sound of the man's shrieks, the orc clubbed the black-steel helm with his useless arm. The metal rang and an indentation formed in the sallet helm. Brunner shook his head against the bludgeoning blow.

The bounty hunter's sword sank to the hilt in the meat of the orc's thigh. The monster released his grip on the bounty hunter's shoulder to wrench it free. Given the momentary respite, Brunner spotted the bolt protruding from the orc's knee. With a roar as savage as any the orc had given voice to, the bounty hunter kicked his steel-toed boot into the bolt. The steel spike sank through the orc's kneecap, and the monster toppled onto his side.

Brunner staggered back, breathing heavily, pulling the serrated knife from his belt and another throwing dagger from the bandoleer across his chest. The orc snarled at him from the ground, his clawed hands already closing about the grip of his choppa. The orc lifted himself to his feet, foam drooling between his steel fangs. Then his head snapped around and a deep bellow of wrath rumbled from his throat. Brunner listened to the sound, then heard the shrill note that had alarmed the orc. The bounty hunter's battered body shook with laughter.

Gnashrak's voice was raised, shouting deep roaring commands in his own brutal language. But it was too late. His mob had also heard the call of the horn. Their bloodlust whetted by the slaughter of the Bretonnians, they were already racing from the mound, across the clearing toward the sound, eager to sink their blades into more human flesh. The orc cursed again, then spun about, his remaining eye locking onto Brunner's.

Then the massive brute loped away – not towards his mob, but into the trees. Three other orcs spotted him and gave chase, their loyalty and fear of the warboss overcoming the bloodlust surging through their frames. Brunner saw them disappear into the trees, then watched as Etienne de Galfort and the rest of his command burst from the tree-lined path, lances at the ready. Lost in the madness of their frenzy, the orcs did not appreciate the slaughter that ensued, not until they were reduced to a field of crushed, broken bodies.

ETIENNE DE GALFORT looked down at the work of his men, then raised his gaze to the mound. He shouted a greeting as Brunner staggered into view. The knight rode toward the bounty hunter, removed his helmet and smiled.

'We won,' the Bretonnian laughed. 'Just as you said, they couldn't resist the bait. And once we whetted their appetite, they wouldn't be able to control themselves and run when we came upon them!'

Brunner nodded his head. 'I was starting to think you weren't coming,' he said, his voice heavy with fatigue.

'I waited until the sands in the glass were half gone,' the noble replied. 'Then we came galloping at all speed.' Etienne suddenly looked closer at the bodies strewn among the stones upon the mound. 'The others?'

Brunner shook his head. 'No.'

The smile died on Etienne's face. 'Still, at least we beat them.'

'You'd have caught their leader if you had come a little sooner,' the bounty hunter said after a pause.

'He escaped?' Etienne asked, suddenly sick in his stomach. The bounty hunter just slumped onto the ground. He raised a hand to his damaged helm and pulled it free, running a gloved hand through the close-cropped brown hair. The glove came away streaked with sweat and blood.

'Don't worry,' the bounty hunter said, fixing Etienne with his piercing blue eyes. 'He's finished. Among orcs, only the strong lead. The injuries I dealt that monster...' Brunner shook his head. 'By tonight, some young bull is going to be calling himself warboss and cooking this brute for dinner.'

'Then it's over,' Etienne said.

'It's over,' Brunner agreed.

NIGHT SETTLED ABOUT the mountainside of the Vaults like a magician's cloak. Four figures sat about the small fire, their beady red eyes gleaming in the flickering light. One of them moved, pushing another log upon the fire. But as he did so, the greenskinned face stared not into the fire, but at the massive shape of one of his companions, a figure from which only one eye gleamed.

Gnashrak let another sigh shudder from his huge body and put a finger into the empty pit of his face to scratch at the irritating eye socket once again. Thoughts were already swirling about in his thick skull. Thoughts of revenge. He would return to this land, burn and pillage it as no orc had ever done. He would gather an army this time, a mighty war host with boar riders and siege engines, packs of trolls and shrieking hordes of goblins to soak up the Bretonnians' arrows. Then he would rip the heart from the man who had cost him his eye and hand. He would take his throbbing heart and eat it before the human's fading eyes.

The gleam of ambition burned in Gnashrak's eye, more fiercely even than the fire before him. The orc yawned and stretched his massive frame. As he finished stretching, he looked about for a place to sleep, then his eye caught the gaze of his remaining followers. For the first time, fear wormed its way into Gnashrak's savage heart. The look in the eyes of the other three orcs was one Gnashrak recognised only too well. It was the gleam of ambition.

Gnashrak reached for the slender Bretonnian sword that he had been reduced to carrying since he lost his hand, noting as he did so the furtive knowing looks of the other orcs. There was still some fear in them, but not much. Not enough.

With the sword in his hand and sleep tugging at his mind, Gnashrak settled down, wary of his companions.

BLOOD MONEY

I ENTERED THE *Black Boar one evening, looking for my literary contact, a hulking Norseman-turned-pirate named Ormgrim – a surprisingly loquacious man, for all his resemblance in appearance and odour to a mountain bear. I had been considering a collection of stories recounting the reaver's exploits, from his days upon the Sea of Claws, stalking the shores in the fabled dragon-boats, to his time as a pit fighter in the lawless fighting arenas of the Border Princes. I dearly hoped that I would be able to catch him early in his cups, before drink would sodden his small brain. Otherwise he would only be able to utter three word sentences in crude Reikspiel that many goblins would find laughable. It would be but a short step from there to the kind of violent outbursts that had resulted in a week of bedridden misery for this unlucky writer who was not nimble on his feet.*

As it transpired, however, I had a much more lucrative prospect than another night of Ormgrim's half-coherent drunken ramblings. Seated at a back table of the smoky, tunnel-like beer hall, I spied the black-helmed shape of Brunner. He was sipping at a small bottle, which I did not doubt contained schnapps. I had seen him like this before, and knew that this was how he indulged himself after a particularly successful hunt. I at once made my way toward his table. The bounty hunter looked up at me, then gestured with a gloved hand, indicating that I might sit. I asked him how he was faring, and if he might share his good fortune with a friend. He smiled at me, unoffended by the directness of my words and began to relate events that had transpired recently in the realms of the Border Princes.

It was a tale long in the telling, and as he spoke, I found my eyes continually drawn to the large wooden cask that rested beside him on the floor. My horror of the object grew steadily as the story unfolded, for I came to understand that Brunner still had merchandise to dispose of...

A LONE RIDER made his way through the timber gate that led into the town of Greymere. The guards atop the walls eyed the man with looks of suspicion, for in the realms of the Border Princes it paid to trust no stranger. War between men in these lawless regions was almost as common as war with the marauding tribes of orc and goblin. The rider paid his coin to the sergeant at the gate, and suspicion or no suspicion, the man was allowed to enter the town, leading a dappled grey pack horse behind his own black and brown bay.

The merchants and peasants that ambled about the muddy lanes of the town paused to favour the stranger with curious glances, for he presented a compelling, almost sinister, sight. The man wore armour about his lean frame, his head was encased in a helm of blackened steel, and knives and other blades hung all about his body. On either side of the man's saddle, sheaths had been attached: one bore a large crossbow, the other a wood and steel frame of a blackpowder weapon. His second horse laboured under assorted burdens, barrels, packs and rolls of cloth. But with one look at the man, all could tell that those packs did not contain merchandise, and that he was not some sort of wandering peddler.

The stranger stopped before the crude timber face of the town's only inn. He dismounted. Casting his visored gaze about the street, as if challenging any thieves who might be watching, he left his horses and stalked into the building. Although several sets of eyes cast covetous looks upon the animals and the gear they carried, none did more than look.

Shortly afterwards a man emerged from the inn, his face as white as a sheet. Quickly and cautiously the man slunk away from the building into the nearest alleyway, losing himself in the confusing spaces between the town's maze of huts and pigsties.

Brunner, the man thought, smoothing the front of his leather tunic and wiping the perspiration from his swarthy brow. The Tilean licked his lips and placed a reassuring hand on the sword at his side. Then, a sudden thought of just who it was he feared brought a fresh burst of speed to the man's steps. *By Ranald and Morr, what is he doing here? Whose head is he after?* The answer came to Vincenzo's mind almost immediately. The meagre price on his own head would not have dragged the bounty hunter away from the city states, but there was someone in Greymere who did merit such a price.

THE GREY-HEADED MAN swept a bone brush through the massive moustaches that crouched upon his lip, training them back into the upward-pointing horns fashionable among the nobles of the Empire. It was unwise, he knew, to affect such an appearance, but years of habit were hard to escape and the former Baron of Kleindorf was not about to give up the few, miserable trappings of his former station that he was able to maintain. Not for the first time, the man who had once been Bruno von Ostmark, and now called himself Drexler, considered his surroundings with a snort of disdain. The house he kept in Greymere was lavish by the standards of the Border Princes: it had a stone façade and wooden floors and roofing that did not consist of thatch and straw or logs thrown across support beams. Only the keep of the ruler of Greymere, Prince Waldemar, was more extravagant and sumptuous. Yet, the baron could not help but remember the castle that had once been his, the estates and private forests that had been his possessions. Even his kennels had been larger than his present home.

Drexler finished sweeping his moustaches into the desired shape and began to dress himself. Here, too, he thought of his fall. Once, three servants would have busied about his person, preparing him to face the day in whatever raiment he chose from closets larger than the bedroom he now sat in. The exiled baron sighed loudly and slumped into a velvet-backed chair and slowly pulled a leather boot onto his foot. Such extravagance was beyond him now. The few servants that he could afford had more pressing duties – matters of business, that would keep Drexler from slipping down the ladder of life. For the nobleman was realistic enough to understand that, miserable as his surroundings might seem, there were far more wretched levels of squalor into which he could sink, and never emerge.

A sharp knock at the door interrupted the nobleman turned merchant as he stuffed a stocking-covered foot into his other boot. He turned towards the door, snarling at this intrusion upon his routine. Drexler stifled the impulse to hurl the shoe at the door as it opened. The men now serving him were hardly domesticated, and hardly as meek as those who had cowered before the Baron von Ostmark. One had to be careful about berating and insulting them, lest the dogs snap at the hand of their master.

The wiry, dark-skinned shape of Vincenzo, Drexler's Tilean aide, assistant and confidant slipped through the portal, slowly closing it behind him. Drexler stared at the Tilean, suspicious of his furtive manner and quiet steps.

The merchant reached under the fur blankets of his bed, fingering the dagger hidden within the bedding.

'Well?' the merchant demanded. 'What news is so important as to drive you to disturb me before I have properly risen? What troubles you that you cannot await a more decent time to speak to me?' Drexler tensed his grip on hilt of the dagger as Vincenzo sidled across the floor towards him. The Tilean licked his lips and a cold sweat glistened on his face. Drexler could practically smell the fear dripping off the man.

'Have you ever heard of a man named Brunner?' the Tilean said at last. Drexler shook his head, staring at the thief and smuggler with a questioning gaze.

'He is the most notorious bounty hunter in all of Tilea,' Vincenzo explained.

Drexler pursed his lips in thought. 'And you think this killer, this Brunner has come to Greymere looking for the Baron von Ostmark?'

'The reward offered by the Count of Stirland is quite substantial,' Vincenzo pointed out. 'What other reason could there be for the bounty hunter to come to Greymere?'

A troubled expression grew upon Drexler's features. He pounded his fist in his palm. 'No, of course. Somehow he heard of me, found me. But he won't get me!'

'I could ask Savio to attend to it,' Vincenzo offered. Drexler smiled.

'Yes, do that,' the merchant said. 'I have never seen a man who could match Savio's blade. Now, leave me. We have to negotiate with the dwarfs again regarding the transport of their beer to the Moot and I want to look my best.'

THE STRANGER SAT at a small table in the rear of the large tavern that dominated the ground floor of the two-storey structure. A few off-duty soldiers from the prince's guard eyed the armed bounty hunter with thinly veiled antipathy. Mercenaries were a common sight in Greymere, and their arrival often heralded the replacement of one of the other soldiers in the pay of Prince Waldemar. The other occupants of the tavern, a trio of dishevelled peasants who were nursing their beers in order to savour the expensive luxury for as long as they could, did their best to avoid looking at the black-helmed man.

A buxom barmaid made her way between the largely empty tables and set a stein of beer before the bounty hunter. The visored head lowered, staring at the frothy mug for a moment before setting a few copper coins on the table. The woman leaned forward, scooping up the coins with one hand, while her eyes maintained their hold on the face. The cloth covering her massive chest hung loose as she bent over the table, and the woman licked her lips with a wet, pink tongue. She hesitated a moment, lingering over the table, watching for any sign of interest the warrior might exhibit.

The bounty hunter reached a gloved hand forward and closed it about the body of the clay stein. He drew his hand back and raised the frothy drink to his lips. The barmaid stood, shaking her head in an angry gesture and stalked away – hopes of supplementing her wages diminished by his indifferent air. As she turned, Brunner let a slight smile play on his face. It had been a long ride here from Remas, but not that long.

The door of the inn opened, bearing with it the smell of dust and excrement from the street outside. A single man entered: short, but with wide shoulders and muscular arms. He was wearing a foppish-looking cap of red silk, with a purple falcon's feather sticking out from a gold button on its left side. A shirt of chainmail encased his body, the skirt falling to his thighs, where green leggings completed his costume. Leather shoes with bright brass buckles set a jingling echo across the tavern's earthen floor with each step the man took.

Bright blue eyes set in the dark-skinned face of a Tilean considered the tavern and its inhabitants. The face of the man was dominated by a bristly black beard, cut to a point. When his eyes closed upon the figure of the bounty hunter, the beard became distorted as his mouth curled into a predatory smile. The Tilean let his gloved hands caress the hilts of the long-bladed dagger and rapier that hung from his belt. He shrugged and the red cape he wore fell from his shoulders and onto his back. The man strode across the room, each face in the tavern watching his every step – save the bounty hunter, who continued to quietly sip at his drink.

The Tilean stopped beside the table, staring down at the seated warrior. Slowly, Brunner set the stein down, and peered up at the Tilean through his visor.

'Your name is Brunner?' the Tilean asked, his tone arrogant, his accent that of the merchant princes of Tobaro. Brunner let his left hand emerge from beneath the table, his small crossbow pistol now visible in his gloved hand.

'Who would like to know?' his icy voice asked.

The Tilean pulled a velvet glove from his hand. 'My name is Savio,' the man said, dropping the glove on the table. A light of recognition blazed in Brunner's cold eyes as the Tilean spoke. 'I make my challenge. If you are a man, you will face me.'

'Not in here!' bawled the massive bald-headed innkeeper from behind the bar. 'It stinks bad enough without blood seeping into the floor.' The off-duty guards seemed to share the innkeeper's thoughts, and Brunner let his grip on the crossbow relax when he heard the men draw their swords.

'It seems here is not the best place,' the bounty hunter said. The duellist nodded back at him.

'I shall await your pleasure outside then,' the man said, spinning about and retracing his steps across the tavern. Brunner watched him go. As soon as the door had shut behind him, the innkeeper strode to the bounty hunter's side.

'Whatever you have done to earn the notice of Savio,' the man shook his head. 'He is the most feared swordsman in all the Border Princes. He has killed more people in Greymere than dysentery.' The man's expression changed to one of mock regret. 'Could you please settle your bill before you go outside? And if you will add a little extra, I can send a boy to fetch the priest from the shrine.'

'That won't be necessary,' the bounty hunter said. He reached below the bench he sat on, and pulled a leather-wrapped object onto the table. The innkeeper stared as the bounty hunter removed a heavy object of steel and wood.

'If you don't pay for the priest, they won't bury you,' the innkeeper muttered. 'They'll just strip your body and toss it over the side of the wall for the wolves and the crows to pick at.'

'Well, they have to eat too,' the bounty hunter said, not looking at the bald man. He removed a small tube of paper from a pouch on his belt. The ends of the paper tube had been twisted closed. The gloved hands tore one end of the tube open and up-ended the paper cylinder over the mouth of the steel weapon. A foul-smelling black grain-like substance poured into the barrel. 'And if I can choose, I'd rather feed wolves than worms.'

'I am happy that you can joke about it,' the innkeeper said, wringing his hands on his apron and looking anything but happy. 'But if you think you can match swords with Savio, then you have no idea who you are facing.'

The bounty hunter packed down the grain in the barrel with a long wooden rod. He set the rod down and removed an iron ball from another pouch on his belt. 'I know who Savio is,' he said. He dropped the steel ball into the weapon, packing it down again with the wooden rod. 'In Tobaro, in Miragliano, in Luccini, his name is reckoned as that of the greatest duellist to ever practise the art of the vendetta.'

The innkeeper's eyes grew wide with alarm as he heard Savio's name associated with such great cities. Suddenly the professional swordsman had become more frightening than even the innkeeper had imagined. 'There is a back door,' the bald man said. 'You could slip through it and be out of Greymere without Savio seeing you go.'

A loud voice called from the street, demanding that Brunner emerge, and berating the bounty hunter as a rogue and a coward without honour.

'And keep him waiting even longer?' Brunner asked. He removed another packet of paper from a third pouch on his belt. He tapped the light, flour-like powder from the folded square of paper into a covered pan at the rear of the gun, just below the steel latch of the hammer. The bounty hunter rose from the table, bearing the loaded handgun with him.

'What are you going to do?' the bald man asked, voicing the question on the mind of everyone in the tavern.

'Before he left Tilea, Savio killed the son of one of Luccini's most prosperous guildmasters,' the bounty hunter replied, snatching up a shabby cloak from a hook beside the door, and draping it over his right arm to hide the weapon he now carried. 'More than enough to pay for the replacement of a bullet and some powder.'

Savio stood in the centre of the muddy lane, men and animals giving him a wide berth as they passed. The thin-bladed, lightweight sword was gripped in his still-gloved hand. His other arm was covered by the heavy fabric of the red cape, the slender fang of his dagger gleaming from the fist that emerged from the folds of the cape. As the duellist saw Brunner emerge from the tavern, he uttered a short, sharp laugh.

'I was thinking that maybe I would have to go inside and drag you out,' he laughed. 'Many is the time when some churlish cur would refuse to answer the demands of honour and unman himself before the duel even began.' The Tilean's blue eyes focused on the shabby cloak draped about the bounty hunter's right arm. 'Oh? You think to fight me in the style of a Tilean streetfighter?' The duellist laughed again. 'The trick is to employ the cape as not only shield but weapon. Catch your enemy's blade in its folds, if you can, but there is many another trick.'

The duellist made a quick swipe with his sword into the empty air, then pranced a pace forward, whipping the edge of the cape forward, like a boy cracking a wet towel. 'Strike the hand of some handsome noble and watch them recoil from so minor a blow, dropping dagger or sword from fingers stung by so little a thing.' The Tilean withdrew, then danced forward a step, unfurling the cape and casting it about an invisible foe, as the sword lashed out again. 'Then one can always cast one's cloak about the enemy. He will panic, trying to fend off your cloak, and exposing himself for one instant to the steel in your hand.'

'Your swordplay is as extravagant as your mouth,' Brunner's voice sneered. The Tilean lost the playful expression, and his words their jocular tone.

'I have never met my equal with the sword,' the duellist said, staring at the armoured figure of the bounty hunter.

'And you never will,' Brunner stated. He lowered the gun held upright at his side. The hammer responded to the tug of the trigger, smashing into the pan and the powder contained there. The powder lighted under the impact, in turn igniting the gunpowder in the barrel. The black powder exploded with a flash and boom, forcing the iron ball from the weapon. The bullet shot across the few yards separating the two men and crashed into Savio's breast, tearing through the chainmail shirt as though it were not there. The duellist toppled backward, his head crashing into a pool of mud and horse urine.

A stunned silence settled upon the street as the echoing report of the handgun slowly faded away. Brunner stalked across the mud, crouched down beside the body of the Tilean and pulled the large knife from his belt. The serrated edge gleamed in the light for a moment before he brought the blade against the neck of the dead man. A woman screamed as Brunner set about his gruesome labour.

'Always make sure that the man you want to kill is playing by the same rules,' the bounty hunter said as he lifted Savio's head from the corpse.

Brunner looked about the street, his gaze canvassing the horrified onlookers. He settled upon a young boy standing near the door of the inn, and tossed a gold coin to him.

'Fetch me a sack of salt,' he told the boy. 'Keep a few coppers for yourself, but bring the rest back to me.' The boy rushed off, the menace in the bounty hunter's voice ensuring that he would return as speedily as his young feet would allow. Brunner pushed open the door of the tavern with the still-smoking barrel of his gun and disappeared into the darkness with his trophy.

ON THE EDGE of Greymere, a crude amphitheatre of wooden tiers had been erected for what passed as cultural pursuits in the brutal and savage realm of Prince Waldemar. Vincenzo quietly made his way through the noisy, raucous crowd seated in the wooden benches that rose above the muddy ground. Far below the wooden tiers, in a stone-lined hole, a nearly naked man held a shortsword in a massive fist, his other hand encased in a razor-sharp cestus. Five wiry creatures circled the man, their red eyes gleaming in the light of the torches set about the pit.

Vincenzo ignored the sight below and made his way toward the front of the viewing stand. He could see several soldiers clustered about the front seats, heedless of how their armoured figures might intrude upon the view of those sitting behind them. Vincenzo kept his hands at his side, in plain sight, as he advanced upon the warriors and the two men seated in the middle of them.

Prince Waldemar was young, his frame powerful and muscular. He wore a robe of wolfskin, his dark red hair bare save for the simplest circlet of gold. A slim scabbarded sword was resting across his knees as he craned his sharp-featured face forward to look at the spectacle unfolding below. Beside the prince, Drexler roared his enjoyment of the fight. But his roar faded as he spied Vincenzo worming his way toward them.

'Excuse me, your lordship,' Vincenzo said to the prince. Waldemar hardly paid the merchant a second thought as Drexler rose. Down below, one of the slender-limbed green-skinned creatures darted towards the pitfighter's belly with a wicked sickle of steel. The goblin's face exploded into a mash of green paste as the gladiator smashed the studded arm-guard of his cestus into the monster's long, narrow nose. The spatter of dark green blood flew to where the prince was seated and Waldemar howled his appreciation.

'You are making a habit of appearing where you are not wanted,' Drexler told his underling as they stepped away from the royal box, if such a formation of guards could be so called.

'It is Savio,' the Tilean said, his voice low and grave.

'Tell him to wait. I'll pay him after the fight,' Drexler turned to return to his seat.

A gasp of shock rose from the crowd behind the two men. Down in the pit, the goblins had worked their way around the gladiator. Three of them jabbed at him from the front and to his left while the fourth circled the man's back. The sinister titter of the greenskins echoed gruesomely from the stone walls of the pit.

The gladiator chanced a look over his shoulder and was rewarded by a sharp stab of pain as one of the goblins, armed with a spear, dealt him a slash across his side as payment for his inattention. The pitfighter snarled in pain and batted away the goblin's weapon. The goblin behind him took the opportunity to leap onto the man's back, raking his naked flesh with its black-nailed hands, and digging runnels into his skin. The goblin's grip held as it locked its legs around the man's waist and soon the greenskin's fanged mouth was snapping at the man's shoulder.

The gladiator bellowed his rage, the sound causing the other three goblins to nervously retreat back from their adversary. The goblin on the man's back looked up, its green mouth smeared red with blood. A look of horror worked itself into the inhuman features as the goblin saw its fellows back away. Had they remained steadfast, they could have easily penetrated the gladiator's guard, but now, due to their craven souls, the opportunity had been lost. Moreover, the goblin on the man's back would pay for that lost opportunity.

The pitfighter let a savage war cry rumble from his throat as he launched himself into motion. Running at full speed, the man charged backwards, smashing into the stone wall of the pit. A sickly liquid sounding crunch rose from the arena. The gladiator stepped away from the wall, not bothering to look at the dark green smear marring the rocks, nor at the limp and broken thing that slipped from his back to twitch pathetically as life fled its broken, shattered form.

'No, you don't understand,' Vincenzo muttered. 'Savio is dead!'

An incredulous look gripped Drexler's features. 'Dead?' As Vincenzo nodded his head in affirmation of the fact, the exiled baron slumped against the low wall bordering the pit. His limbs trembled as though a chill wind licked at them. 'Dead?' He shook his head. Then he stared at Vincenzo. 'The bounty hunter killed him?'

'Shot him down in the street like a wild dog,' the Tilean replied, his tone mirroring the merchant's fear. 'Savio challenged him. Brunner put a bullet in his heart, then cut off his head.'

'Cut off his head!' Drexler put his hand to his mouth, biting down on the horror that welled up within him.

'There is quite a bounty for Savio in Luccini,' Vincenzo explained.

In the pit down below, the remaining goblins tittered maliciously as they jabbed at the barrel-chested gladiator with their weapons. The scar-faced man fended off the more well-directed blows, knocking away the point of one goblin's spear, and smashing back the sword of a second with the return sweep of his blade. A wicked smile spread across the leathery face of a third goblin, displaying a massive set of needle-sharp teeth. The goblin rushed in, a notched iron axe gripped in his green hands. But as the creature came close enough to strike, the pitfighter's booted foot rose and delivered a savage sideways kick to the small monstrosity.

There was a loud crack and the goblin's leg snapped at the knee. The greenskin howled in agony, letting his axe fall from his hand. Eyes upon the still armed goblins, the pitfighter circled around the pit until he stood above the wailing creature. He brought his booted foot down once again, smashing the goblin's neck beneath his heel. There was a final snap of bone and a froth of dark green liquid bubbled from the goblin's over-sized mouth. The laughter of the last goblins turned nervous as the cheering of the spectators rose to a thunderous clamour.

'Perhaps it was Savio he was after?' offered Drexler, weakly. Vincenzo shook his head.

'Were that so, then why is he still here?' the Tilean asked. 'Savio was a bonus to him. But whoever Brunner is after, he has yet to collect them.' A crafty look entered the Tilean's eyes. 'I have an idea,' he said, his voice dropping to a conspiratorial whisper. 'I know of a man in Adlerhof. We could hire him. He could be here in three days.'

Drexler ignored his companion, looking down into the arena below. The gladiator was charging at his remaining greenskin foes. The goblin with the spear shrieked, threw his weapon at the massive pitfighter and raced to the nearest wall, black-nailed hands scrabbling desperately for purchase on the smooth stones.

The other goblin swung his sword, trying to hamstring his human opponent. The gladiator leapt over the goblin's blade. The man's shortsword gleamed in the light as he brought it down to the goblin's head. The creature did not even have time to scream as the force of the man's blow split his skull in two, green blood and greasy brain matter spilling from the goblin's head.

The last goblin cast a terrified look at his comrade's demise and scratched at the wall with an even greater frenzy. The gladiator sneered at the little creature. He bent down and picked up the goblin's discarded spear. With a snort of contempt, the man hurled the spear across the pit, smashing its point into the goblin's back, pinning the greenskin to the wall.

Sparing the dead no further thought, the pitfighter raised his arms over his head and revelled in the joyous roar of the crowd.

'Do as you like, Vincenzo,' Drexler said, his eyes glittering with cunning as he cheered the triumphant pitfighter. 'But an idea has just occurred to me as well.'

BRUNNER EMERGED FROM the inn, his helm catching the sunlight as its golden rays briefly penetrated the haze from hearths and cookfires that hung over Greymere like a shroud. The bounty hunter considered the peasants and merchantmen rushing about the muddy street. It was a habit of his to study every face, each person he encountered for some trait that he might recognise. It was the telltale mark that would put a name to the face and transform the person from just another member of the mob to a piece of merchandise to be acquired and sold.

After a moment, the bounty hunter moved on, stalking down the muddy lane toward the stables where his animals had been taken. He did not trust any hand but his own with his horses – the magnificent Bretonnian bay, Fiend, and the dour, overworked packhorse from Tilea, he called Paychest. It was the bounty hunter's routine to inspect his animals daily, and to ensure that those he entrusted with them had not abused that trust, or his property. The bounty hunter had very high expectations for his animals and woe betide the stablemaster whose care was negligent.

As the bounty hunter turned from the inn, he did not see the barrel-chested, scar-faced shape detach itself from an alley and follow him. The scar-faced man had traded the loinclout of the pit for a set of leather breeches and a sleeveless black tunic that displayed his massive arms. The shortsword that had done such deadly work the night before swung from his belt, and the look in his close-set eyes was no less murderous than that with which he had favoured his inhuman adversaries.

The bounty hunter entered the darkened stable, the odour of animals and dung wafting from the cave-like gloom. He marched across the straw-strewn floor, paying scant notice to the grizzled stablemaster until he was only a few feet away. Brunner addressed a few cold words to the man, inquiring where his animals could be found. The dirty man pointed a brown-stained hand deeper into the building and shambled off to return to whatever duties Brunner's arrival had interrupted.

Brunner found his steed and packhorse tethered to a wooden post set into the wall, forming a stall that separated the animals from their fellows. The massive Bretonnian bay snorted happily as the bounty hunter's gloved hand stroked his flank.

Brunner examined the animal's body, looking for the telltale signs of lash and whip. Then he examined each of the horse's hooves, checking that the shoes had been replaced, and the horn tended to. Satisfied with his examination, he moved toward the grey packhorse. As he rose, however, the bounty hunter noticed the figure of the stablemaster slipping out of the front door. A premonition washed over Brunner and he turned just as a massive figure closed upon him.

Brunner caught the wrist of the hand that gripped the shortsword just as the scar-faced man was thrusting the blade toward his belly. The bulging muscles on the pit-fighter's massive arm were like steel cords, and before the man's strength, the bounty hunter found his own restraining grip thwarted, the fat-bladed sword inching closer towards his vitals.

The bounty hunter twisted his body, catching the pit-fighter off guard. The gladiator's massive body now pressed against Brunner's back, the shortsword thrust away from the bounty hunter's belly.

The gladiator snarled, catching Brunner's neck in the crook of his free arm. Like the legendary pythons of Lustria, his powerful arm began to constrict about the bounty hunter's throat, choking the breath from him. Brunner released a hand from the pitfighter's wrist to rake the man's eyes, but swiftly returned his hand to the wrist as the sword began to turn back towards his body. The gladiator grunted and increased the pressure about the bounty hunter's neck.

The contest continued for a long while, the men's feet jostling in the straw and dung for greater advantage, or some purchase that might tip the balance. Finally, the bounty hunter went limp, his grasp on the sword slackened. The gladiator sneered and increased the pressure on his throat. But the bounty hunter's head suddenly snapped backwards, exploding the pitfighter's bulbous nose with the steel crown of the helmet. The killer released his prey, staggering back a pace. Brunner gasped for breath, but even as he sucked air into his starving lungs, he managed to smash his steel-toed boot into the stunned gladiator's knee. The scarred man crumpled and as he rose, a second kick caught him under the chin. Teeth and blood scattered across the stable, adding to the agitation of the animals.

Brunner stood over the man, and watched the rise and fall of his massive chest. As his icy eyes narrowed, the bounty hunter smashed the toe of his other boot into the side of the gladiator's head. There was a sickening sound like an egg cracking and the pitfighter's body trembled. Again the boot kicked out, this time caving in the side of his foe's skull. The rise and fall of the man's chest eventually grew still.

The bounty hunter crouched, sucking in more precious air, one gloved hand massaging his ravaged throat. He was studying his prey, taking in the build, the scars and what remained of the face. A smile, like that of a wolf as it spies a lone sheep, spread across the bounty hunter's face. There was something familiar about this one. The gloved hand left his throat and grasped the hilt of the long knife hanging from his belt.

THE BOUNTY HUNTER made his way back toward the inn, every eye on the street watching as he walked past, with the dripping head of the gladiator swinging from his left hand, where he gripped it by the hair. As he neared the inn, the wiry shape of a young boy detached itself from the shade of a haycart and scrambled toward him, straining to make his small legs keep pace with Brunner's lengthy stride.

'Will you be needing more salt, master?' the boy asked, a tone of eagerness in his voice. Even at his tender age, he had witnessed death often enough, and heads of criminals adorning pikes set before the town's main gate were commonplace. The gory object in Brunner's hand disturbed him less than the gaggle of flies buzzing about a nearby pile of dung.

Brunner paused, staring down at the boy. The young face stared back at the steel visage. 'Ever seen him before?' the bounty hunter asked, holding the pitfighter's mashed face forward for the boy to get a better look.

'No,' he replied after a moment. 'I am sure that he was a stranger, from outside Greymere.' Brunner continued to stare at the boy, then reached into a cloth pouch on his belt and tossed the child a copper coin.

'Let me know if you see any more strangers,' the bounty hunter's cold voice said. Without a further look at the boy, he proceeded on his way to the inn. As he passed, the child bit the flat wedge of metal, to see if it would bend. When it did not, a gleeful expression washed across his face and he raced off, to be lost in the dingy streets of Greymere.

The bounty hunter was deep in thought as he pushed open the log door of the inn. Since he had arrived here, two men had tried to kill him. The duellist, Savio, had been known here. But the brutish man who had ambushed him in the stable apparently was not, assuming the boy and the stablemaster were to be trusted. Brunner did not doubt that there would be a third attempt.

DREXLER BOLTED DOWN the glass of Estalian brandy as if it were cheap marshbrew from the inn. He cast a withering look at the attending servant and the man hastened to refill his glass. The door of the parlour opened and the exiled Imperial nobleman turned his head, his hand slipping away from the glass to fumble for the crossbow leaning beside his chair. He breathed a sigh of relief as he saw Vincenzo enter, and the ashen pallor faded slightly from his face.

'I have not left this room in two days,' the merchant growled, fear making the sullen tone more whiny than intimidating. 'He killed the pitfighter.' To punctuate his last statement, Drexler drained the glass of brandy.

Vincenzo nodded his head, removing his cloth hat with a hand grey with traildust. 'I could have told you that it would turn out like that. You hired a killer to do an assassin's job.'

'I encouraged the prince to arrest the man,' Drexler said, looking down at the floor. 'He would have done so, had the bounty hunter not already appeared before him. It seems this pitfighter was once a Sartosan corsair, with a price on his head in every port in Tilea.' Drexler sighed, waving his hands in an expressive gesture. 'If it had been the bounty killer's word alone, perhaps I might have prevailed upon Waldemar to arrest him, but the pitfighter's manager came forward to affirm the hunter's claim! Damn fool was hoping to share in the reward, and gain some last bit of profit on his fighter!' Drexler shook his head. Ordinarily, he would have admired such limitless avarice, and the ability to ferret out the last copper from an investment, but this time boundless greed had worked against him.

Suddenly Drexler raised his head, and turned to face his Tilean friend. 'What did you say a moment ago?' he inquired, a subtle tone to his query.

'I made contact with Louis,' Vincenzo replied. 'He will arrive in two days' time.' Drexler shook his head, waving away his words.

'No, you said something about this being an assassin's job,' he said, a sinister gleam in his eye.

He thought for a moment, motioning for Vincenzo to be silent. A smile cracked his face and he nodded. 'Perhaps we do not need to wait two days.'

'What are you planning?' Vincenzo asked, not following the merchant's thoughts.

'Drugo,' the exile said, his smile broadening as he saw the frightened look in Vincenzo's eyes.

'Drugo?' he scoffed. 'Prince Waldemar will never stand for that. You may as well send for Vogun and have him do the job – and smash down half the town in the process.' The Tilean shook his head. 'Besides, Drugo is locked away in the prince's dungeon, to entertain us all on Pflugzeit when he is drawn and quartered.'

The calculating look remained on Drexler's face as he stood from his chair. 'I am very old friends with Waldemar. I think he will find that it is easier to catch an assassin like Drugo than it is to keep him.' He laughed, snatching the bottle of brandy from his attendant and pouring a measure into his glass. 'At least he will after I finish speaking with him about it.'

'This bounty hunter considers killing a business,' Drexler snickered. 'Let us see how he fares against someone who considers it a religious experience.'

A FIGURE OF blackness watched from the shadows beside a ramshackle wainwright's as the last light on the upper floor of Greymere's inn went dark. The face grinned in the darkness as widely and hideously as any goblin from the Bad Lands. No laughter accompanied the manic leer as the shape detached itself from the wall against which it had been pressed. A shadow crossed the muddy street. It had the faintest suggestion of a man's figure, cloaked and hooded in a garment cut from midnight itself. It crossed the street, fading into the looming darkness before the inn. No sound accompanied it, not the sound of breath, the squelching of mud under booted sole, or even the rustle of fabric. The heavy door of the inn, firmly secured from within, was covered by darkness for one fleeting moment. Then it opened by the smallest margin. The shadow slipped through the opening and the heavy door shut behind it.

Drugo replaced the bar his thin, wire-like hook had lifted and scanned the silent building. A dog lying near the door did not even raise its head as the assassin stalked past. The man grinned down at the animal, fingering the dagger clutched in his hand. It had been two weeks since he had slaughtered anything, and the last blood he had drawn had been from his jailer when he bit off his fingers as he spooned food into his mouth. The assassin's tongue darted out, licking his chin and cheeks, as if to recall the taste. The man leaned towards the dog, a murderous urge rising within him. But the moment passed and he turned away, gliding up the narrow stairway that led to the rooms of the inn.

He had been forced to swear oaths before the grey moustached man had released him. Oaths to his patron god, Khaine, the Lord of Murder. The only oaths he would honour, and the man had known it. He had sworn to leave Greymere, sworn never to return, sworn to kill no more of its denizens. With one exception: the bounty hunter.

Drugo knew that his prey would be found up here, in one of the private rooms. It was to be expected. Poor men never warranted a sanction, never rated the expense of hiring a killer. Gold given for the services of an assassin of Khaine was sacred, and only a large amount was acceptable. For who would dishonour a god by offering up a pittance?

Drexler had been most upset at Drugo's insistence that his freedom was not enough, and still more upset when he heard the price. But he had paid, in the end. When the fear set upon them, they always paid.

The assassin glided down the hall, his approach so stealthy that a rat scurried past him along the opposite wall without turning a whisker in his direction. He reached the first door on his left and paused a moment to defeat the lock. He pushed the door open by the slightest of cracks, then closed it again, the brief intrusion unnoticed by those within. The fat man had certainly not been a bounty hunter, his companion even less. The assassin glided away, passing from one door to another, pausing at each, before moving on.

Finally, he reached the room he sought. There, on a battered table, rested the helmet he had had described to him by the merchant. There was a body in the bed, the heavy blankets pulled about it to guard against the chill of the night.

Drugo's blood surged and pounded through his veins. He shut the door behind him and silently moved to the bed. At last, his breath came hot and hard to him, the killing frenzy seething through his body. It had been far too long since he had made an offering to Lord Khaine!

The assassin's dagger slashed downwards, into the blanket, into the spot where Drugo judged the neck to be. It was a killing blow, but the frenzy was upon him, and the blade struck the blankets again and again. The grinning leer became still more wicked and depraved, the gleam of madness still more maniacal as his dagger rose and fell, rose and fell. Then, the smile died, the gleam faded. The assassin's hand reached out, tearing away the blankets. He watched as feathers slowly flew from the butchered pillows, feathers, but no blood, pillows but no body upon them. The assassin leaned forward, unable to believe his eyes.

There was a loud explosive sound and the assassin fell backwards, half his face turned into a charred, gory mess. Flecks of black powder sizzled in his flesh, as his blood dribbled into the floorboards and leaked down to the tavern below.

The bed creaked as a form emerged from beneath it. Brunner lit the lamp beside his helm. The smoking gun was clenched in his hand, mirroring the smoke rising from where he had fired through the raised pallet that served as a mattress. He lit a cigar on the lamp, and as the dark smoke rose from the stubby tube of dried weeds, he bent over the dead man, to examine what was left of his face.

There was a din and clamour in the hall outside, and a frenzied battering at the door of his room. The bounty hunter stalked over to the door, opening it, staring into the bald visage of the innkeeper.

'Just an uninvited guest, maybe you know him,' he said, motioning for the innkeeper to enter and look at the man he had just killed. The man gave a gasp as he recognised the carcass.

'That's Drugo!' he exclaimed. 'A cultist of Khaine. But he is supposed to be locked up in the prince's dungeon!' The man did not protest as Brunner gripped his arm and led him back toward the door where the faces of the rest of the staff and guests peered in.

'Then he might be somewhat appreciative when I return Drugo to his custody in the morning.' Brunner started to close the door.

'My sheets!' the innkeeper shouted, suddenly realising what else he had seen in the room.

'Yes, I'll need a new set,' the bounty hunter said. 'But you can give them to me in the morning.' With that he shut the door in the face of the innkeeper and those behind him.

Brunner walked across the floor, back toward the bed. He reloaded his firearm, then, cradling the weapon against his chest, slipped under the pallet, letting the sheets once again drape over the edge. The bounty hunter was not unused to hardship, with many months every year spent hunting things that were almost men, and men who were barely human. A soft bed, even a not so soft bed, was now too strange to enjoy. And, besides, there was always some jackal ready to murder a person in his sleep. It was always best to give him a tempting target, but never the right one.

THE BALD MAN with the grotesque paunch reached to the shelf behind him and twisted the tap on the cask of beer. The light, urine-hued liquid sloshed into the clay stein. The man set the stein down upon the counter of the bar with such violence that the white-topped brew rolled over the sides of the cup.

'Careful,' the cold voice of the man on the other side of the counter admonished the bald bartender. 'You are spilling my drink.' The innkeeper turned on the bounty hunter, an angry look on his face.

'You can have this one at my expense, just so long as you do not spend another night under my roof!' the man exclaimed. 'Half of my guests left this morning, and the other half have demanded I reduce their bills. All because of you and that visitor of yours last night.'

Brunner regarded the man with a face that was as expressionless as the steel mask of his helm.

'You would think that I had not done your community a great service this past night,' the bounty hunter said. 'Kept you all from being murdered in your beds as I nearly was.'

'As you should have been,' the bald man retorted. 'Beds are meant to be slept on, not to be crawled under! What kind of place do you think I am running here?'

'I am glad that your prince was more appreciative,' the bounty hunter's voice warmed as his hand caressed the slight bulge in the breast of his tunic. 'Twenty gold crowns is not my best work, but then my commissions are seldom so obliging as to come to my rooms looking for me.'

Brunner looked over as the tavern door opened, one hand slipping to a throwing knife, grasping its hilt. The bounty hunter relaxed slightly as he saw the salt boy enter. The boy caught the man's eye and ran over.

'I saw another stranger, like you asked about,' the boy said. 'Riding into town.' Brunner dug a silver piece from his belt, holding it in his upraised hand where the boy could see it.

'Now,' the bounty hunter said, 'describe this stranger for me.' He looked over his shoulder at the innkeeper. 'And I may be wanting to use that back door you spoke of earlier.'

THE SLENDER MAN rode his white horse through the muddy streets, stopping well short of the inn that was the first place of interest to visitors to Greymere. He was a young man, his brown hair worn short, in the rounded bowl pattern of a Bretonnian peasant. But the suit of well-tended leather armour that clothed him, the metal boots, the slender blade at his side, the hard set of his features – these belonged to no peasant. The man slipped down from the saddle of his steed, tethering the animal to a post.

He stared up at the high wooden tower of the building beside him, then glanced back down the street, his hawk-like gaze training on the door of the inn. He turned, removing a long curved length of wood from the saddle of his steed.

The man carried the length of wood with him as he walked into the building. There was no one about in the little timber temple to the goddess Myrmidia, as he had hoped. The Bretonnian paused, and drew a long cord from his belt that he fixed to one end of the haft of wood. He studied the wooden shaft, admiring the grain of its surface, the shape of its cut, the intricate carved runes and script that flowed along its length – too precise, too artful to be any man-made construction.

Straining, the Bretonnian bent the shaft of wood into a bow shape that transformed it from a length of wood into a deadly weapon. The string, made of the hair of elf maidens woven together with consummate skill and craft, was made fast at the other end of the bow.

Louis had dwelled long in his homeland, with his family, on the very edge of the Loren Forest. They had known the forest folk, as few men did, and the bow had been gifted to his father by one of the wood elves. It was that bow that had cost his father his life, when their knightly liege had demanded the weapon, claiming that such a bow was unfit for peasant hands.

Louis smiled, recalling how the knight had died, drowning in his own blood, how he had reclaimed his father's bow, and how he had made the armoured lords of Bretonnia pay for their cruelty and oppression. At last, the feared archer known as the Black Feather – after the crow feathers he adorned his arrows with – had been forced to leave his homeland, to range far across the Known World to escape the vengeful grasp of the king.

Louis walked over to the simple ladder that would take him into the tower. Now he was an assassin for hire, employing his skill and the elegant weapon he bore for the crude pursuit of gold. But some day, he would return to Bretonnia, and cause his former masters to again fear the forests, to fear the death that struck from afar, without warning.

The marksman made his way into the small stand atop the tower, and crouched down onto his belly. He pulled a black-feathered arrow from the quiver at his side, putting it to the string of his bow. He sighted down the street, fixing his gaze on the door of the tavern.

He stretched the arrow back, keeping the string taut and the sight at the door of the inn. When the bounty hunter came out, he would never see the arrow that pierced his heart.

Long hours passed, the sun lowered in the sky. Still the Bretonnian kept his arrow nocked, ignoring the strain of his muscles, and the tension and fatigue setting into his limbs.

Louis waited, still as a statue. Eventually, the bounty hunter would emerge. Then he would die.

'Intent on holding that thing back all night?' a cold voice asked from behind the Bretonnian. The stillness of the archer seemed to actually increase. Louis turned his head slightly, seeing a black boot at the edge of his vision, resting on the edge of the sloped roof.

'Wondering how long I've been here?' the bounty hunter asked. 'Almost as long as you, waiting for you to make a move.' There was a steel edge in Brunner's voice. 'I finally got tired of waiting.'

The Bretonnian didn't move as the man he had been hired to kill spoke, as his sword touched the small of his back. 'When I learned that a stranger had ridden in, alone, sporting a fancy bow, I reasoned it out: that you were here to kill me. That you would be up here, the highest ground in this mud hole. I would be here too if I were going to put an arrow in somebody before they could do something about it.'

The Bretonnian craned his neck around, to glare at the bounty hunter.

Brunner stared back, his face unreadable in the dark. 'Don't even think about it,' the bounty hunter said. 'You move a muscle, and you're dead. And I'm sure you'd rather have your bones rest back in Bretonnia, Louis.'

The use of his name enraged the former peasant. The tone of the bounty hunter's voice echoed his former lord's. With a snarl, the archer turned, gasping as Brunner's sword stabbed into his side. The elegant bow slipped from the archer's shocked fingers, toppling back down the dark pit of the tower. Louis clutched his side, blood seeping between his fingers.

'Now,' the bounty hunter's chill voice spoke again, 'what I want to know is who paid you to kill me.' The words dripped with the promise of death if they were not obeyed. Again, Louis heard the echo of the knight's voice as he demanded his father's bow.

Louis's hand flew to the hilt of his sword. Brunner lashed out with his foot, kicking the man in the chest. A strangled scream howled from the Bretonnian's lips as he was pushed from the tower.

The bounty hunter heard the dull thud of the man's body in the mud far below. He peered over the edge of the tower at the body down in the street, its limbs skewed about it in unnatural, broken angles. He shook his head.

'Well, at least your head will make it back to Bretonnia,' he said, caressing the hilt of the long knife at his belt.

DREXLER SAT UPON the back of his horse on the low hill just outside Greymere, six of his men clustered around him. He had spent a day and a half hiding out here, less afraid of the denizens of the wild than he was of the seemingly unkillable bounty hunter. The sweat of fear dampened his brow as he thought of the man and the massive knife, and the use to which he put it.

Drexler pulled the small steel flask from his belt and drained away more of the Estalian brandy. A few of his men muttered something under their breath, but a withering gaze silenced them.

'You have something on your mind?' he snarled.

'Yes,' one of the men, a one-eyed thug who had been a bandit before Drexler had turned him to the marginally more legitimate trade of smuggler, replied. There was a defiant, worrisome tone in his voice. Some of the other men grumbled their support.

'Out with it,' Drexler demanded.

'If you go ahead with this,' the eye-patch thug went on, 'there is no way Prince Waldemar is going to let us keep on operating in Greymere. Things have been good for us here, the town is a secure haven, close to the trade routes and caravan trails from the coast.' The man looked over at his comrades. 'You should wait this thing out. Hide until he gives up looking for you.'

'Hide?' the question rumbled from Drexler's breast. 'Like some damn rabbit?' The level of outrage in his voice caused the one-eyed man to start. Drexler was all the more upset because he had been doing just that since the death of the marksman Louis. 'I'll not hide. Nor wait for this murderer to pull me from my hole in the middle of the night and cut my head off with that knife of his! No, we finish this thing! And if we must move on afterwards, then so be it.' The glare in Drexler's eyes told his men that there would be no further debate on the matter. Suddenly all eyes turned from the merchant as a horseman rode up. It was Vincenzo. Beside the Tilean lumbered a massive, brutish form.

It stood well over ten feet tall, its monstrous shoulders easily as broad across as the bed of a wagon. Thick arms, like dirty tree trunks, burst from the vest of tanned hide that clothed the bulging, muscular torso. Legs like pillars crunched across the ground, leaving clawed footprints inches deep in the hard earth. A vacant face considered the assembled men from beneath a low, bony brow. A cap ripped from the back of a bear rested on the creature's head, flies swirling and dancing about the rotting fur. The slash-like mouth displayed the broken, rotting, jagged stumps of tusk-like teeth, one of them digging into the leather-like cheek beside the bulbous, squashed nose.

Two beady, grey-hued eyes stared from sockets set deep in the thick skull. Vogun the ogre let his hand twitch – a hand that gripped a club larger and more massive than any two of the men staring at him in a mix of awe and fear.

'I see you found Vogun,' Drexler said, trying not to betray his intimidation. He had used Vogun before, both to protect his own caravans and to prey upon the wagons of his rivals, but he never failed to be awed by the sheer size of the brute. 'Does he know what to do?'

Vincenzo looked at the ogre. 'Down below, in Greymere…' he began. The ogre's brow knitted as he tried to puzzle out the meaning of the words. The Tilean pointed his hand at the town below. 'Down there, Greymere,' he said. The ogre followed Vincenzo's hand, nodding as he saw the town, but once again became muddled when the Tilean called it Greymere. 'The town,' Vincenzo explained. 'In town, there is an inn,' once more Vogun's brow knitted in concentration.

Vincenzo rolled his eyes in disgust. He rode to the ogre's side, his horse snorting in aggravation as the stench of the behemoth's clothing struck its nostrils.

'See?' he asked, pointing his finger under the ogre's nose. The ogre leaned forward, sighting along the line of the Tilean's finger like an engineer aiming a cannon. He saw the finger stabbing at a two-storey structure in the middle of the town. Vogun nodded his massive head.

'Yer, da place dat looks like a lunchbox. Vogun see it,' the ogre's deep, rumbling voice growled.

'There is a man there,' Vincenzo went on. 'In the building. His name is Brunner. He wears a black steel helmet shaped like a bowl. It covers his face,' the Tilean gestured with his hands, trying to show the ogre what he meant. Vogun put a bony knuckle against his brow, as if pressing against his skull would enable him to make some meaning of the Tilean's words.

'By the grace of Morr!' Drexler exclaimed, reining his horse beside the ogre. 'Do you see that building?' the merchant asked. Once again, Vogun bent forward, sighting along Drexler's pointed finger.

'Yer, da place dat looks like a lunchbox. Vogun see it,' the ogre rumbled.

'Go there. Kill anyone inside.'

The ogre nodded enthusiastically. Here were orders he could understand. Drexler tossed the ogre a leather pouch and the creature's face broke into a toothy smile as he saw the glittering coins inside. With a deep bellow, the brute turned and lumbered off down the slope toward the town. Drexler turned in his saddle, facing the incredulous looks of his men.

'We'll be leaving Greymere anyway,' he said.

THERE WERE SHOUTS of alarm in the street. Behind the bar, the balding innkeeper cast a curious look at the door, wondering what was going on outside. He noticed the lamp hanging beside the door begin to jump on its hook. Ponderous steps thudded up to the door. Then the portal was smashed open. A hulking shape bent almost in half, moving sideways to fit through the doorway.

The face of every man in the tavern stared, mouths dropping wide with horror. The ogre straightened up to his full, towering height, hitting his head on the low ceiling. Then he bent his neck down and rubbed a gnarled hand against his bearskin cap.

Complete silence ruled the tavern, not a man dared to move a muscle. Vogun stared at the men, his beady eyes passing from one frozen figure to the next. He stuck a thick pink tongue between his lips, trying to concentrate. The boss had sent him here to do something. Something important. A name flickered in the ogre's addled memory, and with it came the recollection of what he was supposed to do.

'Brunner!' the ogre bellowed, raising his club and smashing it backhanded across the nearest table, scattering a pair of off-duty guardsmen.

The ogre lumbered forward, backhanding a third guards-man as he charged at him, the powerful blow caving in the man's ribcage, and sending his body hurling across the room with such force that he dented the timber wall where he struck it.

'Brunner!' the murderous roar boomed from the ogre's mouth. His club crashed down onto another table, send-ing a shower of splinters and debris across the long room. Men were on their feet, screaming, shouting and running in all directions away from the ogre.

'Brunner!' the ogre rumbled again. For a second, he paused, his club raised in mid-strike, a trembling peasant huddled beneath him. The man dared to look up, saw the puzzled look on the ogre's face, and scurried away, crawl-ing between his column-like legs and running through the smashed door behind him. The ogre's lips silently worked as his mind tried to remember what the word he was shouting meant. He shrugged and smashed the club down where the fleeing peasant had stood.

'Brunner!' the deep voice boomed once more. The hulk turned, stomping towards the bar. The bald innkeeper heard the monster coming, reached beneath the counter and retrieved the last bottle of Bugman's Brew in the place. He downed the fine, expensive beer and mouthed his lips in a silent prayer.

'Up here,' a cold voice called out. The ogre turned, paused a moment, trying to remember if he was here to kill someone or just destroy the place. He shrugged again, he would just have to do both. But first he would kill. Even the ogre understood that a building doesn't run away.

Vogun lumbered back into the hall, scanning the long common room on the other side. There was a loud whistle and the brute turned, facing the stairway. He looked up and saw a man in armour standing at the head of the stairs. The ogre's thick fingers tensed about the grip of the club.

'Brunner!' he bellowed again. His massive foot smashed down on the bottom-most stair. The wood splintered and burst under his mammoth weight.

'That's right,' Brunner's cold voice called down to Vogun. The bounty hunter puffed away at his cigar, then revealed the object he held in his hand: an unhooded flask of oil from the lamp in his room. The ogre stared stupidly at the earthenware pot, then stepped forward again, crushing another stair in his advance. The bounty hunter smiled, hefted the flask and threw it full in the face of the oncoming brute. The ogre snarled, gasping in pain as the oil stung his eyes. He dropped his club, grasping at his face, trying to batter away whatever had stung him with his fists. On the stair, Brunner sighed. He lifted a twisted paper taper to the end of his cigar. Another puff, and the paper took flame. The bounty hunter let it linger for a moment, until it was well and truly on fire, a thick orange flame quickly eating the taper.

'Hardly worth the effort,' the bounty hunter said, tossing the flaming taper at the oil-soaked ogre.

'How long do you think he will be?' Drexler asked his confederate as they sat looking down at Greymere from the top of the hill.

'That depends,' Vincenzo replied. 'Do you think he will be able to find his way back here?'

Drexler clucked his tongue. 'I should have told him that I would pay him when he got back. Like as not, I could have convinced him he had already been paid for the job if I had done that.'

'Look!' exclaimed one of Drexler's thuggish hirelings. Down below, the streets of Greymere were once more plunged into chaos. A massive, flaming shape staggered through the middy streets, blindly groping its way.

'Drop to the street,' Drexler cursed under his breath. 'Douse yourself in mud.' But the burning ogre just staggered on, bellowing in agony.

'Well,' commented one of the hirelings, 'so much for the ogre dealing with Brunner.' Drexler cast a withering gaze on the man.

'Perhaps he finished him off before the bounty hunter got him,' Vincenzo offered. 'Ogres take a long time to die. I've seen many a man fighting an ogre that had an axe-blade in his skull.'

Drexler thought for a moment, then whipped his horse down the hill. 'Yes, we must see for ourselves.' The hirelings and Vincenzo quickly followed their employer towards the town.

THE FRONT GATES of the fort were gaping wide. The mashed remains of the watch captain who had thought to turn back the ogre were lying in a puddle in the middle of the road. The rest of his command was still hiding in whatever burrow they had fled to. As Drexler wheeled his horse around the gory remains, he considered just how inept peace had rendered Greymere's soldiery. Perhaps it was just as well that he was moving on. Because next time the orcs came up out of the Bad Lands, he doubted if Prince Waldemar's men would repulse them.

The riders made their way to the inn. The streets around them had grown silent, only the occasional face peering from a doorway telling them that people yet lurked in the town. The burning corpse of Vogun smouldered beside the road, his enormous vitality and dull nervous system at last overcome by the fire that still chewed on his flesh. Drexler did not give his former lackey a second glance, but reined his horse before the battered doorway of the inn.

Vincenzo and his henchmen followed Drexler into the deserted building. They made a cursory examination of the lower floor, but found nothing. Then Vincenzo set up a shout. He had discovered a trail of blood leading away from the bar, up the shattered stairway and to the hall above. Drexler smiled and ordered his men to follow the trail. If nothing else, the ogre had wounded the bounty hunter. Terrible as he might be, Brunner would be no match for Drexler's mob wounded.

The trail of blood led to a room at the end of the hall. The men filed into the chamber, looking about. The room was empty save for a bed, a small rickety looking table, and a large lamp. The men wrinkled their noses at the rotten smell in the room. The henchmen looked under the bed, examined the small chest set in one corner, as if their prey might have crawled into it.

'Where did he go?' Drexler demanded. The trail of blood led into the room, there could be no doubt about that. Vincenzo looked away from the chest, back at his employer. Then the Tilean's eyes grew wide with alarm. Drexler turned to see what had upset him, and all the colour left his face.

The lamp, its wick burning away, was no lamp. It was a small wooden keg. And, as the wick burnt away, carrying the flame into the keg, the stench of gunpowder overwhelmed the vengeful men.

OUTSIDE, BRUNNER STARED up at the inn, slowly counting down. He reached three when there was a loud explosion. The bounty hunter spat his cigar into the mud. 'Cut the fuse a little short,' he commented to himself, and strode across the street, drawing his sword.

Brunner marched up the stairs, toward the end chamber where smoke still boiled. He peered into the room, his eyes studying the moaning, dying men and those already past their suffering. Then he nodded in satisfaction, gripping the chin of the nearest body, lifting the face to study its features. The dying thug's moan grew to a shriek as the bounty hunter forced his neck to crane upward on the savaged flesh that connected it to his chest. He let the man's head fall back. No money to be had from him.

The rest of the room was a shambles, and Brunner idly considered the steel balls embedded in the timber walls. It would take some doing to remove the steel bullets from the walls. Most likely the innkeeper would leave them, perhaps throwing some planks or paint over them to conceal them from his next patron.

The improvised bomb had been a trick borrowed from a dwarf he had known. His entire supply of steel bullets had been loaded into a small keg, then filled with black powder. A crude, but highly effective way to attend to the gang of would-be murderers.

Brunner had guessed that the ogre represented the last hopes of whoever was trying to kill him. He surmised the man behind the whole thing would come to see for himself if the bounty hunter was dead, bringing enough muscle with him to feel safe. The bounty hunter had borrowed some blood from the dead soldier in the tavern below, thinking he would not mind anymore. It would be necessary to get them quickly to his room, lest the bomb detonate before they were inside, or close enough to be stunned by the explosion. He smiled again. It seemed that his bomb had got the entire mob, which was more than he had hoped for.

A wheezing breath brought the bounty hunter spinning around. He stared at a ragged lump of human debris that had crawled away from Brunner's room, leaving a swath of blood behind him like the trail of a snail. The man raised a gory hand to his moustache, smoothing the curved horns of hair. He glowered at the bounty hunter, his fading eyes burning with a sullen defiance. The steel helm of the bounty hunter nodded as the eyes behind the visor drank in the wounded man's face. There was an unmistakable air of authority about him that was evident even in his dying state. Clearly, this was the person behind all the attacks against Brunner.

Drexler glared at Brunner, waiting for him to draw his butchering knife. Now that death had set upon him, he found that he was prepared for it. He would enter the realm of Morr knowing that he had fought to the last.

'Why?' the bounty hunter's cold voice rasped.

Drexler's eyes grew wide with shock. The killer didn't even know who he was! The bounty hunter hadn't come to Greymere looking for him at all!

The dying man began to laugh at the absurdity of it, but the sound faded as a bubble of blood rose in his throat and burst. He had walked into his own death!

Drexler's head slumped against the floor with a thud.

Brunner turned away from the dead man and headed back into the room, pulling the headsman from his belt. There were a few faces in the chaos he thought he recognised. One might even belong to a Tilean thief named Vincenzo, on whom some petty sum was being offered in Miragliano. And there was no sense in letting perfectly good money rot in the bellies of crows and wolves.

A FEW HOURS later, a dark armoured figure rode through the gates of Greymere, where a group of soldiers was clearing away the remains of the former watch captain. Behind him trailed the dappled grey packhorse, a large barrel strapped across its back. The kidnapper Brunner had been waiting for would never show his face in Greymere now, not with alarm rampant in the town. It would take weeks for the place to calm down again.

Brunner cast a look over his shoulder at the barrel. He might not have met up with the man he was hunting, but at least he had turned a profit by his dalliance in the border prince's town. The bounty hunter smiled. Besides, there were those who would pay ten times more for the collection of salted meats he carried than the price on the kidnapper's head.

The bounty hunter lashed the reins of his steed and set out on the long road back to the city states of Tilea.

THE TYRANT

LATE ONE EVENING, *I made my way along the dingy streets of Miragliano, bound for the Black Boar. A cluster of dwarfs was deep in debate with a narrow-eyed Marienburger, their voices hushed and low. A hairy Middenheimer and a moustached Ostlander were tossing hatchets at a target set against a wooden support post. A sinister-looking man in the colourful robes of the Colleges of Magic was intently studying a black-bound volume, some treasure no doubt procured that very day from some crafty Tilean book dealer.*

As was usual for the tavern, there was a raucous crowd of men from all across the Empire drinking and telling lies of their exploits in the Tilean states. But I had eyes for none of these men, whatever tales they might have to tell, for I found my prize sitting at his usual table. The bounty hunter was sipping from a small glass, which I knew must contain his beloved schnapps. Seeing him thus engaged, I at once determined that his spirits must likewise be high, and advanced upon his table. Those infrequent periods when Brunner was in a good humour had provided me with a great wealth of material for my pamphlets.

For a certain loquacious impulse would overcome him, and he would regale me long into the night with tales of his past enterprises.

The bounty hunter looked up at me, gesturing for me to sit. The gloved hand that beckoned me then caressed the sheathed blade that rested across the table. I stared at it for a long time, remarking its elegance. It was a longsword, that trusted blade of the Empire, its hilt crafted in the shape of a dragon, its guard forming the outstretched wings of the beast, the pommel forming its horned head. Hilt, guards and pommel were all gilded, the golden surface glittering in the dim light of the tavern. Brunner's gloved hand again slid along the length of the blade.

'It is magnificent, is it not?' the chill voice of this grim killer asked me. I nodded my head.

'I have seldom seen so fine a weapon,' I confessed. 'Even in the court of Karl-Franz, I doubt if you could find its better.'

'It is named Drakesmalice,' the bounty hunter's voice spoke. 'A weapon borne by one of the noble houses of our homeland, bound to their bloodline, a part of their very being. It is said that it was forged during the Great War against Chaos, that it was carried with the crusading army that followed Magnus to the very gates of hell.' The gloved hand patted the gilded dragon. 'They say there is magic in this steel, magic that awakens only in the hands of those whose birthright it is to wield it.'

I stared again at the magnificent sword, imagining its long and bloodied history of noble service to the Emperor. There was a power, a lurking strength within that sword, far beyond the might of steel.

'How did you come to possess this impressive blade?' I asked. Brunner stared at me, his face expressionless. A lengthy period of silence passed between us. I was certain that I had somehow offended him, that he was not going to answer me. But at last, the tense quiet was broken and the icy voice of the bounty hunter began to speak of events far from Miragliano, in the lands of the Border Princes…

FIVE GRUNTING, STRAINING bodies filled the narrow lane that wound its way between the mud-brick hovels. The men were of vastly different ages, ranging from those who had just become men to an old grey-head. But beyond their ages, the men were alike. They wore filthy breeches of much patched crude wool, held about their waists by the merest length of rope. Sweat glistened upon their bare muscular chests and trickled into the scarred grooves in their backs where the lash had done its work. The men were clustered about the wooden bulk of an ox cart, their backs bent as they tried to lift the overladen wagon. One of their number was to slip a new wheel upon its axle, and replace the splintered disk that rested against the wall of one of the hovels.

A grim-visaged man observed their labours. His face too was scarred by a long slash that ran from forehead to cheek. Unlike the peasants', his was the mark of a sword, not a whip. The overseer wore a suit of dark brigandine armour, a collar of chain and an open-faced bowl-like helm. A narrow-bladed longsword rested against his hip. The man's features were hard, his nose broad, his eyes small and cruel. His skin, like that of the labourers, was dark, marked by the attentions of the hot Tilean sun. The mercenary fingered the grip of the heavy leather whip that hung from a loop on his belt.

'Let's not be all day!' the soldier snapped. 'The baron wants this grain in the keep and accounted for before the sun sets.' The Tilean's words were sharp and lashed at the straining peasants like the whip he carried. A few turned their heads to stare at the quickly declining sun.

Suddenly, the sound of horses made every man turn away from the disordered wagon to face the three mounted men who advanced upon the accident. The peasants hastily diverted their eyes when they saw the lead rider, staring at the ground with the intensity of frightened beasts. Their overseer bowed his head, but kept a wary eye on the nearby peasants.

The leader was a lean man, just beginning to show signs of a paunch. His face was thin, his cheeks high, his brow furrowed by wrinkles. The man's hair had the salt and pepper hue of black hair becoming white, and was cropped close to his skull; he clearly enjoyed the regular attentions of a barber's knife. His nose was a sharp beak, perched above a sharp slit of a mouth. His eyes were wide and glittered with a feverish intensity as his gaze swept over the tableau that filled the narrow lane. Velvet gloves covered his long fingers, white fur trimming the crimson garments. He wore long boots of black leather that rose to mid-calf. A sombre-hued hose and tunic completed his garb.

A slender sword hung from a jewelled scabbard at his side, fixed to a wide leather belt by a slender silver chain. The hilt of the sword was gold, cast into the semblance of a dragon, with the guard shaped like outspread wings. The golden hilt glittered in the fading light of the sun.

The two guards were dark-skinned like the overseer, but their commander had a fair northern complexion.

'Lord baron,' the overseer said.

The man raised a gloved hand and removed the blue cap that covered his close-shorn hair. He cast an indifferent gaze across the ox cart and the human beasts of burden beside it, trembling in their naked feet. The rider's gaze settled upon the Tilean mercenary. There was a cool, expressionless look in the man's sapphire eyes.

'Aldo,' he said, his voice flat, almost petulant. 'The keep is proving most tedious this evening.' The rider let a sigh whisper from his chest. He began to idly turn his hat about. 'I was wondering if I might borrow one of these creatures.'

'My lord baron,' the Tilean replied, nervousness entering his voice. 'Do you think that wise? I… I mean there… there is still much work to do… to bring in the harvest. And you have already, ah, entertained twice this week.'

'Aldo, I was wondering if I might borrow one of these creatures,' the rider repeated as though the Tilean had never spoken. The mercenary swallowed loudly, bowing even lower before the rider.

'Of course, lord baron,' he said. A thin smile slithered across the rider's face. He turned his gaze to the cowering labourers. The eyes of each man stared up, though not one dared to raise his head.

The rider replaced the blue cap, smoothing it into place, and began to wag his finger playfully from one peasant to another. At last, the finger stopped and settled upon one of the younger peasants.

'Yes, I think you will do,' his deep voice stated. The peasant looked up, fear warring with hate for command of his dirty, scarred features. Hate won and before the rider could move, a blob of spittle landed squarely on his boot. Aldo and the two mounted bodyguards moved forward. The scar-faced Tilean brought a booted foot crashing against the knee of the defiant peasant, forcing him to kneel. The grey-headed peasant looked up, a look of horror and anguish twisting his tired face.

'My lord baron, I beg you!' the man implored. 'He is only a boy!' The rider favoured both men with a withering stare. The other three peasants turned their eyes back to the ground, as if to distance themselves from the events. The rider nodded and his two mounted guards dropped down from their horses and caught both of the older man's brawny arms.

'You know,' the rider said, training his angry gaze upon the old man, 'I do believe that you are right. You will provide much better sport than that vermin.' The rider turned his gaze to Aldo. 'Gut him,' the rider snapped. The old man shrieked, straining against the two armoured mercenaries holding him. The overseer brought a dagger from his belt and raked it across the belly of his captive, finally letting the dying man pitch forward into a pool of his own blood.

'Emil!' screamed the old man, watching as his son twitched in the dirt. He looked once more at the rider. 'Bastard!' he roared. The guard gripping his left arm kicked him in the stomach, forcing the wind from his lungs. The old man bent double, gasping for air. The rider raised his hand when the other guard prepared to deliver another kick.

'Now, now,' the rider reprimanded. 'If you break him, he won't be any good to me. Take him to the keep.' The rider did not wait to see his guards remove the gasping man, but turned his eyes once more to Aldo.

'This mess,' the rider said indicating both the ox cart as well as the corpse lying in the street. 'Have it cleaned up right away.' He cast a wrathful look at the three remaining peasants. 'And see that this lazy rabble attends to it.'

'My lord baron,' the Tilean spoke. 'Five men could not repair the cart, how will three manage it?'

The rider smiled, wheeling his horse about, to face the animal towards his timber keep. 'Just tell them that if they don't, they will be joining the old man. That should give them an extra burst of vigour.' Chuckling at his own jest, the rider galloped back towards the timber fort.

An hour later, Albrecht Yorck, self-styled baron of Yorckweg, sat down in the padded seat resting atop a small awning-clothed viewing stand. It overlooked a small, timber-walled arena beside the tyrant's timber-walled fortress. The Imperial renegade had taken many years to secure his small holding in that lawless region known as the Border Princes. He had fought long and hard against man and beast, orc and goblin, even the wilds themselves to make his township survive. He had little to show for his efforts, but Yorck was determined to enjoy what small pleasures he could wring from what fruits his labours had provided.

This tyrant of Yorckweg looked at the frail peasant girl at his side, whose eyes stared at the timber floor of his viewing stand. He gestured with his hand and the girl quickly filled a horn cup with dark Tilean wine. He gestured again and the woman slunk to her former posture. Yorck let the fluid sit in his mouth a moment before letting the warm taste slide down his throat. It was as if, with every glass, he could taste the terror of the peasants who created it. It was a taste that was much to his liking.

He had known terror, once, and it was that memory that made the fear of others pleasing to him. He knew that he was now the source of fear, that he was the dread sovereign who held the life and death of hundreds in his hands. He understood now what pleasure fear must have given his former noble masters; it was the power to destroy a life with a simple word.

The tyrant leaned forward as the old peasant man from the road was shoved through the log door at the far end of the arena. The portal closed at once behind him. The old man stared about him, with horror in his eyes, then he looked up at the viewing stand. Yorck smiled down at him, the cold, humourless smile he had seen real barons and counts make into an art form.

Again, memory struck Yorck. He could remember his last moments before such a paragon of nobility. It had been in the throne room of the Viscount Augustine de Chegney, following the successful completion of the viscount's brief campaign of expansion into the Empire. Yorck's role had been instrumental in the campaign, but it was a thankless role, and the viscount had no intention of honouring their arrangement. There would be no elevation of Yorck, no rise for the spy and turncoat to a position befitting a gentleman. No, the viscount had shrewdly decided that a man who could betray a good master would betray a wicked one just as easily. Yorck could remember the Bretonnian lord's laughter as he pleaded for his life. But it was not Yorck's words that stayed his hand, rather it was the look of hate from the man he betrayed that saved his life. The hate between the viscount and his prisoner was deep and it would stoke the fires of rage in the prisoner's heart if the viscount let him go, and so it had been done.

Yorck stroked the dragon-hilted sword at his side and the cruel smile spread across his face. 'If you beg for mercy,' he called down, 'I may spare your life.'

The fear in the old man's eyes was at once replaced by hate. The man spat at the distant figure of the tyrant, the spittle falling far short of its target. Yorck shook his head.

'Come now,' he goaded, reaching into the small wooden bowl at his side, and removing a handful of small stones. 'You must have something to say.' The tyrant threw a rock at the peasant, stinging his arm. He repeated the attack, but the peasant refused to beg, or cry out as the small missiles struck his body. His hateful glare remained focused on his tormentor.

'Insolent,' the tyrant declared with a disgusted tone. He dropped the few remaining stones back into the bowl. He reached for a rope that hung from the wooden awning that screened the viewing stand. 'Go join your son, you filthy cur,' Yorck snarled, pulling the rope.

A section of the arena wall below the viewing stand rose upwards and two massive creatures slunk forward from the darkness. They were dogs – monstrous war hounds from faraway Norsca. Each of the canine giants was nearly four foot at the shoulder and twice as long. Their pelts were brindle, sporting a brown field with darker black patches and stripes. The hides were drawn close about their lean bodies and were marked by bare grey patches of scarring where the lash had done its work. The skin was tight over the ribs and the heaving of each animal's chest was quite visible as they loped into view. The massive, wide jaws dropped wide, letting thick tongues loll forward as streams of drool dangled from their jowls. The two animals began to pace towards the peasant in an eerie silence: the tyrant had long ago had their vocal cords severed.

The peasant looked away from the dogs as they advanced upon him, and trained one last, wrathful glare at the chuckling Yorck. Then, the hounds fell upon him, pulling him down to the earth. Yorck snapped his fingers as screams rose from the arena floor. Averting her eyes from the gory spectacle below, the serving girl refilled her master's cup.

ELSEWHERE IN YORCKWEG, shabby figures carefully made their way through the shadow-lined streets of the village to an old disused barn. It was a structure Yorck had given his peasants long ago to hold surplus crops; a surplus that never materialised no matter how large the harvest. By ones and twos, the silent figures made their way to the darkened meeting place. A few, hearing the sounds of screaming from the fort, turned back, retreating to the mock safety of their hovels. But many more heard the cries and strode even more purposefully toward the barn.

There was no light inside, for the eyes of Yorck's guards were everywhere, yet each person managed to find a place, leaning against a wall or sitting upon the floor. Several crawled onto the roof, to act as sentries should one of the mercenaries stray too near the meeting place.

In low, fearful whispers, the men began to speak. It was not so much a debate – it had already been decided what must be done. But it was no easy thing to act. The baron was ruthless and cruel when given little cause. If they should fail to oppose him they would bring even greater misery upon their heads. Yet, who among them did not cringe in terror every waking moment, fearful of the sadistic whim of their master that could see them spirited off to his torture chambers, and thence to the arena and the bellies of his dogs? Fear reaches a point where it can grow no greater, and it ceases to be bearable. The peasants of Yorckweg had reached such a point.

The small stash of coins was removed from its hiding place in the barn. Gathered over five years, stolen and hidden from Albrecht Yorck and his soldiers, the tiny hoard represented the last hope of the villagers. A quick debate was held, a swift conclusion decided upon and a young boy, one who might not be missed, was selected to bear the coins away, to the neighbouring settlement of Brezano and hire a warrior – a professional killer – to rid Yorckweg of its merciless tyrant.

The decision reached, the men stole once more from the barn, in ones and twos, disappearing into the night. The chosen youth, a lad named Jurgen, stood for a moment with his father, then set off, carefully making his way toward the perimeter wall and one of the small holes burrowed beneath the timber palisade. His father watched him go, proud of his boy, but fearful that the entire endeavour might be for nothing.

Another pair of eyes also watched Jurgen depart. Geier was an old man; a crippling blow from Yorck's soldiers had made him more wretched and poor than his fellows, a beggar among beggars. It shamed Geier to live off the charity of those who had nothing to give. And that shame steeled the man's maimed shreds of pride. Carefully he stole his way towards the baron's timber fort. Yorck might pay well to know what had occurred at the meeting, well enough that Geier would not have to beg – well enough that the cripple might feel like a man once again. There was no real hope that the boy would actually find anyone, and this way, at least one of the people of Yorckweg would prosper from their desperate scheme.

THE YOUNG PEASANT made his way through the massive stone walls, staring in open-mouthed marvel at the large iron-bound gates either side of the wall. A sentry, wearing

ring mail and a scarlet tabard, began to make his way toward the boy, but noting his shabby dress and dirty countenance decided that there was little chance of collecting either duty or bribe from the wretch. He hastened back to the shade beside the gate.

As a town, Brezano was much larger than Yorckweg, and Jurgen was amazed at the activity in the streets. Carts and beasts of burden lumbered along the way, carrying sacks of meal, bolts of cloth, casks of wine and other goods he could not even begin to recognise. There were soldiers rubbing shoulders with wool-garbed shepherds, who manoeuvred their flocks with the aid of small yapping dogs. He saw vendors standing beside wooden buildings selling chickens and other fowl to every man that looked to have coin in their pocket.

As he slunk along the press of people, he saw a pair of diminutive figures wearing dark, sombre armour and carrying wide-bladed axes upon their shoulders emerge from a large twin-storeyed building. The peasant had heard of dwarfs before, in folk-tales, but never before had he laid eyes upon one. He stared openly at the two as they lumbered through the throng. Turning around, he looked at the building the two dwarfs had emerged from and decided to investigate.

Jurgen peered into the darkened interior, marvelling at the fact that the building had a wooden floor. He stood in the doorway, gazing across the rows of tables, and narrow benches. The room was the largest he had ever seen – larger even than the barn in which he and his confederates had met, and it was filled with a noisy crowd of people. Raucous laughter and calls for more ale, beer and mead rose from every table. Jurgen smiled to see such merriment, a thing he had never experienced in Yorckweg. But the smile was banished in an instant when a massive, barrel-chested man appeared before him.

The man looked at Jurgen from beneath thick bushy eyebrows and at once laid a paw-like hand on his shoulder.

Before the boy could react, the bouncer spun him around and booted him through the door with a savage kick.

'No beggars,' the bouncer snarled. 'If you can't pay, you can't come in.' The huge man turned on his heel and stalked back into the tavern.

Jurgen watched as the bouncer's broad back disappeared into the gloom of the building. Without thinking, he reached into his pocket, pulling out the coins he had been given. But it was too late: the bouncer had already gone. Jurgen hastened to return the coins to his tunic and rose to his feet, wiping the dust of the street from his clothes.

'You don't want to drink there anyway,' a slender man said from beside Jurgen. The boy jumped in surprise. The man beside him was tall, a full head taller than the boy, but lean. His clothes were much patched and a slim dagger graced his leather belt. The man's skin was swarthy, darker than most Tileans', and his hair was a mass of oily black curls. His mouth was screwed into a wide smile that displayed a set of blackened teeth. 'I can take you to a place where they don't put half so much water in their beer.' The man laid his hand on Jurgen's shoulder and led him away from the crowded street.

'Thank you,' muttered Jurgen. 'But I am looking for someone.' The Tilean's face brightened and a look of surprise entered his eyes.

'Oh? Perhaps I have seen him?' the man said, gently nudging the peasant boy around the corner of a small brick building. 'Or is it a *her* you're looking for?' The Tilean's beady eye snapped shut in a knowing wink.

'No, it's nothing like that,' Jurgen responded. 'Actually, I am not sure exactly who I am looking for.'

The Tilean stared back at Jurgen, the smile withering on his face. 'Well, I know who I have been looking for,' the man hissed, drawing the dagger from his belt. 'I'll have that silver you are carrying.'

Jurgen gasped, looking from the threatening thief, to the confining walls of the alley the man had guided him into. Seeing no avenue of escape, Jurgen put a protective hand on the pocket that contained the coins. 'You can't,' he almost screamed.

'None of that,' the Tilean snarled. 'If you make a noise, I'll have to cut you. More trouble for both of us.'

He took a step forward. Then the dagger slipped from his fingers. The thief's eyes grew wide, staring at Jurgen without seeing him. A bloody bubble burst from the man's mouth and he slumped into the dirt, toppling on top of his discarded dagger.

A man appeared behind the fallen body, wiping blood from the knife he had stuck in the thief's back. The newcomer wore a suit of brigandine armour, a breastplate of dark gromril covering his chest. A steel sallet helm of blackened metal covered the upper portion of his head and face. The man finished cleaning his knife, then replaced the blade in a leather belt across his chest.

The bounty hunter did not spare a glance at Jurgen but instead knelt beside the body of the man he had killed. He pulled an even larger knife from the belt around his waist – a massive blade with a serrated, saw-like edge. 'This time you will stay caught,' an icy voice said from beneath the blackened helm.

Jurgen looked away as the bounty hunter brought the edge of his blade against the neck of the dead man. In only a few minutes, the bounty killer had cleaned his knife and returned it to his belt. He produced a sack and dropped the Tilean's head into it, twisting the end closed. The armoured figure then stood and turned, heading out of the alley.

'Wait!' Jurgen cried out, hurrying after the withdrawing figure. Brunner turned his steel-clad head, to stare at the peasant from the slit-like visor. The boy slunk away from the terrible gaze, his limbs trembling.

The bounty hunter turned again and began to stalk from the alleyway. Jurgen bit down on his fear of the intimidating figure and hurried forward. The armoured head twisted around slowly, the cold eyes narrowing on the boy.

'Th… Thank you,' Jurgen managed to force the words from his mouth. The look in the icy eyes remained the same and more words stumbled their way from the boy's lips. 'For saving me from… from that…' The boy cast a look at the headless corpse lying in the alley, its blood draining away into the dirt.

'Don't thank me,' the cold, flat voice of the killer rasped. 'If that maggot hadn't had a price on his head, he could have cut your heart out and offered it to the Blood God and it would have been none of my affair.' Brunner turned away again, slinging the sack over his shoulder.

'You killed that man for money?' Jurgen gasped, horrified and excited by his harsh emotionless words. 'You're an assassin?' he added in a slight whisper.

'I'm no assassin,' Brunner snapped, a cold fire in his voice. He rounded on the boy, glaring down at him. 'I'm a bounty hunter, and there is a difference, though a moron peasant looking to get his throat slit in a back alley wouldn't be able to understand it.' Again, Brunner headed toward the street. Jurgen hesitated a moment, then followed the bounty hunter.

The press of bodies was no less than it was before, but Jurgen noticed as he followed the bounty hunter that merchant, peasant, soldier and craftsman alike all made way for the grim figure. Slipping behind in Brunner's shadow, the boy discovered that his own passage was not so unobstructed and found his body squirming between the foot traffic as the people closed ranks and resumed their travel.

Brunner walked back down the street, toward the tavern from which the burly guard had so summarily ejected Jurgen only minutes before. As the boy advanced toward the building, the steel face of the bounty hunter turned towards him again.

Jurgen squeaked with fright as he saw that Brunner's gloved hand was closed about the hilt of his fat-bladed sword and that an inch of steel gleamed where he had begun to draw the weapon from its scabbard.

'I trust you have a reason for following me,' the bounty hunter challenged, every inch of the trained killer tensed for action. Jurgen began to back away, but the sudden image of his home, his family, the frightened, desperate faces in the gloom of the barn forced him to hold his ground, to raise his face and stare defiantly at the bounty hunter.

'Yes,' the boy said in what he hoped was like the commanding tone he had heard the baron employ so very often, but which emerged as the high-pitched yip of a frightened fox. 'I want to hire you.'

Jurgen thought he saw a flicker of amusement twitch across the hard mouth below the line of his helm. But it was only for a brief moment. The armoured figure turned and strode through the door of the tavern, waving a gloved hand for Jurgen to follow.

The boy re-entered the tavern. The huge bouncer again rose from his stool, striding toward the doorway, smacking one meaty fist into the palm of his other hand. But the bully had taken no more than a few steps before he saw the man waiting for Jurgen inside. A fearful look made the bouncer's eyes grow wide and the hairy man returned to his stool, studiously avoiding the peasant boy and hardened killer who had preceded him into the drinking hole.

Brunner advanced to a table in the corner of the room, resting his back against the wall. He casually dropped the sack containing the head of the thief upon the table, paying it no further attention. He motioned with his hand for Jurgen to sit at the other side of the table, then snapped his fingers. An ashen-faced barmaid walked toward the table, her steps reluctant, her bodice heaving with short, frightened gasps. The bounty hunter barely looked at the young woman, as he snapped an order for a stein of beer. The barmaid cast a look at the peasant boy, then back at the bounty killer.

'He can drink after I am paid,' Brunner snapped, dismissing the woman. Leaning forward, the bounty hunter's cold blue eyes stared at the peasant boy. 'So you have a job for me?' There was nothing mocking in the killer's tone, only a deadly seriousness. 'You should know that I don't come cheap.'

Jurgen reached into his tunic, pulling the coins from the inner pocket his mother had sewn above his heart. It held the combined wealth of the town's oppressed people. The boy reached toward the bounty hunter, but Brunner tapped the table instead of reaching for the boy's hand. Jurgen nodded and set the coins down next to the rough cloth sack. Brunner's gloved hand hovered over the coins, turning each of them over with a finger. Then he stared into the boy's eyes.

'And what could be worth so much to you, I wonder?' his cold voice asked.

A light gleamed in Jurgen's eyes. Was this man, this horrible killer, really considering helping them? He had been told that they could not trust to greed alone to dispose of their cruel tyrant, but also to the compassion of a noble heart, to the sense of justice that moves some men with no thought of reward. But Jurgen dared not hope that any such emotion stirred within the heart of this fearsome man.

'My village lies only a few days from here,' Jurgen began. 'It was called Elsterholz, and our lord was the Count Schlaesser. But about five years ago a man came, the leader of some soldiers. Our lord hired them, for there was rumour that wild tribes were on the march again. But the man had no intention of protecting the count – he seized control. They killed the soldiers loyal to the count, then their leader hung our count from the village gate and declared himself our lord. The Baron Yorck.' Jurgen fairly spat the name. The bounty hunter leaned forward, his face inches from the peasant boy's.

'Describe this Yorck for me,' Brunner hissed. As the boy recounted the visage of the grim tyrant, the steel head of the bounty hunter nodded in affirmation of each detail.

'He wears a sword, does he not?' Brunner asked, interrupting the boy. 'A nobleman's blade? A slender fang of steel with a hilt of gold fashioned in the shape of a dragon with outspread wings?'

The boy nodded, amazed that he had so exactly described the baron's sword. A moment of silence hung in the air. At last, Brunner nodded his head. 'I will consider this commission you have offered me.' Some of the hope drained from Jurgen's face.

'If the money is not enough, we can offer more,' the boy hurried to explain. 'We have food and mead and some of the girls in the village are very beautiful.' The boy's face dropped as he saw that Brunner's expression had not changed at all. 'And there is more! The baron has all manner of treasures in his fort. Gold from the dwarf mines and silver and gems from the south.' Brunner snorted. Jurgen misunderstood the expression, thinking the imaginary wealth was still not enough to entice the hunter. 'The baron has the horde of a dragon in a secret chamber, from his days as a mercenary and adventurer. If you help us, the town elders will let you claim all that you can carry!'

'I said that I would consider your offer,' Brunner repeated, leaning back against the wall again. Jurgen reached forward to reclaim the coins, but Brunner's gloved hand intercepted him. 'Leave those. They will help me in reaching a decision.'

'But that is all the money we have!' the boy exclaimed. 'That is all the wealth we have been able to steal and keep hidden from the baron's men!'

'Then I know that you won't be seeking to hire some other while I make my decision – unless you can find some fool who will work for unseen dragon gold,' the bounty hunter said. 'Return to your village. You will have your answer in a fortnight.'

The boy rose from the table, slumped in defeat. As he walked away, he cast a last look at the bounty hunter. Brunner was drinking from the clay stein that had been brought to the table, his eyes staring at the other denizens of the tavern. The coins remained on the table, gleaming in the feeble light. The last hope dripped from Jurgen's body.

At least the man in the alley had been an honest thief.

* * *

IT WAS DARK when Jurgen slipped through the crack in the perimeter wall of Yorckweg. It was a burrow dug by the children of the village long ago to escape the notice of their parents and slink unseen into the woods to play their secret games. But now the hidden hole in the wall served a much more important role and those who used it could no longer be properly called children.

Jurgen made his way along the deserted, muddy lanes. His tattered clothes were slick with sweat and covered in the dust of the road. He stole cautiously to the flimsy plank that served as the door of the mud-walled hovel he shared with his parents and three siblings. He paused, listening to the sounds of soft sobbing coming from inside. The boy was certain that it was his mother's voice. A sudden sense of urgency filled Jurgen and he pushed the plank aside.

Jurgen saw his mother kneeling beside the cooking fire that dominated the main room of the hovel, stirring the contents of the iron pot. Her face was drenched in salty tears, their snail-like trails glistening in the flickering light. There was no sign of his brother and sisters, who should have been sleeping on their straw-lined pallets against the far wall. The boy could hear a stirring in the back room, but a thin blanket over the opening of the room obscured his view.

The woman looked up as she heard her son enter. The look on her face was of utter horror. Her mouth opened to scream, to warn her son away, but another voice silenced her. Mother and son both looked to the opening of the back room. The blanket was pulled aside, but the man standing in the doorway was not Jurgen's father. Though wearing only a long white nightshirt, a sword was clasped in his hand.

'We missed you, Jurgen,' he said in a low, mocking voice. 'I understand you have been far away and have much to tell.' Aldo stalked toward the stunned youth. 'I think the baron will be most interested to hear what you have to say.'

* * *

ALBRECHT YORCK EMERGED from his stone-walled chamber beneath the timber fort. There was a contented smile spread across his cruel features. The wailing sobs of guilt mixed with groans of pain sounded from the cell he had left. They replaced the shrieks that had echoed through the halls for the last two hours. A burly Tilean appeared behind Yorck, fastening a chain and lock to the wooden door. The bare-chested man then turned to his master, wiping the sweat from his brow with the back of a hairy hand.

'Get a little wine and some food,' Yorck said. 'We'll have another go at him in a few hours.' Yorck's smile curled into a vile leer. 'Just to be certain he told us the truth.' The torturer bowed and departed. The tyrant turned and faced the henchman who had waited outside the cell for his master's orders.

'Did he tell you anything?' Aldo asked.

'We knew much of it from that idiot Geier,' Yorck laughed. It did his wicked heart good to recall the peasant who had informed him of the plot. Purely out of loyalty, Geier had claimed, though he seemed quite eager when Yorck mentioned a reward.

And Yorck had been most generous, giving him fifty gold crowns for being such an altruistic and loyal man. Of course, Geier had been a bit alarmed when the gold coins were brought to him on a wooden plate, as a meal... Poor man, it seemed that his eyes were bigger than his stomach. Or at least his throat. That was one lesson Yorck had learned from the Viscount de Chegney – never trust a traitor. 'But the boy did fill in some of the gaps, more so than his father or any of the others. It seems he found a man in Brezano willing to kill me. A bounty hunter, or so the rascal claimed.'

Aldo's scarred features narrowed. 'A bounty hunter?'

Yorck nodded his head. 'An expert killer, according to the boy. Get some of your men together. Ride for Brezano and kill this scum. Bring his body back, so we can show this rabble what happens to those who oppose me.'

The Tilean soldier bowed and turned to leave when a nagging thought stirred in what passed for the man's conscience. He turned to his despotic leader. 'What are you going to do with the boy? Hang him in the gibbet with his father?'

Yorck smiled with chilling excitement. 'Dear me no, he might be able to wiggle his way through the bars. No, I think he should have a spot of sport with my pets. It has been some time since they were fed.' The tyrant laughed at his own jest, then turned sternly to his henchman. 'I have my affairs to get in order and you have your own to pursue. I suggest that you go find this man. The boy won't make much of a meal for the dogs.'

THAT EVENING FOUR riders set out from the main gate of Yorckweg. Aldo had chosen his companions both for their martial prowess and their experience as cold and ruthless murderers. These were men who would not shrink from putting a dagger in a sleeping man's back or striking out with a crossbow bolt from the shadows. Each man bore an expression of cruel determination. Long years serving their usurper lord had driven whatever compassion and rectitude they had from their souls. They had done far worse things under Yorck's orders than murder an unarmed man in cold blood – one more crime would weigh no more heavily upon their already blackened hearts.

Aldo's scarred features scanned each of his armed cutthroats. 'Remember,' he cautioned, 'we must bring his body back. The baron wants to make an example of this bounty hunter, and to let the villagers know that no one can oppose his rule.' The rider to Aldo's left bowed his head, the steel of his rounded kettle hat gleaming in the feeble light cast by Mannsleib and its darker sibling. But just as he raised his face, a spike of steel slammed through his nose, crunching through the cartilage and bone. The soldier fell from his horse, clutching at his wound, an inarticulate bubbling gurgle frothing from his face.

Aldo shouted for his men to take cover, but even as he did so, a second crossbow bolt tore through the chest of the man to his right. The mercenary screamed, slumping down in his saddle as his steed raced off into the darkened countryside, frightened by the sudden slaughter.

The remaining soldier turned his horse about, making to ride back to Yorckweg. Aldo saw the bright flash of a black-powder hackbut exploding from the tree line, and he heard the loud crack of the report echoing. He watched as the bullet took the soldier's steed in the neck, dropping it instantly. The man was crushed beneath the animal's weight, pinned to the earth and screaming piteously from above his crushed legs and pelvis.

Aldo did not wait for another attack, but leapt from his saddle and dived into the brush. He landed hard, twisting his foot. He bit down on the pain, and drew his sword, cursing as his horse raced away, bearing his crossbow on the back of its saddle.

The man pinned beneath the dead horse was still screaming when Aldo heard hooves drawing near. The sound of hoofbeats stopped, then only the occasional rattle of chain-links or the scuffing of an armoured boot upon a loose stone indicated that someone was coming closer.

Aldo watched as a dark figure cautiously advanced, stalking toward the wounded soldier with all the caution of a lone wolf on the hunt. The scar-faced Tilean gave a start when he saw the man: the blackened steel sallet helm and the dark gromril breastplate. Somehow he had known that it would be him. Only the bounty hunter would have had cause to ambush them; only he would have had the skill to accomplish such a feat.

Aldo had chosen his band of killers well, but he had not reckoned with facing an even more callous, cunning and ruthless adversary. The bounty hunter closed upon the wounded soldier, raising a small hand crossbow. He pointed it at the wounded man's head and silenced his screams of agony. There had not been even a second of hesitation, a moment to consider mercy, to pity the man he had broken with his gunshot.

Aldo lifted himself from his hiding place, hoping to slink off into the night. At the sound of the rustling movement, the bounty hunter spun about, dropped his crossbow and drew a blackpowder pistol from a holster across his belly in one fluid movement. There was another loud report and the barrel of the pistol erupted into flame.

Only one thing spared Aldo's life from the shot – his injured foot gave way beneath his own weight, causing him to topple just as the bounty hunter fired his weapon. Brunner did not hesitate to address the misaimed shot, holstering the pistol and pulling his fat-bladed falchion from its scabbard. Aldo lifted himself to meet the charge, with a dagger in his left hand, and a longsword in his right.

Brunner closed upon the Tilean with a sinister silence that unnerved him more than any orc's brutal war-howl. With the speed of a viper, the bounty hunter struck out with his heavy sword, the blade barely intercepted by Aldo's much lighter longsword. The bounty hunter strained, pushing the Tilean's sword to the side, exploiting the mercenary's weakened leg to offset the man's superior brawn.

Aldo snarled, the scar on his face livid with anger. He sent his dagger-gripping hand forward toward the bounty hunter's vitals. But a gloved hand closed about his wrist, pushing the blade back, and twisting the point of the dagger back at its wielder. Aldo felt his grip being turned and reasserted his strength, turning his hand around in the gloved grasp, even as he sought to free his sword from the weight of Brunner's falchion.

The two men jostled for position in the shadows, each struggling to subdue his foe. In the darkness, the dagger stabbed into flesh and a dry gasp escaped the throat of a man who was clearly dying.

THE GUARDS ATOP the gate of Yorckweg hailed the lone rider who made his way toward their post. It was still dark, but they could easily recognise the distinctive helmet and armour of Aldo. The mercenary sergeant led a second horse behind him, a body thrown across the saddle. The commander of the watch called out his congratulations on his successful and speedy hunt, and hastened down from the tower to examine Aldo's prize. One of the other guards followed the officer, sharing in the excitement of the moment. He left only one man to work the heavy counterbalance that would raise the timber gate.

'Didn't think to see you back so soon,' the officer said, sparing only a brief glance at the mounted Tilean before hastening to the packhorse. 'Are the others behind you, or did they go on to Brezano for a bit of rest?'

The officer laughed. There was little enough entertainment to be had in Yorckweg, and what little there was, the baron hoarded for himself. It took very little to get any of the men to take an unauthorised furlough to any of the neighbouring settlements. The armoured Tilean just nodded his head, and began to dismount from his horse.

The officer reached for the body slumped across the saddle. He lifted the head, and stared at the face beneath the black visor of the sallet helm. A deep gash spread from beneath the armoured helm to the end of his cheek. It was a scar that the officer had seen many times before. Even as the soldier turned to confront the imposter, six inches of Tilean longsword were driven into his gut. The officer's cry of alarm emerged as a low gasp and he slumped to his knees, pawing at the mud with his hands. The soldier who had followed him down from the tower barely had time to see his officer fall before the imposter sent a throwing knife through his throat. The soldier fell onto his back, writhing in his death throes as blood bubbled between the fingers clasping his neck.

Brunner dropped Aldo's sword into the mud and lifted the small crossbow he had tethered to his wrist with a leather lace cut from the mercenary's boot. The lone guard in the watchtower was reaching for the alarm bell when the small bolt struck him in the back. He shouted once, hands clutching at the dart, but was unable to reach it. He staggered for a moment, pain driving out thoughts of alerting his lord and master.

Brunner calmly reloaded his weapon, and sent a second bolt smashing into the man's face. This time, the shot was fatal and the soldier pitched forward, his body hanging over the wooden railing of the tower, his steel helmet falling from his head and landing with a moist thud in the muddy mire below.

Loading the weapon for the third time, the bounty hunter removed his own heavy falchion and its scabbard from the packhorse. He pushed Aldo's body into the mud and belted the weapon about his waist once more. Stooping to retrieve his black helmet from the dead man, Brunner attached that too to his belt, shifting it so that the helmet rested against the opposite hip from his sword. The bounty hunter cast a long look at the timber fort that rose above the village, nodded his head grimly, then stalked down the muddy path that wound its way between the peasant hovels and ended at the fort of their tyrannical ruler.

Brunner had needed no time to consider the boy's offer. He had followed the peasant back to his home village, keeping behind lest the boy should sight the armed killer on his trail. Then he had hidden himself in the woods overlooking Yorckweg, waiting for an opportunity to gain access to the small village. Aldo and his pack of killers could have been no more timely had the bounty hunter written ahead and requested an invitation.

Now it was time for a long deferred reckoning.

ALBRECHT YORCK SAT in his padded seat, his sadistic, grinning features illuminated by the flickering torches set about the small wooden arena. The man snapped his fingers and a serving maid hurriedly refilled the iron-bound flagon on the short table beside his seat. Wine was well enough during the day, but Yorck felt that something more substantial was in order to fend off the chill night air. The local-brewed mead would serve such a purpose admirably. He had intended to wait for morning before indulging in his favourite sport, but the peasant slattern his troops had brought to him had proven less than acceptable. If it were not for the fact that it would spoil his dogs to give them too much food, he might have added the little witch to the menu. Perhaps in a few weeks' time when the dogs had worked up more of an appetite...

Yorck thought again about the stupid peasant rabble and their audacious plan. For such low-born worms to think that they could actually match wits with a man who had attended a baron of the Empire, who had fought with the Reiksguard in his youth, who had managed to escape the grasp of the treacherous Viscount de Chegney – a feat few men could boast of – it was beyond absurd. Yorck's subjects simply had to learn that they were not his people, they were his property.

The tyrant spared another impatient look at the wooden gate at the far side of the arena. It was taking them quite some time to bring the boy. He might have to see about having one of his soldiers play with the dogs after this, to teach him not to keep his master waiting. Yorck nodded to himself. Yes, that might indeed be a valuable, and highly entertaining, measure to maintain discipline.

The girl at Yorck's side suddenly gasped in alarm. Yorck turned on her, and slapped her with the back of his hand. The girl flinched from the blow, but as the despot recovered from the attack, he saw what had made her cry out. A tall, lean man in armour was standing on the top of the steps that led up to the platform. A dark, black sallet helm covered his head, exposing only the lower part of his face. He clutched a fat-bladed falchion sword in a gloved hand. The other hand held a second helmet and as he tossed it forward, Yorck recognised it as belonging to his henchman Aldo.

'I'm afraid that tonight isn't going too well for you,' an icy voice rasped from below the visored steel. 'First your killers get themselves killed, then someone changes your evening's entertainment.' The bounty hunter took a step forward. Needing no further encouragement, the frightened serving girl darted past the armoured killer and flew down the steps, disappearing into the night.

Yorck stood slowly, backing away. His eyes were wide with fear. He cast a glance toward the log gate in the arena below. Brunner followed the man's gaze.

'I'm afraid that I already met your men,' the bounty hunter stated, his voice carrying all the warmth of an open grave. 'I convinced them that the boy was a little too small for what you had in mind.' The bounty hunter let the point of his sword jab forward. 'It took a little effort to convince them, but not much.'

Yorck gripped the dragon hilt of his own sword and the bounty hunter took another step forward, his icy eyes suddenly blazing into fiery life. The tyrant withered before the glare, hastily raising his hands into the air. For far too long Albrecht Yorck had been content to command the swords of others, for far too long he had taken life in cold blood rather than hot. The warrior Yorck had once been – the bold scheming villain who had betrayed one throne and seized another – had become a petty, hedonistic reptile that now shivered before the threat of honest battle.

'Whatever they are paying you,' he stammered, sweat cascading down his forehead, 'I will triple it!'

A low snarl roared from Brunner's chest and he sprang forward. Yorck lifted his hands still higher even as he sank to his knees, trembling in terror. Brunner set the point of his falchion against the tyrant's belly. The man flinched from the cold metal. Brunner's free hand closed upon the buckle of the man's sword belt, unlatching the clasp, pulling the belt free. He held it in his hand with two fingers as the others worked loose the clasp of his own sword belt. The worn leather fell to the timber floor and Brunner placed the other sword belt into its place with one hand.

'You like that sword?' Yorck muttered, fear cracking through his voice. 'It is yours! I want you to have it! My gift

to you!' Brunner's eyes narrowed and he pressed the point
of the falchion a bit deeper so that it indented the flesh of
the usurper's belly. 'Anything you want!' Yorck squealed.
'You can be the baron! Just let me live!'

'The word of some men can't be bought,' the bounty
hunter hissed, his voice dripping venom. The bounty
hunter clasped Yorck's shoulder and with a savage push
plunged the falchion through the tyrant's belly, releasing it
as Yorck slipped away. The man stumbled on his feet, with
three inches of the heavy sword's blade sticking from his
back. The man stared at Brunner for a moment, but the
bounty hunter's steel-tipped boot kicked the man backwards, so that he broke through the low-wooden railing
onto the muddy floor of the arena.

The bounty hunter looked down. Behind the gate
beneath the platform, Yorck's starving pets clawed at the
wood, driven into a frenzy by the smell of their master's
blood.

Brunner turned his gaze to the dying Yorck as he forced
himself to a sitting position. The fallen tyrant bore a questioning gaze. Blood bubbled from his mouth as he tried to
speak.

'How... much? How much... did they... pay youuu...'

Brunner reached into his belt and threw several small
objects to the muddy floor of the arena. Yorck's eyes
focused on the three silver coins and the clutter of copper
groats.

'Everything,' an icy voice replied. His hand now rested
on the dragon-shaped hilt of the von Drackenburg blade.
Yorck was still staring at the coins, beyond comprehen-
sion, when Brunner's other hand pulled down on the
rope and two lean, slavering shapes lunged from the
darkness.

The two gaunt hounds circled their master, fangs bared,
muzzles twisted into the silent snarls. Yorck raised a trembling arm to ward off the huge beast that snapped at his
neck. Its fangs buried themselves deep into the meat of his
arm, worrying the limb away from his body, and leaving

the throat exposed for the other dog. The second hound was quick to seize the opening, hot breath panting from its excited, eager lungs. Yorck shrieked as the animal's jaws closed upon his windpipe, and crunched his neck as though it were an old soup bone.

Like the bounty hunter, the dogs had taken many lives, but never had they savoured the kill for so long, or so well.

HONOUR AMONG VERMIN

I LEFT THE *city of Miragliano as I had quit the Imperial city of Altdorf – a frightened cur with its tail tucked between its legs. I had terror in my soul, and prayed fervently to Sigmar that I might pass unnoticed by the powers of the Old Night.*

It happened late one evening. I had been speaking with Brunner for many hours. We were situated in a small wine shop near my own rooms. The hour was late when the bounty hunter at last declared that I would have to question him further some other time. We left the wine shop, the light of Mannsleib bathing the filthy streets in a pale silvery light. My companion, as was usual for such a predatory nature, carefully considered the night streets, his piercing gaze covering the entire street at a glance. He did not linger over any one person, nor upon any window, doorway or darkened alley mouth. Yet I had the feeling that he saw as much with his quick glance as I would in an hour of close examination – his keen mind picked out every detail. Brunner had, as I have mentioned, an amazing memory and a craftsman's eye for detail.

Abruptly, Brunner asked if there were any free rooms at the boarding house where I lodged, for we were quite close by. I replied that I believed that there were, and the matter was settled. The bounty hunter led me through the dark streets, saying that he would see for himself what manner of luxury his recollections furnished me with.

We reached the boarding house and Brunner secured a room quite close to my own, at a price considerably lower than my own. Once more, I reflected that the best champion of honesty is fear. I followed the bounty hunter up to the room the landlord had allocated to him. He gave the room a glance, then settled in, taking his leave of me without a word. Feeling for all the world like a dismissed servant, I made my way to my own chamber. However, I had only just begun to tug off my boots when the door opened. The bounty hunter gestured with a thumb at his room.

'It ill suits my level of comfort,' he hissed. 'You sleep there, I'll take your room.' I sputtered out a protest but Brunner reminded me that it was his stories that elevated my livelihood. Like a scolded dog, I gathered up my boots and nightclothes and left the room, hoping that the landlord's daughter Maria did not think to pay me a visit this night. The bounty hunter was capable of most anything. With his ruthless impulses and lightning-fast reflexes, he might kill the girl before he was even aware who had stolen into the room. Or he might welcome the company. I was not sure which scenario troubled me more.

So it was that I woke in the small hours, a foul stench filling my lungs. I did not rise from my bed, for I recalled Tilean tales of the Strigoi, the blood-sucking fiends who smelled of the grave and ripped the throats of their victims as they slept in their beds. After my encounter in Altdorf, vampires held an especial horror for me, and I became as still as a corpse, hoping that whatever exuded such a stench would not notice me. Yet, even in terror my mind was analysing the situation.

The odour was not that of a rotting corpse, but the reek of filthy fur, like an ill-tended beast from a menagerie. My hearing became ever more sensitive as my fear mounted, and I could hear the soft padding of naked feet stealing across the wooden floorboards. The soft, furtive steps drew ever closer towards the bed and with them, the stench filling my lungs increased. I held my breath, trying to wish the intruder away, and screwing my eyes shut desperately, lest I should see what horror now hovered over me.

The shrill titter that sounded from above me chilled my spine; it was a sound of cruel and inhuman amusement. Almost against my will, I opened one of my eyes. In the soft light streaming through the unshuttered window, I saw a hideous shape from the realm of nightmares. It was shaped like a man, though slender and small, its back crooked. A dark cloak covered its shape, and its paws were coated in a verminous black fur. Two red eyes gleamed from the shadows of the hood, and a long, rodent muzzle peeked forward, whiskers twitching as the nose scented my terror. Two long, chisel-like fangs jutted downward from its upper jaw. And I could see the moonlight dance on something metal clutched in its paw.

It was a horror from childhood, a nursery fable given flesh. How often have we tried to frighten naughty children with tales of the skaven, those scheming rat-men who lurk in the shadows, plotting the destruction of humanity? How often do we laugh at their fear at such tales, for we in our wisdom know such tales to be foolish and fantastic? Can we no longer remember our own childhood terrors? When did we decide that such things were not real? And who told us that such things could not be…?

I watched in horror, frozen to the spot by my disgust, by the sudden flooding of my heart with all those childhood nightmares. The skaven drew a long, foul dagger from the worn leather belt about its waist. The red eyes gleamed more brightly and I knew that I looked upon my death.

Suddenly, the door was thrown open. The skaven uttered a sharp squeal of surprise, and leapt from the bed, scrambling toward the window. But it never reached its escape. The dull thok of a crossbow sounded. Once, twice, and yet a third time, all in rapid succession. The monster's body twitched as the first bolts slammed into its mutated flesh, and as the third bolt struck its cowled head, it fell to the floor. A long, naked tail twitched for a moment, then fell still as the vile creature breathed its last.

Brunner walked into the room. He still wore his armour, though he had removed the almost ever-present helmet. I watched his hard, grim face as he stared at the expired monster, turning its carcass over with the toe of his boot. He had the curious repeating crossbow pistol still aimed at the rat-man. He did not seem horrified by the monster's loathsome visage, or concerned at its presence here.

'You knew it would come here!' I accused, my fear giving me enough courage to confront the bounty hunter. 'You used me as bait!'

The bounty hunter reached down and removed a small pouch from the skaven's belt. I heard the jingle of coins as Brunner hefted the sack. He opened it, smiling as he saw the gold it contained. Then he withdrew something else from the sack, a piece of leather that still bore fur on one side. He read whatever message was written on it, then replaced the scrap of leather in the pouch.

'What is this all about?' I demanded. 'By the shadow of Morr, what is that thing?'

Brunner nudged the corpse with his foot one more time. 'Just a messenger, from someone making good on a debt.'

The bounty hunter then began to speak, to spin a tale of what had befallen him in my home city, in Imperial Altdorf, beneath the very feet of the Emperor.

NIEDREG CREPT SOFTLY through the dark room. His silent steps went unerringly past piles of books, tables laden with scrolls and jars, past the dozens of black obstacles that awaited him in the near lightless room. But the young man was no stranger to this environ; he had been this way many times before, though never with such purpose as now moved his thin, lean body.

A small pool of light blazed in the midst of the shadows. Niedreg paused, catching his breath, and stood still, watching, listening, and most of all waiting. His eyes gleamed in the flickering flame of the old copper-bound oil-lamp that had its origins in the desolate wastes of far-off Araby. The lamp was resting atop the large worktable of dark Drakwald wood that dominated the room. Papers were piled in one corner of the table, while books and jars of dark liquids were spread across every remaining edge of the wooden surface. In the only break in the mountain of leather-bound books and glass pots, a stoop-shouldered man was bent forward, his pale, long-fingered hands working within the sphere of light cast by the lamp. The man's head was covered in long grey hair, topped by a rounded cap of black felt marked with symbols and stars of silver and azure.

Niedreg watched as the wizard continued his labours. The old man stabbed a lengthy needle-like device into a small bowl, then removed a tiny scrap of flesh from it. With his free hand he grasped one of the glass jars, and pulled it into the sphere of light. He dipped the needle into the jar, and shook it until the fragment of flesh fell free and slowly sank into the dark liquid. Then he thrust the needle into the blazing flame of the lamp until its tip burned red, then withdrew it and set it upon a sheet of moist vellum, to steam and sizzle.

The old man leaned over the glass pot in which he had dropped the fleshy fragment. Then he turned to a steel frame that held up a thick piece of glass in a brass claw. He raised a wrinkled hand to his head, pulling back the long strands of hair that threatened to slip into his eyes. Looking through the piece of glass, he concentrated on the fragment of flesh, the dark liquid, and what effect their union was having.

Niedreg licked his lips nervously and drew the knife from his robe. It was still in its sheath of dark leather, but the young man imagined he could feel heat ebbing from the blade. He had been warned to keep the weapon sheathed at all times, until the very instant he was to strike. He had been told that the merest touch, the simplest contact with the naked blade would kill, but not quickly, or cleanly. Niedreg cast an apprehensive look at the sheathed weapon and took a deep breath.

The seated figure was so involved in his labour that he did not notice Niedreg's shadow fall upon him. It was almost a summary of their relationship: the old wizard had never paid any but the most cursory notice to his apprentice. Niedreg had served Lothair the Golden for five years, and in all that time his magical training had amounted to little more than hurrying about Altdorf securing the compounds and chemicals his mystic patron required. While it was true that Lothair had shown some compassion by schooling him after the Colleges of Magic had so summarily rejected his application, Niedreg felt that his apprenticeship had been steadily degrading into nothing more than servitude. But now the would-be wizard had found a new patron, one who promised to teach him far more than Lothair ever could have.

The apprentice drew the knife from its sheath. The weapon glistened wetly in the flickering light, its black surface coated with a foul ichor that seemed to ooze from the very metal of the weapon. Niedreg spared the knife only a moment's glance, for the grey head of his mentor had lifted, as though he sensed something was amiss. Whatever warning sense disturbed the old wizard it was not quick enough, for Niedreg swiftly stabbed the black blade into the wizard's back, piercing his heart. A long, low gasp sounded from the magician and he slumped over his table, disturbing the flasks and jars.

Niedreg stepped back, leaving the still-dripping dagger in the old man's back. He watched as green drops slithered from the blade's edge and sizzled on the fabric of the wizard's robe.

Niedreg bent forward to retrieve the blade, but as his eyes fell upon the blood flowing from the wizard's mouth where he had bitten through his own tongue, he flinched away from the dagger. The blood that was pooling on the table was not simply crimson: there was a thick streak of dark foul corruption mingled with it. Once again, the young man recalled his patron's words of caution: *do not handle the blade for longer than you need to*. But he would need to touch it again to accomplish the rest of his task, for his benefactor had told him that the blade must not be found in the wizard's body. Even a charred, blackened skeleton would look the part of a murder victim with a dagger in its back.

Niedreg squatted on the floor, pulling a heavy book from the top of a pile. He opened the leather-bound volume, ripped several pages from the binding, and clasped them in his hand to form a crude mitten. He stood again

and reached for the dagger sticking from Lothair's back.
With as quick a motion as he could manage, he pulled the
dagger from the wound and tossed it onto the table. The
slimy drops of venom still sweated from the gory blade.
Niedreg hastily tossed the pages in his hand over the
weapon. He did not watch as they darkened and curled
when they came to rest upon the dagger. He smiled nervously, fearing and envying the lethal enchantment upon
the blade. He reached toward the flickering lamp, to engulf
the evidence of his crime in fire, when a thought occurred
to him. He was not without his own magic.

Picking up the violated book once more, Niedreg began
to mutter, and rub a dark, salt-like powder between the fingers of his left hand. As he continued his low incantation,
he ripped pages from the book with his now blackened
fingers. He tossed the pages about the room, careful to
place most of them around the dead wizard and, just as
importantly, the subject of his final study. When each page
came to rest, the paper burst into flame. Very quickly, a
dozen small fires were blazing about the room. Very
shortly the entire study would become a raging inferno,
obliterating all trace of Niedreg's crime.

The apprentice paused, admiring the flames his magic
had brought into being. No lesson of Lothair's had ever
been so grand. No, the spell the apprentice had invoked
had been taught to him by his new benefactor – a small
sampling of the secrets and powers Niedreg's new patron
would reveal to him as payment for this night's work.

Shouts of alarm from the street outside brought Niedreg
out of his reverie. The room was now engulfed in flame,
the ancient books and carefully collected relics shrivelling
and cracking as the flames licked about them. At the table,
Lothair's body was burning like a torch, the artefacts on
the table before him already lost in the dancing fire.
Niedreg tipped his fingers to his brow and saluted the old
wizard's corpse as he hurried from the room.

* * *

FROM THE SHADOWS, a pair of beady red eyes watched the flames dance from an upper floor window across the cobbled street. A small hiss of excitement escaped the watcher's mouth as he saw the fire ravage the home of the wizard Lothair. His agent had performed just as he had anticipated, but he had ever been a good judge of men, able to determine their capabilities and find their weaknesses. Now all that remained was to sever the link between himself and the fool turned assassin and he would be in the clear, with no connection between himself and his mistake.

The household of Duke Verletz had been taken ill; indeed most of the household had perished, including the duke himself. His death would firmly put an end to the lunatic idea to renovate the sewers of Altdorf. The duke had a mad notion to install piping and tubing in the hundreds of thousands of buildings in Altdorf, to let the waste of each house be carried directly into the sewers without first being dumped into the street and carried away by the dung gatherer or rainfall. It was the ambitious scheme of a maniac – a maniac with the Emperor's ear. And there were those who did not like such a state of affairs. So, the duke's household had become ill, and the wizard Lothair had been summoned to try and identify the nature of the seemingly sorcerous ailment, and find a way to neutralise it. This too was a state of affairs that could not be tolerated, because an entirely different neck was on the line should the wizard succeed.

The observer fought down the nervous impulse to chew on the object clutched in his hands. There was no need to fear: his error was now going up in smoke and flame. All that remained was to meet with Niedreg one last time and give him the reward that was his due.

The watcher's face twisted into a snarl. The fire was burning quite well now, but still the fool had failed to emerge from the building. Suspense was not something he enjoyed so there would be an extra measure of pain when he caught up with Niedreg for creating such a strain. There were enough causes to instil fear in him, not the least of which were those to whom he himself was answerable. He did not need some one-use man-tool upsetting him so.

The watcher hissed a sharp curse and slid lower in the basement window from which he observed the scene. Niedreg had emerged from the burning house, but he had dawdled too long inside. He was carrying a large chest in his arms and a bulging pack was dangling from one arm. Instead of looking like an innocent witness to the unfortunate fire, it now looked obvious to everyone that Niedreg was a thief and a murderer. The watcher cursed again as a trio of figures in gleaming armour plate with deep rich ostrich plumes flowing from the crowns of their helmets converged upon the idiot. Niedreg tried to run, but did not release his hold on the burdensome chest and pack. The knights easily caught up to him, smashing him to the cobblestones with the butts of their halberds.

Skrim Gnaw-Tail succumbed to his nervous habit and clenched the much-abused end of his long, naked tail into his fanged mouth, nibbling at the scarred flesh with his chisel-like teeth. He slunk away from the window, drawing the shabby cloak of black wool still tighter about his mottled grey and brown fur. He turned his long-muzzled rodent face toward the two larger figures beside him in the basement.

Skrim let his tail drop again, tucking the much abused appendage beneath his cloak with two furry, long fingered hands. He barked a sharp command and the two slaves scuttled forward. They were larger than Skrim – the size of a decently grown human, though leaner and much less broad of chest. The two slaves were naked save for filthy loincloths of tanned rat-hide, and their brown-furred bodies bore the marks of lash and fang. Most horrible of all, their mouths had been sewn shut with a crude cross-stitch of rat-gut.

Skrim gestured imperiously with one of his paws. The skaven scurried forward and pulled up a loose stone in the floor of the basement, exposing the narrow tunnel that wormed its way from the cellar to the vast sewers beneath the ancient Imperial capital. The two slaves stood aside, for their master to go in first. Skrim set a foot on the edge of the pit, then snarled and gestured for one of the slaves to go first. It was doubtful if anything would be waiting for them below, but the skaven would feel better with at least some warning if there were. After the mute rat-man disappeared down the hole, Skrim climbed down, leaving the last slave to replace the heavy stone behind him.

The skaven scampered down the tunnel behind his slave, his keen eyes finding a path even in the absolute darkness. As he hurried along, Skrim's thoughts turned to what he would do now. His luck had betrayed him at every turn in this enterprise. An hour more and that idiot would have fallen into the skaven's paws, removing the last link between him and the duke's death, and the true facts concerning that demise. Nor could Niedreg be arrested by any guardsman. But a patrol of the Reiksguard, the Emperor's own! Which meant that instead of gracing some common keep's dungeon, Niedreg was now enjoying the hospitality of Karl-Franz's own prisons, beneath the Imperial Palace itself, a place Skrim Gnaw-Tail would not risk trying to enter.

Indeed, even the most skilful of the Clan Eshin assassins would be loath to chance the Emperor's dungeons, for measures had been taken to protect the place from Skrim's kind – sorcerous alarms that would react to the presence of any creature of Chaos. Any assassin Skrim sent to finish the job might ask too many questions, and worse, might ask them of the wrong skaven.

No, Skrim decided, as he emerged into the foul-smelling labyrinth of the sewers, a human was responsible for getting him into this mess and it would take another human to get him out of it.

THE DANCING FOX was a sinister-looking building, a three-storey structure that dominated one corner of a broad market square. The narrow windows faced outward like the arrow slits of a castle wall, framed by wooden shutters that had been painted in the same black that coated the exposed support timbers. There was always a crowd in the establishment: merchants fresh from their custom in the square; patrons who managed to have coin within their purses after visiting the hawkers and tradesmen who filled the square each market day; and those of a more larcenous bent: thieves and pickpockets who preyed upon seller and customer alike. But the thieves had their own predators.

Brunner sat at a table, peering from the shadows. He was studying each face as it passed into the vast, triple-tiered common hall of the tavern. A black steel helmet concealed his face and he wore a belt of throwing knives across his chest. A long-barrelled pistol of exceptional craftsmanship rested upon the table before him. From his clay stein some white froth slowly slithered its way to the stained wooden surface of the table.

He watched a pair of men enter the tavern, noting the notched, maimed ear the fatter one had. His memory dredged up a name to go with the ear, and a price to go with the name. He let a thin smile split his face and reached for the beer stein, his gloved finger wiping away the foam to grip the handle of the clay mug. Now he would wait for the fat man to conclude whatever business he had in the tavern. Providing no better mark presented himself, Brunner would follow the fat man as he left. There was not a large contract on the smuggler, but it was enough to justify the three-day journey to the Reikland town where the itinerant magistrate Judge Vaulkberg was currently located.

Brunner watched the fat smuggler boisterously greet a pair of well-dressed men who had the look of the port city of Marienburg about them. Just then a dark shape slipped into the chair opposite the bounty hunter's seat. Brunner gave a start, his hand gripping the pistol on the table. Rarely was the bounty hunter surprised, especially in a tavern and on the hunt as he now was. Yet the wiry figure in the shabby cloak had been so furtive in his advance that even Brunner's cautious, roving eye had failed to notice him. Brunner immediately forgot about the fat smuggler, focusing his angry gaze on the seated interloper, as well as the barrel of his pistol.

The figure raised its hands in a placating gesture. Brunner noted the slender, thin hands, covered by rough gloves of coarse and dirty wool. The cloak was of more crude material, though it had been dyed black at some point. The scent of a cheap, pungent perfume wafted from the figure. As the unwanted guest raised his head, Brunner could see that beneath the hood a mask of black cloth completely concealed his features.

'No harm,' the man said, his voice thin and shrill. Brunner stared at him dubiously, keeping the pistol trained upon him. 'I speak – say,' the man paused, uncertain how to elaborate. 'Need hunter,' he said at last. 'Man-hunter.'

Brunner tried to follow the butchered Reikspiel. The speaker was certainly not a native of the Empire, though even Brunner's wide-faring ears were unable to identify his accent. It was not of Kislev, nor even of the Tilean cities. Nor did the shrill tones suggest the melodious speech of elves or the thin whispers of goblins. But the next words, however poorly spoken, rang like music to the bounty hunter and quieted the questions aroused within his mind.

'Much gold I pay – spend,' the cloaked figure said. The gloved hand scratched within the folds of the cloak and placed a pouch upon the table that chinked loudly with the metallic ping of coins rubbing against one another. Brunner, with one hand still on his pistol, for his doubts had not been banished, reached for the bag. He slid the pouch across the table, undoing the thin cord that bound the pouch. He let his eyes fall to the open pouch, and then looked once more at the masked visage of his companion. He removed one of the gold coins and tapped it against the edge of the table, as though the sheen might scratch away to reveal lead underneath. But the sheen held true, the coin was indeed gold, as were its many comrades in the pouch.

'You have my interest,' Brunner stated flatly.

'Give twice, more when kill – slay,' the voice scratched as the figure leaned back. Seeing Brunner's hand relax on the grip of his pistol, the cloaked head darted about, to see what eyes might be watching their transaction.

'Who's the mark?' the bounty hunter asked. The cloaked figure cocked his hooded head, as though confused. 'Who do you want me to kill?' the bounty hunter explained.

'Wyrd-maker, warlock,' the man hissed.

'A wizard?' Brunner asked. The figure grew silent for a moment, as though considering the bounty hunter's question. Then the head bobbed in a crude approximation of a nod.

'Wiz-ird, yes,' he agreed. A gloved hand slipped into the folds of the cloak, removing a rolled piece of stained leather. 'Prisoner,' the voice added as Brunner unrolled the leather scroll, to reveal a scrawl of lines and scratches. It was a map – a crude map – but a map all the same. 'Locked-kept in Emperor-man burrows,' the speaker paused, again seeming to collect his thoughts, and to translate them into the structure of the Imperial tongue. 'Much-like wyrd-maker not leave burrows,' the speaker said. 'Not have wyrd-maker say-speak to Emperor-man.'

'The map,' Brunner said tapping the leather scroll with a gloved finger. 'A section of the sewers?' The head tipped in a slight, faltering nod. 'Beneath the dungeons? How do I get in?'

A hand pointed at a small scratch mark near one of the lines. 'Tunnel in wall,' the shrill voice explained. 'Open into man-hutch.'

'The wizard's?' Brunner asked. The cloaked shape shrugged, a gesture the figure seemed comfortable doing. Brunner sighed. 'Do you know how large the dungeons of Karl-Franz are?'

'Work – earn gold,' the cloaked man snapped, his temper making his voice even more shrill and unpleasant. 'Not give-all, must look-seek!' The hooded head again scanned the room to see if anyone was listening. Brunner gave a short laugh.

'Alright, I get the idea,' he reached forward and closed his hand about the sack of gold. 'I'll figure out where your friend is.' Brunner set the pouch into a leather box fixed to his belt. 'And send him your regards.' The cloaked head cocked, like a bird puzzling over a worm. The bounty hunter sighed. 'I'll slit his throat. Then he won't say anything you don't want someone to hear.'

The tittering laugh that hissed from behind the mask made Brunner's hand return to his pistol, such was its unnerving, unnatural sound. The speaker flinched as the bounty hunter stared hard into his masked face. The bounty hunter's blue eyes gazed into the red crescents that peered from behind the mask.

'Where do I meet you when the job is done?'

'Alley-run behind butcher-lodge, Fleischer-weg,' the shrill voice replied. Brunner nodded his head.

'When?'

'When wyrd-maker dead,' the shrill voice hissed, 'hunter-man come when dark, when butcher-lodge alone. Hunter-man find gold then. Need wyrd-maker slay-kill soon, or not give-spend gold. Day and night, not more.'

'Alright, but bring twice as much money when you meet me. The death of a wizard is not an easy thing,' the bounty hunter stated, studying the sinister man. In truth, what he had been paid already was enough for him to accept the job. And that was what made him uneasy. The strange figure's reaction to his raising of the fee was not what the bounty hunter expected.

'Gold not problem,' the voice uttered with the same unsettling titter of laughter. 'Small wyrd-maker, easy strike-kill, but gold not problem.' Still laughing, the lean figure rose from the table.

'This wizard have a name?' Brunner asked, a demanding tone in his voice. The cloaked patron froze, cocking his head to one side, as though it was a curious thing to require the name of the man upon whom he had put a death mark.

'Niedreg,' the voice pronounced, before slipping away into the shadowy crowd.

Brunner watched the figure disappear, and considered the gold in his pocket and the mysterious shabby man. He reached forward, tipping the stein to his mouth, to wash away the after-scent of the departed man's cheap perfume.

SKRIM GNAW-TAIL looked from side to side as he scuttled toward the mouth of the sewer. When he was satisfied that no one was looking his way, he dropped to all fours and scampered across the filthy alleyway like the vermin he resembled. He slipped through the narrow opening, dropping ten feet to the dark tunnel of muck-lined stone walls. The skaven's nostrils drank in the stench of the sewer, but even that mighty reek could not entirely drown out the odour of the cheap perfume he had been forced to douse his fur with.

Skrim removed one of his gloves and raised a grey, hairy paw to his nose. His face wrinkled with disgust and he cast a murderous look at the two mute slaves who had been waiting for his return. He slashed his claws against the face of one of them, enjoying the way the brute flinched. It was not their fault that Skrim had been forced to don his unpleasant disguise and walk among the man-things again, but nothing lessened the irritation seething in Skrim's scheming mind. Such petty retribution – even against a hapless lackey – eased the skaven's mood somewhat.

The skaven walked over to the edge of the slime-coated walkway, peering at the foul brown water. The sharp tang of the filth caused Skrim's nose to twitch, but he was more accustomed to this than the overpowering reek of the perfume. To a creature who saw the world through his nose as much as his eyes, it was like being nearly blinded. With another sullen look at his slaves, the skaven dropped into the filthy water, splashing about in the slime for a moment before submerging entirely. When he emerged, clumps of waste and even more unsavoury substances clung to his wet dripping pelt, and a foul odour wafted from his fur, but at least the stinging scent of the perfume had been washed away.

Skrim snapped a command and the two slaves fell into position: one before and one behind their master. The skaven paid his guards no further attention as they made their way through the dark sewers.

He was lost in his own thoughts. The man-creature he had hired was well known amongst the smugglers and traitors Skrim had occasion to deal with, and his reputation was indeed terrible. He would be able to accomplish the task, Skrim was certain of that.

With Niedreg gone, there would be no further connection between Skrim and the unauthorised use of the red pox he had employed against the mad duke. With Niedreg gone, he could stop worrying about the retribution the fanatics of Clan Pestilens would exact upon him if they connected Skrim, the plague-spores that had infected the house, and the plague monk agent who had stolen the spores for him.

Skrim was saddened by the loss of the filthy creature; it was rare to find skaven amongst the plague monks who were capable of being bribed. Still, Skrim believed in the old adage that it is a wise skaven who collapses his tunnels behind him.

Once Niedreg was gone, there would only be one more link to sever. It would be easy enough – humans were, after all, inferior and witless creatures. Skrim raised his tail and began to nibble at it nervously. Still, the stories they told about this bounty hunter were not to be discounted. He looked at the slave ahead of him, then cast a glance over his shoulder at the other one behind. Perhaps he would purchase a few more guards before he met the bounty hunter behind the slaughterhouse to give him his reward.

A shiver crawled through Skrim's body. Yes, he would get some more guards before facing those merciless eyes again. Caution was not cowardice, and even if it were, only skaven with very short lives held cowardice with any manner of contempt.

THE SOUND OF booted feet striding through the inky blackness beneath Altdorf disturbed the dark brown rat as it nibbled at the wing-bone it had wrestled from a pile of dung. The scavenger turned its beady eyes toward the sound, hissing. The vermin cringed from the bright light and with a squeak it abandoned its meal and leapt into the filthy channel of reeking brown water. The rat's naked tail writhed behind it as it swam off, into the darkness that was its proper home.

Brunner strode along the narrow walkway, a blazing torch held before him. He moved with caution, his armoured head turning about, staring at the mouldy walls and foetid water that slowly coursed past only inches from his feet.

The sewers of Altdorf were ancient, dating back almost to the foundation of the city. They had been designed by dwarfs, it was said, as a tribute to Sigmar himself. It was also said that the sewers that served Altdorf were better planned than the streets, as they ran beneath the capital in orderly ranks whereas the lanes and pathways of the capital wound and crossed one another in maddening disorder.

All sorts of strange stories were told about the sewers. It was rumoured that an ancient dwarf steam engine hissed and churned in the bowels of the city to flush the filth through the underground streams. But there were darker stories too, tales of ghouls lurking in the tunnels, waiting to prowl the streets while the city slept and Morrsleib lorded over the night sky. More gruesome yet, it was said that during the siege of Altdorf by the undead hosts of Vlad von Carstein, entire companies of the living dead had entered the sewers, seeking to enter the city from below, and that some of those deathless monsters still wandered in the dark foulness, doomed to spend eternity there.

There were other tales too, of secret covens of profane cultists living beneath the foundation of Sigmar's faith, whose rites summoned up hideous things from the Realm of Chaos.

But Brunner's mind was not on such fears and fancies; his eyes and ears sought more natural dangers such as pockets of mephitic vapour that might explode in his torch's flame, and packs of starving rats that might not be too discerning about their next meal. Crumbling stonework and archways that waited for a victim before succumbing to the ravages of time and damp. To his mind, these were the adversaries to be feared, not the bogies the foolish and the fearful claimed were in the tunnels.

He paused to glance down once again at the map, black powder pistol held at the ready. Brunner studied the scrawled pattern of slashes and curves, then stared at the dark openings that yawned away twenty paces to the left, twenty-five to the right and still again to the left at the very limit of his vision. Each of the brickwork archways appeared equally forbidding; a filthy brown stream crawled from the mouth of every one. He made his way forward, then, bracing himself, leapt across the foul waters, nimbly landing on the narrow ledge opposite. He leaned his body against the muck-crusted wall to steady himself.

Torch in one hand, pistol in the other, the bounty hunter entered the right-hand tunnel, the tunnel that would, in time, worm its way beneath the Imperial Palace itself.

FIFTEEN EYES OPENED as the distant light and the unfamiliar sound of booted feet made themselves known. The eyes blinked – a thin membrane snapping over each yellow, pus-hued orb, dulling the unfamiliar, stinging light. A huge bulk undulated through the water, its mass glowing from the phosphorescent filth that sweated from its lumpy, fungus-like hide. Claws clicked against one another, anticipating the rending of flesh. Sensitive nostrils flared, scenting the almost forgotten odour of man. The hulk slithered through the waste, leaving a glowing wake behind it. Ahead of the thing, rats squealed in terror, scampering away from the unnatural haunter of the dark.

The creature had lurked within the tunnels below Altdorf for many long years, far longer than the reigns of Karl-Franz and his father Emperor Luitpold combined. And in the darkness, it hungered. It did not need food, no, indeed, it was well beyond that simple need, its Chaos-ridden flesh preserved and sustained by no worldly meat. But it still felt the pangs of appetite, the needs of hunger. Its horrible, twisted form was not made for the hunt, however, it was far too cumbersome to track down rats and other vermin; its smell, noise and glowing warned away all the creatures of the sewers well before its approach. In the last year, it had fed only twice: once on a river stork that had flown into the sewers and got trapped. The other time, it had discovered a number of men, loading sacks into a small skiff. They had been too busy to see the peril until it was upon them. Only one of the half-dozen smugglers had escaped. Yet even with the bodies of five men rotting in its gullet, the thing had not been sated.

The torchlight was growing brighter, the footsteps were coming nearer. Body quivering with anticipation, the thing submerged beneath the filthy brown water. It did not understand that even with its body beneath the foulness, it left a film of phosphorescence floating on the water to betray its presence. Even so simple a supposition was now beyond the mind that had once composed volumes of learning and lore and had pondered the true nature of the Winds of Magic.

BRUNNER CONTINUED TO make his way along the embankment, watching his steps as often as he stared at the leather map. The stones were slick and slimy, caked in the filth that had accumulated over the months since the River Reik last swelled its banks and rushed through the sewers, cleansing them in return for the stream of pollution that befouled the mighty river. The bounty hunter smiled. Even if one of Karl-Franz's jailers did know of the secret entrance, he was sure no one would endure the path lead-ing there.

His smile faded as a new stench struck him: a sickly odour like rancid milk mixed with spoiled cabbage and poured over a pile of vomit. Even in this labyrinth of nau-seating stenches, the smell was distinct and overpowering. Tears formed in his eyes, such was the quality of the reek.

Brunner paused to wipe his eyes. The door was not far, at least according to the map. If it were not, he may have decided to quit the sewer entirely until he could equip himself with a fragrant pomander to out the stench. As it was, there could not be more than fifty yards between him and his goal. He would force his senses to endure the smell for such a short distance.

With his gloved hand Brunner wiped his eyes, then retrieved his torch. As he lifted the brand from the small crack in the wall which had served him as an emergency sconce, his eyes fell upon the sewage that slowly flowed past the embankment. There was an odd glow about it, a decidedly eerie green luminance. The bounty hunter cocked the hammer of his pistol and thrust the map through his belt.

The monster rose from the waste, its twin mouths utter-ing a maddening wail, like the mewling of an infant married with the sound of a dying elk. The thing dripped waste and sewage, streams of filth flowing across its mas-sive back, and down its pulpy, shapeless chest. Five groping, slender limbs flailed about from its trunk-like body, each tipped by a series of sharp claws, like the mandibles of an ant. A cluster of short stalks writhed between the limbs, each sporting a leprous eye that blinked in fascination at the man. Two gaping mouths yawned where breasts might be found, were the thing human. The mouths drooled a digestive venom that siz-zled and consumed its own slimy hide. They were toothless and pulpy and seemed to alter shape each time they opened and shut, as though controlled by muscular contractions rather than jaws.

The creature was immense, larger than a bear, and rose from the filth on a set of legs as broad and powerful as those of an ogre. The legs were short, stumpy and loathsomely human in appearance, but they were covered in small pink fibres that fluttered and danced when they emerged from the gangrenous skin of the abomination.

Brunner recoiled as the numerous eyes struggled to focus upon him. He raised his weapon, firing at the clustered eyes. The boom and crack of the weapon was almost deafening, the flash of its discharge blinding in the darkness of the sewer. Brunner did not pause to see what effect his shot had had, but began to race from the loathsome being. He could hear the water sloshing behind him as a tremendous bulk surged through the channel.

Brunner dared a look over his shoulder. The Chaos spawn was nearly upon him, undulating through the water in a hideous, boneless fashion like an eel. The cluster of eye-stalks had been blackened by the pistol shot, a pulpy, fibrous drizzle of yellow pus surrounding the injury. Yet from the base of each ruined stalk, a new eye, the hue of a rotten egg, peered from the gore. And each of the intact eye-stalks now acted in concert, fully aware and focused upon the fleeing bounty hunter.

Brunner spun around, thrusting his torch toward the oncoming mass. The eye stalks snapped shut before the bright glare, but even as the warrior thought the flame might keep the fiendish mutant at bay, one of the snake-like limbs shot forward, wrapping about his arm. He found himself pulled toward the sickly horror, the strength of the thing nearly pulling his arm from the socket. A second tentacle curled itself about his waist as he grasped the dragon hilt of his sword. The spawn pulled Brunner from the brick ledge, and held him above the filthy mire of the channel. The jawless mouths of the abomination slavered, opening and closing with a sickly sucking sound, bubbling fluid sizzling from each maw.

The bounty hunter's hand worked at the trapped sword, straining against the constricting steel coils of the monstrosity. As the beast wrapped tighter about its prey, the breath was crushed from Brunner's lungs. Dark spots blurred his vision and the bounty hunter could feel the icy touch of death. Was he going to die here, devoured by some faceless horror of the dark, all his plans unrealised? Were his bones to fester in filth and dung until they were no more? Wrath blazed in his fading vision. With a burst of hate-fuelled strength, Brunner's grip upon the blade grew firmer and he pulled the ancient sword of the von Drackenburgs from its sheath.

It was an effort fuelled by more than physical strength; it was an effort made possible by the force of will and spirit. And still, the blade only rose a few inches. Yet it was enough. The coil that held arm and sword firm was cut by the sharp steel edge as it crawled from its scabbard. As the cold steel touched Chaos-ridden flesh, it carved its way through the substance like a red-hot knife through butter. The coil sizzled and burned, a foul green mist rising from the wound. The steel seemed aflame, glowing a brilliant crimson.

The Chaos spawn wailed – a sound all the more horrible for its kinship to the cry of a mortal man. The coils withdrew and unwound with a speed that set Brunner's body spinning. The bounty hunter crashed to the floor of the sewer, legs landing in the filthy channel, chest crunching into the brick embankment, the breastplate cracking the mouldy brickwork.

Taking deep breaths to feed his violated lungs, Brunner stood quickly, not allowing his mind to register the many hurts he had suffered. The von Drackenburg sword was held before him and there was no mistaking the writhing fire that crawled about the blade; the mystical flame cast a hellish glow upon the brown water and the crumbling vaulted ceiling above. Brunner let a curse escape his lips, bracing himself for the creature's next attack. And, though the din of its ululating howl still thundered all about him, the ghastly glow of the horror's phosphorescence was receding into the dark.

Brunner breathed a sigh of relief, then stared about him, finding the discarded torch resting, by some miracle of chance, upon the far embankment.

Leaping across the channel, the bounty hunter retrieved the firebrand, then retraced his steps. He dug the map from his belt, employing the hand that still gripped the sword Drakesmalice. Brunner studied the curious scrawl on the map and replaced it in his belt. He was eager to be out of the sewers, for at least the foes he might encounter in the Emperor's dungeons would be human.

TROTZEL STIRRED ON his pallet of straw and lice. The thin, haggard man wore rags that had once been red and blue, though now their colour matched the dirt and grime of his cell. The man's narrow, calculating eyes canvassed the small expanse of his cell: the cold grey stone walls, the bits of bone and rag that littered the floor, the small wooden bowl that served as his slop and the even smaller bowl that held his daily ration of water.

The thief glanced at the heavy oak door with the iron fittings that separated him from the corridor beyond. He was trying to discern sounds and movement from outside. Perhaps one of the gaolers had decided to administer a beating to work off a bout of boredom.

A sound to his left roused him from his disconsolate thoughts. Before his stunned eyes, a section of the wall sank inwards, revealing a blank expanse of darkness.

Trotzel rose from the floor, taking furtive, uncertain steps toward the strange opening in the wall. He had taken no more than a few steps when a gloved hand reached out from the shadows. Even as the thief recoiled, the fist closed about the neck of his tunic. Uttering no more than a frightened squeal, the thief found himself pulled forward, his head smacking against the stonework. Trotzel moaned and slumped to the floor as the hand released him.

Brunner emerged from the opening, casting a satisfied glance at the unconscious man. The prisoner would be insensible for some time, perhaps even hours; long enough to serve the bounty hunter's needs.

Looking the man over, a thought formed in Brunner's mind and a new plan began to form. Turning away, the killer strode to the heavy door, removing a series of small hooks and lead weights from his belt. He expertly assembled the objects, then snaked the slender metal hooks through the small barred grille set in the face of the door. A few moments of play with the hooks slid the bolt of the door back. Brunner retrieved the hooks, then crouched and began to work at the lock with a slim piece of curled metal. There was a click, and he pulled the door inward, peering into the dimly lit corridor beyond, to ensure that no patrol was making its rounds. Then he slunk into the hallway, pulling the door closed behind him and throwing the bolt back into place.

Softly, he crept along the stone passages, moving from shadow to shadow. To every side, the corridor stretched away, lit by torches in iron sconces set at twenty foot intervals. More dark hallways intersected with the corridor along the northern wall for as far as his hawk-like eyes could see. Occasionally, a moan or cry of despair would sound from behind one of the iron-bound doors along the walls, but Brunner paid them no heed. The prisoners could not be expected to have any useful information about the dungeons, the quickest path to the torture chambers or halls of interrogation. He could spend days checking every cell, looking for a man whose name and profession he knew, but whose appearance he did not.

The sound of jangling keys and booted feet brought him to a halt. Brunner crouched in the nearest and deepest patch of shadow, a slender dagger gripped in each hand. He waited as the sounds gradually drew closer, then watched as a trio of soldiers, each garbed in the red and blue of Altdorf's soldiery, with the double-headed Imperial eagle upon his livery, strode the hall. Each soldier wore a sword at his hip, and the leader, a man who wore a bright ostrich plume in his steel helm, marking him as a sergeant,

carried a massive ring of keys on his belt. Brunner listened
for further soldiers and a grim smile flashed across his face.
He slowly set one of the daggers back in its sheath and
removed the small crossbow pistol from his belt. Setting
the other dagger down on the floor, and keeping his eyes
on the three guards, the bounty hunter loaded a quarrel
into the weapon and cranked the steel string back.
Retrieving his dagger from the floor, the bounty hunter
aimed his weapon at the guardsman to the left.

The guard fell instantly. The sergeant and the other soldier laughed, thinking the man had stumbled, that
perhaps he had enjoyed a bit too much ale when they had
visited the guardroom. But the sergeant almost instantly
uttered a low curse as he saw the blood pooling beneath
his fallen trooper. Yet still his thought was of fatigue. Only
when he spotted the small steel bolt protruding from the
man's neck did he understand what had truly happened.
And by then it was too late.

As the sergeant turned his face to alert his remaining soldier, Brunner lunged from the shadows. The soldier had
no time to react, for the first he saw of his attacker was the
bounty hunter's dagger sliding across his throat. The
sergeant pulled his sword from its sheath, opening his
mouth to shout an alarm. But he was too close, and the
bounty hunter pitched the dying body of the other soldier
into the sergeant, both men falling in a jumble of limbs
and steel. At once, Brunner jumped upon the struggling
sergeant, crushing his wrist beneath an armoured boot.
The officer's eyes were wide with alarm, his face ashen
where it was not concealed by thick dark moustaches.
Brunner slammed the palm of his free hand over the
sergeant's mouth as he began to scream, muffling the
sound before it could carry far. He pressed the point of his
dagger against the man's cheek, just below his eye.

'Stop trying to shout,' he hissed. 'Tell me what I want to
know, and I may let you live.'

The sergeant's eyes went wide with fear, but the jaws
beneath Brunner's grip closed. Brunner removed his

dagger and stared into the sergeant's eyes. 'There is a man here, a wizard named Niedreg.' A look of recognition flared through the guard's terror. Brunner smiled inwardly. 'I need to find him.' He put a slight degree of weight on his blade, drawing a bead of blood from the soldier's face. 'I want you to tell me how.' The sergeant nodded his head.

'Th... they brought him in... yestereve,' the man licked at his dry lips. 'He is down in the third level... where they keep all the special prisoners.' The sergeant stared at the bounty hunter, his eyes filled with fear, but slightly narrowed. 'Down this corridor you will find the stairs. Take them down, to the second level. Follow the corridor to a large door with a double-eagle marked upon it. That will bring you to the hallway that leads to the lower level. The wizard is kept in the fourth cell from the third turn to the left of the stairway.'

Brunner leaned back, considering the sergeant's words. 'You are sure that you've told me what I want to know?' The sergeant nodded hastily, emphatically.

'Anything else I should know about? Traps? Guards?'

The soldier shook his head and a slim, cruel smile appeared on the bounty hunter's face.

'You know, if you are lying to me, I will be back. I won't kill you for lying to me. No, I'll not let you off so lightly.'

Pallor crept back into the soldier's face.

'I'll carve the eyes from your head and cut out your tongue. Then I'll sever the tendons in your arms and legs. There will be pain and agony like you've never known, even in this hellhole. But you'll recover, like these poor bastards sometimes do when the torturers have had their fill of them. You'll be a sightless, voiceless sack of meat, not able to see or touch or speak ever again. Just a sack of meat that will beg for death with every breath, but unable to speak that desperate plea.'

Brunner leaned his face downward so his visor was now only a few inches from the trembling body of the sergeant.

'But perhaps you were confused by my question. Perhaps you would like to amend the directions you gave me?'

BRUNNER WAITED IN the dark corridor, watching another three-man patrol pass from view. He had spent a consider-able time dragging the bodies of the soldiers back to the cell, and now he was thankful that he had. The guards might notice the traces of blood in the corridor, but he hoped that they would think the marks had been left by some wretched prisoner. It would not do to have the alarm raised when he was so close to his quarry.

The cell Niedreg was in was on this very level of the dun-geons – not more than a few hundred yards from where Brunner had entered the maze-like halls of darkness and despair. The sergeant had also told the bounty hunter that one of the Emperor's torturers might still be there ques-tioning the arsonist and that one of the dungeon scribes might be in attendance to record any confession. Brunner had thanked him by killing him cleanly with a quick stab of his dagger in the neck.

He crept along the dimly lit halls with slow deliberate steps toward the cell he had been directed to. As he stole forward, he could hear a harsh voice coming from beyond the door. A shout of pain answered the voice, and with it came the sound of sizzling meat. Brunner smiled. The sergeant had indeed spoken the truth when he had changed his story.

The cell door was neither bolted nor shut entirely. It had been left ajar, as much to let the screams reach the nearby cells as to let fresh air trickle in to offset the smell of burned flesh. Brunner's gloved hands pushed the heavy door slowly inward, so as not to draw the attention of those within. As the sergeant had said, there were three men in the cell. Brunner could see a thick bear of a man, his naked chest glistening with sweat, his arms corded with ropes of muscle. He was slowly turning long rods of steel in a brazier of coals. At his side, seated upon a stool, was a nondescript man in blue and gold, carefully scribbling down every word spoken within the room. He was dabbing his plumed pen in a small inkpot on a second stool and using a small wooden board as a writing table. The third man was young, naked, and shackled by iron manacles to the rear wall of the cell. Ugly raw wounds marked the man's body: the burns of the heated irons the torturer had set against the prisoner's bare skin. As Brunner watched, the torturer removed another iron from the fire and advanced upon the prisoner, holding the glowing red point before him.

The bounty hunter pushed the door again, the loud creak bringing the torturer spinning around. The man's ugly twisted face took on a look of outrage, a look that was frozen on his brutal features as the bounty hunter's bolt took him through the eye. The torturer toppled, the brand falling from his hand to set the straw on the floor aflame.

Brunner pounced upon the scribe as he rose, casting pen and parchment aside. Strange words whispered from the man's mouth and an ugly light began to gather in the outstretched palm of his hand. Brunner had suspected that there might be a low-level initiate of the colleges watching over the magician. Still, the initiate's wizardry had not warned him of the danger that prowled the tunnels and corridors below the Imperial Palace. It would take valuable seconds for the wizard to summon even the feeblest enchantment – seconds the man did not have.

Brunner's sword rasped from its sheath and the slender blade slashed through the clerk's neck, painting the wall a bright crimson. The wizard stood for a moment, as though he might ignore mortal injury, but then what magic had been summoned faded and he fell to join the torturer on the cell's dirty floor.

The bounty hunter hurried to stomp out the fire with his armoured feet. Only then did he meet the jubilant gaze of the young magician hanging from the shackles.

'Thank the gods you've come!' Niedreg gasped. 'I knew that Bosheit would not abandon me!' The young murderer watched with some apprehension as the silent rescuer bent to retrieve the scattered pages from the floor. 'I didn't tell them anything,' he hastily explained. 'I have been loyal. I didn't tell them anything, no matter what they did!'

'I can see that,' Brunner said as he collected the pages, scanning a few of them before thrusting them into his belt. He favoured the bound murderer with a friendless smile. 'Whatever you did say,' he added, drawing a dagger and walking toward the prisoner, 'my job remains the same.' Niedreg's eyes widened with fright. A last protest, a last snivelling plea to spare his life formed on his lips, but it died there as the bounty hunter slammed the dagger into his heart. Brunner took a step back, waiting for the corpse to become still, and for the dead apprentice's bowels to empty. Then, drawing the large saw-edged knife he had named The Headsman from his belt, the bounty hunter advanced once more upon Niedreg's corpse.

TROTZEL STIRRED IN his cell, groaning as consciousness returned. The ugly bruise on his skull throbbed with pain. He rolled onto his side, then sat up straight, eyes wide with alarm. Lying beside him in the cell were three dead guards. Trotzel's mind tried to puzzle out who had killed the soldiers. Had the opening in the wall been real then? Had he really been struck by some dark figure from the shadows? A fresh thought drove these questions from his mind: perhaps whoever had killed the guards had also left the door of his cell unbarred! He scrambled to his feet and hurried to the door.

Trotzel reached for the heavy oak portal, but no sooner had he reached it than the barrier swung inward. Trotzel retreated from the door and hurried to the body of one of the dead guards, leaning down to take a sword from the man's belt.

'I shouldn't touch that,' a low, hissing voice snapped. 'Not unless you want to stay here.'

Trotzel turned around, watching as a tall man in armour, wearing a black sallet helm, entered the cell. There was a naked body slung over his shoulder. The thief gasped as he saw that the arms ended in ragged red stumps, and cringed when he saw that the severed hands had been tied around the corpse's neck.

'Come here,' the icy voice commanded. The thief took a few tenuous steps forward. As he did so, the bounty hunter kicked the door of the cell closed with his foot. 'I'm not going to hurt you unless you force me,' he added, ensuring that the threat did not go unnoticed. The thief forced down his apprehension and hurried to the armoured figure.

'Hold this,' Brunner said, dropping Niedreg's body into Trotzel's arms. The thief staggered under the weight, but managed to hold onto the corpse. Brunner strode forward and crouched over the bodies of the dead soldiers.

'Who... who are you?' Trotzel asked, shifting his body to compensate for the weight of the dead man. Brunner did not look up, but instead removed the sword from the dead sergeant, adding it to the ring of keys he had taken earlier.

'Do you care?' the bounty hunter replied. He bent towards the soldier shot with the crossbow, and dug the bolt from his wound, removing his sword as well. 'I should think your freedom would be enough to occupy your mind.'

'It is,' Trotzel admitted quickly, eager not to seem ungrateful lest the menacing man leave him behind. He watched as the bounty hunter strode to the rear wall of the cell and placed his hands against two of the stones set in the wall. Once again, the wall sank into darkness.

'Aren't you going to take his sword?' the thief asked, nodding his head at the unplundered body.

'Two will be enough,' the bounty hunter declared. He nodded his head to indicate the opening. 'Bring the body here.'

'Certainly,' Trotzel replied, hurrying forward as best he could. 'A friend of yours?' he asked.

'No,' Brunner replied, pushing the slim thief through the doorway. The bounty hunter followed Trotzel. A moment later, the wall slid back into place, leaving no trace of thieves, killers or wizards.

* * *

'OH YES,' TROTZEL'S voice crackled with malicious mirth. 'There are quite a few people who are going to be sorry to see old Trotzel again! You can count on it!' The thief let his words turn to another crackle of laughter. Brunner turned to the little man, uttering still another snarl for the fool to shut his mouth. It would serve to cow the man for perhaps another dozen paces or so, and then the thief's eagerness to plot his revenge upon those who had caused him to be thrown into Karl-Franz's dungeons would bring the words tumbling out once more.

The bounty hunter paused, glancing at the map in his hands. A few more turns, and he would be back at the place where he had encountered the monster. For the third time since returning to the sewers, in fact. Brunner cast a disgusted glance at Trotzel and the corpse the little man was carrying over his shoulder.

'I tell you, when I get my hands on Ilsa, it won't be a quick thing,' the thief cackled, resuming his vengeful plots. 'That little trollop! All for a few crowns reward!' The thief hissed a low curse about the caprices of women. 'I'll have a grand time getting even with her!'

A sickly stench brought Brunner's head about. A smile formed on his face. He turned and spoke to the thief once more.

'Almost there now,' he rasped.

'About time!' Trotzel groused. 'Your friend here isn't exactly weightless you know!'

Brunner watched as the phosphorous patch in the slimy water moved towards them along the channel.

'Ranald's blade! What is that smell?' Trotzel exclaimed. 'We must be under the privy for the Count of Ostland's ogres!'

Brunner faced the thief. 'Can you swim?' he asked.

'What? In that?' A look of horror crossed Trotzel's face as he stared at the reeking channel. 'We're going to swim through that?'

'Not "we",' the bounty hunter explained. 'You.' Gloved hands shoved the thief and the corpse he was carrying into the water. The bounty hunter turned from the floundering man just as the slick of glowing scum surrounded him. Brunner could hear the man's shouts of anger and disgust become high-pitched screams, but he did not dally to watch the Chaos spawn devour the man. The creature was quite probably mindless and would perhaps not remember the man who had injured it mere hours ago. And Brunner had no desire to test his strength against that of the abomination a second time.

The bounty hunter looked at the map again, now following it back towards the exit that would take him to the streets of Altdorf. He paused, dropping the keys and swords he had taken from the dungeon guards into the waste-carrying channel. He watched them sink into the reeking mire. Like the bodies of the two men he had removed from the dungeons, they would never be found.

Brunner smiled at his planning. He had left every indication that Trotzel and Niedreg had worked together to escape the prison. Whatever questions might arise from the escape would be blamed on the wizard's magic, and the blame for Niedreg's escape would fall on the shoulders of whichever magician had examined him and pronounced his powers weak and inconsequential. There would be no suggestion that the wizard had died in the dungeon, nor that his slayer had been an intruder from the sewers.

Now there was one last thing to see to. Brunner would have to collect the remainder of his reward from the sinister little man with the unpleasant laugh.

SKRIM GNAW-TAIL peered around the corner of the alleyway. Darkness had settled upon Altdorf, and in the now deserted Fleischerweg, only a handful of streetlamps were lit. There was little custom for beef and pork during the long hours of the night and what foot traffic was still abroad was seeking the taverns, inns and houses of entertainment scattered throughout the Imperial capital. At such an hour, the district of butchers was as lonely as the gardens of Morr. Still, there was always the unlikely chance that a patrol of the city watch might happen by. Skrim would have preferred to end the matter down in the sewers, but there was too much chance that he might be seen; that one of the numerous spies of the other clans and factions of the skaven might see his encounter with the bounty hunter and wonder what was going on.

The skaven could see the bounty hunter in the lonely alleyway, sitting upon a rickety rain barrel that had long ago ceased to serve its purpose. Except for the lines of sheets and towels strung across the alleyway that were used by the slaughterhouses to sop up blood and entrails, and a few battered crates, the man was alone.

Skrim flinched back around the corner, muttering under his breath. His hand began to lift the scarred end of his tail to his mouth, but he dropped the appendage angrily when it touched his wiry whiskers. Why was he feeling so nervous, the skaven wondered? It was only one man, and once he was attended to, there would be nothing linking Skrim to the late Duke Verletz.

The skaven turned his head and snapped a command at the figures lurking behind him.

Brunner stood up as the small cloaked figure stepped into the alley, and advanced a few paces, fingering the small crossbow pistol in his hand.

'I have been waiting for hours,' he said. 'I was starting to think you weren't coming.' Menace dripped from Brunner's voice as he continued. 'I was starting to think I'd have to go out and find you.' The cloaked figure answered with another unpleasant tittering laugh.

'All dead now,' Skrim cackled. 'All gone, but man-killer!' The skaven leader dodged to the wall as six more rat-men scrambled into the narrow lane. They were all lean with filthy, verminous pelts of brown fur clinging to their scarred and malnourished frames. In shape, they were somewhat human, but their hands ended in long claw-like nails and long bare tails snaked from their backs. Their heads were narrow and long, and sported whiskered muzzles and thin, pointed ears. Their mouths had been stitched shut, so that the only sound the creatures could utter was a low hiss. Each clutched a rusty steel blade.

Brunner drew back from the oncoming pack of skaven, and Skrim chittered as he watched the man recoil. Over the centuries, the skaven had been forgotten by the Empire, and reduced to legendary bogeymen to frighten bad children. It was a misconception the skaven constantly tried to foster among the lawmakers and learned men of the great Imperial houses. If confronted by these mythical creatures, even the bravest warrior could be overcome by a superstitious dread that would delay his actions by dangerous seconds.

But there was no such inaction in the human hunter. Brunner fired the bolt from his crossbow, catching the leading skaven in the chest. It fell, twitching in the alleyway, tripping up those scampering behind it. The bounty hunter drew his sword, but did not rush to meet the remaining foes. Instead, he pointed the blade upwards and slashed it across one of the hanging sheets. A rain of small glittering objects fell from the ruptured sack, striking the stone paving of the alley and bouncing across the lane. The naked paws of the charging slaves sank into the spiked edges of the caltrops and they shrieked in pain, several tearing the stitches from their lips in their agonised wails.

Brunner had expected some sort of double-cross, for anyone as free with his money as his mysterious patron might take it into his head to reclaim what he had spent. But he had expected to confront men, not monsters. Still, he had faced inhuman adversaries before, and no matter what shape they wore, he would meet their challenge.

The bounty hunter charged into the injured skaven, his sword passing through the neck of the closest one, sending its head rolling across the alley. The second skaven tried to parry his blow, but it overbalanced and fell against the stones, causing more caltrops to sink into its mangy hide. The slave shrieked, but its cry ended in a low rattle as Brunner's sword transfixed its heart.

The bounty hunter removed his blade from the twitching corpse, glaring at the other attackers, but the fight was over – the injured rat-men limped away as best they could, back to the hidden entrances to the sewers and the comforting safety of the dark tunnels.

A loud snap sounded from the entrance of the alley and something whizzed past Brunner's face, smacking into the wall beside him. He turned as another snap sounded, and staggered as something struck his breastplate, ricocheting off into the darkness. It had dented the almost indestructible metal. He quickly drew a throwing knife and sent it arcing through the darkness to strike the figure at the mouth of the alley. There was a sharp squeal and something clattered to the cobbles.

Brunner strode towards the cloaked figure, watching with some amusement as it tried to tug the knife from where it had caught the garment and pinned it to the wall. The murderous creature had been lucky, the knife had missed its arm.

Brunner stooped and removed the strange-looking weapon the skaven had fired at him. It was similar in some ways to a crossbow, but it had a box-like device set atop the string. The steel string itself had a mechanism that instantly pulled it back after firing. He paused to admire the weapon for a moment, then turned his icy eyes on the struggling creature.

'I suppose you didn't bring me the rest of my money,' he sighed.

The skaven suddenly slipped free and dropped down out of the pinned cloak. Skrim scrambled from the alley on all fours, like the giant rat he resembled. Brunner muttered a low curse, letting the unfamiliar crossbow fall back to the street and grasping for one of his own throwing knives. He had an instant to watch the long, naked tail and grey-furred backside scramble out of sight around the corner. He snarled again, giving chase, turning the corner just in time to see the tip of the fleshy tail slip into a narrow sewer drain.

'No,' the bounty hunter said after gazing at the dark drain. He sheathed the knife and walked away. 'I am not going back down there unless I am sure I'm getting paid.' Still watching for any sign of lingering ambushers, he strode back to the alleyway to reclaim the skaven's abandoned weapon. The exotic weapon would be compensation for the money his treacherous, inhuman employer had failed to pay out.

SKRIM WAS MUTTERING to himself as he sloshed his way through the murky tunnel. He nibbled at the tip of his tail, savouring the taste of his own blood. Flecks of foam fell from the corners his mouth, splashing against the grey fur of his chest.

The human would pay, the skaven swore to himself. The filthy man-creature would suffer untold agony, have the flesh gnawed from his bones by Skrim's own fangs. He would spare no expense to have his revenge. He would set the finest assassins in the Under Empire upon that treacherous cur...

Skrim stopped short, a hunted look entering his eyes. Yes, he could set the nastiest, sneakiest, stealthiest, most skilled assassins in the Old World on the bounty hunter's trail. There were enough warp tokens in his many caches of wealth to afford them. But could he be certain that the killers would stab first and ask questions later? What might they be able to learn from this man-killer before they slew him? For that matter, what might that dolt Niedreg have told him before he was killed? Skrim's head whipped about, his narrow eyes darting at every shadow, trying to see what they might conceal.

He was in the same bind. He could not set one of his own kind after the bounty hunter; he'd have to use another human for the job. Yet even then, there was no surety of killing the man-killer. He had a decidedly skaven-like penchant for distrust and cunning. Skrim had to admit that it was an almost admirable quality. Perhaps he was being hasty in his thirst for blood. After all, those cowardly slaves were more to blame than the man-creature. If they had not been so easily frightened, they might have been able to better the human. It took Skrim quite some time to convince himself, but at last he decided that the escaped slaves were the cause of his humiliation and near-death experience. He'd see them skinned alive for causing such anguish.

As for the man-creature, he seemed to hold no loyalty beyond his need for the yellow metal all the humans lusted after. Perhaps he might be of use at some later time? Enough gold, and perhaps he might even forget about their unfortunate misunderstanding.

Skrim's eyes glistened in the darkness as his devious mind began to hatch new plots and intrigues, plans in which a human bounty hunter was a rather prominent player.

THE BLACK PRINCE

MANY ARE THE *legends told in the misty shadows of the Grey Mountains, that nigh-impenetrable fence between the Kingdom of Bretonnia and the grand Empire. Here was the birthplace of such legends as the infamous Blood Keep and the vampiric red duke. The location of the haunted dwarf minehold of Bhuralidwar is said by some to worm its way through the roots of jagged fangs of rock. And, here too, once stood that monument to the Dark – the fortress of Drachenfels – and the unholy being who inhabited that blighted palace.*

Some of these tales are naught but stories told to frighten young children, and to keep ignorant peasants from straying too far from their masters' lands. But others hold the seed of some dark and terrible truth, some secret the teller of such stories is better off not guessing. For sometimes truth comes at a high price and can raze the fortunes of the most prosperous, sap the strength of the most mighty, and savage the soul of even the most stalwart.

Among the legends of the Grey Mountains, there is the tale of a grim and fearsome haunter of the darkness, a Black Prince, master of a shadowy kingdom of thieves, bandits, murderers, assassins, kidnappers and slavers. A Black Prince who rules from a stronghold hidden within the Grey Mountains, and collects tribute from his nefarious subjects within both Bretonnia and the Empire. Some even say that his spectral reach extends even beyond these great lands, so that cut-purses in Tilea, highwaymen in Estalia, Sartosan pirates and even marauding mercenary free companies in the Border Princes pay their tithe of blood and gold to this man. It is whispered that not all of the Black Prince's slaves are human; that in the dark woods twisted things bray and growl their oaths of allegiance to him. And, it is also whispered, the Black Prince himself is not human, but some creature of the Ruinous Powers, a daemon thing set upon the world to cultivate the seeds of corruption and decay, to weaken the bastions of humanity and pave the way for the next great push by the forces of Chaos.

Chief amongst those tradesmen who harkened to tales of the near-mythical figure of the Black Prince was that hard and brutal breed – the bounty hunter. Though the Black Prince himself might only be rumour, the reward offered for his head was only too real. Held within a vault below the King of Bretonnia's castle in Couronne, the bounty for his capture was the ransom of a king. It had been kept under lock and key for three hundred years following the notorious kidnap and disappearance of the elf envoy from Athel Loren. Yet even after all this time, no man had ever stepped forward to claim the reward, and so the infamy of the Black Prince grew and grew.

The siren lure of the Black Prince summoned that grim and terrible figure, Brunner the bounty killer, to the pleasant land of Bretonnia. And on this epic hunt, I became more than Brunner's chronicler – I became a part of his deeds, a part of the contest between the limitless cruelty of the Black Prince and the unerring ruthlessness of the bounty hunter.

I doubt if I shall ever feel clean again…

One

THE TAVERN WAS full despite the late hour. Peasants spent their meagre earnings on cups of watered-down ale, trying to warm the chill of autumn from their bent, overworked frames. A down-on-his-luck minstrel sat near the fire, despondently plucking away on a battered lute. A pair of caravan guards tested their strength in an arm wrestling contest, trying their best to ignore the whiny-voiced mule-skinner who tried to incite everyone to wager their coin on the outcome. An off-duty watchman bounced an over-weight, middle-aged serving wench on his knee half-heartedly. A woodsman spread a set of skins out on his table, examining them in the feeble light cast by the lanterns on the rafters.

Near the bar, a well-dressed merchant from the Empire ordered another flagon of ale for himself and his son. The merchant sported the elaborate moustaches favoured by the well-to-do of his land. His face was plump and well-fed, but bore the mark of the weather in the hardness of its cast and the roughness of its skin. The eyes glittered with humour, but there was also a mark of sadness in them – a scar left by years of experience in times that were neither so pleasant nor so prosperous as the present.

Otto Kretzer took the two leather mugs from the obese Bretonnian behind the bar and made his way back to the table. A younger man rose to help him, but Otto shooed him away.

'I'm not so old as I can't handle myself, you know,' the ageing man scoffed. He set the flagons down on the table and let a big sigh heave from his chest as he slumped into one of the chairs. 'Of, course, I'm not so young as I used to be,' he admitted with a wink, taking a deep draught of ale from his cup.

'As you are very fond of reminding everyone when it's time to load the wagons,' the younger man laughed.

Josef Kretzer was the very image of the merchant, though not as plump, or as well dressed. A slender branch of black hair curled upwards from the corners of his mouth, framing a sharp nose. His hair was cut short, though not in the military fashion of the older merchant. His leather tunic was not elaborate, but his boots bore a pair of glittering silver buckles that contrasted richly with the simple laces and clasps that graced the older man's leggings.

Josef reached a soft-skinned hand forward and grasped the leather jack. Pulling it toward him, he wrinkled his face. Otto laughed.

'If you are going to take over the route, then you will have to learn to stomach Bretonnian drink,' the merchant sniggered and downed another mouthful of the amber liquid. 'You'll find few enough places that serve beer, and even fewer that serve anything even the lowest dive in Altdorf would dare to pass off as tea.'

The younger man pushed the jack away from him after taking a brief sip. 'I may just have to turn to tea,' he said, ignoring the glowering look the tavern keeper cast at him from behind the bar. 'I don't suppose there would be room in the wagons for a few kegs of decent drink?'

'And lose valuable cargo space?' Otto returned with mock incredulity. His companion smiled and shook his head. As he did so, the younger man noticed a nondescript figure sitting in the far corner of the tavern. Otto followed his son's look and focused upon the solitary traveller.

The figure was slim, almost obscured by the shadows cast by a support beam and a stuffed boar's head mounted on the wall. The man appeared tall; even seated his height was apparent. A worn brown cloak was cast about his head and shoulders, the hood pulled up over his face. Gloved hands rested sombrely on the table before him. The lower part of the man's face was obscured by a wrap of dark cloth; the skin above it was pale and shone like marble in the little light that touched him. Narrow eyes, almost shaped like almonds, stared from above the slender bridge of his nose. They were focused intently upon the door of the tavern. His eyes had their own glitter; they seemed to twinkle with an unholy light.

There was a menace in those eyes, a stamp of death and violence. They were eyes that had seen death many times. They were eyes that had seen murder, many times.

Otto shuddered and turned away, drinking from his tankard. 'Gruesome sort,' he muttered. 'Best lock our door tonight.'

'Who do you think he is?' wondered Josef. 'I see he doesn't drink. Perhaps he's a pilgrim.' A sudden look of horror crossed Josef's face as he considered the covered face. 'Perhaps he's a leper!' he gasped.

'He's probably neither,' Otto replied. 'I'd wager he's a foreign mercenary, a hired killer or an assassin. De Chegney and the Marquis le Gaires may have a treaty, but don't think for a moment that it'll last. Things'll get nasty before too long, mark my words.' Otto winked at his son. 'That'll be good for business. And de Chegney doesn't have le Gaires's prejudice against firearms. We might even be able to unload that cannon from Nuln on him when the time comes.' Otto smiled as he considered what profit that particular transaction would turn.

Suddenly, the heavy door of the tavern was kicked open. Startled oaths died on the lips of guests and staff alike as two men strode into the room. One was a thin, scowl-faced man dressed in animal skins, a heavy crossbow gripped in his hands. The other man was taller, and broader of shoulder. He was clothed in a suit of chainmail. The colourful surcoat of a Bretonnian knight was tied about his waist. He held a huge-mouthed weapon of black steel and wooden stock. The business end of the blunder-buss slowly canvassed the room as the bandit turned his body at the waist. The room grew still and silent as the grave.

The silence was broken by the sound of metal jingling against metal. A tall figure – surely the bandits' leader – strode in from the street, his dark form highlighted by the red glow of the fading sun. An imposing figure, he was clothed from head to foot in armour: boots of lustreless metal rose to his knees, and from his waist hung a skirt of mail, the links of which were so small and fine they looked like scaly hide. His arms were protected by the same fine armour, with long vambraces of dark metal covering his forearms. Sharp spikes marched along the length of the armour pieces, and his ornamented metal breastplate depicted a rampant drake.

The warrior's head was encased in a high-browed helm of black steel, with bat-wing vanes sweeping back from either ear. A crawling trim of gold snaked above the face of the helm, before stabbing downward along the nose to form a vulture-like beak.

His face was hidden by a featureless mask of steel, only two narrow slits for eyes interrupted the polished silvery surface of the visor. A pair of slender, matched blades completed the figure's trappings, one set upon either hip, each sporting a brutal guard of thorn-like spikes.

The bandit leader advanced, stalking past the two mer-cenaries. With every step, the musical tingle of his armour sounded. The denizens of the tavern parted before the advancing warrior, not a soul daring to breathe as he stepped past them. He let an armoured hand rest on the pommel of a slim dagger fastened across his belly and slowly turned his helmeted head. His eyes were alive with a cold fire, a subtle malevolence that caused the soul to shudder.

Other figures entered the tavern behind the bandit leader, but none of the denizens of the room could draw their gaze away from the black-clad warrior. As the warrior stared at Josef Kretzer, the boy suddenly realised how similar the bandit's eyes were to those of the solitary mercenary.

The warrior turned away from the merchant's son and looked into the shadowy corner where the lone traveller sat.

'It is a very long road to walk,' he spoke from behind the shining mask of steel. The voice was beautiful yet cruel. It was a harsh beauty that had nothing in it to warm the soul. It was the voice of a daemon, a sound of the night, the seductive call of the darkness.

'It is a very long road to walk,' the bandit leader continued, 'to find only death.'

The lone figure at the table slowly stepped forward, casting the shabby brown cloak from him. He was indeed tall and lean of frame. His garments were of fine black cloth, his boots of black scaly hide. Three weapons hung from a leather belt round his waist: a long dagger, a barbed sickle-like blade, and a needle-thin hooked shortsword. His head was unclothed, save for the dark mask that covered his mouth and nose. His skin was very pale, contrasting with the inky darkness of his fine black hair. Sharp ears of inhuman length pointed from the long black locks. An elf, Josef realised in surprise, though he had never set eyes on one before.

The elf cast a chill glare upon the armoured warrior.

The warrior spoke again, but no longer in words that were known to any in the tavern save himself and the one he addressed. It was a melodious language, but spoken with great malice. 'What news from home?' the armoured figure asked. 'Do they still allow that feeble fool to babble and rave? Do our people still bow to impotent beings that promise victories they do not know how to achieve?'

The masked traveller drew two of the weapons from his belt: the dagger and the sickle-shaped spineblade. The warrior chuckled mirthlessly, and drew the sword sheathed upon his right side.

'Dagger and ghlaith,' the bandit lord said. 'Are there then no new tricks they teach in Ghrond?'

The assassin moved forward, as lightly as a leaf blown across a graveyard by a midnight wind. As he came closer, the hand with the dagger shot forward, a bright flash of light exploded from the gem that had been secreted in the palm of his glove. The bandits at the door groaned and covered their eyes; many patrons of the tavern screamed, clenching their hands to their faces to blot out the blinding light.

The assassin leaped at the bandit leader, sweeping the sickle-shaped ghlaith in a sideways stroke that should have cut through the bandit leader's mail skirt and ripped his kidneys and bowels from his armoured body. He moved the dagger upwards, seeking his enemy's armpit, hoping to thrust through the lightly armoured join and stab into the lung. The sound of metal clashing against metal echoed above the moans and cries filling the room. As the bright light dissipated, the assassin found both of his weapons blocked and held by the jagged, thorn-shaped blades of his enemy's swords.

'Right now,' the bandit leader said, 'you are wondering how such a thing is possible. I am sure that trick has always worked before. But I am beyond the petty tricks of the witch elves now.'

The elf assassin drew away, spinning about on his heel. The blades in his hands were a blur of motion – such was his inhuman speed. To the returning vision of the watching bandits and tavern patrons, it was like trying to see a gust of wind. The assassin reversed his weapons, slashing the spineblade upwards towards his foe's neck in a move that recalled the decapitating skills of the executioners of Har Ganeth. The dagger slashed downwards toward the groin in a despicable manoeuvre favoured by the man-hating witch elves of Khaine. Once again, the murderous eyes widened with surprise as the ring of metal on metal echoed through the room. His foe had matched the preternatural quickness of his attack, each weapon again intercepted by a thorn-bladed sword.

'Very good,' the warrior congratulated his attacker with the patronising tone of a fencing tutor. 'That was almost exciting.' The bandit leader's armoured hands twisted the swords about, nearly ripping the weapons from the assassin's grip and the elf recoiled, stepping away from his adversary. He raised his right hand, facing the palm toward the armoured warrior and flicked the spent gemstone at him. Matching the same fey quickness of the assassin, the armoured warrior swatted the oncoming missile aside with his sword. The gemstone crashed against the far wall, exploding in a violent discharge of smoke and flame.

The assassin did not hesitate, charging forward, a feral cry roaring from behind his mask. The ululating cry caused the onlookers to cringe, many openly crying out in terror. The tall, black-garbed warrior was unfazed, matching the flurry of blows the assassin struck at him with his own intercepting blades.

'Ah, one of the secret names of Khaine,' the bandit leader laughed. 'Is that supposed to make me tremble? Frighten me?' The steel boot lashed out, nearly catching the elf assassin's knee. He danced back, but this time his enemy followed him. 'I have no fear of your impotent god,' the warrior leader sneered. 'I have found older gods, better gods.' He lashed out with his sword, penetrating the assassin's defences and slashing his right arm. The jagged cut bled freely, but the assassin ignored the disabling blow, lashing out all the more fiercely with his left hand weapon.

'Do you not wonder why the long war continues?' the warrior asked, the tone conversational, calm and unconcerned by the lethal blade that danced before him. 'It is because the ancient fool who rules us does not wish it to ever end.' The assassin redoubled his attacks, and the armoured warrior casually swatted him aside. 'Now, now, you must use your fury, not let it use you,' he scolded. 'The others who came before you made that mistake. I drink feeble human wines from goblets crafted from their skulls.'

The assassin swept the spineblade toward the armoured belly of his enemy, then adjusted his grip, dropping to his knees and trying to slash the back of his legs. The warrior caught the crescent blade with the tip of his sword, and sent it spinning from the assassin's grasp. The weapon clattered against a table before it fell to the floor. The assassin started to draw the remaining blade, but the point of one of the swords nicked the back of his hand, and drew a thin trickle of blood.

'I think the dagger will serve you better than the *lakelui*,' the bandit leader calmly observed.

With a look of withering hate, the assassin bent to retrieve his blade, but as he crouched, his hand darted to the wrist of his injured arm, drawing three slender darts from the sheath there. The assassin rolled and threw the small missiles at his enemy. The swords rang out once more, and the three darts thunked into the counter of the bar where the warrior's deflecting blows had knocked them.

'You are becoming tiresome,' the bandit leader said. 'The dagger, if you would.'

Scowling behind his mask, the assassin crept forward to grab the dropped blade. Instead, he rolled forward, lashing out with the thin, jagged *lakelui*. At the same time, he raised his other arm, neither so numb nor so useless as he had led his adversary to believe. He gripped his mask, pulling it down, then rushed the armoured man. The assassin's mouth fell open and he spat a black mist at the bandit leader. The mist settled upon the face of the helm, and sizzled upon the black steel.

The warrior's long blade swept forward, slashing the assassin's hand from his wrist. The assassin screamed in pain and clutched the bleeding stump to his body.

The black-armoured warrior moved forward, sheathing his bloody sword. The poison the elf assassin had spit upon him still sizzled upon his armour, all save the shiny visor that clothed his face, which was unmarked and unharmed. He bent and picked up the severed hand, pulling the *lakelui* from the nerveless fingers.

'I told you not to favour the *lakelui*,' the warrior said, the tone as pleasant as that of a huntsman consoling a comrade upon a missed bowshot. The assassin sank to his knees, cradling the bleeding stump to his breast. As he did so, the fingers of his remaining hand covertly worked their way into his tunic. 'Thinking to offer my soul to Khaine? Yes, I suppose feeble old Malekith would expect nothing less.' For the first time, there was true emotion in the warrior's voice, a wrathful, wicked venom to his tone. 'Still, incompetent kings should not be surprised when their incompetent servants fail.'

The assassin's eyes hardened. Slowly, he worked his hand back from the tunic.

'What new trick do you think to use upon me?' the bandit leader asked. In a sudden blur, the *lakelui* leapt forward, thrust through the assassin's throat, six inches of the long blade protruding from the back of his assassin's neck. The body slumped to the floor. 'I am sure it would have been tedious and boring, in any event,' commented the warrior.

The hand of the assassin fell open and a four-pointed throwing star fell out, edges dripping with a sticky green poison.

The armoured warrior bent down and pulled the *lakelui* free. He raised the bloody weapon before his face, and held it there for sometime, as though savouring the smell of the blood.

'When you see Khaine,' the voice said to the elf's corpse, 'ask him why he failed to protect you. Ask him why my gods kept your tricks from disabling me, and why your wicked skills were not equal to the task.'

The armoured warrior turned away from the body and gestured to the mass of figures gathered in the doorway. A beastman loped forward. Its head was like that of a wide-muzzled dog, its powerful frame covered by greasy grey hair. The creature wore only a simple skirt of braided hair about its waist and a huge double-headed axe was slung over its shoulder. Iron-shod hooves crunched across the tavern's wooden floor, indenting each plank they struck. The creature focused its questioning gaze upon its master.

'Take him,' the warrior chief commanded. 'Leave nothing that was his. Sop his blood from the floor, and bind his wounds. Wrap his possessions in soft wool. I wish to savour every trace of the smell of Naggaroth.' The warrior's armoured head swung around, regarding the beastman again. 'I shall feast when we return and drink that rarest of wines from a goblet made from this one's skull.' A trace of menace entered the melodious voice. 'Urgmesh,' he hissed as the beastman lifted the body of the assassin to his wide shoulders, 'no nibbling.'

The beastman nodded his shaggy head and loped back towards the door of the tavern. Other, more human, figures hurried in to gather up the discarded weapons and sop the elf's blood from the floor boards. The black-clad warrior absently handed one of the men the assassin's *lakelui*.

The armoured warrior cast his gaze toward his followers bunched in the door. They were a varied lot: motley-armed, foul-visaged men in grimy armour and piecemeal mail stood beside mangy-pelted twisted beastmen. But one figure stood out among them, and the black knight pointed an armoured hand towards him.

The figure stepped forward. He was tall, thin and garbed like his master in a fine mail aketon and skirt, a breastplate of steel and a high-browed helm. The helm was open, displaying his finely featured face, its skin pale and smooth like alabaster. The elf bowed as he stepped toward his master.

'Not as entertaining as I had hoped,' the bandit leader said.

'It is well that my lord is unharmed,' the elf replied. The black knight waved away his minion's concern.

'Such as they will never be able to match the gifts of the Dark Gods,' the bandit leader declared, not deigning to look back at the dead assassin as he spoke. 'There will be others, and they shall find the same end awaiting them.' He cast his eyes upon another of the figures gathered in the doorway. He could see the sweat beading on the man's forehead, a nervous twitch in his limbs. 'Still, our country-man came here expecting to meet someone.' He let his voice switch to the harsher, clumsier Bretonnian tongue. 'Someone thought to betray me to my enemies,' he hissed. 'Someone who has not learned how to obey me. I must teach him a lesson.'

The sweating man made to run, his portly frame smash-ing through the bodies nearest him. Before he could make the street, however, the paw of the huge beastman Urgmesh punched the traitor, knocking him back into the room.

'Bors,' the dark noble clucked his tongue, and shook his armoured head. 'You have been with me for such a long time. I elevated you from poaching and thieving in the brambles around Parravon, and this is how you thank me. Such a waste.' Urgmesh lifted his massive axe and held the blade over the stunned traitor. His master called him off.

'No, nothing so quick, nor so crude,' the bandit chief scolded. 'Bind him. He returns with us. I must remind him that his life and death are my possessions, as are all of yours.' The dark noble's eyes considered each of his min-ions. 'To be able to see another dawn is because I have allowed it. He must learn that death is a gift only I can bestow. Only when his pleas for death have become tire-some will I consider letting him die.' The bandit leader waved one of his metal-sheathed hands and two of the watching bandits gathered up their former comrade and carried him outside.

'What of these others?' asked the elf lieutenant. The noble turned, regarding the frightened peasants as if seeing them for the first time.

'This is an unfit stage to host my skill with the sword, and this rabble is an unfit audience,' the black knight decreed. 'Kill them all, and burn this place to the ground.' The noble stalked toward the door. As he did so, shouts of rage and fear sounded from the cowed patrons. One of the mercenaries rose, charging forward, only to be hurled back by the blast of the blunderbuss. Before the liveried watchman could raise his sword or push the obese serving girl from his lap, a crossbow bolt sprouted from his chest.

Otto Kretzer roared his own defiant fury, but before he could take more than a few steps, he was cut down by the black knight's thorn-like sword. As his father fell, Josef Kretzer lunged forward, his sword forgotten in his rage, and his hands held before him in a clutching, choking grasp.

The young merchant collided with the noble as he turned from the body of the older man. His grasping hands closed about the bevor, trying to grip the black warrior's neck. The knight brought his armoured knee upwards, smashing the wind from the youth's midsection. The boy's body slipped to the floor, his trailing hands clutching at the dark armour as his body sank to the floor. When he came to rest, the dark warrior turned and strode towards the door.

'Burn this refuse,' the warrior lord called from over his shoulder. 'We return to the stronghold tonight.'

THE BLACK KNIGHT strode from the building, paying no attention to the screams and cries sounding from the tavern. He raised his armoured head and stared up at the dark, moonless sky. He smiled beneath his metal mask. No, Morrsleib, the Chaos moon, was still there, dark and invisible against the night sky, but it was still there, watching all that transpired in the mortal world. The bandit prince offered up a silent thanks to the generous power that he felt looked down from that dark star of Chaos. Once again, the Eye of Tchar had served him well, as it had so often before.

His body trembled as the sorcerous power ebbed from his limbs, and the magical vitality that had filled him dissipated into the night. It was dangerous to hold such power within a vessel of flesh and bone for too long, and the dark elf was eager to purge it from him. It was the very stuff of Chaos, the intangible corruption that twisted men into beasts and beasts into monsters. He himself had no desire to suffer such an end. Yet the power had been necessary – no vital – for the duel. Only with such other-worldly aid could he have matched and bested one of the murderers of the temple of Khaine. That, too, he had seen with the Eye of Tchar.

The elf noble strode to his steed, a huge black maned stallion, taken from the icy wastes of the north – the blighted region men called the Troll Country. There was something of the Ruinous Powers about the creature, for even in Naggaroth, the dark elf had never seen its match. It was as savage as any of the reptilians, but without their dull wits and cold-blooded reactions. The horse snorted as its master stroked its mane. He removed a small morsel and fed the scrap of meat to the stallion's fang-ridden jaws. As the animal chewed the flesh, the elf wondered what thoughts stirred within its head. Was it still a horse in its mind, or was it now something else? How much of the Dark Ones' favours could one command before one was no more? Did he command the Power, or did it command him?

The noble shook his head. They were the old thoughts, the old fears. He was Druchii – for him, there should be no fear. He had seen mere humans wield the power, so how could he doubt his own command of it? The Eye of Tchar was his, he was not the Eye's.

The bandit leader lifted himself into the saddle and turned his steed's head. He looked back at the tavern, and watched the first tongues of flame lick about the windows. He watched his slaves hurry from the building, and mount their own horses. He gestured with his hand and the entire force galloped away from the burning structure.

Once again, his enemies in his homeland had thought to strike him down. Even after three hundred years, they still remembered him. He sighed. He had been among humans too long. For them, three hundred years was almost beyond their ability to imagine. For elves, it was nothing – the space between youth and manhood. As he had said, there would be others.

There would always be others. For his enemies would never forget him.

They would never forget the Black Prince.

A RAGGED FORM crawled from the burning tavern, taking in the dull, dirty faces that watched the building burn. He wormed his way into the street and rolled about in the mud to smother the flames that rose from his garments. The peasants and tradesmen considered the survivor with expressionless looks. None of them moved to help the man, just as none moved to fight the fire that was consuming the tavern.

Josef Kretzer rose to his knees and glared at the spectators. He opened his mouth to hurl abuse upon the craven mob, but only a wracking cough escaped his lungs. As he coughed, he became fully aware of the object he clutched in his hand: the long, thin blade in the curious black, fish-skin sheath. His groping hands had torn it from the belt of his father's killer, after the black-garbed figure had smashed his knee into Josef's body.

The young merchant studied its curving, thorn-like shape. He felt some satisfaction as the eyes of the idle spectators grew wide with alarm and they backed away from him. He returned the dagger to its sheath and set the weapon on the ground before him, covering it with both his hands.

Josef bowed his head toward the burning ruin and spoke in a slow, heavy voice. It was an oath – an oath to all the gods of the Empire – he would find the one whose blade he now bore. He would find his father's killer. He would bury the dark knight's own dagger in his black heart. And he would ask no further favour of the gods than this, that Josef Kretzer might live just long enough to watch the life fade from the killer's eyes as he had seen it pass from his father's.

Two

Dour-faced villagers quietly shuffled down the lane that passed for Falbourg's thoroughfare. Occasionally, one of the peasants would pause to stare at the wood-frame expanse of the village's tavern, when another cry of pain exploded from behind the building's walls. But even these curious minds found that their errands required haste after all when the door of the tavern opened and a grim figure in armour and helm emerged.

Brunner strode from the tavern, wiping blood from his glove onto the scrap of cloth he held in his other hand. It had taken a bit of persuasion, but he had finally persuaded the recalcitrant brother of the notorious highwayman Gobineau to confess the whereabouts of the outlaw. Indeed, Brunner considered that it had been a fairly profitable morning. But the sound of booted feet at his back caused the bounty hunter to forget thoughts of profit and prey. With a single fluid motion, he spun about, tossing the cloth from his bloodied hands.

'If you have a name, you'd better use it,' he ordered, his hand pulling his gunpowder pistol from its holster and pointing the weapon at the man who stood only a few paces away.

Framed in the sunlight of morning was a young man wearing a shabby and worn-looking hauberk of toughened leather reinforced by steel studs. A round kettle hat perched atop the stranger's handsome features, a thin fringe of closely-cropped black hair peering from beneath the rim of the heavy iron helmet. His face was set with a harsh scowl of cold determination, and his brown eyes were narrowed in a penetrating look of intense scrutiny. The man's smooth-skinned hand rested casually upon the steel pommel of the broadsword sheathed at his side.

'I understood that I can find the bounty hunter called Brunner here,' the young man said, adjusting his stance so that he might be able to draw his weapon easier. 'I am Josef Kretzer, son of Otto Kretzer of Imperial Schrabwald. If you are indeed the man I seek, I have come to hire you.'

'Indeed,' Brunner said, his voice dripping with doubt. 'It is a very skilful or a very lucky man who can find me when I am already on the hunt.' Menace overwhelmed the bounty hunter's tone. 'Either way, it is a very foolish man who intrudes upon my business.'

'I came here to retain your services, not to be threatened,' Josef snapped, arrogance seeping into his words, mingling with the rage that lurked just beneath his cool veneer. 'I wish to hire you to lead me to the murdering bastard that killed my father.'

'Does this man have a name?' Brunner asked, keeping the pistol trained upon Josef.

Josef paused, gathering his thoughts, recalling the frightened whispers of the peasants in Gambrie. 'It is my understanding that this animal is known as the Black Prince.'

A trace of amusement crawled across the bounty hunter's face, and tugged at the corners of his mouth. 'You come all this way chasing a fable. There is no Black Prince.

Better to ask me to bring you the head of Thorgrim Grudgebearer, the dwarf high king, boy. At least he is real.'

'I have seen him!' Josef roared. I watched him kill my father with my own eyes. With my own hands I took this from him!' Josef reached to his belt and drew the thorn-shaped dagger from its scabbard. Brunner's gaze fixed upon the weapon.

Brunner returned his pistol to its holster and stalked forward. He motioned for the boy to hand over the dagger. The bounty hunter stared intently at the weapon, turning it over, letting the light of the morning play across its dark metal surface.

'You took this from the Black Prince?' he asked.

'He was very substantial for a myth,' the youth shot back. Brunner snorted a brief chuckle.

'If this really came from who you say it did, then we should talk.' The bounty hunter stared at the young merchant. 'Meet me in the stables.' Brunner reached forward and tucked the dagger back in its scabbard on the boy's belt. 'And don't go showing that to anyone else.'

'Then you will help me?' Josef asked, his voice still flat, betraying neither hope nor suspicion.

The bounty hunter had to admit that the young merchant was very good at giving nothing away. He nodded his armoured head.

'That remains to be seen, but you have my interest now,' the bounty hunter replied.

BRUNNER FOUND JOSEF Kretzer sitting upon a low wooden box beside a pile of yellowed hay in the shadows of the village stable. The building stank of dung and the sweat of animals, yet the bounty hunter could detect no sign of displeasure on the merchant's face. Perhaps he was a bit tougher than his soft-skinned hands indicated.

Brunner strode past the youth, not pausing to greet him as he rose from his seat. He walked straight to the massive bay tethered to the rear wall of the wooden stable, the animal's reins looped through a simple ring of iron. The bounty hunter laid a soothing hand on his steed's neck, stroking away some of the horse's tension.

'Have you considered my offer?' Josef asked, following the bounty hunter as he stepped away from Fiend and made his way over to his sturdy grey packhorse, Paychest. Brunner removed a small carrot from one of the pouches on his belt, giving the treat to the often over-worked animal. He looked up, staring at the youth.

'That dagger you stole,' Brunner watched as a venomous quality fought its way through the boy's calm façade. The bounty hunter chuckled. 'Let us say *claimed* then,' it was as close to a word of apology he had given for five years. 'Do you have any idea what it is?'

Josef drew the knife again, trying to discern what the bounty hunter gleaned from the weapon during his brief examination of it. 'The balance is wrong, the space between hilt and pommel is unwieldy for a single-handed blade,' Josef observed. 'Probably some foreigner's weapon, where they have curious ideas about warcraft and swordplay.'

Brunner nodded his head, reaching to the massive burden that was balanced upon the back of Paychest. He undid several straps and a long length of leather fell open, displaying an elegant-looking bow and a number of steel arrows, their heads barbed.

The bounty hunter undid the thongs that held the bow and lifted the weapon from its pack. The bow was slender, crafted in pale, almost white wood. Engravings scrolled across almost all its length.

It was quite possibly the most beautiful weapon Josef had ever set eyes upon, more like a work of art than a tool of war. The bounty hunter tossed the weapon to the merchant. Josef studied the bow, again astounded by the curious grip and the awkwardness the weapon was imbued with. A sudden realisation made him look back at the bounty hunter.

'It is like the dagger,' the youth exclaimed. Brunner motioned for Josef to return the weapon.

'I took that from a hired killer in the Border Princes a year past,' the bounty hunter said, 'but it was crafted for no human hand.' Brunner let that knowledge sink in a moment as he returned the bow to its place and refastened the leather roll to his pack horse's burden.

'Elves?' the boy gasped. He had seen elves a few times in his life: tall, graceful and impossibly beautiful beings. There were a few who could be found in Altdorf, and a veritable community of so-called Sea Elves in the city-state of Marienburg. Josef thought again about the unwieldy grip of the dagger. Shaped for hands longer than those of a man, for fingers thinner and more delicate than the harsh paws of a mere human?

Brunner nodded. 'It is the only thing that makes any sense.' The bounty hunter stepped away from Paychest, facing the young merchant. 'How much do you know about this Black Prince?'

'Only what I have been told by the villagers in Gambrie and what the Viscount de Chegney told me when I petitioned him for aid in hunting down my father's killer.' Josef thought again about that humiliating encounter in the viscount's castle. De Chegney had been displeased to hear about the entire affair, but had done no more than provide Josef with a set of battered and discarded armour and a feeble horse that must have been selected as supper for the viscount's kennel before he had given it to Josef. Only one other thing had the viscount given him, a word of warning that he should forget about everything and return to the Empire and enjoy his father's estate.

Brunner shook his head at the mention of the viscount, but kept his thoughts to himself. Instead, he spoke in a low, icy voice. 'They have been telling stories about the Black Prince for hundreds of years,' he said. 'He is always described as an arrogant, tall, slender figure in black armour. An expert swordsman able to best even the noblest of knights. He commands men and beasts; he is a bandit host that preys upon the land like a murderous plague.' The bounty hunter let a thin laugh rasp from his throat. 'You have heard, no doubt, of Bretonnia's grail knights, who search all across the kingdom in quest of the holy cup of the Lady of the Lake? The Black Prince is a bounty hunter's holy cup. Three hundred years ago, the then king of Bretonnia placed a price of five thousand pieces of gold for the head of the Black Prince after the death of the envoy from the forest realm of Loren. Yet in all that time, no one has claimed that reward. Most men of my calling consider him a myth, a bogeyman called upon by inept sheriffs and larcenous caravan masters to explain every theft this side of the Grey Mountains.' Brunner paused, staring at the boy again, a crafty look narrowing the icy eyes behind the visor of his helm. 'Tell me everything that happened that night, exactly as it happened.'

Josef began to relate the events of the night his father died. He told of the sinister traveller and his duel with the leader of the bandits. He told of the impossible speed with which both of them moved and the amazing swordcraft of the Black Prince. He told of the monster's cruel mockery of his overmatched foe and of his equal savagery when he casually commanded his minions to burn down the tavern and its occupants. He especially detailed for Brunner the strange armour the Black Prince wore, that was at once hideous and beautiful. When he had finished, the bounty hunter moved toward Fiend, untying the animal from the iron ring.

'You will help me then?' Josef asked as the bounty hunter led his animal from the stall.

Brunner removed a rag from the pack on the side of his saddle and tossed it to the boy. 'With five thousand gold crowns in the balance, I may not even charge you.' Brunner pointed a gloved finger at the dagger. 'Cover that up, and don't show it to anyone unless I tell you.' He smiled. 'We don't want anyone else getting any ideas about where that dagger came from.'

THE SEATED FIGURE gazed towards the balcony, watching the morning sun turn the grey stonework white as its rays banished the shadows. Such a glorious morning: not a cloud in the sky. Once again, the noble on the black throne felt melancholy spirits tugging at his normally steadfast heart. Once again, he thought of the perpetual darkness and gloom of his home, the icy northern gales that howled through the towers and battlements of his city like a legion of screaming banshees. They bore with them the soft white snow of the north, which glittered with the chromatic taint of the Chaos Wastes – magic captured by the clouds and born to the south by the power of Naggaroth's sorcerers.

Dralaith sighed and adjusted the sleeve of his long silk *khaitan*, as he remembered his lost homeland. He would return some day, not as a corpse, or as a prisoner. He would return as a conqueror. Even the Dark Gods would not deny him this. For were they not the cause of his exile? Were they not the reason he had become the Black Prince?

He cast his eye upon the locked box of blackened teakwood that rested upon a cushion beside his throne. It was an heirloom of his family, captured by some long-dead ancestor during a raid on Cathay. Within the box, however, was an artefact of far more recent vintage, captured by Dralaith himself, and torn from the neck of a Norse seer when Dralaith's ship had met the barbarian's dragon boat.

Dralaith thought back to that day, when he had led the corsairs down onto the deck of their captured prize. The Norse were rugged and powerful for humans and far more manageable than orcs in the mines and slave pits. The dark elves fought a bitter battle, hindered by a reluctance to kill too many of the barbarians lest their slave-taking be reduced to unprofitable levels. In fact the corsairs had been almost bested by the Norse. Then withering blasts of eerie blue light had come, and the flame that struck down dozens of corsairs, left their armour steaming, but their skin unmarred.

Dralaith had fought his way to the prow of the ship as his corsairs perished all around him. There he had found the cause of the sorcerous assault: a huge human dressed in a mangy black robe of dyed leather, the leering skull of some fanged and horned beast over his head like a helmet. The seer had been a massive, powerful man once, but now he was like a withered giant. Weak of arm or not, as the seer turned about, his clawed hand opened to reveal the gleaming jewel it held. Dralaith knew that he was dead then. Yet it was not the dark elf's eyes that showed fear, but those of the seer. He snarled a brutal oath, but the jewel in his hand did not obey – sheets of mystical fire did not consume Dralaith's body.

The dark elf had not waited for the seer to recover, but had darted in at once and removed the Norseman's hand. A pair of corsairs lunged forward to secure the maimed mystic while Dralaith recovered the jewel from the pools of blood that swamped the deck.

He had learned later, after his torturers had administered their art upon the seer – that the jewel was called the Eye of Tchar. The Eye acted as a focus for mighty powers, powers that could instil vitality and strength in a man, powers that could summon daemons from the nether realms to rend the flesh of the wielder's foes. But this was not the greatest of its powers. He had learned that it showed its owner the future, that the depths of the gem would reveal any danger that threatened, and that it would show the owner of the jewel how that danger might be undone.

But there had been one question that had troubled Dralaith. Why had the Eye of Tchar not warned the seer about him? The seer had laughed then, laughed until the torturers had broken him beyond the point of return. Only as life seeped from his mutilated form did the Norse stop laughing. He smiled up at the dark elf noble. He commended Dralaith on his wisdom, but he could give him no answer, for the seer had never thought to ask that question when he had taken it from a marauder chieftain long ago before he was a sorcerer.

The Black Prince gazed back to the long table set before his throne. A nervous human was seated there, his garments reeking of filth, his hair greasy with dirt and grime.

The dark elf tried to recall the man's name, but could not. He could not even remember why he had been imprisoned in his dungeons. He dismissed his concerns. Whatever he had done, it was unimportant. The Black Prince snapped his fingers. Four servants shambled into the chamber. The first carried a crystal bottle, something that had been salvaged from the cellars of the tower when the Black Prince had reclaimed it from the goblin vermin who had lived there for centuries. The dark elf smiled as he saw the dark crimson liquid within the bottle. The second servant bore a large goblet, its surface covered in silver. The cup of the goblet was crafted from the skull of the latest assassin that sought his life.

The last two servants laboured under a heavy tray, upon which a pile of meat steamed. The Black Prince inhaled, savouring the odour. Then he snapped his fingers and all three objects were set before the prisoner.

'You are hungry,' the Black Prince declared. 'See what a feast I have prepared for you?' The man looked up at the dark elf, then cast his eyes again at the steaming roasted meat before him. 'Eat,' the dark elf commanded as the man hesitated. One of the servants began to pour the thick red liquid from the bottle into the skull-goblet, careful to spill not a single drop, lest he too be asked to join in the hideous repast.

Trembling with loathing and terror, the prisoner clutched at the goblet, and fought down his disgust as he let the salty fluid pass his lips. As he did so, the seated lord began to murmur almost inaudibly, the melodious sounds drifting across the room with a life of their own. The almond-shaped eyes of the Black Prince began to glow with a mystical light and he let out a satisfied hiss. 'Exquisite,' he declared. 'Now try some of the meat.' The prisoner moaned, but reached forward and tore a small morsel from the tray. The Black Prince smacked his lips as the diner reluctantly ate.

It had been hundreds of years since Dralaith had savoured food with his own mouth. The venoms with which the nobility of Naggaroth coated their bodies invariably killed the senses of taste and touch. Only by sorcery, or by forcing his mind to bond with that of another, could the Black Prince experience the taste of food and wine. It was not something that he could do often, for there was always a toll exacted by such frivolous use of magic. But sometimes there arose occasions when he would indulge himself.

The Black Prince considered what the Eye of Tchar had shown him upon his return to the stronghold. One of his bandits, a weaselly little Bretonnian named Ferricks, a close confederate of the traitor Bors, had not returned with him. The Eye of Tchar had revealed the thief hastening back to his home village. He was filled with terror that Bors would implicate him in their crude little plot. But what the Eye had shown him afterwards, the way the Black Prince might steer events, that had been truly enlightening. The dark elf smiled, not even noticing that the diner had stopped eating and was trying his best not to vomit up what little he had consumed.

It was such a simple plot, and the Black Prince was astounded that it had never occurred to him before. And the Eye of Tchar had not shown him such a scheme before this. Not for the first time, the dark elf wondered if he was in control of the jewel, or if it was in control of him. The Black Prince dismissed such concerns as soon as they took shape. It was a talisman, nothing more. And there was nothing he needed to fear with it guiding him. Certainly there was nothing he had to fear from some coarse human bounty killer.

The Black Prince pointed a slender finger at the diner, then pointed again at the steaming ribcage on the tray. 'More meat,' his melodious voice commanded.

The Black Prince settled back in his throne, adjusting his body on the fur coverings. He would enjoy to the fullest measure this meal. It was not every day that he had meat from Naggaroth to savour.

Three

JOSEF FOUGHT TO stay awake and remain upright in the saddle of his horse. The bounty hunter had left the village almost as soon as they had met. They were riding south, despite Josef's words of protest. After their talk in the stable, Brunner had become silent. Not a word had passed between them in all the long miles they had covered since the morning sun had faded into darkness. Whether the bounty hunter was in some foul mood or whether his mind was lost in thought, the youth could not decide. Josef had long ago resolved to stop trying to disrupt the killer's silence.

Abruptly, a dark expanse rose ominously before them, stretching as far as Josef's tired eyes could see. A forest rose from the expanse of meadows and fields like a living wall. Josef could see small dark objects scattered between the edge of the forest and the meadowland. In the darkness he could not decide if they were merely boulders or something of design, monuments or cairns perhaps. Josef's horse stopped as Brunner brought his own animals to a halt. Josef rubbed his eyes, trying to force awareness into his mind. Without a word to the youth, Brunner swung his leg over the horn of his saddle and dropped to the grassy ground.

Somewhere in the night, an owl hooted. Brunner strode forward, advancing toward the dark boulders. Josef wondered idly if he should follow the bounty hunter, but decided that in his state he would be more likely to fall in a hole than be any assistance if anything was lurking in the shadows. For a moment, alarm raced through his fatigued frame, fear that a horde of beastmen and goblins might erupt from the dark expanse of the trees. But the fear quickly died away. As tired as he was, Josef could not care less. His head sagged forward, his chin resting on his chest. A moment later, the boy slipped into a half-sleep.

Brunner made his way through the old standing stones, not pausing to consider the curious markings that had been burned into the rock. Instead, he bent down to gather some small white pebbles. When he had a fistful of the small stones, he began to clear a small patch of ground by kicking rocks and twigs away with his boot. He crouched down, carefully arranging the small pebbles on the ground. Then he stood up again, and stared down at the design he had marked out with the stones. He looked up, his icy eyes considering the dark, brooding shadow of the forest. Then he turned and walked back to Josef and the horses. Brunner climbed back into Fiend's saddle and reached a gloved hand over, to shake Josef back into a semblance of wakefulness.

'Wha... what?' the youth spluttered.

'We're done here,' the bounty hunter stated. 'If we make good time, we can be at Haustrate's inn for the night. Not the best, but better than sleeping under the light of Morrsleib.'

Josef did not argue. He merely indicated with a tired wave of his hand for the bounty hunter to lead the way. Soon all three horses were moving down the dirt road at something approaching a run.

Behind them, in the shadows of the forest, an owl
hooted its cry into the night.

JOSEF FOLLOWED BRUNNER into the dark coaching inn – a battered, faded wooden sign proclaiming it to be Le Canard
Etranglé. A large, two-storeyed building, the inn was protected by a tall stone wall, a fortification absent in many of
Bretonnia's villages and townships. The inn served travellers on business and those on pious devotion. And there
were enough itinerant peddlers and pilgrims wishing to
view the sites where the grail was seen to keep René
Haustrate a busy, and very prosperous, man.

Even at this late hour, the coaching inn was far from
deserted, its guests far from asleep. A pair of Bretonnian
knights with colourful surcoats covering their suits of mail
were seated at one table. Their loud, boasting voices carried across the room. A pair of green-garbed squires, their
dark hair cut in the bowl-shape favoured by the common
folk of Bretonnia, hastened to ensure that the two knights'
tankards never went dry. They constantly fetched fresh
pitchers of ale as the lords drained the old ones dry. A
wiry-looking man, with a face cast in a perpetual scowl,
slowly sipped at a mug of ale while idly toying with a
small tin box he had removed from the bulging pack at his
side. Near to the tinker sat a group of fur-clad trappers,
each of the burly, smelly men describing some adventure
in the wilds with his hands, having realised that there was
no hope of talking with the noisy knights so near.

Brunner strode to the counter, ordering a tankard of ale
when he discovered that Imperial schnapps was not to be
had. Josef joined him, placing his own order that the
pleasant-mannered barkeep was happy to meet when he
saw the youth's coin. Josef turned his back to the counter,
mimicking the bounty hunter's movements. His eyes also
canvassed the room, studying every face.

Josef did not know what he was looking for. Then it suddenly occurred to him what his companion might be
hoping to see. A face, a scar, a peculiarity of dress that

might identify an outlaw to the bounty hunter's elephant-like memory.

Josef continued to study the other denizens of this common room, then caught his breath. Seated at a table at the back of the room was a tall, slender figure garbed in a dull green cloak. Josef could make out the pale skin under the hood of the cloak. The hands were folded beneath the table, though Josef could not tell if they held a blade or not. A leather jack of ale sat on the table, but the silent figure did not seem interested in it. Josef leaned forward, trying to see if the lower half of the cloaked figure's face was covered. A gloved hand pressed against his chest and pushed him back.

'Easy,' the bounty hunter's voice hissed. 'Turn around and enjoy your drink.' The bounty hunter turned round to face the counter, and Josef followed his lead. 'Now, I am going to take the dagger and go have a talk with our friend over there.' Josef could feel the bounty hunter's hand take the covered weapon from where he had thrust it through his belt. 'Just stay here. I'll be right back.'

From the corner of his eye, Josef saw Brunner walk across the room, nimbly dodging the two squires racing past to secure another pitcher for their drunken lords. He headed straight toward the table where the sinister figure was seated. Josef could see that the bounty hunter's gloved hand rested lightly upon the hilt of his sword, but he wondered just how loose that grip really was.

The figure did not stir as Brunner sat down opposite him. Josef could see Brunner's lips moving, but no trace of a whisper managed to fight its way back to him over the boisterous knights. He watched Brunner speak and had the impression that the cloaked figure was also conversing. Then the bounty hunter withdrew the wrapped dagger. With careful, deliberate gestures, Brunner removed the blade from its cloth covering and then its leather scabbard.

The cloaked figure leaned forward. Two thin, pale hands closed about the weapon and pulled the blade towards him. The stranger stared down at the dagger, turning it around and around in its hands. The head rose again, and Josef could see Brunner voicing a reply to some question. Then long, inhuman fingers carefully returned the dagger to its sheath, and wrapped the cloth around it once more. The cloaked figure hesitated a moment and Josef could see the bounty hunter speak with violence. Slowly the hooded head nodded and pushed the dagger back into the bounty hunter's care. Brunner rose from the table and made his way back to the bar.

'What was that about?' Josef asked. 'Was he an elf? Like the other one?' Brunner stared at his young companion.

'We'll get rooms here tonight. Continue on in the morning, for Parravon.' The bounty hunter lifted his neglected tankard and drank deeply.

'But who was that?' Josef turned to indicate the cloaked figure, but as he looked, he saw the table was now empty.

'Someone who answered a question for me,' Brunner replied. 'Though he was not very happy about it.' The bounty hunter drained the last dregs of his ale and would say no more about the man in the green cloak.

JOSEF ROLLED OVER, clenching the coarse wool blanket still tighter about his body, trying to defend himself against the chill morning dew. A booted heel pushed the boy onto his back. He spluttered into a dim sort of awareness, snapping his bleary head about in a series of quick side-to-side motions. The man who had awakened him strode away, to examine the harness on his warhorse.

'Learn to sleep more lightly,' Brunner called to the boy, 'or you might not wake up at all.'

Josef emerged from under the blanket, and wiped the dirt and grass from his clothing. 'It is a wonder I was able to sleep at all,' he groused. He looked about, not seeing any sign of a fire. The boy sighed and walked over to his pack, removing his belt and weapons. 'No breakfast today either?'

'If you wanted breakfast, you should have stayed at the inn,' the bounty hunter reminded him. He had tried to impress upon the boy that he should forsake continuing his little quest for revenge and allow the bounty hunter to continue unimpeded. But Josef was not about to listen to such talk, however valid Brunner's arguments might have been. Josef had a suspicion that the hired killer was not really eager to lose him, either – though what use the killer intended to put him to, Josef could not hazard the slightest guess.

It had been a long, hard ride from the inn. They had been on the road two days now heading northward. Before them, like a distant shadow, the dark peaks of the Grey Mountains steadily grew larger and more imposing. To their right, the vast expanse of the forest of Loren edged to the road itself. It was a dark, forbidding mass of greenery whose branches and leaves permitted not even the slightest glimpse of what might lie within.

Josef could not put the vast forest from his mind, imagining all sorts of nameless things watching them from the shadows. Each night they had camped under the stars. The bounty hunter had slipped into sleep almost as soon as they made camp. He attended to his horses as if he was not troubled in the slightest by the nearness of the forest and the fell creatures that might walk its shadowed paths. For Josef, however, sleep was much more elusive, and he spent hours watching the shadows, listening to the rustle of brush, the calls of night birds and the chirping of insects. Only when fatigue at last dulled his wary senses would he finally sink into a fitful sleep.

'We should reach Parravon today,' Brunner stated. 'By early afternoon, if the viscount's nag can keep up the pace.'

'What is in Parravon?' Josef asked, thrusting the wrapped dagger into his belt.

'A… a friend,' the bounty hunter said after a pause. He faced Josef, staring into the boy's eyes. 'Someone who might be able to tell us a bit more about this Black Prince of yours.' Suddenly, Brunner spun around, his left hand gripping his pistol, his right hand closed about the hilt of his drawn sword.

'If I intended to kill you,' a soft voice said, 'you would never have seen the morning.'

Josef watched in amazement as a tall, thin figure emerged from behind a patch of berry bushes. The figure was garbed in a long green cloak, but this time the hood was drawn back, exposing a fine-featured face with a long sharp nose, a high brow and thin eyes. Long, flowing gold hair cascaded about the figure's shoulders. Josef could see that a slender sword with a hilt of polished horn was sheathed at the figure's side and the stranger was carrying a carved bow of the same white wood the bounty hunter had shown him when they met.

The elf wore a tunic and breeches of fine, smooth brown leather, a fur-lined quiver hanging from his side by a shoulder-strap.

'Lithelain,' Brunner said, keeping his weapons at the ready. 'I can hardly say that I am surprised to see you. You will forgive me if I remain suspicious.'

The wood elf smiled, an expression that seemed subtly mocking and haughty. 'I am afraid that you have more pressing concerns,' the elf said, his voice retaining its soft tone. 'Your steps have been dogged by more than myself. Five riders have been on your trail for the past day and a half.'

'Would you care to elaborate?' Brunner asked, keeping his pistol trained on the elf's forehead.

'I should be very foolish if I did that without compensation,' Lithelain responded.

'I am not giving up the dagger, or my chance at the Black Prince,' the bounty hunter snarled.

Brunner's words caused Josef to clutch the wrapped dagger more closely and draw his own sword. He ignored the fact that the bounty hunter seemed to consider the dagger his own property, and concentrated on the suggestion that the elf had come to take it.

'Of what concern is he to you?' the elf's voice had a harsh, angry quality to it now. 'For you he is just another bounty, but to me, he is a matter of honour, a slight upon my race.'

'For me he is enough gold to choke a dwarf,' the bounty hunter corrected. 'If you think I am going to give that up, you've been out of the business for far too long.' Brunner's mouth twisted into a sneer. 'Don't worry, I'll bring proof to you that he is dead after I collect the reward.'

Lithelain sighed, but the tenseness in his posture seemed to wilt away. As the elf relaxed, Brunner became more wary.

'You may keep your filthy blood money, Brunner,' the elf said. 'But it will be my hand that slays him.' There was no mistaking the threat in the soft, musical voice.

'Are you proposing a partnership?' Brunner asked.

'Wait,' protested Josef. 'That bastard is mine to kill!' The bounty hunter and the elf considered the angry merchant for a moment, then both let a brief flare of amusement flicker across their faces. Brunner holstered his weapons.

'He does have a prior claim,' the bounty hunter said. 'You'll have to wait your turn.'

Lithelain looked intently at Josef, his copper-hued eyes considering the young boy. The elf's graceful features shifted into a look of sadness. 'I admire your determination,' he said, ' but there is enough innocent blood on the Black Prince's hands already.'

Josef began to voice an angry protest, to tell this arrogant non-human creature that when he met the Black Prince, it would be the villain, not he, who would fall. But Lithelain had already turned his attention back to Brunner.

'These riders, they should catch up to you in another few hours,' the elf stated.

'I don't like being hunted,' Brunner said. 'I think we should wait for our pursuers. Maybe turn the tables on them. Perhaps ambush them on the edge of Grimfen.' The bounty hunter paused again, considering his options. 'Do you have any idea who they might be?' The wood elf shook his head.

'I saw them only from a great distance,' Lithelain admitted. 'I could tell only that they were following you.' Brunner nodded as the elf spoke.

'Well, I think this time you will get a better look at them.'

THE THREE MEN crouched amongst the rocky rubble of a wall. Fifty years ago, the local duke had tried to make this section of road between Quenelles and Parravon a toll road. The terrain was ideally suited for his purposes. To the east, the impenetrable and vast expanse of the Forest of Loren loomed – an intimidating barrier to travel, a haunted and ill-reputed land populated by all manner of fey creatures by the imaginations of the Bretonnian people.

To the west, for several miles, the gently rolling landscape sank into a deep depression, the meadows and fields giving way to a foul, stinking morass known as Grimfen. The morass was a bowl of mud and twisted, stunted trees. Small wooded islands dotted the dismal swamp – refuges for boar and wild cats from the arrows of Bretonnian hunters. Vast stretches of grey mud crawled between the islands and the deep pools of black, scummy water. Only the lightest of birds, fishers and web-footed cranes, could navigate the mud flats with any manner of impunity; any heavier creature would find itself gripped by an implacable grasp, pulled steadily downward into the greedy mire. There were reputed to be navigable channels through the fen, but only a handful of peasant hunters and poachers knew how to manoeuvre their shallow skiffs through the swamp.

Between the swamp and the forest was a narrow track of solid land. Under the orders of the duke, that land had been undermined. Much of it crumbled away, expanding the limits of the fen until only a slender path remained. Then the duke had constructed his tower and his gate, demanding tribute from all who travel 'his road'.

The duke's toll road existed for less than a year. Some said that vengeful spirits, offended by the duke's greed, emerged from the forest and cast down his tower. Others told of some hulking atrocity – a creature of the Dark Gods that lumbered out from the depths of Grimfen and reduced the fort to rubble in a frenzied attempt to slay the soldiers within. A less popular story held that the duke's own soldiers set fire to the tower, hoping that its destruction would see an end to their lord's plans for the road and would also see an end to what they viewed as a loathsome and intolerable posting. Brunner could see the possibility in that tale, for he could not imagine any man being able to endure the stench of the fen, much less live with it for months at a time.

Lithelain placed a thin finger on Brunner's shoulder and nodded at the road. In the distance, Brunner could see a small group of mounted figures making their way towards them. The bounty hunter sighted along the length of his crossbow, casting a sidewise look to ensure that his spare crossbow and loaded handgun were still propped against the rock at his side.

'Make out any details?' the bounty hunter asked.

'They do not look out of the ordinary,' the elf replied. 'Armed peasant rabble, it would seem. None of them appear to have more than a sword and bow upon them.' The elf paused, squinting his eyes. 'Wait,' he said. 'I think there may be a knight with them, though he wears no tabard and his horse is not clothed.' The elf concentrated upon the armoured rider. 'He is certainly their leader. I don't think he is a Bretonnian, however. His skin is too dark.'

Brunner scowled, maintaining his aim. He spoke from the corner of his mouth. 'He is wearing a suit of plates, and his head is covered by a large brimmed hat. The man's face is marked by pox-scars and he wears a cavalry mace and a small crossbow at his side.'

'You see him then?' the elf asked, a trace of astonishment in his melodious voice.

'I certainly can't make out much,' Josef spoke. He had tried to impress Brunner to give him one of the crossbows, but had been refused. With only the broadsword given him by the Viscount de Chegney, Josef was feeling ill-equipped for the coming battle. He briefly thought that perhaps the bounty hunter was trying to protect him. But then he realised that Brunner was merely worried that he might announce their presence too soon if he was given a ranged weapon.

There had been quite an argument when Josef heard the bounty hunter wanted to ambush the riders and kill them all before they had time to react. To Josef, it seemed a dastardly and despicable way to fight. The bounty hunter had snarled that the graveyards were full of men who thought battle a nobleman's game. A smart man didn't worry about how he killed an enemy, as long as it was his enemy and not himself who felt the kiss of steel.

'The leader of those men is an Estalian. It is Osorio,' Brunner sighed.

'I thought you killed him,' Lithelain said, watching the five riders approach.

'So did I,' the bounty hunter admitted. 'If he comes back from the dead again, he'll have me believing in that daemon god of his.'

'Excuse me,' interrupted Josef, 'but who exactly is this Osorio? I mean, if he is trying to kill us, I'd at least like to know why.'

'He's a bounty hunter,' Lithelain stated. 'Same as Brunner.'

Brunner glared at Lithelain. 'I'm nothing like him,' he spat. 'Osorio is a fanatic, a butchering maniac. A self-styled witch hunter in the service of Solkan, the Fist of Retribution.' Brunner uttered the name of the god of vengeance as though it had laced his tongue with foulness as he spoke it.

'I understood that you worked with him once,' Lithelain said, staring at the nearing riders.

'Aye, two years ago,' the bounty hunter replied, following the elf's lead and returning his eyes to the road. 'We were both hunting the daemonologist Dacosta, who was said to have relocated himself to Tobaro after fleeing the king's guard in Magritta. We came upon one another in the dae-mon-haunted crypt Dacosta had claimed as his new lair. We made an agreement to combine our strength against him. But after overcoming Dacosta's daemons, and after my bullet had stilled the wizard's heart, Osorio turned on me, saying that the reward belonged neither to me nor him, but must be given to Solkan's temple in Remas. He tried to put a bolt through my head, but I put my steel through his chest first. I left him there, in that forgotten crypt beneath the streets of Tobaro. I heard rumours that he survived, but did not credit them.'

'Now is your chance to try again,' Lithelain said.

The riders were only a few dozen yards from the heaped mound of rubble. As the elf had observed, four of them were rustic, ill-kempt Bretonnian louts, rusty swords thrust through a loop of rope tied about their waists. Each of the men had a quiver of arrows lashed across his back and a long, curved Bretonnian bow lashed to his saddle. They all wore tunics and breeches of homespun wool and leggings crafted from fur. Their faces were cruel, the harsh features set in a greedy leer.

The leader of the men was obviously the armoured fig-ure that rode behind them. He was clothed from shoulder to toe in a suit of dull steel plate armour, his powerful frame seeming to strain the metal that encased it. A brutal-looking mace hung from a leather thong fastened about his wrist while a small, compact crossbow was fitted to an iron hoop on his belt. The man's height was further emphasised by the tower-like broad-brimmed brown hat that clothed his head. His features were dark, baked to a leather-like consistency by the hot Estalian sun. Crater-like scars littered his face, remnants of a childhood pox. The man's eyes were dark green, with a low, hairy brow. A crooked nose, like the bent beak of a hawk, dominated the hardened features.

Brunner stared at his one-time ally, and fingered the trig-ger of his crossbow. He saw the other bounty hunter's green eyes narrow with suspicion as he and his men drew closer to the heap of rubble. As soon as Brunner saw the Estalian pull back on his mount's reins, he fired. The bolt caught the horse in the neck, pitching the wounded animal sidewise, and carrying itself and its rider into the black morass of the fen.

Even as the horse's cry of terror and death sounded, Lithelain leapt up from concealment and sent an arrow through the face of the foremost Bretonnian. The man did not even gasp as he fell from his horse, his body crashing into the dust. Before any of his comrades could act, a second arrow was already nocked and fired, pitching a second rider from his saddle, with an arrow through his chest.

Brunner retrieved his handgun, and aimed it down at the last riders. The weapon discharged its deadly missile with a loud explosion.

The roar and boom of the gun caused the Bretonnians' horses to rear upwards in fright and terror. One of the men was thrown screaming into the black water. The other clung desperately to the neck of his animal as the animal raced past the mound of rubble. Brunner sighted his other crossbow at the fleeing man, but as he did so, he saw the hands gripping the horse go slack and the rider fall. The gory wound caused by the bounty hunter's ball wept from the Bretonnian's breast.

A shriek of anguish rose from the fen as the last Bretonnian struggled upward from the mire. A brown leathery mass the size of a fist was stuck to the man's face and Josef watched in horror as the Bretonnian's hand ripped the giant leech off, pulling away a round chunk of his own cheek. Lithelain did not hesitate, but sent an arrow into the fen. The Bretonnian was knocked from his feet and sloshed backwards as the arrow hit him. As the dead man's body rolled over in the water, a half-dozen leathery bubbles of flesh could be seen clinging to his back.

A whistling sound caused Brunner to spin about. As he did so, a crossbow bolt smacked into a stone block a few

feet away. The bounty hunter could see Osorio throw the
spent weapon away from him. The Estalian's armour was
dripping with slime and he was having difficulty moving
through the mire. The brown hat was gone and blood
flowed from a wound in the man's scalp, where he had
torn one of the rapacious leeches from his body. As Osorio
sloshed his way forward, he wiped his mailed hand across
his brow, trying to keep the blood out of his eyes.

'You faithless spawn of a maggot!' the Estalian cried out.
'Face me, Brunner! We'll fight for the dagger.' Brunner
stared down at the enraged killer, maintaining a stony
silence. 'I know all about it! I spoke with Gobineau's
brother.' Osorio paused, breathing heavily. His violent fall
into the fen was making breathing difficult. The Estalian
paused, gathering his strength. 'You are not worthy to face
the Black Prince!' Osorio screamed.

'I told you,' Lithelain smirked. Brunner shook his head.

'Face me like a man, Brunner, you bastard!' roared
Osorio, sloshing his way forward, the cavalry mace gripped
in his right hand. Brunner lifted his crossbow and aimed it
down at the Estalian.

'I would,' the bounty hunter sneered, 'if I was challenged
by a man and not a dog.' Brunner fired, the bolt smashing
through the dented armour above Osorio's knee. The
Estalian screamed, pitching forward into the foul dark
water. A steady stream of obscenities rose from the fen. 'I
only hope you don't make the leeches and crows sick,'
Brunner said, turning away.

'You're not going to leave him like that?' Josef asked,
horrified. 'At least put him out of his misery.'

Brunner fixed an icy glare upon the youth. 'Don't ever
tell me my business again, boy. If that scum had done even
a single decent thing in his miserable life, I would. But
there isn't a hell foul enough for that kind of bastard.'
Brunner pointed a gloved hand to where they had hidden
their horses. Josef could see that Lithelain had already
mounted the magnificent roan stallion that he had called
from the forest when they had ridden from their camp that

morning. 'Mount up. I want to make Parravon before nightfall.' Brunner pushed Josef ahead of him as he gathered up his weapons and strode toward the horses. Behind them, Josef could hear another cry of rage sound from the morass of Grimfen.

'We've wasted enough time here,' Brunner said. The bounty hunter's jaw was set and Josef fancied that he saw a look of dreadful satisfaction in the eyes that peered out from behind the visor.

THE SHADOWS STRETCHED across the high-ceilinged hall, as though trying to grasp at the chamber's sole occupant. For long hours, the thin figure upon the black throne had sat immobile, staring intently at the faintly glowing contents of the box he was clutching.

A sound like chimes brought Dralaith's attention away from the fascinating scene he had witnessed within the Eye of Tchar. Even his dark heart was filled with a certain sense of admiration for the ruthlessness of the bounty hunter, however crude his methods. The Black Prince hesitated for a moment, then closed the lid of the teakwood box. The chiming continued. It was familiar, a sound that recalled the halls of his castle in lost Naggaroth. For a moment, the dark elf enjoyed the nostalgia, then a foul humour settled upon him. He rose from his throne just as two armoured figures strode towards him.

The slim figures bowed their heads, and slapped their hands to their breasts in the manner they had been instructed; a gesture that showed due fealty and deference to a Druchii lord.

The Black Prince stepped down, his dark silk *khaitan* flowing about his slender figure. He looked at his lieutenants. The two virtually identical faces were so very like his own. Both elves were dressed in full armour, mail aketons worn over their own sombre-hued robes of silk, with breastplates of polished steel.

The Black Prince reached a pale hand out, and idly played with the small steel barbs that dangled from the shoulder guards of his lieutenants' armour on delicate silver chains. He stared at the jagged, thorn-like hooks. He had not seen their like since leaving Naggaroth.

Savagely, the Black Prince slapped the face of one of his minions.

The lieutenant did not flinch, though his pale flesh began to colour. The Black Prince smiled at his slave's resolve. He reached out with both hands, tearing the array of flesh hooks from the armour of both elves. With a contemptuous gesture, he threw the ornaments across the room.

'Where did you get those?' the Black Prince asked.

'From Slaich, my master,' the dark elf that had been struck answered.

'He crafted them for us,' the other lieutenant added. 'He said that they were the emblems of your family, that all the knights who serve our master wear them into battle.' The Black Prince stalked forward, gripping the elf's chin with his hand, digging his fingers into the delicate skin.

'And are you a knight? Are you nobles, you two mongrel curs?' The Black Prince flung the lieutenant from him. 'If you ever again forget your place, I shall cut your tongues from your mouths and sew them to your foreheads, that all may see what becomes of ambitious fools!' The Black Prince waved his hand. Without another word, the two dark elves turned and marched from the chamber.

The Black Prince watched his servants depart. What did they know of nobility, what did they know of the longest war? What did they know of Naggaroth? Only what Slaich had told them.

The Black Prince turned his eyes to the discarded flesh hooks, those talismans of heritage and badges of honour. They had been crafted by Slaich. A feeling almost of sadness came upon the dark elf. Slaich had been with him for many years, more years than any of his servants. The old torture-master had served his own father before Dralaith had assumed mastery of his house – before the Eye of

Tchar had shown him how to safely murder his sire and place the blame where it would profit him most.

Slaich had not been a part of the events the Black Prince had foreseen in the Eye of Tchar. Slaich had much knowledge in his old white-capped head, knowledge that could undo his master's schemes. The dark elf sat back in his black throne, resting his hands on the rests, sinking deep into thought.

It was not how to dispose of Slaich that was troubling him, it was how he should be prepared... Perhaps basted in his own blood? That might provide an interesting dining experience.

Four

THE GREY HAZE of smoke rising from the city of Parravon was visible long before the city itself came into view. More of a fortified town than a city, Parravon was a thin sprawl of houses and buildings nestled between the Upper Grismerie River and the white cliffs that marked the beginning of the Grey Mountains. So near did the white cliffs loom, that many houses had been built right into them; only their doors and windows and sometimes a narrow portico marring the sharply sloping barrier of rock. Jagged chasms dropped away on two sides of the city. The walls of the Grey Mountains and the narrow finger of the river formed the settlement's remaining boundaries. Tall walls of stone, supported by still taller towers formed further defences against attack. A small dock was cut into the riverside wall, allowing traders to make their way along the Grismerie to unload their merchandise in Parravon.

As Brunner and his companions rode nearer, the sound of thousands of birds could be heard – the multitudinous flocks that nested in the cliffs above the Bretonnian city and who were the bane of the many gardens kept by Parravon's great and noble.

A large fort crouched upon the only landward approach to the city. It was a massive bridge, an ancient relic from the days of the elves, and was still as strong as the day it was built. Josef was struck by the slender, gracefully arching ribbon of stone stretching across the boundary of one of the chasms. He was amazed that such a functionary structure could have such a sense of poise about it. The merchant idly wondered how much such a construction had cost, and how wealthy the kingdom that could have afforded such a frivolous expense.

'I shall await you here,' Lithelain announced as they rode towards the gatehouse to petition the guards for access to the bridge. There was a look of distaste on the elf's face, as his eyes stared at the sprawling mass of thatched roofs and tile-topped towers. 'The smell of the place is offensive enough from here. I shall never understand how men can dwell in such confinement and squalor. And to think that you call such filthy places cities and speak of them with pride.' Lithelain shook his long hair.

'City?' scoffed Brunner. 'This village? You need to travel more. This isn't a city. In the Empire, there they have cities.' The bounty hunter turned Fiend about and began to walk the horse toward the gatehouse. 'Stay here if you want,' he called back. 'We'll not be more than a day if my friend hasn't moved on.'

Josef lashed his nag forward, catching up with the bounty hunter just as he was paying the watchmen within the yawning mouth of the gate. He did not pause, but dismounted and led his animals across the slender bridge. Josef fumbled for the coin the gatekeepers demanded then hurried to catch up with the bounty hunter.

The two men walked their animals across the bridge. Although slender, there was enough room for the men and their mounts to walk abreast. There was little traffic this morning and the two were alone save for a distant figure in a torn grey mantle pushing a rickety handcart toward the city.

Josef risked a look over the side of the span, and recoiled in fright as he beheld the distant bottom of the chasm they now walked over, and the jagged, fang-like rocks that covered it. Heights had always been one thing that the young merchant did not enjoy dealing with. He turned his attention back to the bounty hunter, and locked his gaze on him.

'I've not had dealings with elves before,' Josef said when they had traversed half the length of the bridge. 'Can he be trusted?' Brunner's steel face regarded the boy for a moment, his reaction masked by the black metal of his helm.

'It depends what you wish to trust him to do,' the bounty hunter said, staring ahead at the nearing streets of Parravon. 'You can depend upon Lithelain to honour his word, a rare thing for those who ply my trade.' Although Josef was certain that Brunner spoke of himself, he could detect no trace of self-reproach as he implied that he was a man who did not honour his own word. The thought made Josef's eyes narrow, and he gazed with a new suspicion at the hired killer. Until that moment, the boy had not fully appreciated how much he had come to trust Brunner's judgement and allow himself to be led by one who was a stranger to him.

'Who are we meeting here?' the young merchant asked at last, trying to keep his words even and level.

'An old… friend,' the bounty hunter answered.

'You seem a bit uncertain about this "friend",' Josef observed. Brunner faced the young avenger.

'I have not seen him in over a year's time,' the bounty hunter said. 'When we parted, it was not on the best of terms. Still, there is no better man to speak with about legends and myths, and what seeds of truth might lie buried under centuries of embellishment and invention.'

Brunner turned away again as they reached the other side of the bridge and its fortified gatehouse. Beyond the crouching barrier, they could see the handful of narrow, twisting streets that formed the township of Parravon.

* * *

BELLS TOLLED IN the streets, summoning the folk of Parravon to their morning devotions. The man seated at the table in the centre of the small bar looked up from his scattered sheets of parchment and squinted at the light streaming in from the open window. He looked about for the landlord, seeing the powerfully built man stumbling his way down toward the bar.

The man blinked his eyes, staring for a moment at the bottles of Bretonnian wine and Estalian sherry arrayed in ordered ranks behind the counter. The landlord grunted with disgust and reached over the dark wood of the counter. He retrieved a clay jar from beneath the bar, pulled the cork stopper from its mouth, and took a deep swallow of the contents, coughing as the fiery liquid burned its way down his throat.

The man at the table wrinkled his nose as the strong smell of Kislevite vodka wafted up from the jar. 'How can a man drink that vile brew so early in the day?' he observed.

The landlord wiped the sleeve of his shirt across his mouth and resealed the jar, setting it back behind the counter.

'You should talk,' the landlord laughed. 'You do see that the sun is up? I don't know why I charge you for your room; you never use it. Unless of course Yvette is around,' the innkeeper winked lasciviously at his patron.

'The duc wants this history of Parravon completed in a few weeks,' the man at the table said. He reached for a leather cup resting amidst the scattered documents and a half-filled inkwell. 'Complete with all but the most outrageous lies his forefathers have handed down over the centuries.' The scrivener frowned as he observed the depleted nature of his cup. The landlord chuckled and nimbly retrieved a bottle from the rack and made his way to the table.

'I mean why commission a historical work if you don't even care if the facts are correct?' the writer complained. '"And nothing about elves, if you please,"' the man continued, mimicking the voice of his benefactor. '"We find them a most dull and insignificant part of our city's lineage."'

The innkeeper laughed again and made his way across the wood floor of the bar. 'Best to keep such talk to yourself,' he warned. 'Otherwise you'll be without a patron and I'll have to throw you into the street.' He smiled, but the writer did not doubt that the man would be as good as his word if the duc's silver were to suddenly dry up.

The innkeeper moved toward the door, intending to let some fresh air into the building to clear some of the stink from last night's patrons. As he opened the door, however, he found himself staring into the dark metal of a steel helmet. The man beneath the helmet pushed his way past the burly innkeeper. A smaller, younger man followed the warrior inside. A protest formed on the innkeeper's tongue: the inn could not open until after the morning devotions had ended at the chapel, but a second look at the sinister figure caused him to rethink his choice of words.

The writer looked up, his face growing slightly pale. He reached for his cup, almost draining it in one swallow. The armoured intruder stared down at him, the eyes behind the visor of his helm burning into the seated man. After a moment of tense silence, the bounty hunter spoke.

'You look well, Ehrhard,' the steel voice rasped. 'Parravon seems to agree with you.'

Stoecker nodded his head, some of the colour returning to his features. 'Brunner,' he said. 'I did not expect to see you again.'

'The world is full of unpleasant surprises,' the bounty hunter stated. He cast a side-wise look at Josef. 'Show him,' Brunner ordered. Josef hesitated, annoyed by the killer's tone, but withdrew the carefully wrapped dagger from his belt. Stoecker reached forward, taking the weapon from the youth. The writer gasped as he unwrapped the blade, marvelling at the elegant, thorn-like edge, and examining the engraved hilt and pommel.

'What can you tell me about this?' Brunner asked.

'It is elvish,' the writer responded. 'I can't make out the writing, however. I doubt there are many men who could.'

'I already know it is of elf make,' Brunner said. 'If it is any consolation, even an elf was unable to decipher that script. He did say that it had certain similarities to family honours inscribed in the heirlooms of his own people, however.' The bounty hunter gestured at the weapon with a gloved finger. 'He also said that it is an especially ugly thing, tooled to rip and tear, to leave ugly wounds that will bleed greatly and not close if the blade is stabbed deep enough.'

'I've seen items like this before,' Stoecker said, still turning the dagger about in his hands. 'Though never an example so fine.' He looked up, focusing his gaze on the bounty hunter. 'In collections and museums in Marienburg and Brionne, you may see such things, scavenged from the field of battle and carefully preserved. Swords, axes, spears, all with the same thorn-like look, all with the hooked spurs at the mid-point of the edge. They are the arms of the dark elves, the corsairs who sail from across the sea to wage their campaigns of slaughter and pillage.'

'This did not come from a battlefield,' Brunner stated, retrieving the dagger and handing it back to Josef. 'This boy took it, from the Black Prince himself.'

'The Black Prince?' Stoecker exclaimed, a look of profound interest dispelling the last lingering traces of trepidation. 'Are you certain?'

A look of suspicion entered the writer's eyes. 'Is that why you came? You already knew about the dagger's likely origin from your elf friend. You came here to ask me what I know about the Black Prince.'

'You've been here long enough to have collected every hag's tale and minstrel's fable,' the bounty hunter answered. 'Unless you've changed since Miragliano, I imagine your chambers must be cluttered with myth and nonsense.'

'I have changed since Miragliano,' Stoecker said, reaching for his cup once more. 'I learned things it was better not to know, if you recall.' The writer sighed, collecting the scattered pages of the duc's manuscript and setting them into a neat stack. 'Still, you are right, I have collected many stories about the Black Prince.'

'Then let us see if you are as good at sifting truth from legend as you are at weaving lies from true life,' Brunner said. The writer rose from the table, looking from the bounty hunter to Josef and back to Brunner.

'There will be a price,' the writer said.

'I will meet it,' the bounty hunter replied. 'Provided,' he raised a gloved hand, and stabbed a finger at the exiled Imperial novelist, 'your information is of value.'

FOR SEVERAL HOURS, the three men sat in the small garret Ehrhard Stoecker had leased from his Bretonnian land-lord. Stacks of parchment, paper and vellum were cast all about the tiny room as the writer sifted through the hap-hazard arrangement of legends and travellers' tales he had been recording.

It was long, tedious work, but the elusive image of the Black Prince began to form around them. At times, Stoecker would ask Josef about the being that killed his father, then he would seize upon some small detail and tear through the documents for some scrap of story that might relate to Josef's attacker, even if the Black Prince had not been associated with the account.

In the end, however, there was little of value in Stoecker's exhaustive collection of tales. The Black Prince was alter-nately reputed to be the bastard son of the former Bretonnian king, Charles de la Tete d'Or III, or some sinis-ter agent of the Empire, who was trying to destabilise the frontier between the two great nations. Some tales said the Black Prince was a creature of the great enchanter, contin-uing his dread master's work even after Drachenfels's demise. Still others claimed that the villain was in the ser-vice of another of Bretonnia's adversaries, the wicked Lichemaster, Heinrich Kemmler, who was using his acts of banditry, securing magical artefacts of unholy power so that the necromancer might continue his war against the king.

No two accounts were the same, and those that told of the possible hiding place of the Black Prince were even more contradictory. According to the legends, the Black Prince's lair was as near as the haunted and forsaken Blood Keep, or as remote and far off as the blighted Cripple Peak. The few truths amounted to little more than a rough idea of when and where the vile creature had first set foot upon Bretonnian soil. Nearly five hundred years ago, a dark elf fleet had ransacked the countryside in the vicinity of Bordeleaux, and it had been at about this time that the oldest stories of the Black Prince had originated. This information was far too little to appease the bounty hunter.

'It seems I have wasted my time coming here,' Brunner snarled. 'I would do better trying to track down one of his men and beating what I want out of him.'

'That might be difficult to accomplish,' Stoecker said, setting the last of his string-bound bundles of parchment on the side of his bed. 'It might take you years to find him that way, for I doubt if any but the most trusted of his minions is shown his stronghold.' The writer smiled. 'And don't forget, while you are looking for him, he might come looking for you.'

'If you have another plan,' Brunner replied, 'speak. I have no time to spare in fencing words with you.'

Stoecker paced the room, then looked over at Josef. 'There was something interesting in your account. The man who the Black Prince said betrayed him; his description was interesting. I believe he may have been a man named Bors, once a fairly notorious highwayman in these parts.'

'How does that help us?' the bounty hunter asked.

'You will agree to my price?' Stoecker answered. The bounty hunter nodded his head. Stoecker breathed deeply, gathering his thoughts. 'This bandit, Bors, had a partner, a man named Ferricks. A week ago, this Ferricks appeared in

Parravon and was arrested by the watch. A rather interest-ing coincidence, don't you think?'

Brunner considered the writer's words. 'Indeed, a very interesting coincidence. You are thinking that if his friend was behind this plot to kill the Black Prince that Ferricks might also have had a hand in it?'

'Indeed, and that would explain why he fled and was captured here!' Josef exclaimed.

'More to the point, gentlemen,' Stoecker spoke, in a lec-turing tone, 'if Bors knew the location of the Black Prince's stronghold, then most likely Ferricks does as well.'

'Then I think this Ferricks is someone I need to speak with,' Brunner stated.

'That may be somewhat hard; he is to be hung at the end of the month. They are keeping him in the duc's dungeons until his execution date arrives.' A crafty look entered the writer's eyes. 'But I have met the keeper of the duc's gaol, a knight named Sir Lutriel Tourneur. I have even recorded some of the lies he tells about how he became a knight of the realm. He is a – shall we say – ambitious man. Include him in our little compact, and I think he might very easily arrange a pardon for Ferricks.'

'And split the reward still further,' Brunner's voice rum-bled from his throat.

'I care nothing about rewards, only that this monster meets a just end,' declared Josef. The bounty hunter did not spare the youth a glance.

'There might be enough treasure in his stronghold to off-set whatever demands your partners make on the king's bounty,' Stoecker offered. Brunner nodded his head.

'Very well,' the bounty hunter said, 'we'll see your gaoler.'

THE DUNGEONS OF the Duc of Parravon were located beneath one of the watchtowers nestled between the half-timbered houses of the townsfolk. The guard on watch at the tower at once recognised Stoecker, though he cast a suspicious eye at his two companions. The guard told the men to wait while he spoke through the grille in the front of the heavy oak door, to someone inside in the thin, nasally tones of the Bretonnian language.

After a few minutes, the door opened. Five soldiers wearing rounded steel helmets and coats of chainmail beneath their colourful heraldic surcoats emerged from the tower; each man bore a long, hatchet-headed halberd. From the midst of these soldiers, a sixth man strode forward. Tall, imposing in his suit of plates, the man wore the colourful surcoat of Parravon, but with a golden thread edging the chevrons and fleur-de-lys depicted upon fields of blue and yellow. Mixed with the symbols of the city, the knight's mantle also bore three other symbols – marks of his own battles and achievements: a rampant wyvern, a black star, and a silver raven. The man's face was hard, framed by a mail coif that covered his head and dripped about his neck. His harsh eyes regarded the three men who sought entry to the tower. The knight's upturned chin was thrust forward as he studied the men who accompanied Stoecker.

'Ah, Stoecker, my friend,' the knight said at last, turning his attention fully upon the writer. His voice was deep, suave and had a self-assured and condescending tone. 'What brings your esteemed self to my humble post?'

'Sir Lutriel,' Stoecker answered, bowing his head. 'I was telling my companions about your noble self and your important position in the duc's trust. They simply had to meet such a fascinating figure.'

'Indeed,' Sir Lutriel said, a crafty gleam winking from his eyes. But his tone suggested that he had not believed a word of the writer's flattery for a moment. 'Perhaps we might retire to my quarters where we can sample some of the duc's wine. It is not well to be on the streets of Parravon after dusk,' he added, his tone dropping into a warning whisper.

Very soon, Brunner found himself standing in a lavishly appointed chamber that served the knight for entertaining guests. His critical eye appraised the value of the tapestries and soft rugs he was standing on. A few statues, all nudes, nested on tables between glass carafes of dark, sombre looking brandy and bejewelled boxes. Brunner did not doubt that the keeper of the duc's prisons was corrupt, but he was surprised at how openly he flaunted his willingness to accept a bribe. The bounty hunter guessed that there could be but one reason for the knight's lack of subtlety: that any in the hierarchy of Parravon in a position to reprimand him must be thrice the thief that he was.

The knight settled himself in a tall-backed chair behind an extravagantly carved table. He rested his hands on top of the table, steepling his fingers, and stared at his guests.

'Now then, what did you really come here for?' he asked, his tone as condescending as before.

'You have a prisoner here,' the bounty hunter answered. 'A thief named Ferricks. I want him.'

Sir Lutriel's face spread into an amused smile. 'And what if I am not prepared to hand him over to you?' The crafty look returned to the Bretonnian's eyes. 'I wonder what Brunner, the notorious bounty killer, wants with such a miserable and insignificant villain. I don't think the duc ever offered more than three pieces of gold for the reptile, and he will hardly offer such a sum for him again.'

'He may be able to lead us to the lair of the murdering swine that killed my father,' snarled Josef. Sir Lutriel turned his gaze on the boy, the amused smile returning to his face.

'It has been my experience that revenge rarely pays well, certainly not well enough to fabricate an acceptable lie for the duc when I fail to produce this man for the noose next week.'

'This man was one of the Black Prince's captains,' Stoecker stated in a flat, almost mater-of-fact tone. The statement brought a look of surprise to the smug knight's face. The man rubbed at his chin with a gloved hand.

'The Black Prince?' he mused aloud. 'Perhaps in this instance revenge does pay well. Very well indeed.' He stared hard at the writer. 'You are certain of this? But of course you are, otherwise Brunner would hardly have come here.' The knight allowed himself a chuckle, the sound rattling about like bones in a grave. 'I think perhaps we might be able to do business after all. Of course, I shall expect a generous portion of the king's bounty.'

'How much?' Brunner's voice hissed.

'Oh, I am not a greedy man,' Sir Lutriel gasped, his tone putting the lie to his words. 'The king is offering a tidy amount for this brigand prince. I think that two thousand is not too much to ask for me to play my role in this enterprise.'

'You'll get one,' the bounty hunter's voice rasped.

'Shall we split the difference?' Sir Lutriel retorted. 'I will accompany you to ensure the return on my investment. Or perhaps I should just take this man and try and find the bandit's stronghold on my own?' The threat lingered in the air between the two men. The bounty hunter stared long and hard at the knight, but even his murderous gaze was not enough to sway the Bretonnian. After a few tense moments, Brunner turned from Sir Lutriel.

'Take me to Ferricks,' he said. 'Before I change my mind.'

Sir Lutriel smiled, enjoying his small victory over the infamous killer. But Stoecker wondered about the ease with which the knight had made his point. He had never seen Brunner back down from anyone before. He doubted the bounty hunter had ever allowed another man to get the better of him.

The writer wondered if Sir Lutriel had truly gained something, or if he had done exactly as the bounty hunter wanted him to.

THE DUNGEONS WERE a maze of dank, narrow halls that wound below the tower in a winding, spiral fashion. Rats scurried from cracks in the walls, snapping at the light cast by Sir Lutriel's torch before scurrying back into the shadows. Stoecker broke into a sweat every time the rodents appeared; he was unpleasantly reminded of another such creature he had seen in the bounty hunter's company.

The knight led the men down the spiral of uneven stone steps, deep into the dismal shadow.

As they passed one cell, a thin, pleading voice cried out. Brunner turned, staring at the cell door. He walked over, and peered into the chamber behind the iron grille. A thin, bedraggled figure with a pointed beard stared back at him.

'Brunner!' the prisoner cried. 'It's me, Mahlinbois! Praise the Lady!' A set of thin, pale fingers clutched at the bars of the iron grille. 'You have to get me out of here! They mean to burn me at the stake for consorting with daemons!'

'And have you been?' Brunner asked, his voice betraying a spark of humour.

'How can you ask such a thing?' Mahlinbois responded. 'I am an honest conjurer.' The grimy figure drew himself up with all the pride his tattered raiment would allow.

'A friend of yours?' Sir Lutriel's snide voice interrupted. 'It is a dangerous thing to be too familiar with sorcerers.' The bounty hunter turned on the knight.

'Open the door,' he ordered. A smug expression appeared on Sir Lutriel's face, as though a fox had just asked a watchdog for the keys to the chicken coop.

'You overstep your bounds, Imperial.' The stress the knight placed on the last word left no doubt that it was said as an insult. 'This is my tower, filled with my men. I give the orders here, not you.'

'We need him,' the bounty hunter stated. 'Unless you wish to face a sorcerer without any magic of your own?'

'I should think we would be better off with the duc's pet wizard,' Sir Lutriel sneered. 'This wretch was hardly worth capturing.'

'And yet you say he summons daemons,' Stoecker pointed out.

'If your swine had not waited until I was sleeping off a night of ill-advised excess at the brothel, they would never have laid a hand on me!' snapped Mahlinbois, his words fiery with outrage.

'Perhaps he is no daemonologist,' the knight continued, knowing that such was the case. 'Still, it does the people of Parravon good to see a wizard burned at the stake from time to time. It shows that their lords are doing something to combat whatever fiendish things stalk the streets at night.'

'Perhaps you care to explain to the duc exactly why you need to borrow his own magician?' Brunner interrupted. Some of the smugness left Sir Lutriel's face and he advanced on the door, removing the heavy ring of keys from his belt and opening the door slowly.

'You understand, my price is back at two thousand now, and I shall expect an equal share of whatever we find in the Black Prince's stronghold,' the knight said as he opened the door.

'The Black Prince!' exclaimed Mahlinbois as his thin figure emerged from the dark cell. 'Is that why you need me?' The unlucky magic-user tugged at the door, trying to close himself back in his cell.

'You're the closest thing to a wizard I could find on such short notice,' Brunner said. Sir Lutriel's hand closed on the prisoner's shoulder and pulled him from the cell.

'Ranald's Cloak! I'm an illusionist, Brunner. Nothing I create is real!' Mahlinbois was shoved to one side as Sir Lutriel made his way back to the head of the group. 'I'm no graduate of the College of Wizardry! My mentor was just a petty charlatan, playing with the very smallest drafts of the winds of magic! I'm no match for a sorcerer!'

'Perhaps you would rather stay here and be burned?' Brunner hissed back.

'Actually, I think I would,' the frightened illusionist agreed.

'Too bad, the choice isn't yours to make,' Brunner turned, gesturing for Sir Lutriel to proceed. 'But when this is over, I can bring you back here and they can burn you.'

Mahlinbois waited for a moment, then followed Josef and Stoecker down the stairs.

'Why couldn't I just have been an honest thief like my father?' the magician grumbled as he descended after the bounty hunter.

* * *

FERRICKS WAS A rat-faced, spider-like man. As Sir Lutriel hauled him from his cell, and the greasy man blinked up at the group, Brunner found himself wondering if skaven ever sired offspring with goblins.

'I understand that you haven't told us quite everything,' Sir Lutriel said, glowering down at the little man.

'What? I've told you everything I know, about things I haven't even done and people I never even met,' the thief uttered his words without pausing for breath. 'Whatever you want to know now, I did it, and whoever you want to pin it on was there as well.' The thief uttered a sharp bark of fright as he saw the thorn-like blade Josef had unwrapped.

'No! I know nothing about that! Not a thing!' Ferricks's eyes were wide with fright. He wiped his sweaty palms on his filthy breeches.

'These men say otherwise,' Sir Lutriel scoffed. 'Perhaps some more time on the rack might jar your recollections?'

'You're a dead man already,' Brunner said, stepping toward the little bandit. 'Does it matter if they hang you here, or if the Black Prince does it later?'

Ferricks looked about him with a shifty, narrow-eyed expression trying to recover from his start at hearing the Black Prince named. 'What are you proposing?' the thief's whiny voice asked.

'It is within my power to pardon you,' Sir Lutriel said, acting as if the thief's decision was of no concern to him. 'Tell us what we want to know, and you will be a free man.'

'Sure, and then the Black Prince's men will find me and kill me, but not quick and nice like your hangman.'

'Not if I kill him first,' Brunner's murderous voice rasped. Josef turned, eyeing the bounty hunter.

'If you kill him?' Ferricks laughed. 'He's not human. He's been around hundreds of years and nobody has been able to put him on the spot. Why should you be any different?'

'Ferricks, may I introduce Brunner, the bounty hunter. I rather imagine that his reputation precedes him?' Sir Lutriel enjoyed watching the small thief slink away from the bounty hunter much like a man who has nearly stepped on a snake.

'If anyone can do this thing, it would be Brunner,' Stoecker said. 'Besides, do you really have any other choice?'

'I show you on a map where the Black Prince's tower is, and you let me go?' Ferricks said, trying to make certain he understood.

'No,' Brunner's icy voice spoke. Even Sir Lutriel stared at the bounty hunter with a look of open surprise. 'You guide us there. That way anything that happens to us, happens to you as well.' Ferricks cringed back still further, his back against the stone wall. But he found himself nodding in agreement.

'If I help you, I want a share of his treasure,' the thief said.

'If you help us,' Brunner's voice snarled, 'I'll consider not bringing you back to the Viscount de Chegney for the reward he has on your scrawny neck.'

FROM HIS DARK throne, the Black Prince watched the lithe figure of the slave girl strut and whirl across the floor. He smiled as he considered her smooth, unblemished skin. Truly, it had been such a shame to loose Slaich. Such a master with the whip! It had taken him years to get this animal to perform, years of discipline with the lash. Yet there was not a mark on her body, as the brief garment that clung to her hips allowed the elf to determine. True, the girl might be reckoned a beauty to humans – for what they knew of such things – but the real measure of her worth was the way in which she performed. It was the savage dance of the witch elves, those maniacal temple maidens of Khaine in his native Naggaroth. But there was an added element lacking in the dances of those dangerous elves, an element that thrilled the Black Prince and made his breath short. It was fear. The girl exuded it, as the memories of the pain Slaich had inflicted upon her added to the frenzy of the dance.

The Black Prince looked away from the sweating, wide-eyed woman, his eyes falling to the teakwood box. The lid was open and the gleaming gemstone of the Eye of Tchar stared back at him. The dark elf smiled. The bounty hunter had discovered Ferricks, just as the Eye had foreseen. It annoyed the elf to allow the traitor to draw another breath, but he knew that the vermin's days were numbered. He had seen that as well within the Eye.

The Black Prince raised his new goblet, and let the last of Slaich's blood slip past his pale lips. The rest had been imbibed by one of his slaves, so the dark elf might savour the taste, but this last cup he would drink himself. It was a final honour to bestow upon his old servant.

Slaich was the first of the sacrifices his current scheme would force him to make. It had been the hardest one, taking the dark elf a few heartbeats to decide upon. Those which were to follow would not disturb him in the slightest.

Five

THE SMALL GROUP of riders left Parravon early the following day, just as the first gleam of pre-dawn began to glow above the peaks of the Grey Mountains. By nightfall, they had camped in a break in the woods that clothed the base of the trees. Running a cold camp, the bounty hunter had allowed no fire. The encampment was a tense place, made all the more so by the distrust and rivalry festering in the hearts of the members of the small band. Mahlinbois loathed and despised Sir Lutriel, who in turn was quite open about his own suspicions about Lithelain, who he believed would betray them to seek his own, separate vengeance. Ferricks was in obvious terror of the Black Prince: he started at every shadow, terrified that the evil creature's reach would find him. The wiry thief was also in obvious terror of both Brunner and Sir Lutriel; as fearful of the two men as he was of the brigand lord he was betraying. And Josef, too, harboured his own suspicions, wondering if he could trust the bounty hunter.

Only the writer, Ehrhard Stoecker, seemed without prejudice. He flitted from one person to the other, engaging each in conversation. Josef wondered if this was why the bounty hunter had allowed the man to accompany them. Not to indulge Stoecker's desire to have some grand adventure of his own, but to keep the bounty killer's company from cutting each other's throats in the night.

Eventually, Stoecker finished his circuit of the camp, and seated himself beside Josef. The young merchant looked over at the writer. Stoecker must have noticed the boy's glance, for he smiled and asked what was on Josef's mind.

'I can understand why everyone is here, except for the elf,' the youth confessed. 'Ferricks and Mahlinbois are being driven by their fear of the hangman or Brunner. Sir Lutriel wants a share of the bounty. You are here to experience one of the adventures you write about. But why is Lithelain with us?'

Stoecker smiled, nodding toward the elf making his way into the trees, to take his position for the long night watch. 'I've spoken with him before, a few years ago, in Miragliano.'

'Miragliano?' the youth asked. 'Why would a wood elf be in a Tilean port-city?'

'The same reason he is here now, the same reason you are here. He is looking for revenge.' Stoecker noted the start Josef gave as he heard the declaration. 'You see, many years ago, centuries actually, the wood elves sent an envoy to the king of Bretonnia. But she never returned to Athel Loren. She was ambushed, her retainers and guards killed by the Black Prince. For a hundred years, Lithelain searched for the envoy, but all he could discover were rumours, and legends about a shadowy bandit king. Then, one day, as he followed yet another lead, he met a rider on the road. The rider was silent, and wore a silk robe that clothed her from head to foot. As he drew nearer, the smell of death struck his nose, and the buzz of flies sounded in his ears. The rider was a corpse, lashed to the saddle. A wooden frame held it upright. As Lithelain looked closer, he saw that the corpse was that of the missing envoy, and it was only hours old. I will not mention the atrocities that sorry body bore witness to, but cut into the flesh were savage, twisted elf runes, runes that spelled out a simple message: Compliments of the Black Prince.'

Stoecker fixed Josef with a stern, saddened gaze. 'The envoy was his sister.'

Josef stared up at the tree the elf had climbed into, with a sudden understanding in his eyes. He might not be certain about whether Brunner would cheat him of his revenge, but he could be certain that nothing would keep the elf from killing the Black Prince with his own hands. Josef knew this because the same determination filled his own heart.

JOSEF AWOKE WITH a start, a clammy hand clamped across his mouth. He stared up into the face of Sir Lutriel.

'Don't make a sound, or we are undone,' the knight's calm voice whispered. He removed his hand. Josef sat up, seeing that the knight was fully dressed, his sword sheathed at his side.

'What's this about?' the youth asked. The knight gave him a knowing, superior look.

'Tell me, do you honestly think you have any chance of getting what you want if you stick with Brunner?' Sir Lutriel replied. 'Do you honestly think the elf is going to let you cheat him of his vengeance? Or do you think that Brunner is going to allow you to jeopardise his chance of collecting the bounty on the Black Prince's head?'

'A bounty which you want for yourself,' Josef observed.

'Naturally,' the knight admitted. 'But I am rather loath to share it.'

'What do you intend?' the merchant inquired, his mind racing, trying to see where the Bretonnian was leading him.

'I've just had a most illuminating discussion with our friend Ferricks,' Sir Lutriel confessed. 'He told me about an old goblin tunnel that burrows its way into the Black

Prince's stronghold – a tunnel that is never used, and never guarded. He also told me how to find the valley where the Black Prince's stronghold is hidden. It might be possible for two determined men to make their way in and collect that valuable head.' The knight smiled. 'Actually, Ferricks came to me with the idea. It seems he is inordinately fond of the idea that the Black Prince might already be dead when Brunner drags his sorry hide back there. In fact, he even said that he would keep the bounty hunter riding in circles for a few days, to give us enough time to kill his former master and be away before Brunner can do anything about it.'

'Why me?' Josef wondered, suspicions rising in his mind. 'Why not do it yourself?'

'I need someone to watch my back. I have no idea what risks might be involved. I need an accomplice.' Sir Lutriel's voice dropped still lower. 'And you are the only one I can trust. The others are too connected to Brunner, and if I take Ferricks, I lose my decoy. Brunner would be after me like a shot in that event.' The knight paused, studying Josef's reaction to his words.

'It is the only way you'll get your chance at the murderer of your father,' he said.

'You will let me face the Black Prince?' There was a note of disbelief in Josef's tone.

'Oh, by all means. And when he kills you, there will be no one to share the reward with,' the knight admitted, his voice as friendly and superior as ever. Josef considered the brutal honesty of the statement.

'Very well,' the youth said. 'Give me a moment to gather my things.'

JOSEF AND THE knight made their way down the narrow path, careful not to dislodge any of the jagged stones that lined it. It was a secret way into the small valley where the Black Prince had made his stronghold; a way supposedly known only to Bors and Ferricks, though Sir Lutriel had expressed his doubts, and had kept his sword ready. It was not only men that served the dark elf, and the knight knew enough about beastmen to know that if their minds were less than human, their senses were more than human.

The path had started in a grove of tangled trees, then climbed up the side of a hidden, narrow ravine that laced through the Grey Mountains. On one side, the narrow path was bordered by soaring dark cliffs, on the other it dropped away into a deep chasm. The surface of the trail was damp and slippery, forcing the two travellers to move very slowly, lest they lose their footing and tumble to their deaths on the jagged rocks below.

It was a highly defensible route, and Sir Lutriel did not doubt that it would indeed take an army to force their way into the valley should its inhabitants be aware of their approach. But Sir Lutriel had never been one to take the direct approach when a knife in the back or a loose saddle-strap might serve his purpose just as well.

They had left the horses hobbled in the small grove of trees, where the Bretonnian hoped they would not be discovered, and had then set upon the winding trail that Ferricks had described. They climbed the grey rock of the mountain, at times nearly vertical with the face of the grim rock, then descended by a treacherous path to the valley floor.

The valley itself was small, but again proved perfect for the purposes of the bandit lord. A small stream ran down from the mountains, rolling across the rocky, barren ground before plummeting down the deep gash that snaked its way across the valley floor.

The narrow crack was decidedly unnatural in appearance, much like the runnels cut into the valley floor. But where the runnels showed the remains of ancient trenches and earth-works, the crack was an altogether different sort of scar left by a long forgotten battle. The crack started at the opposite side of the valley, in the shadow of the mountain, and ran almost to the valley's centre.

The crack was the last vestige of an ancient tunnel dwarf sappers had blasted in an effort to reach the stronghold of their enemy – before the unnatural wards and defences of their foes had caused the tunnel to collapse and crumble into the caverns under the Grey Mountains. The collapsed dwarf tunnel had left behind a long jagged cut twenty feet wide and hundreds deep.

Rising from the centre of the barren valley was a slender round tower of white stone. Fluted buttresses supported the crown of the tower, where a tiled roof enclosed the upper parapet. Several balconies opened out from the sides of the tower at varying heights, each edged by triangular crenellations that added to the symmetry of the structure. In places, the stone was chipped or fractured, but it was still an imposing and fabulous sight, a relic of the days of elf rule over the Old World, before the War of the Beard caused them to abandon their colonies and withdraw back to the enchanted shores of Ulthuan.

Neither of the men who gazed upon the tower for the first time could guess how many battles it had seen unfold. Nor could they fathom the deep satisfaction its present occupant drew from claiming such a relic of his cousins for his own. As they observed the tower, a pair of gangly, man-sized creatures silently circled the spire on grotesque bat-like wings. It was difficult to make out any detail at such distance, and neither of the men desired a closer look than their position allowed.

Sir Lutriel pulled Josef close, motioning with his hands how they would next proceed. Ferricks had told them of an underground passage, a tunnel built by the goblins during their infestation of the tower, that wormed its way from the mountainside to the stronghold. He did not know if the Black Prince knew of its existence, but Ferricks was certain that his former master had not put the old tunnel to any use. There might be other secret ways into the tower, but this was the only one Ferricks had ever learned about.

The knight and the merchant made their way carefully across the open expanse, casting fearful glances at the tower, wary of any sign of watching sentries. The ground they had to cover between the trail and the opening of the old goblin hole was not far, but it was the most dangerous. Both men sighed with relief when they gained the cover of a cluster of rocks. Between a pair of massive boulders, the dark, gaping mouth of the goblin tunnel beckoned to the men.

The opening itself was tight, and Sir Lutriel found himself obliged to squirm his way between the rocks, not daring to fill his lungs as he slithered through the tight passage. The tunnel itself was an equally miserable experience: a low-ceilinged affair, with an uneven floor and frequent disorienting changes in pitch and direction. The men had to bend double with their backs parallel to the ground, their swords held before them. Josef lit a small torch he had brought with him to illuminate the jagged passageway. Old bones, the last remains of the original inhabitants, were crunched into powder beneath their boots.

After what seemed an eternity in the clammy, dark silence of the tunnel, the ceiling suddenly grew much higher, and the men could stand upright. The tunnel had opened into some sort of chamber. Josef could see that a great pile of goblin bones rested against one wall, while the other opened into a deep, sloping passage. The remaining wall was remarkable as well, for it was smooth, moulded by skilled hands rather than gouged from the living earth.

Josef looked at Sir Lutriel. The knight nodded, dropping the face of his helmet down and firming his grip on the hilt of his sword. Josef set the torch down and began to rub his hand across the smooth surface of the wall. Down near the bottom, his palm encountered a slight spur, a blemish in the face of the wall. There was a faint, barely perceivable *click*, and a section of the wall slid outward.

'Remember, he is mine,' Josef whispered, then stepped through the opening. He could see that the door had opened upon a hall, its walls, ceiling and floor crafted from the same smooth white stone. As he took in his surroundings, a bright flash of light exploded before his eyes.

Stunned, the youth was unprepared when a clutching hand tore the sword from his hand. Josef could hear a grim Bretonnian curse, and guessed that Sir Lutriel had also been captured and disarmed. Burly limbs wrapped themselves about Josef's arms and the boy was savagely pulled into the centre of the hallway.

'It seems I have visitors,' a melodious voice purred.

Josef found himself staring into an inhumanly handsome face. It was not unlike the visage of Lithelain, in many ways, but to call them identical was to call a swarthy-visaged Arabyian a pale Kislevite nomad. The paleness of the speaker's skin was more marked, it was more pallid than the creamy hue of the wood elf. There was a harsh cruelty about this elf's features, a stamp of wickedness that tainted the fine sharp lines with menace. The hooded eyes regarded Josef and Sir Lutriel with an almost bored expression.

Josef let his gaze fall from the elf's face, starting as he saw the black armour, the twin swords, and the long dangling length of silk and steel skirts. He had not seen the face of his father's murderer before, but he recognised the garb of the Black Prince.

Rage surged through his lean frame and the boy struggled against the grip holding his arms. But the powerful hold could not be broken.

The elf smiled, drawing his thin lips tight. He idly flicked a lock of long black hair from his face. 'Whatever shall I do with my delicious guests? It is so seldom that I am called upon to entertain.' Coarse laughter echoed in the Black Prince's words and Josef became aware that there were others with him. Hard-faced men, wearing all manner of motley armour filled the corridor behind the bandit lord. Two more elves, their faces mirroring their master's, their armour fashioned to echo and mimic that of the Black Prince, flanked the dread figure. Their own beautiful faces were twisted into sneers of sadistic amusement. Other figures, twisted and inhuman, loomed above the elves and men, or slithered their warped shapes between the bandits to get a better view of the prisoners.

'But look,' the elf exclaimed with mock astonishment. 'One of my guests has brought a gift.' The Black Prince's thin hand reached to Josef's belt, nimbly plucking the covered dagger from him.

The elf held the dagger beneath his nose, and closed his eyes as he savoured the smell of the Naggaroth steel. 'I much regretted the loss of my dagger,' he said. 'It is an heirloom of my family, and there are few enough of those left to me, in these less prosperous times. I thank you for its return.'

'The Lady's curse be on you!' roared Sir Lutriel, struggling to free himself from the embrace of the hulking beastmen that held him fast. The Black Prince turned and faced the Bretonnian.

'The Lady?' the dark elf asked. Then his eyes widened as if with sudden recollection. 'Ah yes, that heathen deity you animals pray to. Truly, can you do no better? I have borne curses bestowed in her name for centuries now. Now, I ask you, even for a god, don't you think that is a bit slow to act?'

'Damn you!' Sir Lutriel snarled. 'Give me a sword and I'll cut that smirk from your face!'

The Black Prince laughed. 'I fear that such a contest would be quite dreary. I've faced your sort before, even your masters. In Naggaroth, they would not have even been allowed to cross swords with a cripple.' The knight roared anew at the villain's mockery, but the Black Prince had already turned his back on the man. 'Do not fear, I shall arrange for you to show me just how skilled you are with the sword.'

'We will be avenged, my father will be avenged!' cried Josef as the Black Prince began to withdraw into the shadows along with his retinue. The elf paused, considering the boy once again with his disdainful face.

'Surely you do not mean the bounty hunter and his comrades?' the Black Prince laughed. He watched with amusement as the rage on the boy's features faded into shock. 'Yes,' the elf's voice sank into a soothing whisper, 'I know all about them. In fact, I was just going to arrange a proper welcome for them.' The reptilian smile returned to the monster's face. 'It is so rare for me to receive visitors.' He looked at the beastmen holding the two prisoners. 'Take the boy to my audience chamber.' He pointed a slender finger at Sir Lutriel. 'Take that to the pit, and prepare it for this evening's festivities.'

The Black Prince did not pause to watch the beastmen drag their burdens away, but regarded his two attentive lieutenants. The elves bowed their heads as the Black Prince stared at them. 'Drannach, Uraithen, attend me. There are things we must discuss before my other guests arrive.' He walked away, the two dark elves following a respectful ten steps behind their master.

THE BLACK PRINCE stood at the gate of the tower, once again armoured for battle. He was flanked by Lieutenant Drannach and the hulking hound-faced beastman Urgmesh. Before him, mounted on a coal-black steed, the other dark elf lieutenant stared down at his master. Like the Black Prince, he was garbed for battle, his fine, sharp features staring out from the open face of his helm. Behind him, a dozen grizzled horsemen awaited his command.

'Hunt down these swine and bring him and his companions back to me, alive,' the Black Prince's melodious voice intoned from behind the mask of his helm. 'I have already despatched the harpies to watch the mountains, lest the worm think to deceive us by taking the more difficult road. But I think it most likely that he will try the pass.'

'And if they should elude us?' the lieutenant asked.

'We keep a watch here,' the Black Prince gestured with a slender, mail-clad finger, pointing above his head. 'I shall post watchmen above, to warn us should our visitors approach the tower, and keep a force below to greet them should they use the tunnel.'

'I think you should find a single sentry of more service,' the lieutenant offered. 'A single watcher might go unseen and unnoticed. One sentinel with keen eyes would be more certain to carry warning than a dozen, who would surely be seen before the bounty hunter emerged from cover.' The lieutenant grew quiet, then spoke again. 'Perhaps Gruzlok; his eyes are the best of all your servants.'

'The beastman is also simple,' the Black Prince scoffed. 'A dog would be hard pressed to maintain a discourse with Gruzlok.'

'It takes no great wit to detect a company of riders approaching the tower,' observed the lieutenant. 'And his phenomenal vision may prove of great benefit.' The Black Prince nodded his armoured head.

'Quite so,' he said. 'I shall act upon your suggestion.' The elf waved his hand in a dismissive gesture. The mounted lieutenant looked over at his men, inclining his head, and motioning for them to follow him.

The line of riders galloped from the tower to the narrow floor of the valley. The Black Prince watched them for a moment, then faced Drannach. 'Come, let us see how our guests are faring,' he said. The two dark elves withdrew back into the tower, the gate closing behind them.

THE BLACK PRINCE smiled. Things were proceeding just as the Eye of Tchar had revealed. Very soon now, the events he had allowed to unfold would speed to the conclusion he had seen. The harpies – if the miserable gruesome Chaos beasts he had secured from a travelling menagerie could honestly be allowed to bear the name – would nestle amongst the crags of the Grey Mountains, to await his command to return. He had not seen them in the Eye of Tchar, so he did not want them close by when his present scheme came to fruition.

As for his lieutenants, well, they were another matter.

THE BLACK PRINCE entered the great hall of the tower, striding past the bowed heads of his bandit soldiers and misshapen beastmen, not sparing a glance at any of his servants. Drannach and the beastman Urgmesh followed at his heels.

The bandit leader walked to a low dais set before a great gaping pit. With measured strides, he climbed the steps, seating himself on the high-backed seat that was a copy of the chair in his throne room. The elf considered the fiery gaze directed at him by the young boy chained at the foot of the dais, by a large dog-collar fixed about his neck. The Black Prince chuckled as he felt Josef's hate wash over him.

'In good time,' the bandit lord said. 'But first, you should enjoy the hospitality of the Black Prince.' The elf laughed again as, with a flourish, he spread the skirt of his aketon and robe and took his seat. The noble brought his steel-clothed hands together in a single, metallic clap, then gestured with one of his hands to the pit below.

Josef hesitated for a moment, glaring at his oppressor, then risked a glance at the pit. It was a large, circular depression in the floor, some twenty feet deep, lined with steel spikes all about its upper lip. The base of the pit was covered in sand, the walls pitted with deep scratches and stains that were certainly that of spilled blood.

Bones, cracked apart by some tremendous pressure, were scattered about in the sand. The unpleasant thought occurred to Josef that they had been snapped to get at the soft marrow within. But the most terrible sight was the lone figure standing in the centre of the pit, staring at the gloating minions of the dark elf lord with eyes that were as filled with rage and fury as Josef's own. Sir Lutriel had been stripped down to a loincloth, his back bearing the dark bruises of his treatment at the hands of the beastmen. The defiant Bretonnian knight's gaze shifted to the massive wooden portcullis that dominated the far wall of the pit. A sound, like the shuffling of some enormous being, sounded from the darkness beyond the portal.

'I understood that I would be given a chance to display my swordsmanship,' Sir Lutriel bellowed. His voice was calm and still carried a note of superiority and scorn. The Black Prince laughed and gestured to one of his human brigands. The grimy killer stepped to the rim of the pit. Laughing boisterously, the bandit tossed a long-bladed knife to the sandy floor below. Sir Lutriel bent down and retrieved the knife.

'Thank you for your graciousness,' the knight said, bowing to the seated lord. As he rose, Sir Lutriel's hand came upwards, hurling the blade at the Black Prince in a single, blinding motion. The steel turned end over end, then was caught by an iron-clad grasp inches from the breastplate of the dark elf. The Black Prince handed the knife to Drannach without even glancing at it.

'You can hardly fault me for trying,' Sir Lutriel's voice rose from the floor of the pit. Another shuddering step mixed with a low snarl sounded from behind the gate. The knight turned to the portcullis.

'A pity,' the Black Prince's musical voice purred, 'now you shall have to face Marius without the benefit of that swordsmanship you were so boastful of.' The elf clapped his hands again, the sharp ring of metal upon metal echoing across the hall. A pair of human brigands at once leapt into motion, gripping a great wheel set into the wall. With quick wrenching movements, the two men turned the wheel. In the pit below, the wooden portcullis rose.

THE DARK ELF lieutenant led his riders down the narrow neck of the valley, spurring his steed onward. His keen gaze was able to discern the slightest detail at a great distance. He studied the terrain, watching the rocks and trees for any sign of movement or anything unusual. He did not expect to find the bounty hunter's little band of would-be assassins at the very doorstep of the stronghold, but caution was something in his very blood.

The lieutenant wondered how things were faring back in the tower. Had the bounty hunter already arrived? Was he even now confronting the Black Prince? The elf allowed himself to smile. But his amusement swiftly faded as he turned his body around, staring with suspicion at a nearby stand of trees. He cursed himself for his lack of attention. He had travelled this path more times than he could count, yet never had there been a stand of trees where he now saw them.

The elf shouted a warning to his followers as he pulled back on the reins of his horse. But it was too late. A loud boom sounded from the trees. The dark elf felt a powerful impact strike his chest, lifting him from the saddle. His shifting mass unbalanced the startled horse, its footing already disturbed by the lieutenant's hasty pull on the reins. The animal nickered in terror as it fell sideways. With inhuman agility and speed, the elf leaped from the saddle, determined not to be crushed under the weight of the animal. But the horse was not falling toward the ground, it was toppling over the lip of the collapsed dwarf tunnel that snaked its way down the breadth of the valley. The elf's leap carried him further over the precipice and his scream of horror was added to that of his animal as both fell into the rift.

As the bandits watched their leader fall, they were set upon. Arrows whistled from the trees, smashing men in their throats and chests, pitching them to the ground. Before the men had even begun to react, three of their number lay on the ground, dead or dying, a fourth slumped in his saddle, his hands clutching at the arrow embedded between his ribs. The sharp report of a crossbow was added to the whistle of the arrows, and two more of the men fell dead as they spurred their horses back toward the tower. The remaining bandits retreated, another of their number falling as an arrow caught him in the back.

'A good shot,' mused Brunner as he reloaded his crossbow. Lithelain nodded solemnly.

'I loathe striking an enemy in the back, but it will perhaps convince them to keep going,' the wood elf said.

'You could have got more of them if you'd given me one of your crossbows,' moaned the weaselly thief Ferricks. He was sitting on a large rock, idly drawing in the dirt with a twig. 'After all, I have proved that you can trust me. I'd have nothing to gain by betraying you at this point.'

Brunner considered the thief. 'I feel better knowing that I don't have to keep an eye on you,' he declared.

'Do you still need the trees?' gasped the illusionist Mahlinbois. Sweat dripped from his brow, and his breathing was laboured. For nearly half an hour Mahlinbois had maintained the illusory woods, concealing the bounty hunter and his companions – ever since Lithelain had reported riders emerging from the tower. The phantom trees had seemed real enough to anyone gazing upon them from a distance of ten or more feet away, but within the area of the illusion, the trees had been nothing more than a slight, shadowy mist-like apparition, offering only the slightest impediment to the vision of the bounty hunter and his comrades.

'No, your sorcery has served its purpose,' Brunner said. Mahlinbois sighed, closed his eyes, and snapped the small branch he had held in his right hand to focus the illusion. The phantom trees dissipated like mist rising off a morning lake.

'I am no sorcerer,' Mahlinbois snapped. 'How many times must I remind you of the fact? I am no equal to a sorcerer!'

'We'll find out, won't we?' Brunner said, his voice colder than usual. The illusionist drew back, words of protest dying on his lips. The bounty hunter stalked over to where Ehrhard Stoecker stood, holding the reins of the company's horses. He advanced upon Paychest, removing a long black cloak from a leather bag at the side of the animal. As he turned to walk away, the bounty hunter caught the sullen look with which the writer stared at him. He turned on the man, staring into Stoecker's disapproving face.

'Something bothering you?' the bounty hunter demanded.

'You knew they were coming,' Stoecker stated. 'Even before Lithelain saw them, you knew they were coming. I have to wonder, how did you know? And where have Sir Lutriel and Josef gone?'

'You ask too many questions,' the bounty hunter grumbled, starting to walk away. Stoecker reached out, grabbing the bounty hunter's shoulder turning him back around. He did not flinch as he saw Brunner's hand close about the dragon-hilt of his sword.

'You used them,' the writer accused. 'You knew they would go off on their own, try to beat you to your precious bounty and get captured.' A sudden thought brought an angry hue to Stoecker's face. 'You've been using that boy all along! You've never cared in the slightest about his quest to avenge his father! At least Lithelain is seeking justice for his sister. You're just trying to line your own pockets. Tell me, if Sir Lutriel hadn't come with us, would you have sent the boy on his own to lure out the riders?'

'Maybe I would have sent you with him,' the bounty hunter answered. He left Stoecker, walking back toward Lithelain, the long black cloak in his hands.

SIR LUTRIEL RETREATED from the opening gate, the smug defiance falling from him as his eyes began to appreciate the massive shape moving in the shadowy chamber beyond. Slowly, the form emerged into the light. First came a sharp, black beak of bone. Behind the black beak came a massive head, clothed in dark brown feathers and edged in white. The feathers were caked in filth and blood. The bird-like head turned from side to side, in a monotonous, idiot motion. Open holes of scarred flesh marked where the beast's eyes had once stared from the avian skull.

Two powerful, feathered legs stepped from the shadows onto the sandy floor. Six-inch claws of sharp black tipped each digit upon the foot. The body moved forward, exposing a powerful chest that was also covered in feathers, where it was not marked by welts and scars. Two raw, disgusting growths sprouted from the shoulders above the forelegs, the plucked remains of once mighty wings.

The idiot motion of the creature's head stopped abruptly as it caught the scent of the knight. The griffon uttered a sharp, shrieking roar and stumbled the rest of the way into the pit. The rear quarters of the beast were covered in a yellowish fur, where they had not been branded and scarred. The lean, lanky body was like a leopard, the ribs pushing the feline skin from within. Great dewclaws tipped each talon of the rear legs, but the long feline tail had been cropped, worn down by a jagged cut to a small stump. Even in its mangy, tortured state, however, the maimed griffon was an impressive sight. Fifteen feet long, and six feet at the shoulder, it was still a magnificent and terrible creature.

The Black Prince laughed as the griffon shrieked again. 'Don't you wish you had your knife now?' he hissed at the frightened knight.

The griffon hobbled forward, one of its rear legs displaying a debilitating break that had never healed properly. The blind head snapped forward, the beak shutting with a sharp crack. Sir Lutriel knew that it would take a single bite from those jaws to rip an arm from his body.

The knight began to slowly move around the edge of the fighting pit. There was no plan of attack. Even the possibility of retreating into the monster's den was denied as the bandits lowered the portcullis once more. The knight merely hoped to win as many more minutes of life as his agility and strength might allow.

The griffon shrieked once more, a sound that was echoed by the wasted gurgle of its famished belly. The beast lunged forward, and only a last moment dive saved Sir Lutriel his life. The griffon, still smelling its adversary, lashed out with its forefoot, scraping its claws along the stone wall, leaving a series of deep scratches in the rock. Realising its error, and with surprising quickness, the monster turned, its blind head bobbing about for a moment before scenting the knight again. Once again, the claws just missed the knight as he dodged aside.

From above, Josef watched the uneven contest with open horror. There could be no doubt as to the outcome of this contest. It was like baiting a bear with terriers. The laughter of the Black Prince's men as they watched the pathetic display sickened the boy, and gnawed at his soul. He turned his eyes once more to the figure of the dark elf on the throne. Somehow, some way, by Sigmar and all the gods of the Empire, he would kill this gloating fiend.

FROM HIS POSITION atop the tower, the goat-headed brute watched the small group of riders slowly approach the tower. He had spied them some time ago, but he was still trying to decide exactly who they were. The black-cloaked leader might be the departed dark elf lieutenant, Drannach or Uraithen, the beastman never could tell the two apart. There were fewer riders than there had been before, and the monster was certain that some of them were not men who had left the tower with the elf. The monster considered alerting his master, but the thought seemed somehow elusive. As soon as it occurred to him, it slipped away. No, he decided, best to make certain who was approaching the tower before bothering the Black Prince. The beastman grunted as he thought about that. It was almost as if it was not his own thought, but the idea of someone else.

The brute stared down at the riders. The leader certainly looked like Uraithen, or Drannach, but then again, he didn't… He should alert his master. Or not… The beast-man shook his head, trying to clear the muddle of thoughts rattling about in his thick skull. He reached over, pulling the chain that would lift the gate from the entrance down below. If the elf had to wait to gain entry to the stronghold, he would receive a beating. But was he certain that it was the dark elf? The monster grunted once more in confusion, bashing a fist against his horned head to try and force his thoughts into some semblance of order.

One of the riders, a tall human wearing a black helmet, pulled a small device from behind his back. A steel bolt shot upwards from the small crossbow, smashing through the beastman's eye. The brute fell from the balcony, strik-ing the ground without a scream.

'Nice shot,' Lithelain congratulated Brunner. 'Especially with such a clumsy weapon.' The elf cast the cloak from his shoulders, and handed it back to the bounty hunter.

'Remember, he is mine,' the wood elf warned.

'You can have everything but his head,' Brunner responded, reloading his weapon, nudging his horse toward the open gate.

The party slowly made their way past the entrance, eyes alert for any sign of other guards. Last of all came the illusionist, Mahlinbois, who was wiping away the tarry residue from the small gunpowder-laced candle he had used to disorder the beastman's mind. The magician was discomfited by the ease of their entrance to the tower. The Black Prince was a master of sorcery, so it was said. Mahlinbois appreciated that magic of any sort thrived upon misdirection and confusion. Were they the hunters, or were they the prey? Were they walking into the Black Prince's lair, or were they walking into his trap?

Once again, the illusionist cursed the day he had ever set eyes upon Brunner. There was an aura of invincibility about the man, but Mahlinbois knew only too well that such protection would not extend to himself, or any of the bounty hunter's allies. Indeed, he knew that to Brunner's way of thinking, they were all expendable, just like the boy and the gaoler.

THE WATCHING BRIGANDS hooted with laughter as Sir Lutriel again narrowly escaped the lunge of the crippled griffon. The monster's neck craned about as the man dived away, the beak snapping inches from the knight's back. Sir Lutriel's body was caked in sweat and sand, his breathing heavy. The effort of avoiding the lethal talons and jaws of the griffon was telling on him. Fatigue clutched at him with a suffocating grasp that would kill him if he succumbed to it. The knight doubled over and gulped air into his lungs while keeping a frightened watch on the hulking shape of the monster.

The griffon too was suffering from the speed and nimbleness of its prey, its movements becoming slower and more clumsy as it lunged and leaped about the arena, trying to fill its starving frame with the fresh meat it could smell just beyond its reach. The harder it tried to fill its belly, the more impossible the task became. As the griffon ran towards the knight, flapping the plucked stumps above its shoulders in a sorry reminder of when they had been wings, it stumbled, landed heavily on its belly, one of its legs twisting beneath it. The monster raised its head, as if to cry out in pain, but sound was beyond its infirmity. As the blind eagle-head turned about, it happened to face toward the knight as he gathered his strength. The griffon stumbled back onto its feet, taunted by the nearness of the man's scent. With hobbling, awkward steps, the blind monster walked toward Sir Lutriel.

On the dais the Black Prince extended his hand. Without a glance or a word from his master, Drannach placed the knife the knight had discarded into the Black Prince's outstretched hand. The mailed fingers closed about the hilt.

'This has become tedious,' the Black Prince stated, his voice dripping with scorn. With a quick, blinding move, the elf lifted his hand and hurled the knife down into the arena. The blade sank into the meat of the Bretonnian's leg. The knight crumpled, his voice opening in a scream that was born more of terror than of pain. The griffon, only five steps from him now, suddenly went mad as the smell of blood reached it. It reared up on its hind legs, and emitted a deep clacking roar that was like the scream of a hawk and the bellow of a bull.

Sir Lutriel tried to leap to the side as the monster barrelled straight toward him, but his injured leg gave out. He crumpled to the floor of the pit and began to crawl away, but it was too late. His agility was gone now, while the griffon, driven berserk by the smell of blood and the gnawing hunger that wracked its frame, had found a new strength.

The beast fell upon the knight like an avalanche. One of the paws smashed into Sir Lutriel's back like a dwarf steam-hammer, pulverising his pelvis and spine. The black talons sank deep into the flesh and bone. Even as a bloody cry of agony bubbled from the Bretonnian's lips, the powerful neck of the griffon craned downwards and the beak closed about his head. The jaws closed with a snap, and the knight was instantly decapitated. The griffon raised its head, swallowing Sir Lutriel's head whole. Then the gore-stained beak descended once more, tearing bloody goblets of flesh from the mangled body beneath its paw.

'Mongrel cur!' roared Josef, lunging at the seated noble, the chain about his neck arresting him so that his clawing fingers were just unable to reach the Black Prince. 'He didn't have a chance!' the youth accused.

'I know,' said the elf, his melodious voice rising above the coarse merriment of the bandits despite its softness. 'But that spectacle was becoming uninteresting. I shall have to think of something more special for you.' The dark elf's armoured visage stared down at Josef, and he cringed away from the merciless cruelty in those almond-shaped eyes. Then the Black Prince stared at the farther end of the hall. A cry of alarm sounded from one of the bandits near the southern extremity of the chamber, a cry that trailed off into a scream.

BRUNNER LET THE arming mechanism of his repeating crossbow pistol load a second bolt, and took aim once again. Not for the first time, he considered the weapon a fair exchange for the gold the skaven had cheated him of. At his side, Lithelain held his bow at the ready. Stoecker gripped his sword with a steady look of determination, while Ferricks licked his lips as he fingered the small sword the bounty hunter had given him. His eyes darted from one side to another, looking for some avenue that would take him away from the bounty hunter and the armed brigands that now faced them. Behind all of the men, the illusionist Mahlinbois readied another of his curious firework-candles. Only the sweat beading on his forehead betrayed the calm, concentrated effort the magician put into his work.

Before them, the long chamber was filled with the followers of the Black Prince. Thirty armoured brigands
stared in a mixture of surprise and outrage as the man
Brunner had shot writhed on the floor, clutching at the
bolt buried in his belly. The lows and grunts of the beastmen added to the snarls of the bandits. Men began to draw
their swords, a few scrambled toward the walls of the
chamber to pluck spears and halberds from ornamental
brackets set into the stonework. On the dais, the armoured
figures of the Black Prince and his lieutenant glared at the
intruders.

'Kill them,' the Black Prince commanded. 'Kill them all.'
He gestured with his hand, stabbing a clawlike finger at
Brunner. The bandit throng roared and surged forward.
Even as the first men began to move, the bounty hunter
fired. The bolt sped across the hall, smashing into the
breastplate of the bandit lord. The Black Prince staggered
for a moment, then turned, glaring at the bounty hunter, a
dent marring his engraved breastplate. Brunner did not
have time to send another shot at the dark elf, for the
oncoming bandits demanded his attention more.

'You have a sorry notion of a fair fight,' complained
Mahlinbois, still fiddling with his magical implements.
The illusionist risked a look up, seeing three more bandits
lying on the floor: two with the feathered shafts of the
wood elf nestled in their bodies, a third with a bolt
between the eyes.

'Then do something to balance matters,' snarled
Brunner, firing the last bolt into a mangy-pelted beastman
that was nearly upon him. The monster staggered away,
mewling as it pawed at the spike of metal jutting from its
cheek. Brunner spared the monster not a second thought,
and drew Drakesmalice from its sheath in a flash of steel.
Beside him, Lithelain sent a final arrow speeding into
another bandit, then tossed his bow aside, drawing his
own sword.

The Black Prince watched for a moment as his minions
crashed into the flashing steel of the bounty hunter and his

allies. He could hear the sounds of conflict, howls of pain and cries of triumph as men matched swords. He had seen its like often before. But he had not expected it this day. The bounty hunter should never have gotten so far, not with the precautions that had been taken. The dark elf smiled beneath his armour. Of course, he had been betrayed. How could he have been so stupid? He had been reared on treachery and double-dealing, it was in his blood. How could he not see it when it stared him in the face? But he would know how to deal with his betrayer.

'This battle vexes me,' the Black Prince said, his tone redolent with boredom. Drannach looked up at him, a puzzled look marring his fine features. 'Attend to this,' the noble declared, stepping down from the dais, the silk robe swirling about him. The Black Prince strode the short distance to the door, disappearing into the dark corridor beyond. The lieutenant watched him go, then drew his sword, stalking away from the dais and toward the knot of fighting men.

Left alone on the dais, Josef struggled against the iron chain that held him. As he struggled, his eyes turned to the open doorway. The sight of the corridor down which his father's killer had gone let a new strength, an energy of pure hate, fill him. The young merchant tore at the spiked collar, his hands becoming raw and bloody as the spikes bit into his flesh. But despite his determination, the metal held fast.

BRUNNER'S SWORD LASHED out once more, clipping a bandit's hand. The man fell back, cursing, then screamed as he stared at the red stumps of his fingers. Brunner had no more time to consider the man, however, for other opponents were filling the space left by the maimed man. At his side, Lithelain was keeping seven enemies on their guard, the elf's astounding speed confounding their best attempts to surround and butcher him. But the elf was doing no more than holding his foes at bay. He was unable to do more than deflect their steel, lest he expose himself to another's blade by extending his reach too far. A gash in the elf's side told of where one halberd-armed bandit had been able to momentarily defy the intercepting curtain of flashing steel, but no other had been able to match that feat. The weapon he had wielded lay upon the stone floor, cut in two by the elf's vengeful return.

Perhaps realising that they were almost inconsequential, Stoecker and Ferricks found themselves faced by only a few of the bandits. Even so, the two men were far from experts with the sword, and were hard pressed to preserve their lives. The writer kept his back against the wall, knocking back the swords of the two bandits who faced him. He was trying to recall the time he had spent in the company of a Reiksguard fencing tutor, to slip back into half-remembered patterns of feint, parry and thrust.

The wiry Ferricks, a steady deluge of pleading and begging slithering from his tongue, kept worming around the steel of the men vainly trying to kill their former comrade. Despite his whining pleas, the thief was not averse to striking back, stabbing one through the knee when the brigand's lunge carried him too far forward, slicing another along the side when he wormed his wiry body around the man's sword.

From the pit, the roars and bellows of the griffon rose as the sounds of violence and the smell of blood drifted down to the creature. The monster's cries provided a sinister accompaniment to the battle, and nearly all the combatants paused when the sounds suddenly stopped.

The great brown-and-yellow shape of the griffon lunged upwards from the pit, tearing two of the jutting fangs of steel from the stone-work, one of them digging deep into its shoulder. The monster's hind legs scrabbled at the edge of the pit for a moment, gaining purchase, then it propelled itself upward. The plucked stumps of the creature's wings beat furiously as it stepped forward. The bandits drew away to look in horror at the huge bestial shape that had leapt into their midst. The griffon's blind head rolled from side to side for a moment, then the beaked maw opened once more, uttering a loud, frenzied shriek.

The griffon leapt forward, pinning an ape-like beastman beneath its mass, and crushing its ribcage with a loud crack. The griffon's jaws snapped around, slashing through the armour and collarbone of another bandit, and dropping him in a screaming pile of wreckage.

As the bandits scrambled to attack this new and unexpected adversary, Brunner gave voice to a cry of his own. Two bandits found the bounty hunter's steel in them before they remembered their original opponents. At his side, Lithelain pressed his attack, racing through the men who had held him at bay, sweeping his sword in a blur of motion that none of the brigands could individually counter.

The bounty hunter watched the elf's actions with some misgiving. Lithelain was not seeking to finish off his enemies – he left many of them with only painful scratches or disarmed. The elf was only trying to make his way past the men, towards the door at the far end of the hall. Brunner brutally smashed the dragon-hilt of his sword into the nose of his current enemy, splattering the man's face with his own blood. As the man clutched at his disfigured face, the bounty hunter kicked his groin with his steel-toed boot. The bandit doubled over and Brunner flung him aside, over the lip of the fighting pit.

A shriek and a satisfying liquid impact carried up from the arena.

Beyond the edge of the battle, Mahlinbois watched as the griffon wreaked havoc among the bandits. The huge monster was bleeding from dozens of wounds, not the least of which being the great tear in its shoulder where the spike had bitten into the beast's flesh. But the frenzied monster seemed not to even notice the many injuries that had befallen it. It was a berserk engine of death now; already seven mutilated bodies lay strewn about it, where its claws and snapping jaws had done their work. Only death would stop it now.

Perhaps, in some way, the monster was exacting its own brand of vengeance against the Black Prince for the suffering that had been inflicted upon it. The illusionist smiled, snuffing the candle out with his finger. There was no need to concentrate further: in its current state, the griffon was beyond any of his mind-tricks. He had employed his craft to convince the creature to forget the crippling injuries done to its wings, to convince it that its feathery body was whole once more. So simple a mind, it was easy to disorder the past. The griffon had recalled the time when it had soared high above the Grey Mountains, when it had dived from the heights to fall upon prey its keen gaze had found far below. Convinced that it could fly once more, the griffon had lunged upwards, towards the sounds of battle, the smell of blood; its conviction drove it with a strength that its captors had believed beyond its tortured form.

The illusionist considered the battle at large. Stoecker, the writer, was matching swords with a single bandit now, and gaining the better of the man. Able to concentrate his attention on one man, Stoecker was proving himself a capable swordsman.

Ferricks was nowhere to be seen, though Mahlinbois could see one of the men the thief had been fighting lying on the floor with a deep gash in his belly. The magician's gaze followed the battle back to the griffon. He watched as Lithelain made his way past the hulking monster, ducking under the sweep of the beast's claws as he matched swords with another bandit. The elf spun about, catching the bandit's steel on his own. He twisted his hand and rolled the blade past the man's steel, ripping into his face. The injured bandit dropped, howling, and the sound was his undoing. As the bandit looked up from his mutilated face, the griffon's claw disembowelled him with a sweeping slash. But the wood elf was already beyond the beast.

Brunner had advanced around the flank of the griffon, carefully keeping his distance from the monster. He lashed out at another bandit, puncturing the man's lung with the point of his blade, then hurled the injured man into the pit to join his comrade. A slender fang of steel struck the edge of Drakesmalice, and the bounty hunter found himself staring into the inhumanly slender face of the dark elf lieutenant. The creature sneered at him.

'You shall regret coming here, animal,' Drannach spat. 'I shall carve every inch of your flesh before I allow you to die.'

The bounty hunter pushed the elf back, blocking his return with a hastily drawn knife. 'You're not worth a shilling to me,' the bounty hunter snarled. 'Step down, and I may let you live.' The man's words brought a look of outrage to the pale features of the elf and he lunged forward, catching the bounty hunter's knife on the projections on his vambraces. He turned the blade and broke it with a snap. Drakesmalice and the elf sword groaned as they slid across one another, as their wielders glared at one another from behind the crossed steel.

The dark elf suddenly twisted his blade, escaping the guard of the bounty hunter. Then he dropped low, sweeping his blade at the bounty hunter's legs, seeking a crippling blow. The sword slashed at Brunner's calf, but he dodged backwards just as Drannach made his attack. The bandit's steel scraped across the surface of Brunner's leg armour. Drannach hissed, lunged forward, then twisted his sword about at the last instant, turning the feint into a sidewise slash.

The sword cut into Brunner's shoulder guard, nearly penetrating the metal. The bounty hunter counterattacked, but found the elf's sword about to intercept his own. Taking a note from his foe, Brunner dropped low, letting the blade slide across the top of his helmet. The dark elf at once realised his exposure and brought his sword whisking downward to intercept any new attack.

Instead of lashing out at Drannach, Brunner thrust with his sword to his side and rear, slashing at the furred flank of the embattled griffon. The dark elf's eyes grew wide with fright as the monster turned about, snarling, ropes of gore dribbling from its claws and beak. The smug self-assurance of Drannach faded and the elf brought his sword up to block the talon-ridden paw that slashed out at him. The blade broke as the griffon's ponderous blow batted it aside. The paw smashed into the dark elf, throwing him across the hall and into the far side of the pit. Drannach's fall was arrested as his body struck the fangs of iron that framed the pit, the force of his impact impaling his body on the spikes. The minion of the Black Prince spat thin, greasy blood, then grew still. As life faded from his frame, his dead weight caused his body to slowly slide from the spikes and complete its descent to the sandy floor.

Brunner took advantage of the griffon's attack on the dark elf to dive under its legs, choosing the most dangerous, but most certain route away from the monster's snapping beak. A kettle-helm wearing bandit attacked him as he rolled clear of the monster, but the bounty hunter's left hand grasped a throwing knife as he completed his roll, and it was but the blinking of an eye before the bounty hunter had hurled the weapon deep into the bandit's chest. As the man sagged to the ground, two of his comrades closed on Brunner, while the rest of their number, led by the hulking beastman Urgmesh, desperately tried to stop the griffon's rampage.

LITHELAIN SKEWERED THE throat of the last bandit foolish enough to get in his way, and sprinted toward the open doorway. As he ran, a voice from the direction of the Black Prince's throne called to him. The elf hesitated, seeing Josef chained to the dais, his hands outstretched in a pleading gesture. The elf muttered a low curse and ran to the boy. He raised his sword as he reached Josef, then brought the edge against the taut length of chain with a swift and steady strike. The chain parted, the severed link flying off into the shadows. Lithelain nodded his head solemnly at the freed youth, then turned to continue his pursuit of the Black Prince. But no sooner had he turned, than a solid weight smashed into the back of his skull. The elf gasped, then slumped on the dais steps.

Josef let the length of chain he had coiled about his hands fall slack, and stooped, removing Lithelain's sword from his slackened grasp. Josef looked down at the stunned elf, his face a study in hate and determination.

'I'm sorry,' he said, 'but the bastard is mine.'

Firming his grasp on the curiously balanced sword, Josef jumped from the dais and ran into the dark corridor.

THE GRIFFON CONTINUED its onslaught, catching another spear-armed bandit and slashing the man in half with its claws. The bandit beside the butchered man gave a cry of terror, turning to flee. But he found his retreat blocked by a massive, shaggy form. Urgmesh ripped the halberd from the man's hands, then flung him aside.

In silence, the huge beastman closed upon the griffon, allowing the monster to be distracted by the war cries and screams of a cluster of human bandits who were trying to attack its flanks. The dog-headed brute lumbered forward, raising the halberd over his head, and watching as the griffon swung its own head from side to side, swiping with first one paw, then the other. With a snarl, the beastman attacked, letting the heavy axe-blade smash through the thick bone of the griffon's foreleg.

The griffon screeched in agony as the maimed limb hung limp and broken. It snapped at Urgmesh, but he had already withdrawn, growling for the human rabble to attack. A half-dozen swords and spears stabbed into the tortured creature's flesh. The griffon stumbled about, its movements slow and even more ungainly than before. Blood cascaded from the punctures along its body, drenching its fur and feathers with gluey red gore. The griffon's beak opened and a great bubble of blood burst from its stained beak.

Urgmesh snarled a new command, and a bandit who had kept himself from the fighting thus far advanced. He wore the colourful surcoat of a Bretonnian knight tied about his waist, and in his hands he held a wide-barrelled contraption of steel and wood. Alone among the bandit throng, he had come armed with more than sword and dirk. He was carrying his valuable blunderbuss more to guard it against the thieving inclinations of his comrades than any premonition of trouble. Now the brigand crouched and aimed the weapon at the wounded monster. A murderous smile split the man's coarse features as the blind head of the griffon swung in his direction once more. The man released the hammer of his firearm and the mouth of the blunderbuss spat a gout of smoke and flame. The griffon howled in agony as a hail of metal shrapnel tore through its face, digging pits into its skull. It reared onto its hind legs, roaring in fury and pain, then slumped onto its side, smashing a bandit beneath its dying bulk. The other bandits attacked the monster's body with a vengeance, stabbing it again and again.

Brunner watched the griffon fall, and uttered a curse on all the fickleness of all the gods of battle. He looked about the chamber. Stoecker was duelling with a lone bandit, a heavy-set lout with a wolfskin cap. Mahlinbois was fumbling in the leather satchel that held his implements, desperation now filling his face. Looking at the dais, the bounty hunter saw that Josef was gone. Ferricks and Lithelain were likewise nowhere to be seen. But there was no dearth of enemies: fully a dozen of the Black Prince's scum were still in condition to do battle. The bounty hunter cursed again, drew his pistol from its holster and prepared to meet the onslaught of the brigands.

Urgmesh roared, the sound bestial and triumphant. The beastman's misshapen head turned about the chamber, looking for another foe to slay. His eyes fell upon the dark haired man fencing with one of the bandits. The monster snarled again, eager to kill. Urgmesh rushed forward, charging past the rest of the brigands. He closed upon the embattled writer. The first sweep of the halberd nearly beheaded both men, as it swept above them, striking sparks from the stone wall. The bandit gave a yelp of fright, withdrawing from the hulking beastman's advance. Urgmesh ignored the rogue, his rage-filled eyes locked on Stoecker.

The writer adopted a defensive stance, not relishing his chances against the inhuman bruiser. The beastman snickered derisively as he saw the swordsman prepare himself, enjoying the sight before hurling his huge body at the writer. The halberd slashed downwards, only narrowly missing Stoecker's body as the writer forced the cleaving blade aside with the flat of his sword. The beastman grunted, then lashed out again. This time, the strength of the monster's blow pushed Stoecker back several steps, and he groaned with horror as he saw the deep notch the axe-head had made in the metal of his blade.

The first rule of swordplay, the writer recalled, was to keep all emotion from your blade. Fear, anger, could turn even the most skilled sword into the clumsy choppa of an orc. A swordsman who was in complete command of himself, who knew he would triumph over his foe, was more deadly than the most flamboyant Talabheim rake. Stoecker tried to cling to the half-remembered speech the fencing instructor had made, but with the hulking, stinking beastman inches from his face, its hot breath washing over him, he felt anything but calm.

At the very edge of the battlefield, Mahlinbois wrapped the length of musty grey cloth about the gunpowder candle. Muttering a prayer to Ranald the Trickster, the illusionist began his incantation. The cloth had been torn from the shroud of a reputed necromancer. Now the Bretonnian magician would discover if the man's deeds had indeed been as vile as rumour had coloured them.

Brunner closed upon the bandits, the shot from his pistol blasting apart the skull of his first enemy. He reversed his grip on the firearm, wielding its heavy butt like a mugger's sap. He met the attack of the men advancing upon him, smashing the sword from one man's hand with the pistol, crushing the bones of his fingers. Meanwhile he swept the edge of his blade through the knee of one of his companions.

The bounty hunter was under no illusion about his ability to overcome so many foes, but he was determined that he would give them such a reckoning before he fell that those who walked away from this fight would speak his name with fear all the rest of their days. As the men continued to slash at him, and as he found himself hard pressed to block their attacks, Brunner's eyes beheld the bandit with the blunderbuss reloading his weapon. There was a sneer on the rogue's face as he rose from his crouch, aiming the loaded weapon at the bounty hunter. Brunner cursed once more, realising that there was little chance of avoiding the weapon's blast. It might not kill him at this distance, but even a minor injury would leave him open to the swords of the blackguard's comrades. And the bounty hunter knew that the bandit would not hesitate to fire, even with his companions in the way.

Suddenly, the face of the gunner grew pale. The bandits facing Brunner grew similarly fearful, as they gazed in horror at the corpse of the griffon. The body was twitching, and rippling with motion. As the rogues watched, the skin spilt apart along the monster's back, like the rind of a melon under the attention of the hot Tilean sun.

From the tear in the beast's flesh, something gaunt and white emerged. First, a claw, then a long leg bone. From the corpse of the slain monster, its skeleton crawled forth, animated with some hideous mockery of life. The griffon's skull, pock-marked by the blast of the blunderbuss, swayed from side to side. Then the neck craned about, holding the skull rigid. The sightless sockets of the griffon's skull stared at the bandits with a soundless malevolence.

The bandit with the blunderbuss screamed, firing his weapon at the undead horror, heedless of the men before him. Three bandits squirmed away as the blunderbuss roared, two clutching at painful burns and gashes in their sides, a third writhing on the floor, clawing at the weeping back of his head. The skeleton was unmoved; the shot had only dug new pock-marks in the bones. The creature took a step forward, loping toward the brigands.

The silent advance of the skeletal abomination was too much for the men. Screaming, the gunner dropped his treasured blunderbuss and ran from the chamber. Those of his comrades who were able to, followed as best they could, injured men forcing maimed legs to work despite their wounds. Brunner watched the men flee, casting a suspicious look at the skeletal horror looming at his side. A smile flickered on his face.

STOECKER BATTED THE cleaving blade of the monster aside again, feeling the jarring impact rattle his very bones. Urgmesh grunted, showing his fangs. The beastman would rip the meat from this one's bones for making him work so hard to kill him. The writer's sword was notched and ruined, his strength was failing, and his movements slowing. He would not last much longer. But every second he denied the kill to Urgmesh was an insult to the brute. He felt the old man-hate, the fury the Black Prince had taught him to quell, welling up within him once more. The beastman reared his head back, and uttered a deep lowing roar. He recalled the howls of devotion to the Dark Gods he had uttered long ago at the sacred herdstones of his kind. He saw a satisfying look of terror on the face of the frustrating little man, and knew that it was good that the man should know fear. It would make his flesh taste all the sweeter.

It was the last thing Urgmesh saw. A heavy mass of steel and wood crashed against his head, smashing in the side of his skull, bashing his head against the stone wall crumpling it, as it impacted with the hard wall. The beastman sank to his knees, sliding down the wall, leaving a gory slick behind as he fell. Brunner took no chances, however. He lifted the blunderbuss over his head with both hands and brought it crashing down into the beastman's skull once more, snapping his neck. The bounty hunter looked away from the foul corpse, and stared at the writer.

'Happy you came along now?' the bounty hunter asked. 'Not quite like one of your stories, is it?'

Stoecker offered no reply, staring in horror at the skeletal thing that had emerged from the corpse of the griffon. The writer pointed a trembling finger at the apparition.

Brunner followed the extended finger, chuckling as he saw the source of Stoecker's terror.

'I think you can cease your conjuring,' the bounty hunter said. Almost at once, the skeletal thing disappeared. Where it had been, the corpse of the griffon still sat, unchanged from its moment of death.

'I do not believe I could have maintained the illusion much longer in any event,' Mahlinbois gasped as he walked toward Brunner and Stoecker. His step was shaky, his limbs trembling with their effort to maintain enough strength to keep him on his feet. Sweat fell from the magician's pale face.

'You did well enough,' the bounty hunter said, handing him the battered blunderbuss. Brunner turned, striding toward the doorway near the abandoned dais.

'Where are you going?' the illusionist and the writer said almost simultaneously.

'After my money,' the bounty hunter answered.

'But what if they come back?' asked a frightened and outraged Mahlinbois.

'Threaten them with that,' Brunner replied, pointing at the blunderbuss.

'But it isn't loaded!' complained the magician.

'Convince them it is,' commented the bounty hunter, striding into the shadowy corridor.

THE BLACK PRINCE stood in his throne room, crouched above the teakwood box. He burned with fury. He saw the shape of things now, saw how he had been betrayed, and led to the edge of ruin and death by deception and trickery. But he would set matters right. He would get his revenge. The dark elf threw open the teakwood box, then stepped back.

Empty. It was empty! A cold, lethal fury gripped the Black Prince as he looked at the cushioned vacancy of the chest. He was still staring at the empty box when, with an almost casual move, he intercepted the sword that sang through the air, whirling towards his neck, catching the

blade on the spines on his vambrace. His armoured face
turned about. Cruel eyes stared at Josef as the Black Prince
closed the steel glove of his free hand about the blade of
the stolen sword. The Black Prince tore the weapon from
Josef's fingers, casting it aside like a piece of garbage, then
he backhanded the boy with his other hand. Josef landed
in a jumble of limbs, his lip split and bleeding. The Black
prince rose from his crouch, hand almost casually falling
upon the pommels of the twin swords sheathed at his
side.

'I am not in a fair humour,' the elf's melodious voice
stated. 'Curse whatever gods you hold dear that you are the
first to find me in such a mood.' The elf drew one of the
thorn-bladed swords from its sheath. Josef spat blood
from his lip at the monster's feet.

'You killed my father!' the boy snarled. The elf stood
immobile for a moment, as though taken aback by Josef's
outburst. Then the disarming sound of the fiend's laughter
echoed through the chamber.

'And you are ungrateful enough to curse me for such a
boon?' the Black Prince shook his masked head. 'You
should thank me for preserving you from the lies and
machinations of your elder. Only with the passing of the
father can a son truly become all that he is destined to
become, only then can he emerge from the shadow that
hovers above him.' The elf laughed again, noting the
enraged fire in Josef's eyes. 'But this is something I myself
did not learn until this very hour, and you are but vermin
and will find no value in the truth.' The Black Prince
stepped toward Josef, watching as the boy scrambled away,
crawling before him like a mouse scurrying before a cat.
The elf lifted his sword, preparing to stab the steel downward into Josef's body.

'Face me if there is a drop of courage in your craven carcass!' a soft, yet thunderous voice called out. The Black
Prince hesitated, then turned his body, so that he might
keep one eye on the vengeful youth, and another trained
upon the challenging voice.

'You shall atone for your misdeeds, monster!' declared Lithelain, stooping to retrieve his sword from where the dark elf had thrown it. The wood elf extended the blade, pointing it at the Black Prince. The dark elf bowed with mock graciousness, stepping toward Lithelain.

'Ah, a more worthy adversary presents himself,' the dark elf declared. The Black Prince held his sword against his side, drawing the second blade from its sheath, gripping it by the point where blade and hilt met. Lifting the blade, out to one side, the Black Prince made as if to discard the weapon. But just as he began to toss the weapon aside, he reversed his hold upon it, hurling it like a spear at the wood elf. The thorn-bladed sword nicked the side of Lithelain's leg, cutting through his leather breeches.

'So, you are one of those filthy tree-dwelling aborigines,' the Black Prince stated as Lithelain recovered from the unexpected injury. The wood elf swung at the gloating fiend, but the Black Prince's sword easily caught Lithelain's blade, and turned it back with a slight push. 'No Druchii would have fallen for so obvious a deception. But why should I expect cunning from one whose kind could not even outwit those disgusting dwarfs?' The Black Prince sneered, lashing out with his sword. He met Lithelain's intercepting steel, twisted about it, and slashed the elf's shoulder.

'This would already be over if we fought in Naggaroth,' the Black Prince's voice laughed. 'They duel with envenomed blades there.' The Black Prince struck out again, feinting high, then lunging forward, catching the arm that held Lithelain's sword with his own free arm. He pulled the wood elf's body in close and slashed his belly with the fighting spines of his vambrace, while he dug the thornlike projections of his sword's pommel into the wood elf's back. The dark elf released his foe, spinning about as he backed away to again intercept the wood elf's steel.

'But one must make concessions for savages,' the Black Prince said. 'Otherwise there is no sport in butchering one of your kind.' The Black Prince lashed out again, Lithelain parrying the fiend's blow aside. Turning his body, the wood elf avoided the fighting spines of the dark elf's other arm. The wood elf smashed the hilt of his parried sword into the reflective visor of his enemy. The dark elf staggered back.

'You shall pay for every drop of blood you have spilled,' the wood elf swore, attacking once more. The Black Prince intercepted the avenger's sword, catching it between his vambrace and sword.

'Shall I?' the dark elf sneered. 'Then I must have run up quite a debt.' The Black Prince surged upwards, throwing the wood elf aside. The dark elf's sword flickered toward Lithelain, barely intercepted as the fighter recovered. 'But do you think that you shall be the one to collect it?'

Lithelain spun his body about, sweeping his sword in a low arc. The Black Prince leapt above the striking blade, thrusting his own sword through the wood elf's breast. The Black Prince pushed his body forward, digging the steel deeper into Lithelain's chest. The wood elf gasped, fighting for breath, his eyes widening with rage and disbelief.

'This has been utterly boring,' the Black Prince declared, his face only inches from the dying elf's face. He twisted the blade about in the wound, bringing a fresh spasm of agony to the gasping elf's features. 'There are people I must find, and kill,' the Black Prince stated. He tore the sword from Lithelain's body, and a great flood of blood bubbled from the triangular cut. Lithelain dropped, his fading eyes locked on the figure of the Black Prince.

'Don't worry, your bones will feed the crows and your memory will become a jest told to your children when I tire of making them scream.' The Black Prince stepped away, his foot sliding beneath the naked steel of the wood elf's sword. The dark elf worked his toe under the blade and flicked it across the chamber once more. The sword clattered across the floor to where a horrified Josef had watched the swift, brutal fight. The boy reached toward the sword.

'I hope you were paying attention,' the Black Prince's musical voice said as he strode away from Lithelain's corpse. 'I expect better from you.' The dark elf walked toward the boy, sword held at his side. 'Though I doubt that I shall receive it.'

A roar and crack thundered through the Black Prince's throne room. The dread figure of the bandit lord shuddered as a red mist burst from his chest. The sword fell from suddenly lax fingers. A shaking hand rose to the wound that marked the very centre of the Black Prince's chest. The mailed hands probed the aperture, coming away and rising before the reflective face-plate. The eyes behind the metal mask stared in wonder and disbelief at the crimson staining the metal fingers. The Black Prince turned, falling to his knees as the strength failed in his legs. With an effort, he looked up as his killer walked toward him.

'Sorry,' the icy voice of the bounty hunter reached the Black Prince's ears, 'I was getting bored myself.'

Brunner returned the smoking pistol to its holster and strode forward. The Black Prince coughed within his helm, red liquid seeping from the joins of his visor and gorget. 'And there are people waiting for me, and that ugly head of yours.'

The Black Prince slumped forward, his death rattle gargling in his throat.

Brunner watched the dark elf expire, then fingered the grip of the long-bladed knife he morbidly termed The Headsman. Before beginning his macabre task, the bounty hunter looked up at Josef.

'I could have let you have your chance at him,' the bounty hunter said. 'But somehow, I don't think you'd have liked that.' Josef nodded his head, a surly look of guilt and anger mixing with profound satisfaction on his face.

'Now come over here and help me get this bastard's armour off,' Brunner called out. 'I want to make a good cut. After all, it has to be pretty enough for a king.'

EHRHARD STOECKER SAT his battered body down in the chair, casting a furtive look around the bar of the inn. There was no sign of Yvette, however. The woman had been rather upset at him when he had returned to Parravon, after leaving for weeks with no warning, and she had used more than words to express her ire. She had been most unwilling to listen to his explanations. Even the gold he had brought back with him had done nothing to assuage her anger when she had discovered the bruises the writer had earned in his brief combat with the beastman.

Stoecker sighed and sipped his wine. His share of the Black Prince's booty had amounted to more than a few hundred gold pieces, a tidy fortune before the duc's tax men had decided what their portion should be. Perhaps he should have gone with Mahlinbois and Josef after all, and returned to the Empire. But, no, there were too many reasons for him to stay as far from Altdorf as he could. He recalled only too well the old Imperial proverb that all roads led to the Emperor's city.

Once again, Stoecker found himself lamenting the fortune that must have once been hidden within the Black Prince's vaults. But the fleeing brigands had had a considerable headstart, and they had known where to search. The bandits had further benefited from the skills of the thief Ferricks, who, having excused himself from the battle, had slunk down to the treasure rooms, disarming the many cunning devices set to protect them. All except the last one. Stoecker didn't think he had ever seen a more surprised look that the one on Ferrick's corpse when they found him stuck to the wall by a spring-launched javelin.

They had split what the bandits hadn't taken – at least he, Mahlinbois and Josef had. Brunner had angrily stated that he worked for his money, and wanted no part of the plundering. Stoecker had thought the bounty hunter foolish, but, as it turned out, the price on the Black Prince's head had far exceeded what they could loot from his tower. After they had parted company with Mahlinbois and Josef, Stoecker had suggested to Brunner that he might split the bounty. The bounty hunter had laughed, responding that he never asked Stoecker for any portion of what he earned from the lies he wrote about the killer.

Stoecker shook his head, wondering where the fearsome warrior was now. He cast an eye at the door of the inn. He laughed to himself and sipped at his wine. It did not matter where Brunner was. Sooner or later, the writer was certain, he would again walk through that door. Stoecker had never been more certain of anything in his entire life. And strangely enough, he found himself eagerly anticipating that meeting, found himself wanting to hear about every treacherous, ruthless step of the bounty hunter's travels.

A SHAPE SHROUDED in black moved through the darkened chamber, disturbing the flies that buzzed about the headless corpse rotting on the floor. The shape did not pay the corpse a second thought, but moved toward the dais. It looked over at a smashed teakwood box and smiled beneath its hood. Then it climbed the steps to the throne-like chair. A slender, pale hand caressed the armrest, sliding its fingers along the length of the wood until there was a click. The hand reached into the hinged opening of the seat, removing the silk-wrapped object within. The apparition's eyes glittered as they stared at the Eye of Tchar. The slender hands drew the gem back to the cloaked body, and the magical scrying stone disappeared in one of the pouches on the figure's belt.

The shadow turned away from the throne, stopping this time beside the headless corpse. The black-garbed shape bent down, and lifted the discarded helmet from the floor. The face under the hood smiled as it considered the helm. It almost dropped the piece of armour, but a stray thought caused it to tuck the helmet with its reflective visor beneath its arm.

All had unfolded just as the Eye of Tchar had shown him. News of Dralaith's death would reach Naggaroth. There would be no more assassins, for he knew that one day, one of their number would succeed and all his plans would come to ruin. He had sacrificed much to accomplish the deception, but gold was trash, easily collected by

one of his skill and intelligence. His followers were likewise trash, and easily replaced. He cast another look at the
headless corpse of Uraithen. It was not the first time he
had cause to allow one of his lieutenants to momentarily
assume his guise as the Black Prince. But it would certainly
be the last. It was no matter, the two departed elves were
nothing but mongrel half-breeds sired upon a filthy abo-
rigine. No true Druchii would ever have allowed
themselves to be so easily deceived. In death, his sons had
proven how pathetic and unworthy of his blood they truly
were. Dralaith spat on the floor, a gesture denoting the
contempt he felt for the spirits of such worthless beings.

Only one thing disturbed him. It was the thought that
somewhere, a miserable human was walking the earth,
boasting that he had killed the Black Prince. Indeed, he
very nearly had. The dark elf had nearly fallen to his death
when his horse had toppled over the precipice, and it had
taken him several hours to climb up from the chasm. It
alarmed him somewhat that the Eye had not shown him
that particular event. Once more, Dralaith pondered the
Norse shaman's laughter.

A most vexing thought, the dark elf mused as he left his
throne room for the last time, and walked the empty halls
of the abandoned elf tower. It was an itch that would have
to be scratched – one day.

ABOUT THE AUTHOR

C. L. Werner has written a number of Lovecraftian pastiches and pulp-style horror stories for assorted small press publications. More recently the prestigious pages of *Inferno!* have been infiltrated by the dark imaginings of the writer's mind.

Currently living in the American south-west, he continues to write stories of mayhem and madness in the Warhammer World.

More Warhammer from the Black Library

The Gotrek & Felix novels
by William King

THE DWARF TROLLSLAYER *Gotrek Gurnisson and his long-suffering human companion Felix Jaeger are arguably the most infamous heroes of the Warhammer World. Follow their exploits in these novels from the Black Library.*

TROLLSLAYER

TROLLSLAYER IS THE first part of the death saga of Gotrek Gurnisson, as retold by his travelling companion Felix Jaeger. Set in the darkly gothic world of Warhammer, TROLLSLAYER is an episodic novel featuring some of the most extraordinary adventures of this deadly pair of heroes. Monsters, daemons, sorcerers, mutants, orcs, beastmen and worse are to be found as Gotrek strives to achieve a noble death in battle. Felix, of course, only has to survive to tell the tale.

SKAVENSLAYER

THE SECOND GOTREK and Felix adventure – SKAVENSLAYER – is set in the mighty city of Nuln. Seeking to undermine the very fabric of the Empire with their arcane warp-sorcery, the skaven, twisted Chaos rat-men, are at large in the reeking sewers beneath the ancient city. Led by Grey Seer Thanquol, the servants of the Horned Rat are determined to overthrow this bastion of humanity. Against such forces, what possible threat can just two hard-bitten adventurers pose?

DAEMONSLAYER

FOLLOWING THEIR adventures in Nuln, Gotrek and Felix join
an expedition northwards in search of the long-lost dwarf
hall of Karag Dum. Setting forth for the hideous Realms of
Chaos in an experimental dwarf airship, Gotrek and Felix are
sworn to succeed or die in the attempt. But greater and more
sinister energies are coming into play, as a daemonic power
is awoken to fulfil its ancient, deadly promise.

DRAGONSLAYER

IN THE FOURTH instalment in the death-seeking saga of
Gotrek and Felix, the fearless duo find themselves pursued
by the insidious and ruthless skaven-lord, Grey Seer
Thanquol. DRAGONSLAYER sees the fearless Slayer and his
sworn companion back aboard an arcane dwarf airship in a
search for a golden hoard – and its deadly guardian.

BEASTSLAYER

STORM CLOUDS GATHER around the icy city of Praag as the foul
hordes of Chaos lay ruinous siege to northern lands of
Kislev. Will the presence of Gotrek and Felix be enough to
prevent this ancient city from being overwhelmed by the
massed forces of Chaos and their fearsome leader, Arek
Daemonclaw?

VAMPIRESLAYER

AS THE FORCES of Chaos gather in the north to threaten the
Old World, the Slayer Gotrek and his companion Felix are
beset by a new, terrible foe. An evil is forming in darkest
Sylvania which threatens to reach out and tear the heart
from our band of intrepid heroes. The gripping saga of
Gotrek & Felix continues in this epic tale of deadly battle
and soul-rending tragedy.

More Warhammer from the Black Library

THE STAR OF ERENGRAD
By Neil McIntosh

OTTO PAUSED, LOST in contemplation for a while. 'The question is,' he continued, 'are you ready to give your all to this struggle for Kislev? Ready, if necessary, to give your life?'

Stefan thought again of the map. In his mind it had become a map of darkness; a wash of black creeping across the face of mankind, slowly obliterating it. He shuddered, but it was a shudder born of anticipation as much as of unease. He had no doubt of what his answer must be.

'What is it that you need me to do?' he asked.

SWORD-FOR-HIRE *Stefan Kumansky is a lone warrior in a dark and dangerous world, driven to destroy the forces of evil wherever they may hide. Now his quest for vengeance has forced him to undertake a perilous journey to Erengrad, a frozen city under siege. Hunted by enemies both natural and daemonic, Stefan must face the greatest foe of his past before he can face an uncertain future of sweeping battle, deadly combat and sinister conspiracy.*

More Warhammer from the Black Library

THE DEAD
AND THE DAMNED
By Jonathan Green

TORBEN SWUNG HIS sword at the inhuman noble. The stroke opened a great gash across the vampire's chest through his shirt. The man stumbled backwards at the blow and collapsed over a gravestone.

'One down,' the mercenary said to himself with a grin, and span to face the other creatures.

Torben suddenly found himself hurled to the ground with the hissing nobleman furiously tearing at his mail armour with its talons. Twisting to one side, the warrior used his bulk to throw the clawing vampire from him. Quickly getting to his feet, he watched open-mouthed as the wound he had dealt the man closed bloodlessly before his very eyes.

'By Queen Katarin's sword!' he exclaimed. 'What does it take to stop these things?'

BADENOV'S MERCENARIES *are a group of hard-bitten fighting men. Drawn from the length and breadth of the Empire, they are held together by a lust for gold and a thirst for glory. Vampires, ghouls, rat-men and the Dark Knights of Chaos all abound in this land, but Badenov and his men will battle on until the last of them joins the dead or the damned!*

INFERNO! is the indispensable guide to the worlds of Warhammer and Warhammer 40,000 and the cornerstone of the Black Library. Every issue is crammed full of action-packed stories, comic strips and artwork from a growing network of awesome writers and artists including:

- William King
- Dan Abnett
- Brian Craig
- Graham McNeill
- Gav Thorpe
- Gordon Rennie

and many more

Presented every two months, Inferno! magazine brings the Warhammer worlds to life in ways you never thought possible.

For subscription details ring:
US: 1-800-394-GAME   UK: (0115) 91 40000

For more information see our website:
www.blacklibrary.com/inferno